Personally or Professionally

The Sterling Series

By
Danielle M. Angeline

PublishAmerica
Baltimore

First printing

ISBN: 1-59286-439-2
PUBLISHED BY PUBLISHAMERICA BOOK PUBLISHERS
www.publishamerica.com
Baltimore

Printed in the United States of America

Pam,

Thanks for all your support & encouragement. I hope you come to love Michael & Casey as much as I have. Happy reading. With much love and many blessings.

Hugs –
Janielle

Acknowledgments

Michael for the sweet memories and encouragement.
Jerri & Anita for their immeasurable editing hours.
Katherine for keeping me aligned and guiding me on this journey.
Susan for reminding me to always go with my gut instinct.
Stacey for endings by taking me back to the beginning.
Debbie for her unconditional help and support.
Kim for the brilliant cover art.
Cheyenne and Sierra for making me laugh,
just when I needed it most.

Publish America for making my dream come true.

Prologue

"They're taking Amy to the hospital." The voice on the other end of the phone was surprisingly calm. The words didn't seem real as a pain stabbed at his chest. Dropping the receiver, Michael Sterling grabbed his keys, making a mad dash out of his office, down three flights of stairs and to the lobby, where he informed Maggie Cowan, "I'm going to Brookshire Hospital. I don't know when I'll be back." And with that he was gone.

Maggie was worried. Michael's speech was riddled with anxiety and he already looked stricken with grief. Immediately, she picked up the phone. "Mr. Logan, it's Maggie. Mr. Sterling is on his way to the hospital. I think this is it." She jotted down Eric Logan's instructions for follow up, if in the event Michael was gone longer than a week. As she hung up the phone, Maggie knew there was nothing more they could do.

Weaving his car in and out of traffic, Michael was bordering on reckless driving as he slipped through yet another yellow traffic light. "Please don't let me be late. Hold on, just hold on until I get there. Please." Miraculously, Michael made it to the emergency room, unscathed. Rushing through the sliding doors, he asked the admitting nurse, "Amy Sterling?"

But before she could respond, Michael's mother was at his side. "Michael..." Ida Sterling was practically breathless. "Your sister's not..." Quickly, Michael escorted his mother to a private waiting room.

"I'm too late. Damn it!" Michael paced as he ran his hand through his sandy waves, his hand resting on the back of his neck.

"Calm down, Michael." His mother scolded, "You're not too late. Now sit down." Taking Michael's hands into hers, she wanted to prepare him, explaining, "Amy and I were at home having tea when she collapsed so I called the ambulance." Even though her tone was even, the pain was apparent. "She's stabilized but her doctor said that there isn't much more she can do."

Michael swiped at his tears that stung his eyes. "Can we go see her?"

"Of course." And hand in hand they walked down the long corridor.

Before entering, they took a deep breath and forced smiles as they entered Amy's room. They had anticipated this moment, hoping it would never come; that there would be some break through with the radiation treatments. But Amy never went into remission and now her days were few.

"Hey sis." Michael greeted as cheerfully as possible.

"Michael..." Amy's sing-song voice was interrupted by a cough as she reached her IV laden hand out to him. "You made it." Then Amy addressed their mother, "Can I have a few minutes alone with my brother?"

"Sure sweetie, I'll be right outside the door." Ida Sterling gave her daughter a peck then smoothed her hand over her bony cheek. "I love you." She whispered then told Michael. "Don't tire your sister out."

Michael nodded as he positioned himself on the edge of the hospital bed, wrapping Amy's hand in his. Amy, barely thirty, looked up at her older brother. "Michael there is something I have to tell you."

"Amy, you don't have to say anything."

"Ssh, just listen to me. First, I love you. I'm glad you're my brother." Amy tried to prop herself up but it was futile. Her body was too weak and she knew she was fighting a losing battle. "Second, Michael, I have no regrets. I've had a wonderful life with you, mom and believe it or not, dad. My career as a dancer took me to places I dreamed of as a child. I'm lucky. I've done everything I've wanted to but one." Again Amy coughed then lifted an oxygen mask to her face, taking in several deep breaths. "Michael... I wish I had loved someone the way you loved Casey."

Stunned, he replied with only one word, "Casey?"

Amy nodded.

"Amy, I understand what you're saying but why? Why Casey?"

A sharp pain shot through Amy's frail body and it was getting too difficult to breathe and she knew she had to tell him quickly. "Out of all the girls... Casey is the one. I know it's true without you saying a word. You had that look."

"But that was a lifetime ago."

"Promise me, you'll find her. Tell her you love her. It's my dying wish that..." Amy never finished her sentence as she squeezed her brother's hand one last time then took her final breath.

Through a river of tears, Michael promised.

Chapter 1

One year later

Looking up, Casey Andrews white knuckled the arms of the ornately designed mahogany chair. Swallowing hard, her throat parched, she barely whispered, "Why?"

"Because Arthur is dead and I'm in charge, young lady! And you're fired! Now, get out of my office!" The elderly man's boisterous voice bellowed as his beady eyes narrowed like a slithering snake that had just successfully attacked its prey.

The cruelty of his words squeezed her chest as her heart raced, making it difficult to breathe. Pain stabbed at her stomach. Clenching her mid-section, the room began to spin and Casey thought she was going to pass out. No, she wasn't going to give The Snake the satisfaction. Struggling to maintain her composure, Casey silently demanded it of herself to hold back the tears that were stinging the corners of her eyes. With conviction, she stood up tall, even though she was only five foot five. Drawing in a deep breath, leaning forward on the edge of Mr. Whitley's European imported antique desk, Casey glared at him. "You'll regret this." Raising an eyebrow, her tone remained even. "And one day you'll want me back. You'll see." Again, she stood tall, proud of her brazen retort. Casey pursed her lips, then as gracefully as possible, praying not to stumble, turned on her heel and simply walked out of the new owner's office. The entire staff looked on in astonishment as she marched towards her own office, avoiding eye contact with everyone.

Julie Warren was so preoccupied reviewing the proposal she had just finished, that it caught her off guard when Casey slammed the door in her face. Cracking the door open with caution, Julie peered into her supervisor's corner office. Horrified, Julie raised her arms in protest, "What do you think you're doing!" As she did so, several pages of the proposal, scattered onto the faded steel blue carpet, that was in dire need of a cleaning. Again, Julie yelled frantically, "What in the world are you doing!"

With trembling hands Casey placed a framed photo of her mother into her gym bag. Picking up the little stuffed Snoopy her niece and nephew had sent her on her last birthday, Casey cradled it, in a child-like gesture for a moment. "Packing." Casey whispered as she placed the little stuffed dog in its new home, all the while wishing her tears would remain at bay. The last thing she wanted was anyone to see her cry, especially over a slimy snake like Mr. Whitley.

"What? Why?" Julie rambled as she stooped to pick up the mess she had made.

"I don't want to talk about it." As she gathered up files, tossing them into the box that was atop her desk, Casey did her best to deter Julie, but her efforts were in vain. Then she emptied the contents of her desk drawers, making sure the one thing she did not leave behind was her Rolodex. It was packed full of clients and contacts she had acquired over many years as an Interior Designer and she was certain, at this juncture, it would be her hottest commodity. Finally, Casey reached for two tubes containing original drawings and sketches she had recently completed but had yet to present to the client. As far as Casey was concerned they were hers until Whitley Designs put their stamp of approval on them. Drawing in another deep breath, Casey felt as if time was moving in slow motion yet it only took twenty minutes to pack years of work into one box.

Casey felt Julie's hand on her shoulder. "Casey, what is going on?"

"Julie, please, just leave me alone!" Her tone was harsh as the words echoed out into the hall. Abruptly, Casey turned away from Julie and pulled the back-up disk out of her computer. Then she switched off the main power without a second thought. Lifting her pocketbook and gym bag onto her shoulder, Casey grabbed the box and with determined swiftness quietly exited. Whispers could be heard among the dozen cubicles as she turned down the hallway towards the elevator.

Catching up with Casey, Julie breathlessly announced, "You forgot your portfolio." Hesitantly she added, "Casey…ah, you don't owe me an explanation, but…am I being let go too?"

"No. I'm sure it'll be your office by tomorrow." Casey twisted her lip as she glared at the numbers above the elevator doors.

"Casey…" Julie frowned then finished off with, "I'm really sorry." Placing the portfolio on top of the box, Julie suggested, "Let's make plans for Saturday night, my treat?" Julie's blue eyes were glazing over. She liked being Casey's assistant designer. Always encouraging and fair, Casey's mantra was maintaining the team effort and everyone admired her, except Mr. Whitley.

"At least let me help you take your things down to your car."

Barely able to press the down button with her hands so full, Casey mustered, "No. I'm fine. Just call me when you get a chance." Hiding her tears behind a fake smile, Casey nodded to Julie when the elevator doors closed.

As the elevator carried her down to the first floor, Casey felt weak. Leaning up against the wall, she closed her eyes and drew in a deep breath. The tightness in her chest was getting worse as the doors chimed opened to the main lobby of the Whitley Building. Collecting what little energy she had left, Casey made her way through the atrium to the main entrance. With her arms full, she leaned against the door and shoved it open with the curve of her hip. Just as she stepped outside, she was hit broadside. The box slipped from her fingertips as she lost her footing and found herself splayed across the rough pebbled concrete along with the rest of her belongings. Raising herself to her knees, Casey clutched her chest, struggling for a breath.

"I'm sorry. Are you okay?" As the man rested his fingertips on Casey's shoulder, it caused an unexpected knee jerk reaction in his brawny body.

Casey's breathing had become shallow and labored when the touch of the man's hand on her shoulder jolted her body.

"Breathe." His tone low and confident tickled Casey's ear. "Just breathe." He repeated again then added, "I guess I really knocked the wind out of you."

"I'll say." Casey struggled. It wasn't long before she had stabilized her breathing and that's when reality struck like an on coming train. "That's it! I just can't take it anymore!" Her shouting turned to tears that drowned out the stranger's voice.

Again the man asked, "Are you all right?"

Ignoring him, Casey reached for her belongings that where scattered across the pavement. Grabbing her bag, she unzipped it, analyzing its contents. "It's broken!" Casey's voice cracked and her misery turned to hysteria.

The sunlight reflected off the fragments of the broken glass. As he stood beside her, the man placed a handkerchief in the palm of her hand, "Here." Intricately embroidered in the corner of the cloth in light blue thread were the initials M. C. S. but Casey shrugged it off as she held the material to her burning cheeks.

Extending a strong hand out to assist her, Casey hesitantly placed her shaky hand in his, a perfect fit. Again, his touch sent a jolt throughout her body like lightning from a hot July thunderstorm. Looking directly at his face, Casey's vision was blurred from of her tear filled eyes. Once on her feet, she lowered her head in embarrassment, trying to hide her stained cheeks. As she stared at the pavement, Casey noticed her sandal had slipped from her foot. Reaching down, she occupied herself, adjusting the strap, avoiding contact with the man that now stood before her. Again, Casey dabbed her brown eyes. Lifting her head, they locked gazes. Her pounding heart sent a rush surging through her body, remembering, only one man who had eyes that green. *"It couldn't be?"* Nibbling on her lower lip, Casey quickly put the thought out of her mind. Looking down again at her belongings, Casey's whole demeanor shifted. "You have some nerve, why didn't you look where you were going?" Her words were precise as she scolded the handsome stranger. "Here, I've got my own." Shoving the handkerchief back into his hand, she avoided contact with those emerald green eyes. Sweeping her coppery curls back from her face, Casey placed her hands on her hips. "Just look at what you did!"

"I said I was sorry. Let me help you." His voice was steady and all too familiar.

"No! I'll get it. Clearly, you're in a hurry, so just leave me alone! I'll take care of it myself!" Casey tried to dismiss him but he did not heed her demand. Picking up Casey's pocketbook and handing it to her, his fingertips brushed against hers. His body shivered against her touch as a chill spiraled down Casey's spine.

The broken glass clinked when Casey retrieved her gym bag and placed it on her shoulder. "I really can't believe this!"

Ignoring her words, he reached for her portfolio, noticing that new scratches had been added to the already worn leather. A soft breeze cascaded across the pages, capturing his attention. Surprisingly, Casey caught herself staring at the definition of his sun-kissed biceps beneath the short sleeved dark blue polo shirt. At that observation, she let out a deep sigh.

He gently placed Casey's portfolio and the drawings into the box then reached for the lid. As he swept it up into his arms, he met with eyes he knew all too well. "Casey?" Electricity surged through her body as he spoke her name.

Stepping back in disbelief, Casey questioned, "Michael?" Without waiting for an answer she repeated herself. "Michael Sterling." Laughing timidly, she rambled, "Oh my gosh! What are you doing…I mean, you're back. Where have you been? Oh my gosh, how long has it been?" Casey rattled on nervously then stopped. Drawing in a breath, she casually straightened her sleeveless white blouse and smoothed her hands over her pale pink skirt that was smudged with dirt.

"Casey, I'm so sorry. Are you all right?" Michael questioned with genuine concern as he trailed his eyes over her, noticing her knee was bleeding.

Narrowing her eyes, Casey bit her lower lip, wondering what he was really apologizing for. "This has got to be the worst day of my life."

"Your knee is bleeding. Let's go sit over there, so I can take a look at it." Michael motioned as he positioned Casey's box of belongings under his arm. Then gently placing his hand on the small of her back he guided her across the outside courtyard to a quaint grouping of stone benches that complemented the landscape of the Whitley Building. Retrieving his hanky again, Michael knelt before Casey. He gently slipped her sandal from her foot, then cupped her ankle in his hand, resting it on his bended knee. "I never did like to see you cry."

Conscious of his actions, Casey curled her lower lip between her teeth as she reached for the only piece of jewelry she always wore. The delicate cross hung gently in the hollow of her neck, always bringing Casey comfort in times of distress. Yet as her mid-section tightened at Michael's every touch, that too lent her a sense of comfort she had not felt in quite some time. "I wasn't crying…" she stammered as Michael slowly ran the soft cloth up her leg.

For an instant, time seemed to stand still as Michael took notice of her matured features. As she raised her arm to her necklace, there on Casey's forearm was the dark brown heart-shaped birthmark. He smiled, remembering how much she had hated it and always proclaimed that one day she was having it removed. For some silly reason, Michael was glad she hadn't. Catching a glimpse of gold flecks reflected in her brown eyes, Casey winced as Michael haphazardly attended to her injury.

"Michael, are you watching what you're doing?"

Clearing his throat, Michael felt like a kid that got caught doing something he wasn't supposed to be doing. As he lowered his eyes, Casey's fiery auburn curls caught his attention out of the corner of his eye. Her hair was longer now and he couldn't help but notice how it gently cascaded over her shoulders, gently framing her face. Contrasting against her pale skin was a splash of freckles that highlighted each cheekbone. The tiny scar Casey had acquired in her childhood was still apparent on her lower lip but to Michael they were still as kissable as he remembered. Shaking his head, he raised an eyebrow at the thought. Clearing his throat again, Michael told Casey, "Well, there is no permanent damage…to your knee but you probably should clean it up when you get home." He smiled. Carefully folding the stained cloth into a small square and shoving it into his back pocket, Michael slowly rose to his feet, casting his eyes over every inch of Casey's exposed skin.

"Thank you. I will." Casey stuttered as she started to stand up but before she could, Michael, without reservation, slid her box of belongings aside and sat down, uncomfortably close. Brushing his arm against hers, she felt a twinge flutter in her stomach and blood rush to her cheeks, turning them hot. Embarrassed to face him, Casey glanced down at her leg then blurted out, "Where were you going in such a hurry anyway?"

"I have a meeting." Glancing at his watch, he returned with, "Correction, had a meeting."

Casey's brown eyes widened, as she cupped her hand over her mouth, "I made you miss your meeting? Maybe if you hurry, you can still make it." She exclaimed as the tug o' war began inside her, wanting him to leave and hoping he would stay.

Michael reached for Casey's hand and wrapped hers into both of his. "Relax. It's not a big deal." He mentioned so calmly. "It's not everyday I run into you." He smiled then added, "So how are you?"

"Good. Real good." Casey responded without any regard to Michael's question as she eyed an older woman exiting the Whitley Building. It took Casey a few minutes to recognize Calandra Kosta, the owner of Calandra's Cuisine, a Greek restaurant. Squinting against the bright sunlight, it looked as if Mrs. Kosta was upset. Quietly, Casey made a mental note to give her favorite client a call.

Raising an eye brow, a perplexed look fell across Michael's face. "That's not what you were saying a few minutes ago." Pointing towards the front door of the Whitley Building, Michael continued, "Didn't you just shout to half of the world…"

Casey noticed that Michael was still holding her hand and in as much as it exhilarated her, it also made her extremely uncomfortable. Slowly she slipped her hand from his as she replied timidly, in a soft tone, "Don't remind me. I'm really embarrassed." Casey did not want to recap today's devastating events. Examining the tiny scar on his chin, she reverted the topic of conversation back to Michael, "Who's your meeting with?"

"Whitley Designs."

"Excuse me?" Casey inched away.

"My meeting is with a Mr. Whitley of Whitley Designs."

"Well, if you ask me, you're out of your mind!"

Perplexed by Casey's wisecrack, Michael crinkled his brow, "What do you mean?"

Wide-eyed, Casey hesitantly responded, "Michael, Mr. Whitley is impossible to work with. You'd be better off with a different designer."

"And you would know this, because...?"

"Because, Mr. Whitley is my..." Casey cleared her throat then quickly blurted out, "... *was* my boss."

"I didn't know you worked for Whitley Designs." Michael grinned then added, "Well, maybe it was meant to be after all."

Crinkling her brow, she stared at Michael, his comment registering in her brain but not quite making sense. "What are you talking about?"

"What are you talking about?" Michael quickly returned.

Mortified, Casey just let the words slip from her lips, "Michael, Mr. Whitley just fired me."

"You can't be serious. Why?"

His probing questions were starting to grate her nerves. Michael Sterling was the last person she wanted to pour her heart and soul out to. She had been vulnerable to him once and vowed never again. Giving it some thought, Casey cleverly replied, "Irreconcilable differences."

"Personally or professionally?" Michael teased.

"Professionally!" Casey sulked as she tightly crossed her arms over her chest in frustration.

Michael then unclipped his cell phone from the belt of his well-tailored trousers, and punched the numbers on the keypad. Turning towards Casey, his eyes smiled with a mischievous glint, "Yes, this is Mr. Sterling. I have to cancel my two o'clock appointment with Mr. Whitley. Tell him I'm going with another designer." Michael's voice resonated with confidence reminding Casey of the first time they met, in high school, twenty years earlier.

> *Casey was overwhelmed by the enormity of the High School as she discreetly glanced down at her class schedule. "Room 112?" She mumbled as she eyed the tiny numbers above each door-jamb, hoping no one would notice she was turned around. Having heard the rumors of Seniors tormenting in coming Freshmen, she was determined not to be one of their targets. "One twenty, one twenty-two...shoot." Turning abruptly, her sneaker squeaked on the freshly polished floor, causing a wave of laughter to resonate through the crowded corridor. Flustered and not paying attention to her direction, Casey bumped right into another student which caused her to stumble backwards. But his quick reaction and strong hand prevented Casey from landing on the floor in total humiliation.*

"Slow down. No need to rush." His deep voice tickled her ear. "If you're late, you're late. Teachers understand that on the first day." He shrugged.

"I'm sorry. It's my...I wasn't looking ..." Casey trailed off as she met with the most beautiful green eyes she had ever seen, with the exception of the contact lenses models wore in the many teen magazines she read religiously but found so difficult to emulate.

"Where you headed?" His voice was deep and smooth.

"One twelve. Ah...Biology?" Casey posed more as a question.

He looked into her brown eyes, noticing flecks of gold that made her eyes dance. Michael took a step back. "Yeah? Me too. You mind? I have to stop at my locker first." Michael stated matter-of-factly as he gestured down the main corridor.

Casey nodded as the hustle and bustle of students scrambling to locate their next class was overpowering her. She had visited the high school once before with her mom, during registration but she still felt lost and out of place. As they walked down the hall, Casey swore that every student that passed them by, greeted Michael in one manner or another. Whether it was a quick hello or a thumbs up, Casey already knew he was one of the most popular boys in the freshman class. Few words were exchanged as they reached his locker. Twisting the combination on the dial, he opened it with ease. Another boy passing by, slapped Michael on the shoulder, shouting above the ruckus, "Way to go and on the first day." Then he gave Michael an a-okay sign and proceeded down the hall, disappearing into the crowd.

Scrunching her nose, Casey asked, "What was that supposed to mean?"

"Ah, ignore him. He doesn't know what he's saying."

Leaning up against the lockers, Casey mumbled, "I haven't even found mine yet." As she held her books tightly against her less than developed chest, Casey couldn't help but notice the smooth fit of his jeans and it made her nervous. As he stood too close for comfort, she could feel her heart rate increasing. Having never experienced such feelings, Casey tried to hide her embarrassment as she ran her hand through her uncontrollable curls. Secretly she wished she had braided her hair this morning and worn something other than a faded pair of overalls and a tee shirt. Surprisingly, many of the students were dressed in the latest fashion, a luxury Casey, or rather her mom, could not afford on a teacher's salary, while raising two daughters.

"I can show you after class. Is it a date...what's your name?"

"Ah..." He caught her off guard. "Casey. Casey Andrews."

"Michael Sterling." It was music to her ears. "One-twelve is this way." He teased pointing down the hall as the bell for classes to begin, rang. Instinctively, Michael took a hold of Casey's hand, as they sprinted down the hall, rushing to their next class. Casey felt a flutter in the core of her stomach as Michael pulled out the chair next to him, "Let's sit here."

"Okay, class, the bell has rung. Choose your seats wisely, because the person you sit next to will be your lab partner for the year." Their new teacher announced. The room erupted with moans and movement as many of their classmates switched seats.

Casey stood up.

"Where are you going?" Michael rested his hand on Casey's arm.

"I thought you'd want one of your friends to sit here. I can go sit somewhere else."

"Nah..." Michael smiled as he patted the wooden chair, encouraging Casey to take her seat again.

"Casey? Casey." Michael waved his rugged hand before her eyes. Catching the intoxicating scent of his cologne, she jerked her head upwards. "You looked a million miles away."

"More like a million years." Casey quipped as she tried to stop herself from staring. His features had remained the same. His eyes were as green as she had remembered and his chiseled features were still striking especially when he smiled. His dimples added a simple boyish charm to his facial traits causing Casey to smile too. Wandering her eyes over his body she noticed the boy she had loved so many decades ago had matured into a virile man. In the afternoon sunlight, Michael's brown waves shimmered with golden highlights and curled just above his shirt collar. As she memorized his face, a small giggle escaped her lips.

"What?" Michael questioned wanting to know what had provoked her laughter.

"Oh…you still have your ear pierced." Casey pointed towards the tiny diamond.

"Yeah, and the scar to prove it." Michael taunted as he rubbed his chin. "I tell people that it was Halloween and the moon was full and the love of my life had this great need to do some damage."

"Michael!" Casey was tickled by his humor and shocked he remembered. Letting out a sigh, Casey stated with seriousness, "Well, it was nice to see you again, but I've got to get going." Casey stood and collected her belongings.

"Casey, wait." Michael gently grasped her arm, just like he had the first day they met in high school. His touch still made her sizzle as the same electrified feeling surged through her body. She shook her head, "What?"

"I was thinking…" It was unusual for Michael to waver. At times his confidence was so impressive it was misconstrued for arrogance. "I couldn't help but notice…your designs…I mean I've always known you were talented, and when I saw your portfolio…" he pointed towards the front doors, "when I picked it up…"

"And what Michael?" Casey was growing anxious, suddenly wanting to be on her way, retreating to the comfort of her home.

"You could come work for me." He stated firmly, believing Casey would not turn down his offer.

"I don't think that's a good idea, Michael." Confusion consumed Casey as she rejected his offer. Yet her head was screaming quite the opposite.

He reached into his back pocket and pulled out his wallet, retrieving a business card. Michael laid it on top of the box that Casey held close. "Call me tomorrow." He paused, glancing at his watch. "No…"

"Well, which is it Michael, do you want me to call or not, because I really need to go." Casey's patience was wearing thin.

Gently placing his hands on Casey's shoulders, Michael looked deeply into her eyes, "I'm taking you to lunch. Downtown. One o'clock." He cocked one eyebrow as the corner of his mouth curled upwards. "You have nothing to lose." His charming smile captivated her senses.

Casey had reservations and wanted to shout, *"Yeah, except my head and my heart."* But she remained silent, simply nodding.

"Casey, business has really picked up and I need someone with your reputation. A real go-getter…"

"…With my reputation…" Casey creased her brow. "How could you possibly know about my professional reputation…?"

Michael's eyes widened, then he stepped back slightly and shrugged, "Your name gets mentioned every now and then and..." He flipped over his business card and dashed off his home phone number. "Here." He shoved the card in her direction. "My office and cell phone numbers are on the front and I put my home number on the back. Call me...anytime." The spark in his emerald eyes, after twenty years, still took her breath away. How could Casey say no?

Her eyes narrowed, glancing down at Michael's business card. "You're Sterling Architects and Construction, Inc.? I should have known." The familiar design on the card caught Casey off guard.

"You've heard of us?"

"Here and there in conversation but I never assumed it... never mind."

"The construction is my business partner's division. Eric Logan. We hooked up about five years ago and decided we wanted to be our own bosses so...do you need a ride somewhere?" Michael abruptly changed the subject.

"No, Michael. My car is just across the street."

He leaned forward and whispered, "Let me help you."

Chapter 2

Anxious and wanting to meet with Eric before the end of the day, Michael headed north on Madison, as he weaved his red Maxima through the early afternoon rush hour traffic. Parking at a metered spot in front of the three-story building, Michael burst into the lobby of Sterling Architects, shouting, "Maggie, has Eric left for the day?"

"Mr. Sterling, you're back." Maggie Cowan stood as Michael breezed by her. With urgency, Michael kept moving down the hallway to the stairwell, not waiting for a response. After his encounter with Casey, his heart had been pounding furiously as he replayed every word they had exchanged. The sound of her voice resounded in his head, and for some reason, even when she was yelling, to Michael it was lyrical. And yelling he deserved. He knew he was going to run into her, he had prepared himself for that for the past three months. But not literally. In all his life, Casey Andrews was the only woman who affected him this way. Michael wasn't sure what it was, but whenever she was around, his emotions always spun out of control.

Pacing back and forth in front of Eric's desk, Michael struggled to form the right words. Suddenly, he found himself blurting out a sentence he thought was incoherent. "Eric, I ran into Casey."

Removing his wire-framed glasses and placing them on the pile of papers that were scattered about his desk, Eric eased back in his chair, looking up at Michael. "That must have been some meeting, because you're awfully fired up. What happened, Mike?"

"I think it's time to expand the business. We've been talking about it for a year now and well, let's just say the opportunity has presented itself."

"You mean your meeting with Mr. Whitley?" Eric questioned with confusion.

"No, not exactly."

"What are you talking about?" Eric was growing concerned about Michael's agitated behavior. He had never seen him this worked up about anything, especially work, during the entire time they had been business partners.

Leaning against the edge of the desk, Michael announced, firmly, "Casey Andrews." Taking a strong pause, he then added, "It's the chance to make something personally wrong, professionally right."

"Mike you're not making any sense." Eric placed his elbows on his desk, folding his arms in front of him.

For the next hour, Michael ranted on about his history with Casey, concluding with this afternoon's events, including the cancellation of his appointment with Mr. Whitley. "Eric, you have to trust my judgement on this one."

Eric shook his head. "I don't know if I can, Mike. We've worked our tails off to build the reputation we now have and you want to play out some ancient personal fight in the professional arena? I don't know if I can allow that. Not when the Brookshire Hospital bid is about to be awarded."

"But don't you see, we'd be getting Casey's professional reputation and probably some of her clients as well. And I know Casey, she'll work hard. It's the perfect opportunity to announce our expansion and we can provide our clients with the whole package. One stop shopping, so to speak. Plus..." Michael trailed off as he swiped his hand through his hair. Drawing in a deep breath, he continued, "We could have Casey draw up some designs on a contractual basis and if we don't land the project, then we don't hire her."

Eric twisted his face at Michael's words and just as he was about to respond, Maggie's voice came over the intercom. "Eric, Mr. Rezabeck is on extension 105 and..." Maggie cleared her throat, "Is Michael in there with you?"

"I'm right here, Maggie, what is it?" His voice was tight.

"Oh, I'm sorry Mr. Sterling but..." Maggie was hesitant.

"Go ahead." Michael had told Maggie time and time again to call him by his first name, but she couldn't seem to bring herself to do so. It seemed as though Maggie was scared of him, but Michael could not recall any moment in which he used fear as a tactic with his employees. He had experienced that himself when he was starting out as an architect and swore he would never be that kind of manager.

"There is a rather irate woman on extension 107 and she refuses to give her name. Do you want to take her call or should I tell them you're in a meeting?"

"No, Maggie. I've been waiting for Mr. Rezabeck's call. Thanks." Eric went to reach for the receiver, "Mike, I'm hesitant but I know you. You're going to do what you think is right, anyhow. But I'll be keeping an eye on you. I own half this company and I won't have your personal life affect me professionally." Eric raised his brow, feeling uncomfortable with his words.

Michael nodded his head and exited silently. With his heart still pounding and his mind racing, he was not thinking clearly. He went downstairs to the lobby and as he breezed by Maggie once again, he informed her, he was leaving for the afternoon. Then quickly added, "Put all my calls through to voicemail and I'll check them later. If anything major comes up, call me on my cell."

Noticing there was a certain edginess to Michael's tone she had never witnessed before, Maggie simply replied, "Yes, sir." Before Maggie could put any thought into Michael Sterling's odd behavior, three phone lines rang simultaneously. "Sterling Architects and Construction. May I help you?"

Michael wasn't used to feeling this edgy, especially when it came to business decisions. It was the one lesson Michael's estranged father had impressed upon him in his youth. Always stay calm and cool when making deals. "Bottom line, never let the other person see you sweat." It was obvious his father lacked eloquence when spouting off one of his many platitudes; nonetheless, Michael chalked it up to his father's generation. An upbringing, absent of displaying any kind of feelings whatsoever equaled yet another generation of non-emotional men, or at least that was the case when it came to Cab Sterling. And while Michael was far from being like his father, he still wasn't quite used to feeling so emotional.

As he marched down the block to The Corner Café, it hit him like a freezing wind in the middle of winter, even though it was nearly summer. Eric and Michael had mulled over the idea of expanding Sterling Architects with an Interior Design division for over a year, long before Michael had planned his meeting with Whitley Designs and running into Casey. He recalled mentioning her to Eric at least a dozen times, so Michael pondered why Eric was giving him such resistance. His only conclusion was that Eric was knee deep in work and was only trying to protect his own investment. Ironically, when Michael had conversed with several colleagues as to what Interior Design firm they referred their clients to, it was always the same answer. "Casey Andrews at Whitley Designs." Convinced she was the one to have on his team, Michael cleverly put his plan into action to strategically steal Casey away from Mr. Whitley. And Whitley had made it that much easier for him, by letting Casey go without his knowledge. What he had not bargained for were feelings he had kept buried for decades.

Entering The Corner Café, Donna the day shift manager, greeted Michael with a wink and a smile.

Michael and Eric had frequented the establishment many times in the past years and had christened it their office away from the office. It had become the ideal place to brainstorm and that's what Michael needed, some time alone to think. Sitting at the bar, Michael asked for a beer, but then changed his mind, "Ah, Donna, just make it a club soda with a twist."

"Sure, no problem Mike." A scratchy voice called out, as she dumped the half-poured draft down the drain. "What is it, hon?" Her Baltimore accent was thick.

Michael shook his head as he took a sip of his drink first. "Kind of slow today, huh?" The melody of a slow tune wafted from the jukebox in the corner and echoed through the almost empty room.

"It's not happy hour yet, it's only four o'clock." Donna gave him a perplexed look. "Well, it must be a woman on your mind, 'cause I've never seen you like this over business."

Michael glanced at his watch then at Donna, noticing for the first time her hair was starting to gray at the temples. "Actually, it's both and I don't know if I've made the right decision."

"Yeah?" The fiery red-head folded her arms and leaned against the bar. Chewing hard on her gum, she stared contently at Michael.

"I want to hire a designer. The firm has been doing well and it's the right time to expand."

"So, what's the problem, hon?"

"I want to hire my ex-girlfriend."

"Melinda Parker?"

"Good God no!" Michael retorted then softened his tone. "This is someone else. We go way back. College, even high school." Michael took a sip of his drink then added, "...and Melinda Parker was never my girlfriend." He stated succinctly for the record.

"So, what's the problem? That was what...twenty years ago?" Donna shrugged and when she smiled, her crows-feet were more apparent as well as a chipped tooth. Grabbing a rag, Donna ran the cloth under the hot water faucet and wiped down the bar.

Michael let out a low chuckle, "Not quite." He drew in a deep breath and continued. "It's not that she's not talented, she is. And I know Casey. She's honest, dedicated and capable of accomplishing anything. Her professional reputation is well known. In fact, a few years ago, she received a Designer's Award at a tradeshow. It was in all of the local papers and trade journals."

Donna raised a brow as she noticed the spark in Michael's eyes as he rambled on about Casey.

"So like I said, what's the problem? Sounds to me like you got a real winner on your hands. If you say she's got the reputation she's got, I can't imagine it hurtin' your business." Donna reasoned.

"I'm afraid it's more personal than professional." Michael hesitantly admitted.

"Now this is a side I've never seen. Let'en that heart rule that head." Donna pointed out. "Why don't you let Eric interview her, then both of you can decide. People change, you know. You want another drink?"

"No, thanks Donna." Michael tossed a five-dollar bill onto the counter. He stood and headed towards the exit, then turned, "Hey, thanks Donna. I know what I have to do."

"Anytime, hon. That's what I'm here for." The forty-something bartender waved as Michael exited and another patron entered The Corner Café.

The warmth of the sun blazed on Michael's back as he slowly walked two blocks past his Architectural firm, to Angelina's Boutique. The bell chimed as he stepped into the quaint little shop. The aroma of Italian spices permeated the air. Michael glanced around, uncertain of what he was searching for, but knowing he would find something. There were cut glass figurines, candle holders and hand crafted jewelry boxes. Michael shook his head as he explored each shelf.

"Michael, it's a been too long. Why you not come visit a me?" The short plump woman stepped out from behind the counter.

Michael joined hands with the elderly woman and kissed her on the cheek, "Mrs. Burchellio. You look lovely as always." Dressed in bright purple pants and a yellow silk blouse trimmed with the same color purple, she clashed against the faded décor.

"You always flatter a me. That's a why I like you so much." Her thick accent cut through the jangle of her bracelets as she shook her short index finger and then winked. "Whata woman are you buying for thisa time?"

"Ah, an old friend."

"Business or a pleasure?"

Michael sharply said, "Business." He glanced around the shop again, and then a reflection of light caught his eye. He moved to the small domestic section, eyeing each selection carefully. Picking up the ornate item he moved over to the register. "Could you possibly wrap it for me, Mrs. Burchellio?"

"For you, anything. But sucha gift? You sure this is a professional and not a personal?" She winked again as she wrapped tissue around the heavy object and gently placed it in the box.

"Believe me, this is perfect…either way." A smile was back on Michael's face. "Please say hello to Phillipe for me." Content with his purchase, Michael stepped out into the late afternoon sun, feeling as if it was the dawning of a new day.

Chapter 3

The heel of Casey's slightly worn sandals clicked across the hardwood floor as she made her way through her condominium to the dining room. Flopping her purse and gym bag onto the dinner table, the broken glass clinked in her bag, reminding Casey of the day she had had. Then she contemplated which was more bizarre: getting fired or running into Michael? Hindsight being twenty, twenty, she had somewhat anticipated she would come to blows with The Snake but crossing paths with Michael Sterling was the furthest thing from her mind. Actually, she hadn't thought of him since she had received an invitation to their ten year reunion, but that was almost three years ago.

As she moved to the den with her box of office belongings in tow, Casey eyed the stack of bills piled up on her computer desk. A twinge of anxiety grabbed at her chest. "Thank God for the savings account," she mumbled, as she dropped the box onto the floor, shoving it into the corner with her foot. Meandering her way to her bedroom, Casey knew she was only kidding herself. At best, the savings account would last a few months, if she was frugal.

After throwing her shoes into the walk-in closet, Casey turned to the pinewood dresser. She pulled out a pair of jean shorts and a red tee shirt. The changing of her attire, did little to ease her mood. Haphazardly, Casey pulled the mauve comforter over the floral sheets and placed the pillows against the white wrought-iron headboard. Making the bed and straightening her bedroom lent her no comfort either.

Entering the bathroom, Casey stared into the mirror. Pulling her long curls up into a ponytail, she stared at her reflection. Reaching for the blue wash cloth that hung on the shower door rail, Casey ran it under the cold water. The coolness of the cloth offered no relief to her stress as she replayed today's events in her mind. *"What are you going to do now?"* She questioned, knowing her reflection would not respond. Rinsing the wash cloth one more time, Casey dabbled it to her scrapped knee. A funny tickle ran up her leg to her mid-section and an unpredictable giggle escaped her lips. It was as if she could still feel his hand on her leg and strangely, it made her smile.

After applying peroxide and a bandage to her knee, Casey returned to the dining room. Carefully, she opened her gym bag, reaching for the damaged frame. "Oh mom." She winced, "How I wish you were here." Laying the photo down on the table she retrieved the trashcan from the kitchen. As Casey placed the broken glass into the trash, there was a knock at her door.

"What are you doing here?" Casey gave Julie a hug. "I'm sorry about earlier."

"That's okay. Are you in the mood for carrot cake and Margaritas?" Julie giggled, flashing her pearly whites as she held up a bakery box and a grocery bag.

Pursing her lips, Casey shook her head, knowing deep down, she could always count on Julie to come through in a crisis. "You are too much. This is great!" Casey smiled as she retrieved the cake from Julie. "Let's get out the blender." Casey's demeanor shifted, now that her tried and true best friend was in her presence. In fact, it elated her. Setting the cake down in the center of the table, Casey shoved her belongings to one side. Moving into the kitchen, she set up the blender, filling it to the brim with just the right amount of each ingredient, making the best Margarita she'd had in ages. Within minutes, Casey poured the strawberry mixture into two frosty glasses and joined Julie at the dining room table.

"The suspense is killing me, Casey. What happened with Whitley today?"

"Do I have to?" Casey moaned.

"Absolutely! After you left, he called an emergency staff meeting. He callously announced you were fired and said I was taking over your accounts. Although, he gave me no indication it was a promotion or that there was a raise along with it." Julie rolled her blue eyes. "So, tell me. I can't stand it one more minute."

"Right after lunch, The Snake called me into his office. He handed me the profit spreadsheet for the past quarter. Highlighted was the remodeling of Calandra's Cuisine. He told me to recheck the figures. I did twice, everything added up. We made a profit, a small one but a profited, nonetheless." Casey took a bite of carrot cake, then gently wiped her lips.

"So, what am I missing here?"

"The Snake almost had a coronary because we made less than half our regular profit. I told him that the profit came in low on this particular design job because she had a limited budget. And when she opens her second restaurant on the Waterfront next year, we will have that job done slightly higher than our regular profit. So, to me, it balances itself out. To the Snake, it was bad business. And I even reminded him that it was Arthur who approved the project before..." Sadness fell over Casey for a brief moment but was interrupted by Julie's question.

"So what happened next?"

"I lost my temper, Julie. But…" Casey gestured excitedly, "Before he fired me, before it came to blows between us, I tried to reason with him. I really did." Casey tried to reassure herself.

"And…"

"And, The Snake does not like being compared to his brother. They are so opposite and if you ask me, he's going to drive Whitley Designs right into the ground. How many clients have stayed because of the staff? How many fires have you, and Bill and Veronica put out…that he started?"

"Don't forget yourself." Julie quickly interjected with her dimple laden smile.

Casey forced a smile, then suddenly felt her heart pounding against her chest. Every time The Snake was mentioned, her blood pressure sky rocketed and her pulse quickened. Drawing in several deep breaths, Casey released each very slowly in an attempt to calm her frayed nerves. Sipping her margarita, she continued to address Julie. "I told him the word around the industry is that no one wants to do business with Whitley Designs anymore. He hit the roof but I really laid it out on the table. There is no way Whitley Designs is going to survive by putting fear into the employees. And Arthur was a far better manager than he'll ever be. But The Snake slithered back into his hole. He didn't want to hear it. And, well you know the rest." Casey shoved her half eaten cake to the side then swirled a spoon around in her partially melted margarita.

"You are direct, aren't you?" A wide-eyed Julie teased.

"I can honestly say, Julie, I don't regret what I said. It was only a matter of time before we clashed. I'm surprised I lasted as long as I did. You know I didn't like his management tactics. And to be honest, you know no one else does either. Anyone who has had a review in the past six months has made it abundantly clear as to how The Snake has treated them. And I guarantee in the next six months, Whitley Designs will be out of business."

Julie dabbed her napkin to the corner of her mouth. "I hope not! Because I'm not planning on leaving anytime soon."

Casey creased her brow but spoke not a word.

"You have to apologize to him so you can get your job back. We need you there. "

"Absolutely not!" Casey glared at her friend for a moment then jumped up, grabbing both their plates, tossing them into the kitchen sink. "I don't want my job back. And my advice to you, start looking." Casey tossed her hands in the air, "Besides, after what I said, I'll never work for Whitley Designs ever again." Folding her arms over her chest, Casey eased back into her chair.

"Never say never."

"It's hard to believe that Arthur and Mr. Whitley were brothers."

"No kidding." Julie agreed.

Casey was quiet for a moment then continued, "I will never forget the day he took over Whitley Designs." Casey cleared her throat, "I am Mr. Whitley, the other brother. And you will *not* call me by my first name. My brother's reign is over and we have work to do. So do it." Julie laughed at Casey's bad impression of Mr. Whitley. "What is his first name anyway?" Casey questioned.

"Snake." Julie giggled then suddenly her mood was more serious. "I really miss Arthur."

"Me too. We were so lucky to have him as a boss. Arthur cared more about us than the company. It was like we were his family, even though he was married. I will never forget what he did for me when my mom was sick." Casey's thoughts drifted back to three years ago.

> *Casey sat at her desk, tapping her pencil incessantly, debating how to approach Arthur Whitley. Looking at her watch, she knew she had no choice. Drawing in a deep breath, Casey rose from her chair and went to Arthur's office. Gently tapping on the half open door, Casey peeked inside.*
>
> *"Casey." He smiled. "What can I do for you?"*
>
> *"Arthur…" her words caught in her throat.*
>
> *"Casey, you look troubled."*
>
> *"Arthur, I ah…I know I've only been here seven months but I have to give you my two week's notice. I just can't work right now." Casey let out a sigh of relief then held her breath again, concerned with his reaction.*
>
> *He wiggled his finger in his ear, "Casey, what did you say? It sounded like you were giving me notice, but I must be mistaken, right?"*
>
> *"No, I'm sorry, you heard correctly. I'm just so tired and I can't keep up this schedule and care for my mom at the same time. I really am sorry." Casey hung her head as she stood to exit his office.*
>
> *Standing at the same time, Arthur moved towards Casey, "Whoa,*

wait a minute." Arthur swept an arm around Casey's shoulders and escorted her over to the blue and yellow plaid sofa. He sat opposite Casey, "What is this about you caring for your mother?"

It was one of Casey's strict rules about business: never get personal. But as Arthur looked at her with his sympathetic brown eyes, she knew she had to tell him everything. "My mom was diagnosed with cancer about four months ago. She's taken all the treatments but she is not getting better. I have a nurse with her during the day and I'm with her at night but I just..." Casey choked back her tears not wanting to show her vulnerability.

Arthur moved over to the small serving cart by his desk and poured Casey a glass of water. "Say no more."

Casey took a sip. "I will help you find someone to replace me before I leave."

"No, that's not it. You're not leaving. You're going to stay right where you are."

"But Arthur..."

"No 'buts' Casey. You are my star employee. We will work this out." He moved over to the console on his desk. "Julie, I need you, Veronica and Bill to come to my office right away, please?"

"Yes, sir. We'll be right there." Julie's voice echoed.

Silence permeated the air as Casey took another sip of water. For once she was rendered speechless by his words. Exhaustion was overwhelming her and guilt was retching at her stomach as Julie, Bill and Veronica entered.

"Have a seat." he commanded. "We have a situation and I need your help."

"Arthur, don't." Casey did not want to involve the staff in her personal life.

"Casey, we are family. And when family needs help we all pull together." There was sternness in Arthur's voice but he still remained polite and respectful. Addressing his staff he continued, "Casey's mother is ill. And unfortunately she is not getting better. A nurse is at the house during the day but that leaves Casey to care for her mother at night. I need each of you to help pick up the slack. Casey will delegate which projects she needs help with. I'm going to break the rules here and let Casey work at home three days a week. Julie, I need you to order whatever office equipment and supplies she may

need. Does anyone have any questions?"

"Just one, Arthur." Julie spoke up. "Casey, why didn't you tell us? I knew something was wrong but I didn't want to pry."

"I'm sorry. I haven't been here that long to put this on all of you. It's my responsibility to…"

"…To what? Drive yourself to pure exhaustion? Come on, kiddo. We'll help you." Arthur rallied.

"Of course we will." Bill chimed in. "In fact, I can come by a couple of hours on the weekend. I'll sit with your mom or help you with whatever. I cook a mean pot of spaghetti." He joked trying to lighten the mood.

"Yeah, that's all you know how to cook." Julie giggled.

"Darla and I can come by after church on Sundays." Veronica added. "You know Casey, I've been there, only with me, it was my daughter. She was three months premature. I was ready to risk it all just to be with her but Arthur wouldn't let that happen. In fact, everyone in the office brought over food. Casseroles, lasagna, and groceries. I didn't cook for months." Her dark eyes brightened, "Arthur let me set my own hours. I came in early, worked through lunch, and left early just so I could be with Darla. The days I took off, I just made up the time at home. Why do you think I've been with this company for eight year. It's because of everyone's kindness and understanding…well, let's just say it's time for me to return the favor."

A tear slipped from the corner of Casey's eye and Julie's too. "Yeah, but…" Casey dropped her head again. "This isn't fair to you all."

Arthur moved closer. "This is your mother. You need to be with her. And if it gets to be too much, call me. Anytime, day or night. Esther and I will come running. You all are the children we never had." Like the affection of a father, he could not resist hugging her.

Julie reached for Casey's hand, "Me too, Casey. Call me, anytime. Promise? Casey?"

She looked up at Julie with gratitude, "Oh, I almost forgot to tell you. You'll never guess in a million years." Casey brushed her hand over the top of her hair as she took another sip of her drink. "As I was leaving, guess who I ran into?"

"Who?"

"Michael Sterling." Julie's eyes widened as Casey continued. "The guy I dated in high school and college? He was the reason I became an Interior Designer, well not the whole reason. But anyhow, as I was leaving the Whitley Building, he knocked right into me. My stuff flew everywhere. At first I didn't even realize it was him. We haven't seen each other in ten years. Not since he left for grad school."

"So what happened? Did he recognize you?" Julie asked, eyeing the open box of cake. No longer able to resist, Julie swiped a finger through the cream cheese frosting then licked her finger clean.

"Oh, yes. Actually, he was acting like I was his long lost best friend, or something."

"So, when are you going to see him again?"

"I don't know, Julie, too much of a history."

"Yeah, so you dated a decade ago. People change."

"Well, I told you we met in high school, didn't I?" Casey rambled, ignoring Julie's rationalization.

"About a million times." Julie confirmed with a nod and a smile.

"Believe me, the college I ended up going to was not my first choice. I wanted to go to college on the Eastern Shore but because the college there was private, my mom really couldn't afford it, so I ended up at University of Maryland with Michael." Casey got up for a moment and came back with the pitcher of margarita mix. "You want some more?" Before Julie could object, Casey filled her glass to the rim. "So, where was I? You know Interior Design was not my first major either. I started out as pre-law. I wanted to save the world. One semester, I think it was my sophomore year, I had to take an art class and Michael convinced me to take the 3-D perspective class with him. From there, I was hooked."

"So what is Michael doing now?"

"He's an architect like I always knew he would be. I remember in high school he used to build all these fancy models just for the fun of it. Now, he runs his own company, like I knew he would." Casey's words were a tad bit sarcastic. "He cancelled his meeting with The Snake, then offered me a job."

"I took that call. What a voice!" Julie giggled then added, "So, when do you start?"

"I don't know, but he's taking me to lunch." Casey had not had time to weigh her options.

"Are you out of your mind? Do it. You have nothing to lose. What is the worst possible thing that could happen? Besides wouldn't it be interesting to see how this plays out… personally?"

"Julie, I am not interested in anything personal with Michael Sterling."

"What about professionally? It sure beats unemployment, job hunting, interviews and draining the savings account. At least see what he has to say. Then tell him what you want. Worst case scenario, you look for another job."

"True, but Julie, I've been thinking about getting out of the industry altogether. I want to do something important with my life. I want to make a difference in this world."

"But you're so talented. Why the change of heart?"

Casey could not give her a justified answer. All she knew was that something was missing in her life and now was the perfect opportunity for a change.

"I know that look, Casey. What are you not telling me?"

The sun was starting to dip behind the trees that surrounded the complex, so Casey turned off the air-conditioning and opened the windows. She turned back towards her friend, "He's living our dream…without me…" Casey was interrupted by a knock at the door. After peering through the peephole, she slowly opened the door.

"Casey Andrews? Sign here please." The deliveryman was direct. He handed her the package and proceeded down the stairs without another word.

With her curiosity piqued, Casey opened the package as she made her way back to the dinning room. Handing the ornate sterling silver picture frame to Julie, Casey asked, "So what do you think of this?"

"It's gorgeous, who sent this to you?"

"None other than Michael Sterling, himself." Casey smiled as she read his simply worded apology.

"I suppose I don't have to ask what you're going to do, do I?" There was a twinkle in Julie's blue eyes.

Casey's face lit up. "I guess I have a lunch date tomorrow. And then I'm going to visit my sister, Hannah."

"Tell Michael to take you to Imperial's." Julie giggled and then Casey joined in.

Chapter 4

Melinda Parker pushed button number thirty-eight on the elevator panel at Empire Tower. It was practically owned by Parker Industries since they occupied two-thirds of the floor space. As the doors opened, Melinda was immediately greeted and escorted to her husband's office by his assistant, Payne Claiborne. He was a short little Donald Trump wanna-be freshly graduated from John's Hopkins with honors with two Master degrees he completed simultaneously. One in International Public Policy and the other in International Business Law. Payne had yet to take his bar exam and used the excuse that he was in the process of mastering a third language, hence the delay. While Payne was impressed with himself and anyone else making at least a couple of million a year, Melinda could have cared less about his credentials. "You're looking lovely, today, Mrs. Parker." Payne complimented as he held the door open to Lyle's office.

"Oh stuff it, you little brown noser." Melinda tossed her head in the air as she paraded across the room to Lyle's desk. Even though Melinda Parker was nearly twice his age, Payne couldn't resist glancing at the sultry sway of Mrs. Parker's hips. The beige material hugged her forty-something body, which caused a slight pang in Payne's twenty-five year old body. He would never admit it out loud, but he found Melinda Parker quite attractive, if only she wasn't such a bitch.

"May I get you anything, Mr. Parker? Mrs. Parker?"

"Yes. Some privacy." Melinda snapped.

Lyle pursed his lips, cocking on eyebrow at Melinda. "Actually, there is Payne. Lyle stepped out from behind his oversized mahogany European import. "Find out everything you can." Was all Lyle instructed as he handed the folder over to Mr. Claiborne.

"Yes sir." And with those final two words, Melinda and Lyle were alone.

"Melinda, how many times have I told you not to talk to my staff that way? It undermines my authority."

"You're authority? Oh please, everyone around here thinks you walk on water."

Lyle now stood face to face with his wife. Running his index finger down her cheek, he questioned in a low tone, "And you?" He leaned in to kiss her, but she abruptly turned away, only offering him her cheek.

Lyle stepped back, knowing the answer to his question without Melinda saying a word. Returning to his chair behind his desk. "What brings you downtown?"

"I was wondering if you had anything for Sterling Architects? Contracts, files, plans that need to be dropped off? Any new projects going on?"

Jumping from his chair, Lyle curled his fingers into fists then leaned against his desk, "When are you going to give it a rest, Melinda?"

Remaining cool and collected, she simply replied, "I'm sure I don't know what you're talking about?"

"The hell you don't. You got what you wanted out of the deal. She's is out of the picture. And we own fifty-one percent of some little independently run Architecture firm. Jeez, just leave it be."

"I'm just making sure our investment stays afloat. That's all."

"Everything's fine, Melinda. Why don't you focus your attention on something where you can do some good." Lyle eased back into his chair. "Now, if you don't mind, I have work to do. I'll see you at home tonight." Lyle did not look up as Melinda silently exited his office.

She knew exactly where she was going to focus her attention next as she pressed the elevator button for the first floor.

Imperial's was an exclusive downtown restaurant that overlooked the Waterfront Harbor. During the week numerous business people frequented it, but reservations for a Friday or Saturday night had to be made weeks in advance. At Michael's suggestion, Casey graciously accepted his invitation. She now sat at a corner table for two, on the upper outside balcony. It was only mid-May but if felt like summer as a beautiful breeze cascaded off the water and gently caressed Casey's fair skin. She had removed her peach silk jacket, revealing a sleeveless cream-colored camisole. The knee length matching shorts rustled against her leg as she impatiently tapped her foot. Glancing down at her silver watch, Casey wondered if Michael was really going to show. As she took a sip of her ice water, a man approached her.

"Excuse me, are you Casey Andrews?"

"I am." Casey nodded.

"Mr. Sterling phoned and said his meeting ran late but he'll be here in fifteen minutes."

"Thank you."

"Can I refresh your drink or would you like to order an appetizer?" The young man's tone was polite and even.

"Actually, do you have raspberry ice tea?"

"We do. Would you like lemon with that?"

As Casey stood to go to the ladies room, she simply replied, "That would be nice."

The young man started to turn away, then added, "Oh, Mr. Sterling was very apologetic."

Casey stared into the mirror thinking she should have pulled her hair back. She fluffed her curls and reapplied her lipstick. The anticipation of Michael's arrival was overwhelming her. Having spent the morning hours calling the airlines, she had thought of everything but Michael's job offer. Now that he was late, numerous rationalizations swirled in her head.

As Casey approached the table, she felt the snugness of a masculine hand wrap around her waist and a whisper tickled her ear, "Sorry I'm late." She turned and was caught in Michael's embrace. Such an affectionate gesture caused an unexpected shiver to trickle down her spine. "And this is the real reason for my lateness." Michael handed Casey a bouquet of freshly cut flowers; an assortment of springtime's finest blooms. Daisies, roses, and tiger lilies, neatly accented with babies breath and fern leaves. As she slipped from his embrace and back into her seat, Michael simply smiled. A smile that could easily melt any woman's heart.

As Michael moved around to the other side of the table, Casey caught herself eyeing Michael's physique and his well-fit trousers. His tan was a sharp contrast to the light blue dress shirt that hugged his broad shoulders. *"He still looks gorgeous as ever…"* Casey thought then quickly looked away when the waiter arrived with her drink and a glass of ice water for Michael.

"What are we drinking to?" Michael questioned with enthusiasm.

"Ah…" Casey was speechless.

"I'd liked a draft, please." Michael exuded assurance always knowing what he wanted and how to get it, even something as trivial as a drink. "Where were we?"

"Michael, first of all thank you for the picture frame and the flowers. They're both quite beautiful, but you shouldn't have."

"I know, but I wanted to, seeing that I broke your picture frame and this cute little old lady was selling flowers on a street corner, I just couldn't resist." He squeezed lemon into his water and took a sip. "I'm glad you like the frame."

"How did you know where I lived?"

"There's only one C.M. Andrews listed so I took a chance." Michael shrugged. Confidence reigned over him. "So, have you given any thought to my offer?"

"Actually Michael, I haven't." She responded to him quickly but it was not the answer he wanted to hear, nor the one Casey wanted to give him. Considering herself a decisive person, her uncertainty was troubling her.

"Why don't you come by my office tomorrow? I can show you around. Introduce you to the staff." Michael stated with certainty believing that once he got her into the offices of Sterling Architects and Construction, Casey could not resist his offer of employment.

"I'd love to Michael, but I'm flying down to my sister's for the weekend. There were only two flights that had availability and since it is going to be such a short trip, I made reservations for tomorrow."

"What time is your flight?"

"Twelve-fifteen." Casey wanted to tell him otherwise, but opted not to.

"Be at my office at eight. I'll show you around. We'll talk, then I'll take you to the airport." Michael commanded.

"I guess Julie can pick me up Sunday night." Casey mumbled, looking over the balcony at the Harbor.

"I'll pick you up and take you out to dinner."

"Michael, let's have lunch first before we start making dinner plans. Besides, my return flight doesn't get in until six-thirty. By time we get to dinner…" Casey could not find a justifiable reason why she shouldn't have dinner with Michael. Granted, she would probably be tired from traveling. All the more reason to accept his invitation but she found it difficult to say yes.

"Why don't you ask your friend to join us and I'll ask Eric. You'll meet him tomorrow." Michael encouraged. "We'll make it a double…" Michael trailed off knowing it was too soon to mention anything more personal then having a meal together.

"Michael? Are you even listening to what I am saying?" Casey's words were terse, then she added, "What are you up to?" Casey's eyes narrowed as she smooth her hair away from her face.

"Crabs, drinks, maybe a game of darts at Bayside. Catching up with an old friend. Why?" There was a mysterious innocence in his tone.

"What an assumption Michael. Considering the length of time that has lapsed since we've seen each other, I think I'm making myself perfectly clear."

His casualness turned cold. "Casey, I haven't had much time for a social life. I need to relax. What's wrong with that?" His charm was indisputable yet his suggestions had Casey perplexed.

"I just feel there is something you're not telling me."

Just then the waiter appeared to take their order. Michael let out a sigh, relieved of the young man's presence. Casey was the one person that knew his intentions, sometimes before he knew them himself. "Are you ready to order?" The young man asked as he placed Michael's drink on the table.

"Can you give us just a few more minutes." Michael stated before Casey could reply to the waiter. Michael lightened the conversation hoping to avoid Casey's last statement. "I love coming down here."

"Me too. Especially on a day like today." Casey's harshness softened as a light breeze whistled across the water. "Whitely Designs did the interior of that building over there." Casey pointed to the building that stood perpendicular to where they sat. The Waterfront Harbor renovation had been completed in three years and the grand opening ceremony had taken place this past April, just in time for the start of the summer tourist season.

"Really? My company renovated the old movie house. Actually, it was quite a coupe. Melinda Parker, who runs the Historical Preservation Society, she nailed the Renovation Committee to the wall. And she got she wanted. Although, she does knows all the right people as well." Michael laughed. "So have you decided what you want?" Casey was taken aback by his question. "For lunch?"

"Oh, ah I'll have the California Club and potato salad."

"I'll have the Turkey Club and potato salad sounds good." The waiter wrote down their order and took their menus.

Now it was Michael's turn to be serious. "Casey, I'm sure the past twenty four hours have been overwhelming for you, but do you think we could start over?"

Melinda Parker handed the store clerk her credit card. As the clerk slid the card through the register, waiting for approval, Melinda, swirled her new diamond bracelet around her wrist. Then she started to count the endless rows of diamonds as the clerk handed her the receipt that required her signature. "Thank you, Mrs. Parker. Have a nice day."

Melinda simply smirked as she stepped outside, the warm sun reflecting against her diamond and emerald watch that bedecked her other wrist. Melinda was pleased that it was early enough and late enough in the day where she could sit quietly and have a martini without question. As she made her way upstairs, she was relieved there was no wait at Imperial's.

"Mrs. Parker. So nice to see you, again. Are you having lunch with us this afternoon?"

"No, Charles. Just a quiet seat in the lounge will do just fine."

Melinda smoothed her skirt underneath herself before she sat down. "The usual." Was all she said, until she caught a glimpse of the couple out on the terrace. Melinda stood straight, blood racing through her veins, teeth clench, her breathing harsh; she saw it all. The flowers, the laughter, the flirting as his hand reaching across the table towards the red-head whose back was to her. "Make it a double."

"So…" Michael questioned, "How is Hannah?"

"Good. Her and her husband, Adam, they live in South Carolina, now. His job transferred them there."

"Yeah, what does he do?" Michael had now shifted the conversation to a more superficial level.

Casey's eyes widened at the question. "You know, I'm not really sure. I know he's a Line Supervisor or something like that. I guess I'll have to ask him when I'm there." Casey joked as she tossed her curls to one side.

That gesture always drove Michael wild and he suddenly found himself feeling like the fifteen year old boy he was when they first met. Letting out a short sigh, he noticed it was getting late and motioned to the waiter for the check. "Well, if we don't get out of here, we're going to end up eating dinner here. Where are you parked?" Michael stood abruptly causing Casey to wonder what was the rush.

"Oh, in one of the many parking garages around here, somewhere." Casey noted nonchalantly as Michael assisted her with her jacket. Accidentally, his fingertips brushed against her bare skin and that feeling took over her body. "Well, I think I'm going to go do a little bit of shopping." Casey quickly rattled off as they ascended the outside steps to the Waterfront's ground level. "I have some things to pick up for my trip." She fibbed, wondering why she suddenly felt so uncomfortable in Michael's presence.

Chapter 5

It was a ten minutes before eight when Casey pulled her car into the parking garage. Glancing into the rear view mirror, Casey gave herself the once over as she dabbed a bit of clear gloss onto her lips. Quickly running her fingers through her bangs, several curls fell into place that nicely framed her face. Comfortably dressed, in a floral print blouse with tiny red, blue and yellow flowers, a navy blue skirt and sandals to match, Casey smoothed her hand over the material before she made her way across the street to Sterling Architects and Construction. As she approached the main entrance, Casey could not hide how impressed she was with the three-story brick building. Conveniently located in a section known as mid-town on the main thoroughfare of Madison Street, with a cluster of businesses on either side, the front façade was welcoming. Potted blossoms were strategically placed on either side of the entranceway while two potted plants hung from the green and white awing. Casey glanced down the street, noticing at the corner of Madison, where it crossed with Calverton, was The Corner Café. The ornate wrought iron, accentuating each building reminded Casey of the South.

Her fingers trembled slightly as she reached for the door and stepped into the reception area. Moving towards the receptionist's desk that was diagonally opposite the front door, Casey took in the décor. To the right of the desk was a large over stuff sofa. It was colonial blue accented with peach flowers. From the ceiling, in front of the bay window hung three Philodendrons, that soaked up the early morning sun. On the opposite wall were two navy blue chairs and a coffee table with a variety of reading materials, including Architectural Today. The walls had been painted a soft peach and the carpeting matched the chairs. Besides the shell shaped wall sconces, the only piece of art that hung on the wall was a painting above the sofa. The woman behind the desk was on the phone, so Casey stepped closer to the painting, wondering if she recognized the artist. Trying to stifle a gasp that escaped her lips, Casey turned back towards the receptionist's desk.

"May I help you?"

"Yes." With composer Casey asked, "Is Michael Sterling in, I'm Casey Andrews."

"Oh, yes. He's waiting for you in his office." The receptionist stood, reaching forward to shake Casey's hand, as she introduced herself. "I'm

Maggie Cowan." She was a tall shapely woman that towered over Casey. Her dark brown hair was neatly french-braid and tuck in at the nape of her neck. Black mascara highlighted her brown eyes and blush accentuated her full cheeks. She wore a lightweight suit in bright Kelly green and beige flats. Her silver bracelets clinked together as she pressed two buttons on the console, "Mr. Sterling, Casey Andrews is here." She paused, "Right away." Again she dialed two numbers, "Beth, I'm taking Miss Andrews up to Michael's office. Can you pick up the phones for a few minutes? Thanks."

Casey fell in step with Maggie as they walked down the hall. "Mr. Sterling's office is on the third floor. Stairs or do you prefer the elevator?" Maggie questioned cordially.

"Oh, the stairs are fine. So Maggie, how long have you worked for Michael?" Casey made idol conversation, as they drew closer to his office.

"Just about two years. I've been taking some night classes at the local Community College but it's hard to do with a family. Besides, I haven't quite decided between interior design and architecture. My husband thinks I should become an Architect yet we want to have more children. At this rate, I'll be a hundred before I get my degree." Maggie giggled softly.

"Oh, how many children do you have?" Casey questioned politely, when knowing whether or not Michael's receptionist had a child was the furthest thing on her mind.

"Just one. Joey. He's three and a holy terror. He just has a mind of his own." Maggie turned left at the top of the stairwell. The décor was identical to that of the first floor. At the end of the corridor the two women entered into an office that was nearly the same size as the lobby.

"Good morning, Mr. Sterling." Maggie greeted in a singsong voice.

"Good morning, Maggie, Casey." Michael stood.

Casey could barely utter the word hello. It was an uncomfortable feeling addressing Michael so formally, especially with their history. However, considering the circumstances, the situation at hand called for Casey to put forth her professional best regardless of how personal they had been in the past.

"Maggie, could you express mail this to Brookshire General Hospital? Also, I am expecting a package; call me when it gets here." Michael inquired as he handed a large envelope to Maggie.

"Consider it done. Can I get you two anything, coffee?"

Casey shook her head but it was Michael who responded, "No. I'll be showing Casey around and then we'll be leaving around ten-thirty but thank you."

Maggie turned to Casey, "It was nice to meet you Miss Andrews. I hope you decide to come on board."

"Thank you, Maggie. It was nice to meet you, too. And please, call me Casey."

Maggie nodded and exited Michael's office.

Michael had returned to his chair. "Please have a seat." Leaning back with his arms stretched behind his head he exuded such confidence as he asked, "So, Casey what do you think so far?"

"It's impressive, Michael, like I knew it would be."

"This is because of you."

"Excuse me?" Casey nearly choked causing her to question, why did he always try to surprise her? On some subconscious level, did he derive some silly amusement from his actions? Casey could only wonder about the answers to the questions that were plaguing her. As she cleared the tickle in her throat, Casey inquired, "I'm sorry. Could I trouble you for a glass of water?"

"Of course." Michael retrieved a bottle of water from his mini refrigerator, twisted off the cap and handed it to her. "Are you all right?" Then returned to his chair.

The cool water soothed her scratchy throat and gave her a moment to collect herself. "Michael, let's just keep this on a professional level."

"Fair enough. I'll play along…for now." Michael grinned then added, "Why don't I take you downstairs and show you around? You can leave your portfolio here. Eric wants to look through it while you're in South Carolina."

As Michael brushed by Casey, his spicy cologne permeated the air. Tickling her senses as it took her breath away, she placed her purse and portfolio in the chair beside her. "Don't lose it. My life is in there." Casey barely managed as she stood to exit his office.

The second floor was a large open space with a half a dozen cubicles. "This is the construction department I told you Eric runs. We have three project managers that work out of this office and four in the field who run the construction sites. Eighty percent of our business is commercial." They continued to move towards the front of the building.

Eric was hanging up his phone as Michael and Casey approached him at his desk, "Hey, Mike, what's up?"

"Eric, this is Casey Andrews. Casey, this is Eric Logan."

Casey's eyes followed his movement as he stood to shake her hand. "It's a pleasure to meet you." Looking up to address Eric, it was obvious he stood nearly six feet tall. Tight blond curls fell to his shoulders and behind wire rimmed glasses were hazel eyes and his blond stubble was speckled with gray. Eric possessed broad shoulders and well-developed muscles. His skin tone bronze, indicated he worked out doors.

"Yeah, and it's about time I met you. Mike's told me quite a bit about you."

Subconsciously Casey started twisting a lock of hair around her finger. Trying to hide her reddening face, she jokingly stated, "All good, I hope." Her eyes narrowed as she cast a quick glance in Michael's direction.

"Absolutely. So, I understand you're coming to work for this guy, huh? Play hard to get." Eric said in jest.

"I will take that under advisement." Casey acknowledged with a smile.

"Don't believe everything Eric tells you. He's a jokester so take *my advice*, be careful." Michael too was trying to hide his embarrassment.

"Joking aside Casey, we kid around but we take our business seriously. Mike has worked really hard to make this company a success. We want to expand with an Interior Design division and from what I've heard you're the best in the business. Did you bring your portfolio with you?" Eric's tone turned serious.

"I did but it's in Michael's office. I can go get it." Casey stumbled over her words as she started to depart Eric's office.

Michael then cut in, "Casey, don't worry about it."

"Well, perhaps I can look at it later." Eric stated with an even tone, addressing Michael more so than Casey. "Well, I hope you decide to join the family."

"We'll see. If I'm here on Monday, you know Michael gave me an offer I couldn't refuse." Casey pursed her lips as she continued to fuss with her hair.

"Well then, I guess Mike is going to have to make you an offer you can't refuse." Eric teased then added, "We're preparing a proposal for the new hospital wing at Brookshire; it would be great if we could include some preliminary design sketches."

"I'll see what I can do." Casey offered.

"Maggie is sending the materials cost sheet over to the Hospital this morning. Good work Eric." Michael turned to leave then added, "I'm taking Casey to the airport in awhile, so if you need to reach me, call my cell phone. I should be back after lunch."

"Oh that's right. Have a safe trip. See you Sunday night. It was nice to meet you." Obviously Michael had already confirmed their plans for dinner at Bayside.

Casey nodded and followed Michael back upstairs. "I'll have to call Julie before I leave. Between calling the airlines, my sister and packing, I completely forgot. I'm sorry."

"Perhaps you'd like to call her from your office?" Michael offered as he stepped into the office they had casually passed by earlier.

For the moment Casey let her guard down. "Oh Michael, it's beautiful." Taken in by the plush mauve carpeting that accented the soft antique white walls, Casey was rendered speechless as she mulled over every detail. Next to the windows was a drafting table. Perpendicular to the table was a desk, similar to Maggie's and in the corner, to Casey's left, were two chairs strategically placed on either side of a small glass table with wrought iron accents. "You didn't do this just for me, did you?"

"This office has been empty for awhile since Eric moved downstairs."

"Michael, you're avoiding my question."

"Well, after I ran into you, I came back here and Eric and I talked for an hour about starting the design division. At first he was hesitant but then he got really excited, so last night a couple of guys from one of the crews, Eric and myself stayed until midnight painting. Eric said he will have the carpeting cleaned this weekend. We still need to order a computer for you but I guess it's Eric's way of saying he wants you to work here."

"Michael this is wonderful and…"

"And…"

"…a bit overwhelming. You have to slow down. I haven't said yes."

"But you will."

Lyle Parker straightened his pale yellow silk tie and propped his reading glasses onto his nose before he opened the file Payne Claiborne had just laid on his desk. He held up two pieces of paper and peered at his assistant. "That's it?"

Payne rocked up and down on his toes, "I'm sorry sir but the only thing I found was that traffic ticket and if my calculations are correct, that ticket was issued when she was in high school. And it was paid for within a week of issue. Her credit rating is impeccable because she pays her bills on time. The only living relative she has is a sister. Single. No children. And…"

Lyle held his hand up, "Enough. I want to know what is going on over at Sterling Architects."

"Simple. He's offered her a job." Payne shrugged. "That's it sir. That's all I could find."

"I want every stone unturned. Parents, grandparents, even great grandparents. Schools, organizations, political affiliation, religious affiliation...I want it all."

Payne nodded. "I understand sir." He exited without comment. Perplexed though, Payne did not understand why Mr. Parker wanted an extensive background check done on someone like Casey Andrews. Payne knew he would find nothing.

"Look, when my wedding was called off, I gave my every waking moment to this company. And well, your name came up in conversation, several times. For some reason, it prompted me to want to expand the company..."

"I was wondering if you were ever going to tell me." Casey cut him off. Even though they had gone their separate ways after college, Casey found it hard to believe Michael had ever considered marrying someone else. But then again life did go on and his obviously had without her.

"How do you know?"

"I ran into Valerie Sorrenson at Hidden Springs Lake, last summer. She went on about how I had missed such a great reunion and you were with your fiancée so at this point, I assumed you were either divorced or you have a very understanding wife. Besides... it's not really any of my business whether or not you're married. I knew you would tell me when you were ready."

"I don't even know where she is and at this point, I really don't care."

"What happened?" Casey hesitated.

Michael drew in a breath and crossed his arms over his chest. "She left me at the altar, literally. No one had heard from her all day. Eric went over to her house and found a note taped to the front door. If you can you believe that. She didn't even have the nerve to face me." There was pain in Michael's voice. With his back to Casey, staring out the window, Michael continued, "She said she couldn't marry me. She was leaving town and I was to forget about her. A part of me died that day. But business was starting to soar so that's been my life for the last three years."

"Michael, I'm sorry you had to go through that." Casey could see the muscles in his back tense against his dark green polo. The need to console him consumed her heart but rationally she knew her actions would be misunderstood.

44

Ignoring Casey's sympathetic words, Michael made his declaration, "Her leaving, made me realize I really didn't love her. It hurt but it was too easy to move on." He drew in a deep breath as he stared out the window. The silence in the room made Casey feel uncomfortable. As she started to speak Michael continued, his voice was smooth and deep, "There's only one woman I've ever loved and I let her go." Michael mumbled, oblivious to Casey's presence until he heard her clear her throat. Michael abruptly turned around; Casey noticed his cheeks were a deep shade of red.

His truthfulness cut through Casey's heart and old emotions churned inside, exactly what Casey feared and her decision became evident. They could not have a professional relationship without it becoming personal. "Michael, I'm flattered by what you've done. I really appreciate the opportunity to work for you. Believe me, it's tempting but I think it would be best for the both of us that I look elsewhere. And...you don't have to take me to the airport. I'm only going to be gone for the weekend so I..."

"Casey..." Michael cut her off mid-sentence, his fists clenched by his side as a wave of embarrassment surged through his veins. He had broken his promise to himself. The last thing he intended was getting too serious, too fast with Casey Andrews, again. "Aw, forget what I just said. But you are right."

"I am?" Casey stomach tightened. She didn't think he would agree so easily considering he had practically demanded she come work for him. "Well, then, I guess I'll see you around."

"Casey, I didn't mean, not work for me. What I meant to say is, you're right; we need to keep strictly professional. Just forget the past. It worked out for the best. Will you take the weekend to think about heading up the design department?"

Chapter 6

"Nice painting, Michael." Her words caught him off guard as they stepped out into the warmth of the sun. Retrieving her sunglasses from her purse, Casey positioned them on her nose as she glared over the rim, waiting for a response from Michael.

Struggling to choose his words carefully, Michael remained silent as he crossed Madison, a few steps in front of Casey.

"Michael, did you hear what I said?" Casey called out as she tried to fall into step next to him.

Standing in the shadow of the parking garage, Michael paused, turning towards Casey, "I heard you. I just don't want to talk about it right now." Twisting his lips, he calmly managed to shift the conversation, "Why don't you get your bags and I'll pull my car around?"

As Michael proceed towards his car, Casey stood motionless, astonished by his aloofness. "That's it!" Casey wanted to scream as she searched her memory. But Casey could not recall a time when Michael had ever been so stand offish with her. Then the realization hit her, she was searching for the Michael she had met and fallen in love with too many years ago. And time had moved forward. Circumstances, good or bad, caused people to change and it was now obvious to Casey that he was not the same person. He had changed. Forcing one foot in front of the other, Casey made her way to her car, retrieving her bags from the trunk. Once her luggage was in the trunk of Michael's car, Casey slipped into the passenger seat. "Michael, is my car going to be safe here, over the weekend?"

Michael noted the concern in her voice, "Give me your keys. Eric and I will take care of it this afternoon. We'll take it to my house then it'll be there when we finish dinner Sunday night." He stated smoothly as he shifted into gear.

Reluctantly, Casey reached into her purse, handing her keys over to Michael.

The events of the past few days had made Casey feel she was on an endless roller coaster ride and at this moment, her head was spinning and her heart was pounding. A deep sigh escaped her lips and not even the warmth of the bright sunny day could relinquish her stress. Thoughts crashed like waves against breakers with no sign of letting up. Silently, she wished she could snap her fingers and be landing in South Carolina right now. The short drive to the airport seemed to take forever and the silence was deafening. Finally, relief washed over Casey as Michael pulled up to the curb for departing flights. Simultaneously, they stepped out of his Maxima. Michael opened the trunk and as Casey reached for her suitcase, Michael's hand landed on top of hers. The intensity of his touch set off a fire that rage through her body in an instant.

"Casey, I'm sorry." Michael's sincerity snapped Casey to attention.

"For what Michael?" Her tone was sharp as she place her luggage down.

Michael moved closer, reaching for Casey. Gently he lifted her chin, gazing into her curious brown eyes, "Casey, don't take this all so seriously. Let's just wipe the slate clean and start anew." Michael's gaze was cold, yet his gesture was heart-warming. "If it is that important for you to know, your painting has gone wherever I have. It's hung in every office I have ever worked. It's been an inspiration and a reminder for me to keep pursuing my dreams. You taught me to never give up."

Shock fell over Casey at the honesty of his words. "Thank you but I think you were born with that instinct." She teased as she lifted her carry on bag onto her shoulder.

As Casey headed towards the terminal, Michael caught her by her elbow. "Casey, I never should have mentioned anything about my engagement to…"

Casey pressed her fingertips lightly against Michael's lips. "Say no more. We make our choices."

The sides of Michael's lips curled into a smile as Casey removed her hand. "I really hope you take the job and I promise, strictly professional." As Michael turned to shut the trunk and wish Casey a safe trip, a passing motorist shouted, "Will you hurry it up and kiss her so we can get a move on here!"

Casey speculated what would prompt such a comment, yet she found herself staring at Michael's lips. She found herself wondering and she found herself wanting to be reminded of what his lips felt like on hers. But before Casey could be so impulsive with such a gesture, her thoughts were interrupted by a boisterous laugh.

"Have a safe trip and I'll see you Sunday night. Tell your sister I said hello."

"I will." Her voice cracked. Casey turned and walked towards the terminal. At the sliding doors she turned and started to wave good bye to Michael but he was already gone.

The flight to South Carolina was three hours with a stop somewhere in North Carolina. Unable to sleep on the first leg of her flight, Casey had barely closed her eyes when she boarded the second plane and now it was taxiing towards the terminal. Feeling listless, Casey turned her thoughts away from the past week and painted on a smile. She reached for her carry-on and proceeded through the gate.

"There she is!" shouted two young voices. Casey was surprised they were at the gate as she bent down on one knee to greet Jason and Emily with hugs and kisses. In return she got two tight squeezes and shouts of joy.

Standing, Casey reached out for her sister, Hannah and embraced her with an endless hug. "How are you?" Casey's gently patted her sister's shoulder. "God, I've missed you. You look great!" Brown curls that had fallen out of her ponytail framed Hannah's round face. Pink blush simmered on her cheeks and matched her lipstick. Her pink tee shirt was neatly tucked into her denim shorts. And as always, once the temperature was above seventy degrees, Hannah broke out her brown leather Birkenstocks.

"They let you down here?" Due do recent events around the world, airport security had multiplied ten-fold. "I'm really surprised. It took me an hour to get through security back home."

Hannah shrugged. "I guess it's because we're not a major airport and there is only this one terminal. We still had to go through a thorough security check."

Shaking her head, Casey didn't want to think about what had happened nine months ago, in New York City, Pennsylvania and virtually, her backyard. It was going to be a fun and relaxing weekend with her family and serious conversation about world events was not part of her agenda. She had shed thousands of tears and her and Hannah had more than exhausted that topic.

"Well, Hannah you look great, as always."

"Not for long. Soon I'll be fat again."

"Hannah! Are you pregnant?" Casey whispered as she covered her mouth to stifle a giggle. "Why didn't you tell me? Oh my gosh, another Nayler on the way."

"Ah, I just got the results this morning. Adam and I had our suspicions and surprise, surprise, number three. But I'm a lot further along than I thought." The two sisters hugged again at the joy of the good news. "It looks like we're going to have a very happy New Year." Hannah giggled.

Casey rubbed her sister's flat stomach. "That's your due date?"

Hannah nodded and smiled at the attention Casey was showering her with, but Hannah's mood shifted when she asked, "Is everything okay?"

"Oh, it's a long story and there will be plenty of time to talk about it." Casey tried to be upbeat, not wanting to downplay her sister's good news. Abruptly changing the subject, Casey asked, "Do you think we can stop for a snack? I skipped breakfast and I was asleep when the flight attendants served lunch. Not that I'll all that jazzed about airline food."

"Sure. Why'd you skip breakfast?"

Hannah didn't miss a thing and even after thirty-some years, she still took Casey by surprise. "I had a meeting this morning."

"You mean The Snake wouldn't let you take the whole day off? Jeez, I would quit that job."

"Not exactly but I'll tell you about it later. Let's get out of here."

Casey's comment confirmed for Hannah that something big had happened for Casey to suddenly hop on a plane but for now she would let it slide. "Adam's making shrimp and ribs tonight and that won't be until about seven. He wants to grill. There's a really great deli by the house. I want to get some red skin potato salad. For some reason, I'm craving it." Hannah snickered. "Wait until you see the deck. Adam did such a great job. We eat outside practically every night." Stars danced in Hannah's eyes, assuring Casey of her sister's happiness.

"Aunt Casey, are you coming to live with us?" Jason asked as he placed his little hand into Casey's. Jason had turned five in January and had become quite the conversationalist.

"Oh, no honey. But I'm here for the weekend. And you and Emily and your mom and dad are going to visit me at the end of the summer."

"Yeah! Do you wanna go to the beach?"

"Can we mom?" Emily jumped up and down with excitement.

"We're going tomorrow, but you can go in the pool when we get home." Hannah stated as she brushed her hand over her daughter's straight brown hair.

"Aunt Casey, can I get your suitcase? You know I'm seven now. I'm a big girl." Emily said coyly.

"I can see that, Emily. I think you've grown six inches since the last time I saw you." Casey was taken in by the innocence of her big brown eyes.

"No, just four inches." Emily joked.

Casey only had one carry-on piece and her purse so they by-passed baggage claim and went directly to Hannah's car. On the way to the house, they stopped at the local deli, Hannah had been raving about, and bought sandwiches. Hannah also purchased, dinner rolls, cole slaw and macaroni salad along with her potato salad for tonight's cookout. "Hannah, you're not feeding an army." Casey laughed with her sister when she saw the enormity of her purchase.

"I know. We can always take the leftovers with us to the beach, tomorrow." Hannah squeaked knowing she was actually being practical. With Casey's last minute decision to fly down for the weekend, the last thing Hannah wanted to do was spend it grocery shopping and cooking. She just wanted to be with her sister.

Casey was excited to be with her family and for the first time in days she felt the tension slip away. Within minutes of their arrival, Casey had pulled her hair into a ponytail and changed into her one-piece black bathing suit and pair of white shorts. Barefoot, she stepped out the back door and onto the freshly built deck. It was partially covered and housed wicker patio furniture. Emily and Jason were already splashing around in an above the ground pool, that was just their size.

"I thought it would be nice to eat out here." Hannah was lounging on the sunny side of the deck nibbling at the tuna sandwich, her and Casey decided to share. "So, tell me Miss Corporate America, how is dear old sweet Mr. Whitley?" Hannah giggled.

"That's Ms. to you." Casey giggled then added sharply, "That Snake let me go."

"He fired you? Oh my…I knew something was up."

"Why do you say that?"

"You always come to visit when something is wrong."

"I do?" Casey actually felt embarrassed that she had run to Hannah's side for comfort without even realizing it.

"Well, not always but I'm glad you're here." Hannah reached for Casey's hand, "I may not be older, I may not be wiser but I will always be here for you."

"Hannah…thank you. That is so sweet. You always were my favorite sister." Casey teased.

"I'm your only sister." Hannah eyed Casey, then her words became serious. "We're all we got. Besides what are sisters for? So what are you going to do?"

Casey's demeanor changed, "Oh! You will never believe who I ran into as I was leaving Whitley's on Wednesday…never, ever guess in a million years." Casey scrunched her nose.

"There's only one person that has ever gotten you this excited. I'll flip out if it was Michael Sterling."

"Yes!" Casey's brown eyes sparkled in the early evening sun as she faced her younger sibling. Hannah's eyes twinkled too, a trait they both inherited from their mother.

Hannah swung her legs around and jolted into an upright position, "Tell me, tell me, tell me! What happened?"

Hannah listened attentively as Casey recapped the past weeks events. "But Hannah, I really want out of the business, altogether. I've been thinking about a major career move. I want to become involved in charity work. Planning special events or something like that."

Hannah understood her sister's dilemma. "Well, Casey, if you want my opinion, I think you should take the job, even if it is only temporarily. For six months. It certainly would look impressive on your resume. Wouldn't that show that you have good planning and organizational skills? Maybe Michael would help pay for a class or seminar? Maybe you could volunteer and involve Michael's company in a fundraiser or…" Casey nodded as Hannah paused in the middle of her speech. "I agree with Julie, take the job!" Hannah gestured towards Casey, as if she were reprimanding a child, "Just be certain that you can keep your feelings out of it."

Casey crossed her arm over her chest, "That's what I'm worried about."

"Oh!" Hannah rolled her eyes. "Please don't tell me you're *still* harboring feelings for Michael Sterling. Casey, as I recall, when he left for graduate school, you vowed and I quote, 'I'm never falling in love again!' and you've been pretty true to your word up until now."

"Up until now my career has been the love of my life. Besides, that was a lifetime ago."

"Exactly my point, Casey. You're the strongest most independent woman I know. Don't let him take that away from you."

"Aunt Casey, Aunt Casey…" Jason came running towards her, beaming from ear to ear, "Look, watch…" He ran towards the pool and jumped over the two-foot wall and into the water.

"Ta-dah!" He threw his arms up into the air and then shouted, "I'm a diver!" The yard echoed with joyous laughter.

Tugging on his tie and unbuttoning the top two buttons of his dress shirt, Adam crept up behind Casey and Hannah, "Hey gorgeous." A deep voice resounded.

"Adam Nayler!" Casey went to give her brother-in-law a hug and to her surprise, he scooped her up into his arms and swung her around. Finally, her feet landed safely on the ground. "Adam, you silly, I see my sister is keeping you healthy and happy." Casey had her arm around his waist as she gently poked his stomach.

"And my beautiful wife." Adam released Casey and pulled his wife close to him. "Kiss me baby." He embraced Hannah as his lips met hers.

"Funny you say that." Casey interjected with a smile.

"What? Baby? We did it again?" Adam questioned as he massaged Hannah's flat stomach.

Hannah nodded to her husband as a tear moistened the corner of her eye. They kissed again.

"Woo Hoo! We have to celebrate. And ladies, do I have a surprise for you. After our cookout and the kids are in bed...Mar-gar-itas are on the house! Although my wife's will be virgin." Adam snapped his fingers and moved back and forth, trying to cha-cha. Hannah and Casey's giggles were joined with the clamoring of Jason and Emily greeting their father.

"Daddy! Daddy!" Being so happy-go-lucky, he gathered his drenched children into his arms and showered them with hugs and kisses not having a care that his dress shirt was getting soiled.

"Hello, my munchkins. Are you two going to help me grill tonight?"

"Really daddy? Oh, you're the best." Emily's long lashes fluttered as she patted Adam's cheeks and returned his kisses. Then she brushed her little fingers through his tight black curls.

"But first daddy has to go change into his chef's outfit." Adam slid his children down to the ground and they ran across the yard. Bursts of shouts and laughter escaped their lips as Emily and Jason jump back into the pool, splashing each other. Adam went into the house as Casey and Hannah returned to their lounge chairs.

"Ah, this is the life." Casey pulled her sunglasses from atop her head and eased back into her chair. "Hannah, you are so lucky."

"Yeah, I am but the grass always looks greener on the other side of the fence. You're lucky, too. And you'll realize it once you say yes to Michael."

Casey did not respond.

The summer-like sun was still above the horizon at dinner time when Adam and the kids lit the grill and started preparing the shrimp and ribs.

Casey and Hannah set the picnic table for their cookout. "You know Hannah it's perfect moments like this, is when I really miss mom."

"I know what you mean but I believe that she is watching over us."

"I don't doubt that for a moment. So, have you thought of any names for the baby yet?"

"I think it's a little too soon for that but you'll be the first to know." Hannah's infectious laughter echoed through the yard.

"Well, how about Casey?" She raised an eyebrow to her sister. "What? It's a good name."

"I think if it is a girl, I want to name her after mom."

"Oh Hannah that would be wonderful."

The evening had cooled after the sun dipped below the horizon. Hannah was inside helping Emily and Jason get ready for bed. Casey quietly cleaned up the dinner dishes as Adam was scrapping the grill. "Hannah tells me you're going to be working for Michael Sterling. That's pretty gutsy, if you ask me."

"Gutsy? Why do you say that?"

"I don't think I could have an ex-girlfriend working for me. What, with all that history? The risk of being the brunt of office gossip. Misunderstood words and actions. Like I said, gutsy."

"Well, to be perfectly honest Adam, I haven't accepted Michael's offer and I am not sure that I'm going to."

Adam and Casey were now seated opposite each other at the picnic table, "Don't get me wrong, I'm not trying to discourage you. Hannah and I just want you to be sure you know what you're getting yourself into, that's all. We just want you to be happy."

"Hey, where's my margarita, honey?" Hannah teased as she approached Adam and Casey.

"Coming right up."

An ocean breeze rustled the trees above so Casey went inside to change into her jeans. She peeked in on Jason and then Emily, giving them each a kiss and hug good night. When she returned to the patio Adam had already served the drinks and was dealing out playing cards for a few rousing games of gin rummy. The evening proved to be relaxing as they exchanged the latest events in the Nayler family. Emily had lost a tooth and was already asking about sleepovers and nail polish, showing she was mature beyond her youth. Jason had expressed excitement about being able to go to the same school with Emily in September.

The timing of Adam's promotion and substantial raise could not have been more perfect with the announcement of Hannah's pregnancy. Hannah had been mulling over the idea of working part-time and had expressed that after the baby was born, that was her intention.

"Well, I'm going to call it a night." Casey gave her sister a hug and a kiss on her cheek and then turned towards Adam and hugged him as well. "Thanks for playing master chef tonight."

"Anything for my favorite sister-in-law." Adam bellowed.

In the spare bedroom, Casey changed into an old worn-out shirt she had found rolled into a ball and tucked away in one of the pockets of her luggage. The tattered material hung loosely over her curves and a smile ran across her face when she remembered where she had acquired it. It was Michael's old college soccer jersey and the only physical evidence she had, that he was once a part of her life. Casey turned out the lights and snuggled up in the rocking chair, staring out the window at the star lit sky. She couldn't help but think about her mom and wondered what advice she would giver her. But deep inside, Casey knew Hannah had already spoken the words. She couldn't help but think of Michael again. The chirping of the crickets soothed her as she crawled into bed, lulling her to sleep. Within minutes Casey was dreaming.

Snow the night before her twenty-first birthday led to classes being cancelled the next day. Michael had been keeping his distance for over a week now and he had yet to mentioned her birthday. Not having heard from him nor seeing him, Casey resolved that this was one birthday that was going to be like any other day. She refused to give him the satisfaction of her anger. After dinner she decided to study for a few hours and then go to the corner pizza place with her friend Susan. It was nine o'clock when there was a knock at the door.

"Are we going? Come on we have some celebrating to do." Susan was always cheerful.

"I don't know? I'm not in the mood. No offense but this birthday is not what I expected." Her words were laced with sadness.

"Oh no Casey we won't have any of this. Get up, get dressed and let's go. We don't have to go to the pizza place. I heard there's a party over in the next dorm. Let's go check it out. If you're not having fun, we'll leave and go somewhere else."

"Oh, all right."

Dressed in a maroon thermal top, jeans, a flannel shirt and boots, Casey and Susan walked across the snowy field to Richmond Hall. The door creaked as they entered the main floor.

"Susan, I don't think there's any party...why are the lights out?"

"I'm almost certain there was supposed to be one tonight. Chris told me about it at dinner. Let's go in the lounge and see if anyone is there."

Casey could barely see as she walked up two steps and turned left. "Susan, this is spooking me. It's too quiet."

"Surprise!" Shouts filled the room as the lights came on.

Casey began to shake and cry from the shouts of her friends. She felt the heat rise to her face as she turned to Susan, "You knew! Didn't you?"

"Somebody get this girl a drink." Susan shouted above the festivities. The two broke out into laughter as Casey gave Susan a hug. Casey brushes the tears from her cheeks as she accepted a glass filled with punch. Swiping a hand through her red curls, Casey scanned the crowd for Michael. There in the opposite corner of the room he stood, simply smiling. Casey quickly crossed the room. "Please tell me this is why I haven't seen you in a week?"

Michael nodded then planted a kiss on her cheek.

Casey brushed her hand against his cheek. "Thank you."

Michael's wrapped her in his arms, his body pressing against hers. Passion swelled in Casey's heart as his whisper tickled her ears. "This is the reason why we haven't seen each other." Cupped in his hand was a small box wrapped in floral paper with a purple ribbon.

With trembling fingers, Casey pulled the wrapping from her gift. Lifting the lid Casey gasped and almost lost her balance but Michael held her close. "Oh Michael, it's beautiful."

"Here, let me put it on you." He slipped the ring onto her finger. The heart shape diamond and amethyst stones glimmered in the light. Michael pulled her close pressing his lips to hers. His parted lips searched her mouth that rocked her most private part. She tightened her embrace as Michael's hands caressed her back. "Let's go to my room." He suggested as he pressed his lips to hers again.

A soft breeze caressed Casey's half-dressed body. At that moment, she laid awake, mystified by her dream.

Casey was awake and dressed before the dawn's first light, a habit she could not seem to break even if she could sleep in. A deafening silence shrouded her sister's house so Casey decided to walk down to the shore. Adam and Hannah lived a little over a mile from the beach, so it was no surprise that that was where Casey ended up. The sun was starting to show itself over the Atlantic as Casey sat huddled up against the empty lifeguard stand. Zipping up her jacket as a cool breeze cascaded off the ocean, she reached for the delicate cross that hung around her neck. Then Casey mumbled out loud. "I was taught to trust you, so here I am, doing just that. If I am supposed to work for Michael Sterling, then I will. I just ask, you keep my heart strong and don't let me lose my head." Calmness fell over Casey as she beheld the sunrise. It was picture postcard perfect, as the sun painted the sky pink, orange, lavender and blue. Relieved, she got up and meandered back towards her sister's house. As the sun became a full sphere on the horizon, a smile graced Casey's lips.

Having returned from her morning walk and none of her relatives were stirring, Casey decided to make breakfast. As she flipped a pancake in the large skillet a scratchy voice mumbled, "Morning Aunt Casey." Rubbing her eyes, Emily hugged her aunt. Within minutes Jason was awake too and hugged his aunt in the same manner. Enlisting the help of her niece and nephew, Casey prepared breakfast in bed for Adam and Hannah.

Emily and Jason both dressed themselves and headed to the back yard to pick some flowers for their parents. When the three of them entered the master bedroom, Hannah and Adam's eyes lit up.

"You shouldn't have." Hannah beamed.

"Oh come on, sis, when was the last time you and Adam slept late?"

"Casey is right sweetheart, we should take advantage of her." Adam teased.

"Adam!" Casey tossed a small decorative pillow at him. And they all laughed.

Before he could retaliate, the phone rang. "Casey, it's your boss." And Adam let out another burst of laughter as he handed her the phone.

"So have you decided." He could not quell the eagerness in his voice.

"Michael, I said I would give you my answer when I return." Casey did not want to discuss her terms over the phone. "I'll see you tomorrow night. Is

Eric going to join us?"

"Yes. What about Julie?"

"She said she couldn't make it until eight but she'll be there."

"Casey, can you at least give me a hint?"

Casey let out a slight giggle, "No way. You're just going to have to wait."

"You're enjoying this, aren't you?"

"As a matter of fact, Michael, I am. I got to go. Just wait outside baggage claim, I'll meet you there."

"Oh, all right. See you tomorrow."

Casey giggled again as she hung up the phone.

The rest of the weekend was filled with lots of activity. After they had spent the day at the beach, Casey, Hannah, Adam and the kids dined at a local restaurant that looked out onto the ocean. The local seafood was fit for a queen. Casey savored every bit of the crab stuff Salmon she had ordered along with mixed salad greens. Hannah ordered her favorite, steamed spiced shrimp, while Adam enjoyed the Surf and Turf special. Emily and Jason were satisfied with the traditional kids fare of fish sticks and french fries. Stuffed to the gills, the kids had fallen asleep on the way home. While Adam put the kids to bed, Hannah and Casey had opted to watch a video.

On Sunday, Adam took Emily and Jason to the park while Casey and Hannah went shopping. The boardwalk was donned with dozens of boutiques and novelty shops. Casey found the perfect sundress, although she struggled with the purchase wondering if she would have the opportunity to ever wear it. Hannah encouraged, "It's perfect. I think you should buy it. But I'm warning you, don't wear it in front of Michael." Hannah teased with an all knowing grin.

Casey had a sour look on her face, "Now, why would you say that?"

"Because, unless you want him to fall in love with you again, I advise against it because you look awesome. It's... you!"

The weekend had gone by too fast yet Casey felt renewed and energized. It was always difficult for Casey to say good-bye, especially to her one and only sister, but Casey knew she had to get back to her own life and deep down inside she was ready to give Michael her answer. "I'm really going to miss you so much. Are you and Adam definitely coming up for Labor Day weekend?"

"We'll be there. You could invite Michael, if you want to. It would be interesting to see him, again."

"Hannah, you are too much. Now you take care of yourself. Get plenty of rest, eat your veggies and take your vitamins."

"Casey, I'm not ill, I'm just going to have a baby."

"I know…" Casey patted Hannah's tummy. "Bye little new niece or nephew. Aunt Casey loves you."

"Aunt Casey, we want a hug." Jason and Emily were both reaching up.

Casey bent and gave them each a hug. "Oh, I had so much fun, you two. I can't wait until you come to visit me. We're gonna go to the lake and swim and fish. You two be good. I will talk to you next week."

"We love you Aunt Casey." Her niece and nephew proclaimed in unison.

Caressing their cheeks, "I love you both very much."

"So gorgeous, you keep that Michael Sterling in line, okay?" Adam leaned forward to give his sister-in-law a hug. "And if you need anything, call us, okay?" Casey nodded in agreement fighting back the tears, thankful Adam had become the brother she never had.

"Well, Casey…I guess this is it. Call me tomorrow night. I want to hear all the juicy details." The two sisters let out a chorus of laughter, then Hannah turned serious, "So are you going to take my advise or what?"

Casey just smiled.

"The weekend was too short." Casey thought to herself as she grabbed her carry-on from the over head bin. Memories of her family weekend danced in her mind, remembering Jason and Emily's silly laughter. *"They've grown so fast."* And Casey realized the faster they grew the more she missed having family around or even a family of her own.

"Are you going to get off the plane? Some of us want to go home." The obnoxious woman stated. She had been seated next to Casey the entire flight and was now shifting her impatient attitude from the flight attendants to Casey and it showed from her sarcastic tone.

Quietly apologizing, Casey jumped out into the aisle and made her way through the airport terminal, not paying attention to the crowd waiting just beyond security.

"Let me take that for you." Michael's smooth voice startled Casey. Looking up into his green eyes, they gleamed as he reached for Casey's bag. "And you can carry this."

Overwhelmed, Casey could not find the right words to respond to

Michael's gesture. She held the bouquet close and became engulfed in the sweet aroma. With a light touch Casey traced her finger over the delicate petals of the three red roses, then the white daisies, and finally the purple violets. His five o'clock shadow tickled her cheek as she found herself wrapped in his embrace. An unexpected ache gripped her mid-section and she quickly pulled away from the warmth of his touch. "Michael they are so beautiful. Thank you, but you've got to stop showering me with gifts... you're going to spoil me." Casey hoped she was making her point without sounding ungrateful.

"And what is wrong with that?" And that was something Casey could not deny. When they were together in high school and through college, Michael found contentment in being able to pamper Casey. And to him, some things had not changed. "I just wanted your week to be better than last week. Regardless of your decision, I know it was rough for you and I just thought...by the way, how was your trip?"

"It's was good." Casey's tone showed her aggravation at how deftly Michael could change the subject. "Getting back to the flowers... " She added quickly. "You thought you could coax me into accepting your offer?"

Michael creased his brow and his dimples disappeared at her remark.

"I take it back, Michael. Let's get out of here." Looping her arm in his, it remained there for a brief moment until Casey had to pull away.

The balminess of the late spring evening surrounded them as they made their way to the airport-parking garage. Casey's sudden silence was making him edgy but Michael knew he could not push her into making a decision. As he turned the key in the ignition, Michael quietly hoped she would give him the opportunity to make things right. He had never forgiven himself for how he had treated her so long ago. Yet, the day before they graduated college was engrained in his thoughts as if it had happened yesterday.

It was exceptionally hot for the early part of May when Casey and Michael had packed a picnic and went to their favor spot, Hidden Springs Lake. They had finished their sandwiches when Michael suggested they take a walk. As they hiked the mountain that over looked the lake, a soft breeze swept over their sweaty bodies. Only the sound of nature surrounded them as Michael pulled Casey into his arms.

"You know I love you Casey."

"Of course...I love you, too. Can you believe it? We did it.

Tomorrow is graduation, then it's the real world for us." Casey's eyes lit up like sparklers on the Fourth of July.

"For you." Michael corrected.

As Casey stepped back a twig snapped beneath her boot. "What are you talking about?"

"I got accepted to Graduate School."

"Michael that is wonderful. We have to celebrate this weekend."
"Not exactly."

"What do you mean not exactly? Cut to the chase Michael. Whatever it is, just tell me."

"I got accepted to University of Southern California."

. "What? You're joking, right?" Casey wanted to believe he was kidding, then it dawned on her, "You mean you took the GRE exam and never told me?" The truth was beginning to sink in. "Never mind. I don't want to know. But what I do want to know is, what possessed you to apply to a college three thousand miles away...away from me?" Casey choked on her tears.

"My father. That's the only way he'll pay for it, if I go to his alma mater." Michael moved towards Casey and wiped her tear stained cheeks. "Casey, listen, we can make it work. You can come with me."

"You know I can't Michael. I start my internship in two weeks. I've already accepted it and it's with one of the most prestigious design groups on the East Coast. Plus I put down a non-refundable deposit on an apartment..." Casey trailed off. "Besides, I can't leave my mom and my sister behind."

"It won't be that long. I'll be back before you know it. I don't leave until August and you know I will come home for Thanksgiving and Christmas." Feeling as if her world was crumbling, Casey sat down burying her head in her hands. Michael knelt before her, "I know we can make it work. Somehow we will make it work." He encouraged, unconvincingly.

Casey lifted her head, "You can go on believing that Michael, but when it comes to your father, he always wins. Always. You know that and so do I. I can't fight him to keep you. And I don't feel I can keep this either." Casey pulled the diamond and amethyst ring from her finger.

"Casey, don't!" Tears now welled in Michael's eyes.

"Don't what, Michael?" He fell silent as he accelerated onto the interstate.

"Michael, did you hear what I said?" Casey shouted. "Six months."

"What? What are you talking about?"

"Six months, Michael. I will work for you until the end of the year. By then I should have your design department up and running and I will have someone trained to take over my position."

"Really?" Michael could hardly contain his excitement.

"There are a few other things like benefits. And, I'm willing to work as many hours as you need but I want the flexibility to set my own schedule. Sometimes, I'm more productive working at home."

"That's fine, Casey." Michael replied coolly, containing his excitement.

"I have a pretty big client list from Whitley Design's and I'm sure most of them will follow me. So I want to negotiate a percentage of the profits I bring into the company. And in order to make it official, I'd like a written contract."

Michael gave Casey a peculiar look.

"Don't worry Michael, I'm not going to bankrupt you. I just want a small…" Casey drew in a deep breath then added, "We'll call it a Christmas bonus. Okay?" Casey's voice was light and ready to burst with laughter. For the first time in months, happiness was running through her from head to toe and she wanted to share it with the world. "And one more thing… "

"Casey, there is more?"

"Yes, Michael and this is important. This is going to be strictly professional. No getting personal. No reminiscing. More then ten years have come and gone and I don't want to look back anymore and guess what could have been."

At first Michael was taken aback by her assertiveness. For now, he let her set the rules. If they got too close too soon, he could lose her forever.

"Do we have a deal?"

"Yes."

Casey reached out her hand and Michael met it with a firm handshake. Casey eased back in her seat feeling triumphant. Ten minutes later, Michael pulled into a parking space at Bayside Bungalow.

Located on an inlet just off the Chesapeake Bay, local residents frequented Bayside all year round. Even though its popularity peaked during crab season, its uniqueness came from the owners eccentric style. From the mismatch décor, that resembled Christmas in Jamaica to Mediterranean appetizers, including stuffed grape leaves and marinated artichoke hearts with jumbo

Kalamata olives, Bayside Bungalow received kudos, year after year.

As Michael held open the car door, Casey couldn't help but tease him. "It's nice to know chivalry is not dead." Casey's mood was a far cry from last week and it showed in her light-hearted manner.

As Casey and Michael stepped inside, the hostess greeted them with, "May I help you?" And a smile.

"We have a reservation, Sterling."

"Yes. I just showed a gentleman to your table."

Another hostess escorted Michael and Casey through the establishment then to the outdoor dining deck. The newly purchased patio furniture was a sharp contrast to the weathered terrace that jutted out over the bay. The water lapped against the pylons as the setting sun cast a shimmer on the water. Eric stood at the railings edge, memorized by every detail of the six-person yacht that was docked in one of the slips.

"Still wishing, huh?" Michael ribbed.

As Eric abruptly turned, he accidentally spilled beer down the side of his cup. "Well, what a way to make a second impression." Eric kidded as he set his drink down on the table next to him. Quickly drying his hands, Eric reached towards Michael, "Let's try this again." He hastily shook Michael's hand then Casey's, asking, "Hello, Casey. How was your trip?" While Eric was interested in Casey's response, he had been eagerly anticipated her answer to his next question, "So, do we have a new Design Manager?"

Casey glanced at Michael and winked, then flashed Eric an ear to ear smile.

"She drives a hard bargain, but she starts tomorrow." Michael looked at Eric, hoping he would remain silent on Michael's declaration to make things right.

Eric let out a howl that made other restaurant patrons look on. But to Eric, it didn't matter. He was excited about the expansion of the business and then offered to purchase a round of drinks. Seated in comfort, Eric was the first to hold his glass up in a toast to Casey.

Flattered Casey had to turn the conversation to a more serious note. "Michael, Eric…"

"Uh-oh, she's getting serious already." Eric comment noticing the immediate tone as Casey addressed them.

"It's not a big deal." Casey reassured then added, "I was just hoping I could wait a week? I usually go to my mom's cabin the week before Memorial Day weekend to get it ready for the summer. Unless there is something I need to get started on right away." Casey tried to hide her disappointment.

Michael and Eric exchanged glances, "Aw Mike, let her go see her mom."

Casey leaned towards Eric and whispered, "It's just her cabin, my mom passed away three years ago." Casey patted his hand in a gesture of gratitude that he went to bat for her.

"What? Casey, you didn't tell me this." There was a nervous tone in Michael's voice.

Casey sat up straight. "Yes, I did. At lunch the other day… I know I told you."

"No, Casey." Michael reached for her hand. "I'm sorry." At this given moment, he could have mentioned he knew exactly how she felt but comparing the passing of Casey's mom and his sister Amy, both lost to cancer, left his nerves raw. It had been a year yet the wound was still open.

"It's okay, Michael. She's in a better place now."

Michael nodded, believing Amy too, was at peace and no longer in misery.

"She's not suffering and well, it might sound corny but I like to believe she's watching over me." Casey looked down at her hand cupped in Michael's. The comforting touch made her nerves sizzle yet she gently pulled her hand away, sweeping it through her tangled curls. "I could have sworn I told you. That's why I didn't go to our ten-year reunion, although she begged me to go. But she was so sick it just didn't feel right leaving her. And that was my mom, unselfish to the end. Luckily, Hannah, Adam and the kids were here." Casey's eyes widened as she finally stated, "Believe me, I'm glad I didn't go to the reunion, because she passed away that night. I would have never forgiven myself had I not been there." There was an awkward silence as Casey looked at Michael, an unfamiliar expression taunting his face, until Casey added, "Oh let's talk about something else. So gentlemen, what jobs do we have on the table for me to get started on?"

She had taken Michael and Eric by surprise at her assertiveness, but before either could answer, their waiter brought out one of many appetizers they had ordered. "Are you ready to order?"

"We're waiting for one other person." Michael replied. "We'll order when she arrives." The waiter nodded then proceeded to light the citronella torches that framed the dinning deck. They not only added extra lighting but the sweet smell permeated the cooling air. "We can talk about business later." Again there was an uncomfortable silence between the three of them. Michael fumbled for something to say or do. Reaching into his jeans pocket he remembered he had Casey's keys. "You're portfolio is in the trunk of your car." As he passed them to her, his fingertips brushed against hers. An unexpected sensation ran through Michael. Shocked by the feeling, he inadvertently retracted his hand, knocking over his beer. Eric and Casey jumped, both wondering what had caused such a knee-jerk reaction.

"Well now, I don't feel like such an idiot. Are you feeling okay, Mike?" Eric chided as he tossed napkins over the puddle of suds.

Through gritted teeth Michael quickly noted, "I'm fine. It was an accident. I'm sorry."

Another waiter rushed over with a wet rag, quickly cleaning the mess and retrieving a fresh glass for Michael. Once the commotion had died down, Michael folded his hands around his drink, trying to make light conversation. "So how's Hannah?"

"I'm going to be an aunt again." There was a twinkle in her eyes as she made the announcement. "She found out Friday morning. It was great. Hannah, Adam and I had a cook out with the kids and went to the beach. Hannah and I did a little shopping. It was a fun weekend. I can't wait until they come up here. We haven't been together at the lake in a long time."

"When are they planning a visit?" Eric inquired.

"The end of the summer. Adam just got promoted, so he's waiting to take vacation time the week before Labor Day. We're going to stay at the cabin. You know, you all should come out there too."

"We'll see." Michael stated abruptly.

Just then Julie approached the table. As she stood there waiting to be introduced, her eyes locked with Eric's. Instantly, he stood and reached out his hand, ignoring Casey and Michael, "I'm Eric Logan, and you must be Julie."

"Yes, Julie Warren." Her cheeks turned pink as her hand lingered in his.

A yawn slipped from Casey's lips as Michael drove back to his house. Her eyes were closed but she wasn't asleep although thoughts of crawling under the covers were at the forefront of Casey's mind.

"If you're too tired to drive, you can always stay here." Michael stated coolly as he parked in his driveway.

"That's quite all right, Michael." Casey's aloofness was no surprise to Michael as he noticed her taking in the sight of his single family home. The newly installed aluminum siding, the neatly trimmed hedges and the perfectly manicured lawn were all evidence that he had done well for himself.

"No, really. I have a guest bedroom and a pull-out sofa in the den. Come on. I'll make you some tea."

Casey dropped her luggage onto the lawn, firmly crossing her arms across her chest. "Michael, what's going on? Are you afraid if you let me out of your sight you're never going to see me again? I just want to go home." Casey whined then added, "I'm tired."

Michael moved from his side of the car, closing the distance between them. "You're reading too far into this. I just thought you might be too tired to drive. That's all." Michael threw his hands in the air. "You are still so stubborn. You won't let anyone help you. You won't let anyone in. I give up. Jeez, who the hell hurt you so bad?"

Casey arched an eyebrow, staring right into his eyes, that now appeared to be muted green.

"Never mind. You don't need to say it. Will you at least call me when you get home, so that I know you're all right?"

"That I can do." And she did.

Chapter 7

It was a beautiful two-hour drive through the mountains to Hidden Springs Lake. The trees and wild flowers were in full bloom and it was by far Casey's favorite time of year. The on set of spring made her feel alive and the extra energy exhilarated her senses. The feeling of the open road, a light breeze caressing her face and the warmth of the sun was already clearing the cobwebs and the horrid image of Mr. Whitley yelling, "You're fired!" Having survived yet another crisis, Casey turned her car with ease onto the main dirt road. In her mind, Casey had come home.

There were two dozen cabins scattered around the lake, each owned by various families, some of which could be traced back to the turn of the century. Casey's grandparents had sold their house in the city and bought the cabin at an auction for a steal. They lived out their retirement days in utter bliss, until they had passed away, her grandmother first then her grandfather two months later.

That was when Casey's mother, Florence had inherited the cabin. In that same year Casey's father had left one morning for work and never came back. At that time, Casey was five and Hannah was ready to turn four. It was an awful year for her mother but rising to the challenge of raising two little girls on her own, Florence Andrews did not give up. By the start of the school year she had obtained a permanent teaching position and kept it until she fell ill.

Many times Casey's mother had wanted to sell the cabin because of the cost of medical care and the financial strain that was being put on both Casey and Hannah, but Florence's daughters would not hear of it. They could not allow their memories to be sold. Casey's last memory of her mother was at the cabin; her passing away quietly in the night with her family by her side. Even though it was one of her saddest memories, it did not cloud all the wonderful summers they had spent together over the years. Hopefully, someday Casey would be able to share this place with her own family.

"An unlikely dream." She mumbled out loud as she passed over the threshold.

The cabin was set back from the main road, in a grotto of pines, directly across from the lake. The scent of the trees always permeated the air and gently blanketed the three-bedroom cabin. On the other side of the lake was a picturesque view of the Appalachian Mountains. There was skiing in the wintertime but it was definitely a weekend hot spot during the summer. As Casey turned to her vehicle, her neighbors, the Kirby's had just step out of their cabin.

From across the way, Mrs. Kirby waved as she approached. "Hello Casey." The older woman greeted her with a hug. "How are you doing?" Mrs. Kirby questioned as she readjusted her straw hat.

"Good Mrs. Kirby. How are you?"

"Casey, how many times have I told you to call me Nancy?" She chided as she unfolded her bright yellow beach towel and tossed it over her shoulder.

"I'll try but you know you'll always be Mrs. Kirby to me." Casey propped her sunglasses on top of her head.

The two let out a little laugh. "So how long are you staying?"

"I'll be here all week. I haven't been here in a couple of months and I don't know how much time I'll be able to spend here this summer but I still want to give the house a good cleaning."

"The job is keeping you that busy, huh?"

Twisting a tight curl around her finger, Casey, for some unknown reason wasn't too anxious to mention her new job with Sterling Architects but before she could stop herself the words fell from her mouth.

"Casey, that's wonderful. What are you going to be doing?"

"I'll be in charge of the Interior Design division."

Nancy pursed her lips, gently tapped her long finger to her chin, "Sterling. Why does that sound so familiar?" Turning towards her husband, Sean, who stood a considerable distance away, Nancy called out, "Honey, do we know anyone by the name of Sterling?"

Casey's stance wavered as the two women awaited his response but Sean only shook his head then returned to inventorying his tackle box.

"Oh, I'll eventually figure it out. Well, that sounds impressive, Casey. Congratulations. We'll have to celebrate."

"Thank you. Are you and Mr. Kirby, ah, Sean, heading down to the lake?" Casey quickly questioned, abruptly turning the conversation around.

"Of course, dear. You know my Sean, he can't go a day without trying to catch dinner. As a matter of fact why don't you join us tonight?"

"I'd love to. I haven't had the opportunity to go grocery shopping since I just got back from Hannah's."

"Oh, how is your sister?"

"Good, really good. Her and Adam are having another baby."

"Land sakes! Her second, right?"

"Third. Emily is seven and Jason is starting kindergarten this fall. They're going to be here for Labor Day weekend."

"Oh, that'll be real nice. We'll have to get together." Nancy glanced over at her husband, Sean, who was anxiously waiting their departure down to the lake. "Well, Casey, I better get going. We'll see you this evening, seven?"

"I'll be there. Should I bring anything?"

"Nonsense. Just yourself, sweetheart." Mrs. Kirby smiled and met up with her husband. He waved too, as they head down the path towards the lake.

Casey finished unpacking and immediately took all her belonging to the laundry room. Sorting through her suitcase, Casey filled the machine with her whites and turned it on. In the meantime she opened every window in the cabin then went to the kitchen to inventory what few canned goods she had left behind from Julie's and her trip back in April. As she diligently made a grocery list the phone rang.

"Melinda Parker."

"I've got the information." Payne Claiborne whispered into the receiver.

"I really appreciate this and this is strictly between you and me, understood?"

"Yes, ma'am." Payne smiled knowing he'd be well compensated for betraying Mr. Parker's trust.

Melinda twirled the phone cord around her finger as she pace back and forth in front of her desk at the office of the Historical Preservation Committee. "What did you find out?"

"Michael Sterling hired her and as for the property at Hidden Springs Lake, it was bought and paid for by her grandparents and her mother."

"And her father?"

"Either Casey Andrew's father vanished without a trace or he's deceased. But I'm still working on that." Payne paused then added, "Is there anything else I can do for you Mrs. Parker?"

"Yes, see what you can find on Amanda Carlyle."

"I'm already on it ."

"Very good." And there was a click in Payne's ear before he could respond.

"Good morning." The voice on the other end chimed.

"Hi, Michael."

"I take it you got to the lake without any problems this morning?"

Casey yawned, "Yeah, I was up before the sun, so I hit the road pretty early. I'm really tired but I'm glad to be here. This is just about my favorite place on earth." Casey yawned again.

"I can't believe you left so early, with so little sleep."

"That wasn't my doing. But I did have fun last night."

"Me too. Did you happen to catch on what was going on between Eric and Julie? You would think it was the Fourth of July."

Casey's giggle was interrupted by another yawn. "It was impossible to miss." Obviously Casey needed to sleep or have a giant cup of coffee. Again she apologized for yawning then asked, "So, what can I do for you Michael?"

Michael's tone quickly shifted, "I'm e-mailing you some documents on the new wing at Brookshire General Hospital. I know you're on vacation, but we could really use some preliminary sketches by the end of the week. Are you up to it?"

"I am. Just not at this given moment."

"I understand. I'll call you tonight after you get some rest." Michael concluded.

"I won't be here." Casey blatantly commented.

"Plans already? Where are you going?" Michael pried.

"Out." Casey stated sarcastically. Her sarcasm was always at its peak when she had been deprived of sleep.

"With who?"

"Michael, what was our rule about personally versus professionally? You're overstepping the boundaries we established not more than twenty-four hours ago. Please respect my wishes, that our personal lives are separate from our professional lives."

"You're right. I'm tossing you a white towel right now." There was a moment of silence. "Did you get it?"

"I got it Michael. Cute. Very cute." Casey giggled then finished with, "I have to go Michael but I'll call you before I go out."

"Thank you." And then Michael hung up the phone.

Casey felt a twinge of guilt being so hard bound to what they had agreed upon, but she had a job to do and Michael Sterling was now her boss. Her superior. Not a friend, not a boyfriend, not a lover. It was strictly business and a paycheck. And an opportunity to collect herself and figure what her next career move was going to be. Basically, she had set a goal and bought herself some time.

Heading towards the laundry room, Casey tossed the finished load into the dryer and another into the washer then returned to the task of making a grocery list. Once that was done, she was going to set up the laptop Michael had lent her and then run down to the Country Store to grab a bite to eat but first she wanted to call her sister, as promised.

"Casey, you're crazy. I can't believe you got home late last night and you're at the cabin this morning." Hannah's tone sounded as if she was scolding Emily or Jason. It was not her intention to be so condescending to her older sister, yet the reasoning behind it was that Hannah envied Casey. While Hannah was quite content with the life her and Adam had carved out for themselves, there were those moments when Hannah wanted the freedom that Casey had. The spontaneity and spunk to go anywhere, to do anything. Casey feared nothing in Hannah's eyes.

"Jeez, you sound like Michael. I couldn't sleep and I just wanted to get to the cabin. I'm a different person when I'm here. I'm more relaxed and after last week…"

"I know." Hannah stated in an understanding mother-like expression. So, I only have a few minutes but what did you decide?"

"I officially start next Tuesday. But Eric and Michael need some preliminary drawings by the end of the week. You and Julie gave me some good advice. And dear sister… for once I listened." Casey paused then added, "Thank you, Hannah."

"Well, Congratulations! Maybe you can spend some of your time this week looking at classes or volunteering. I'm sure summer classes haven't started yet and…" Hannah stopped to take a breath. "You're just so lucky. Your options are wide-open." Hannah was always so direct. And that was just one of her many qualities that Casey adored about her sister.

"Hannah, the grass is not always greener on the other side of the fence. But I do appreciate your support. So, how are you doing?"

"Fine, Casey. Are you going to bug me for the next seven months?"

"Of course. What are sisters for?" Casey giggled.

"You crack me up. Well, I have to go, my other line is ringing. I'll call you later. Love you." Hannah whispered.

"Love you too. Bye."

It was well past lunch when Casey had finished her conversation with Hannah. Before slipping into her sneakers, Casey went to the hall closet and dragged the boxed up hammock onto the porch. Quickly, she finished her laundry then head to the store, deciding she would leave grocery shopping for tomorrow morning.

"Mr. Parker, I'm going to the post office and then I'm going to get lunch. Shall I pick something up for you?"

"No, I'm going to order in."

"Is there anything else, sir."

Lyle Parker rubbed his chin, then simply shook his head. Knee deep in contract negotiations, Lyle motioning for his assistant to just go away.

Payne Claiborne made his way out of Empire Tower, to the bustling streets of the Waterfront. The branch of the post office was just next door and surprisingly Payne was in and out in fifteen minutes. Crossing several streets to his next destination, Payne felt his blood racing through his veins. This was too intriguing and for a brief moment he felt like James Bond.

The bell jingled as he entered. A few customers browsing the new releases looked on but thought nothing of Payne's presences. A business man in a finely tailored suit, in a music store at lunch time didn't phase anyone. A musty smell permeated the air as he made his way back to the jazz section. He thumbed through the racks remembering that the last CD he bought was back at Christmas time and he decided to splurge.

"You're not here to shop." The woman proclaimed in a husky voice. "Did you bring what I asked you to bring?"

"I did. It's all in there." Payne stated as he handed the manila envelope over to Melinda Parker.

Abruptly she turned to leave without another word.

Then Payne shouted out, "Amanda's sick."

Melinda turned, whipping off her Anne Klein sunglasses. "What did you say?"

"Amanda Carlyle? She sick, really sick. She's been in and out of the hospital for the last six months."

Melinda felt her throat start to close but she refused to show any emotion. Gnashing her back teeth together, Melinda simply replied, "That's not my problem." And in the next moment she was gone.

The dirt road hugged the perimeter of the lake and in the distance Casey could hear a group of youngsters down by the dock. Run, jumping, splashing and laughing. To some it was noise, to Casey it was sweet memories of a lifetime ago. Keeping a steady pace down Hidden Springs Lane, Casey passed the camping grounds that were half full of pitched tents and campers. By the weeks end it would be full to capacity with city slickers just like herself trying to interject a little peace and quiet into their over active lives. Despite her lack of sleep and the unexpected one hundred and eighty degree turn her life had taken, Casey's energy was unrelenting.

Realizing that chapter of her life was now closed, she could start writing a new one…with Michael. For a moment thoughts of him crept into her mind and a smile danced across her face. *He looks so damn good!* Giggling to herself, Casey felt the butterflies flutter in her mid-section until she recalled their conversation this morning. Her thoughts were betraying her words. Mumbling over and over in a reprimanding tone, she reminded herself to, "Keep it professional." Casey struggled as she tried to cast images of Michael Sterling aside.

The wooden steps creaked under her feet and the bells chimed as Casey stepped inside The Country Store. Mr. Miller, the owner had renovated the store a few years ago and added the deli right next to the check out counter without interfering with the quaintness of the shop. Casey meandered to the far end of the store, inspecting the deli case.

"How are you my dear?" Mr. Miller inquired.

"Good, Mr. Miller. How are you?"

"Just fine. You here for a while?"

"I'm staying for the week. I'm getting the cabin ready for the summer. Late spring cleaning you might say."

"Well don't work too hard; vacations are meant for relaxation and this is just the right place to unwind." He winked. "What can I gitch you?"

"Turkey on white with lettuce and tomato." Casey strolled through the aisles, eyeing the merchandise then she found herself staring out the window. Off in the distance, a familiar figure was approaching but when Mr. Miller interrupted her thoughts, asking, "Mayo? Mustard? Pickles?" she didn't think twice about the woman heading her direction.

"Pickles on the side would be fine."

"Anything new happening?"

"I start a new job next week." Casey stated briefly but enthusiastically.

"Well good, then you will start your new job feeling refreshed. You know the Welcome Center is having a dance Friday night. Do you want chips?" Mr. Miller jumped from subject to subject without a pause.

"No thanks. But do you have any fruit?" The bell on the door rang causing her to turn. In an instant, Casey recognized the woman that had just entered. "Mr. Miller I have to pick up a few more things. I'll be right back." Quickly, Casey dashed in and out of the aisles hoping and praying that the other woman would not recognize her. Peering over one of the shelves, Casey noticed she had engaged Mr. Miller in deep conversation. Casey's shoulders slouched forward in disappointment. How could she get her lunch and dodge this woman at the same time? Darn it! The door bell rang giving Casey cause to peek around the aisle to see if she had left. To her dismay, two kids entered the store. Just as Casey was about to slip back into her hiding place an all too familiar voice accosted her,

"Do my eyes deceive me or is the work-a-holic actually here on a weekday?"

"Hello, Valerie." Casey turned with a somber tone. Much to Casey's surprise, Valerie Sorrenson rushed towards her and greeted her with a hug, nearly knocking the cereal box and container of milk from Casey's hands. Struggling, she barely returned the gesture.

"What are you doing here?" Valerie's tone was high pitched and squeaky, just like when she was a cheerleader back in high school.

"Oh, you know, vacation. Every year I try to make it out here before the out-of-towners take over." The sudden on-slot of Casey's lack of sleep hit her like a tone of bricks and she found herself not feeling very sociable. A lengthy conversation, especially with Valerie Sorrenson, was the furthest thing from her mind right now. Casey just didn't have enough energy to keep up with her motorized mouth.

Not that Casey hated Valerie, however Valerie had a tendency to act as if everyone was her best friend, yet in high school they were mere acquaintances. They ran in different circles and while they acknowledge each other's existence with a casual hello when changing classes, they never did form a long lasting friendship. At least in her eyes, Valerie seemed to have a different recollection of their high school days.

"Well, you look wonderful. Have you lost weight?"

Startled by Valerie's comment, Casey did not know how to respond.

"Casey are you ready to check out?" Mr. Miller interrupted.

Turning her back on Valerie, Casey rolled her eyes. "Yes. Yes I am." Casey placed the cereal, milk, a container of mixed nuts and a six pack of raspberry iced tea on the counter along side her sandwich and a mixed bag of fruit Mr. Miller had put together for her.

"Are those fruit choices all right for you?"

Casey eyed the bag that housed a few apples, oranges, pears and a banana. "That's fine." Nodding, she dug into the pocket of her shorts and pulled out a twenty-dollar bill and held it out to Mr. Miller, long before he finished ringing up her purchase. After handing her, her change, Casey slipped it into her pocket. Turning around to exit, Casey was surprised that Valerie was still standing behind her.

"So, Casey what have you been up to? We haven't seen each other in so long."

"Work, mostly." Again, she tried to keep the conversation to a minimum.

"Casey's startin' a new job next week. Ain't that right?" Mr. Miller interjected.

"Well, congratulations. With who?"

"Oh no, this was the last thing you needed to know." Casey thought so loudly she was certain Valerie could hear her. Casey could not find the right answer and she knew if she merely mentioned Michael's name Valerie would blow it out of proportion and it would be a lead story on the six o'clock news. Then Casey realized she was the one blowing everything out of proportion. It was, after all, just a new job.

"Well?"

Casey hesitated, "An Architectural Firm." Hoping Valerie wouldn't make the connection.

"How nice. Which one?"

"Sterling Architects and Construction." But no sooner had the words left her lips when Valerie's eyes lit up like the city skyline on a moonless night.

"Why Casey Andrews that is Michael Sterling's company. Well, imagine that, two high school sweethearts, reunited. Why, I haven't seen him since our high school reunion. He was there with that gorgeous fiancé of his...what was her name..." Valerie trailed off as she snapped her fingers trying to remember a name Casey wanted to forget. "Oh, I'll remember it eventually. Must be old age setting in. So, they must be married with children by now. Hhmm, What does she have to say about her husband hiring his *ex*-girlfriend?" Valerie gave pause as she nibbled on her fingernail.

Stunned by Valerie's snide remark, Casey found herself wanting to remove the smirk from Valerie's face. But violence was not of her nature. Realistically, it boiled down to whether or not Casey should reveal the truth of it all. How

Michael was left at the altar, that his fiancée left town without a trace and it left Michael a broken-hearted mess, but she couldn't bring herself to divulge such personal aspects of his life, especially to Valerie Sorrenson. Besides, Michael is now her boss and gossiping about the boss is not very professional.

"Allison! No. Abigail! No…Darn it. Well, I'll just have to give him a call and congratulate him and his well, somewhat new bride." Valerie clucked.

Jolted by Valerie's outbursts, it dawned on Casey that Valerie, the town gossip, was absolutely clueless? How could that be? Valerie knew everything there was to know about everyone. Or at least from their high school. Who married who. Who was divorced. Who had children. Who was cheating… it was as if she had never left high school.

Refusing to give Valerie the satisfaction of marveling at someone else's misery, Casey inched her way towards the door. "Valerie, now's not a good time to call him. He's up to his elbows with work and well I'm only working for him until the end of the year. That's all." Casey snapped as she tightened her grip around the doorknob.

"Well, a lot could happen in six months. Oh, wait until I tell Tina and Deanna, they will do somersaults. This would be a great article for our quarterly newsletter." Valerie was beaming from ear to ear. "I'll entitle it 'Together At Last'. No, wait, even better, 'Professional or Personal?'." Valerie squeezed Casey's arm, jumping up and down with excitement as if they had just won the state championship.

Casey felt she had no choice, as she pulled away from Valerie, her words were laced with an uncommon harshness, "Valerie, don't! High school is over and so are Michael and I. Please leave us alone." Casey reached for the door and thrusted it open. As she started to exit, Valerie followed.

"But think of the free publicity Michael could get. I'm going to give him a call first thing tomorrow morning." Valerie was completely oblivious to Casey's request.

"I give up." And with that final statement, Casey walked away in a fury. Dirt kicked up behind her heels as she briskly walked back down Hidden Springs Lane. Valerie was not going to bend and Casey was in no mood to argue. Michael would have to handle Valerie Sorrenson on his own. By time Casey reached the cabin, her exhaustion had hit its peak. She was not longer hungry just simply worn out. Within minutes of her return, Casey was fast asleep.

Other than waking up later than she had wanted to, the rest of the week was far less eventful. Casey shared a quiet dinner with the Kirby's her first evening at the Lake. Each night she spent a few hours working on the Brookshire General Hospital drawings for Michael and Eric. Later in the week she had joined the Kirby's on a fishing expedition. Because of their generous nature, she could not show up empty-handed and had brought along a picnic lunch. Even though they were old enough to be her parents, she enjoyed their company and considered Nancy and Sean, friends. Sean always told such fascinating stories about his tour of duties in Europe and Nancy talked about the grandchildren, recipes and her Christian Women's Group.

The sun was at its peak on this particular day, as Nancy was telling Casey about her volunteer work with the Women of Hope. "We're working with a local contractor who bought a few row homes at a government auction last year. He's is fixing them up for moderate income housing. Have you heard of the Home and Hearth Project?"

When Nancy had mentioned that, Casey sat up straight and listened more attentively.

"One of the ladies in my group read about it in the newspaper last summer. So we decided to crochet some blankets and embroider pillow covers. Some of the gals have made quilts. I know it's not much, though."

"Not much? Nancy, that's great! You are giving of yourself and you are giving these people a little piece of ...hope. A place they can call home." Casey choked out her words as her eyes began to water. She was feeling overwhelmed with emotion and could not pin-point why. "I wish I could do something like that. Help people." As her feet dangled off the edge of the dock, Casey dipped her toes into the cool mountain water causing a ripple effect. Watching the rings migrate out onto the lake, Casey did not take notice to the glint in Nancy's eyes until she looked up.

"Would you be interested in volunteering some hours?" Nancy quietly asked.

Casey raised an eyebrow as she held her hand to her brow, shading her eyes from the sun. "I don't know how to knit or crochet."

"But you know how to decorate. Nothing fancy. Would you be interested in selecting some paint colors or wallpaper or maybe some borders? I know the decorating committee would welcome your expertise. We work hard but we have lots of fun. And it's such a good group of people. Believe me if this doesn't touch your soul nothing will. You'll be giving a child a sense of renewed hope." Nancy sweetly threw Casey's words back at her then added,

"We're working every other Saturday until the end of the summer. It might go to the end of September but we won't know that until Labor Day. What do you say?"

There was a puzzled look on Casey's face. "You're very convincing, Nancy." Deep down Casey knew this was exactly what she had been searching for and if she said no, she would only scold herself later. "Yes! I'll do it!"

"Before you leave, I'll give you a list of phone numbers and our schedule for the summer. The young man you want to contact is Eric Logan. I think I have his office number with me." Nancy paused then added, "That's where I know the name Sterling!"

Casey crinkled her brow then questioned, "Tall, blond curly hair, wears glasses?"

"Isn't that where you're going to be working?" Nancy held her aging hand to her chest, "What a small world." Then she combed her fingers through her almost all gray hair. "My stars. I can't believe you know Eric."

"Not very well. I just met him last week."

"See Casey, it's fate that you are supposed to do this. Eric is single, you know."

"Yeah, so? What does that mean?" Casey giggled.

"He's a nice fellow, that's all." Nancy smiled.

"Nan, then you should say that." Sean stated firmly. Just then his reel clicked and lurched forward. "Ah, looks like a big one." He grabbed this rod with both hands and braced his booted feet on the edge of the dock. Both Nancy and Casey jumped up and stood behind him, Nancy leaning hard on the lawn chair where her husband sat. It was a struggle but after a few minutes Sean pulled a rather large fish from the lake. It squirmed to break free but Nancy scooped it into the net that lay on the dock. "Dinner anyone?" Sean boasted. And the three of them broke out into laughter.

"Why can't we just send a courier?" Eric questioned as he shifted the battered pick up truck into drive.

"All the way out to Hidden Springs? It's too risky." Michael flexed his brow.

"I think there is something you're not telling me. She is going to be suspicious, both of us showing up and what's up with the overnight bag?"

Michael shook his head, then asked Eric, "Ah, I'm getting a room near the lake. I need to get away. That's all."

"And you just happen to choose to Hidden Springs where Casey is staying with no means of getting home, other than asking her if you can tag along?" Eric glanced in his rear view mirror and then his side view mirror before changing lanes. "I don't think it's a good idea. I just hope you know what you're doing and that you don't mess things up."

"It's for the benefit of the company. Besides, Brookshire Hospital did move up the proposal deadline and I think the preliminary sketches with give us the edge we need to land the contract. What's wrong with that? It is the truth." Michael drew in a deep breath then sighed, "What?" Michael did a double take when he saw the scowl on Eric's face.

"One, I think you're putting all your eggs in the basket, or whatever that expression is and two…" Eric eased up on the accelerator as he exited the highway that led to Hidden Springs Lake. "…I think you're still in love with her."

The rat-a-tat-tat sound of rain falling on the leaves brought Casey out of a deep sleep early Friday morning. Casey didn't want to get out of bed but she had to start packing for her return to the city before the flux of tourists arrived for the Memorial Day weekend. Another week had gone by rather quickly and Casey did not want it to end. The cabin was more home to her than her own apartment. Perhaps it was the mixture of childhood innocence and memories of her mother that lent her comfort. Or the sweet company of the Kirby's that had become her second parents. Or the peaceful surroundings of natures glory and the fresh mountain air. Or her awareness of the chaotic city life. Whatever it was, Casey was determined to come to the lake at least twice each month during the summer. It energized her and always made her see things more clearly. And when it came time to retire, even though that was thirty-some years away, Hidden Springs Lake was the place where Casey Andrews wanted to be.

Slipping the floral sheets off her body, Casey sat up in bed, slowly easing her feet to the hardwood floor. "Do I have to get up?" She pondered only for a brief second when an eruption of noise startled her. Quickly swirling her silk robe around her nakedness, Casey tiptoed towards the closed bedroom door. Cautiously and quietly as possible she turned the handle, peering out into the living room with one eye. Scanning the cabin, nothing seemed out of the ordinary. As Casey inched the door open a little further she heard a soft tapping. Stepping just beyond her bedroom door, she was taken aback by the two figures at her front door. Glancing at the clock on the way, Casey knew it was too early for visitors especially when she wasn't expecting anyone. Her breathing was heavy and it was her natural instinct to turn and run but her feet would not move. It was as if they were glued to the floor. Reaching for the phone on the end table, Casey started to dial 9-1-1 but then she realized it was disconnected as her eye followed the trail of the phone cord to her laptop.

"Casey?" The man's voice was low followed by another knock at the door.

"I told you we shouldn't have come up here."

Casey rolled her eyes and a slight smile formed at the sides of her mouth as she made her way to the front door.

"Did we wake you?" Michael smiled smugly.

"Casey, I'm sorry." Eric apologized immediately. "I had nothing to do with this. It was all Mike's idea." And again he apologized.

"It's all right. I'm just surprised to see you two here. And Why? And at this hour? Good God what time did you leave the city?" Casey ran her fingers through her tangled curls.

"Four-thirty, but we stopped for breakfast." Michael had a sheepish look on his face, then questioned, "Are you going to let us in? It is kind of wet out here."

"Of course." Casey unlocked the screen door. As she reached forward her robe slipped open revealing a small portion of her breasts. Embarrassment washed over her as she clasped the material closed over her skin causing the door to hit Michael in the shoulder.

"Sorry." She mumbled. "Ah…let me get the coffee started and let me put on some…get dressed." Casey stated nervously. Without waiting for a response from Eric or Michael, she slipped into the kitchen. She prepared the coffee maker then escaped to her bedroom while they made themselves comfortable in the living room. Quickly she pulled a tee shirt over her head and slipped on her jean, then pulled her red curls up into a ponytail. Glancing in the mirror, Casey washed her face, accepting fact that there was no time for make-up.

"So, why are you here? Is everything all right?" Casey questioned as she hand them each a towel, making herself comfortable in the oversized recliner with her legs curled beneath her.

"We're sorry to barge in on you like this…" Eric trailed off, then rambled on, "But there is a meeting at Brookshire General Hospital this afternoon for all the contractors submitting bids. Can you believe it? They told us about it yesterday afternoon. We didn't want to show up empty handed so we were hoping that you had some sketches done."

"Oh, as a matter of fact, I do. But I could have come back early or I could have sent a courier to the office."

"We didn't want to chance it." Michael interjected.

Casey shrugged her shoulders then moved over to the dinning room table and thumb through her portfolio. The laptop was still set up so she turned it on, and saved two files to a disk. Handing the drawings to Michael, Casey returned to the recliner. "There's a cost spreadsheet on this disk as well as well as some colored renderings. If you print them on 11 by 17 paper, I think that will be best."

Michael and Eric looked over the sketches; both their expressions said it all. "These are pretty good. What about the financial aspect?"

"Actually, I'm under by eleven hundred dollars. It's not much but under nonetheless. I did some research on the Internet and found that color blue is supposed to be calming and healing. So, I choose various shades along with some traditional storybook characters. Drapery and boarder patterns vary a little from room to room. My thought was to create a peaceful yet playful atmosphere especially with this being a Children's Oncology wing. I also sketched a mural of Cinderella dancing with the prince at the ball, for the wall near the nurses station."

Michael was desperately trying to hide how impressed he was but he could not deny Casey's talents. "You're right on the money. Hospitals are always so drab."

"Well, I think we have a chance of landing this project." Eric smiled from ear to ear, finally feeling confident about Michael's decision to hire Casey as well as interrupting her vacation.

Michael, however, remained speechless. Capturing the glint in Casey's eyes, Michael, barely above a whisper, mumbled, "Thank you."

"You're welcome. Do you want some coffee?" The aroma permeated the humid air. Without waiting for a response, Casey disappeared into the kitchen and returned with a tray filled with three coffee cups, spoons, cream, sugar and the glass coffee pot.

"After this, I better get going. I have a two hour drive and I want to make sure I have everything before I walk into that meeting." Determination rang out in Eric's voice yet his statement piqued Casey's curiosity.

"You're not going with him?" Casey's eyes narrowed as she addressed

Michael.

Michael and Eric looked at each other, "I'm just staying for the night." Again, confidence reigned from every fiber of his being. Flashing his smile, his eyes danced with enthusiasm, an all too familiar look from days gone by.

"Oh really?" Casey managed but all she felt was embarrassment that Michael was putting her on the spot and in front of Eric. How could she say no and Michael knew she couldn't. It was a tad bit unnerving for the moment.

Michael immediately noticed Casey's grip tighten around her legs and presumed from the look on her face, she was pretty aggravated with his announcement. "Eric is dropping me off at a lodge. I saw it on a billboard on the way up here. However, I do need to impose on you for a ride back to the city."

She took a deep breath and the words slipped from her mouth before she knew what she was saying, "Michael, I doubt there'll be any vacancies on Memorial Day weekend. Don't be silly, I have two *other* bedrooms, you can stay here." Casey narrowed her eyes, as if he didn't know she would offer.

"Great. Then I can leave you two in peace?" Eric said in jest yet there was an underlying serious in his voice. "Well, I better get going."

"So soon?" Casey questioned.

"I don't want to risk running into traffic with the weather and all."

"It looks like it stopped raining. Surely you could stay for one more cup of coffee." Casey's words were short of pleading for him to stay.

"Tempting but no, I've had enough. Besides, I want to make the meeting on time, so if I head out now I should be back at the office by ten-thirty. Plenty of time to change my clothes, print your drawings and get a bite to eat before heading downtown. Anyway, I have a date with Julie tonight." Eric's eyes gleamed at the mention of her name.

"You do? Well, tell her I said hello and I'll call her when I…we get back."

"I will. And thanks for working on this, Casey. This should give us some leverage. I have a funny feeling the board is having this meeting just to see who's on top of things. And I am in the mood to show them who is." The grin on Eric's face lit up the cabin as he stood and handed the damp towel to Casey. Heading towards the front door with sketches and the computer disk in hand, he turned, "I'll talk to you all later. Hey Mike, you want to come get your stuff?" Eric nodded towards his pickup truck parked out front the cabin.

Michael was quiet as he followed Eric out to the truck. Casey was suspicious of Michael's intentions and she knew she would have to be on guard for the next forty-eight hours. *Damn, why does he have to look so good?* There were those thoughts again as Casey went to the kitchen to fix breakfast.

"Buddy, I don't know what you are up to, but don't mess with her head." Eric demanded then added, "Remember we all have to work together. I really want this to work out. I really like her."

"Eric, you have nothing to worry about."

"Mike, I will give you this much. Professionally, you made the right decision bringing Casey on board especially after seeing her sketches, but on a personal level, I can't help but question your motives." Eric raised an eyebrow to Michael.

Michael repeated himself, "You have nothing to worry about."

"I just hope you know what you doing. Do you?"

Michael grabbed his duffel bag and left Eric's question unanswered. "I'll talk to you later." Then turned on his heel and head to the porch. The roar of the truck's engine did not drowned out the question in Michael's head, *"Do you know what you are doing?"* He hesitantly opened the screen door and stepped inside the cabin.

Chapter 8

All she wanted was her morning cup of coffee that was sitting on her desk, getting colder by the minute. As Julie Warren sat in Mr. Whitley's office, her arms tightly crossed over her chest, she had become the latest victim of his hissing and she realized it wasn't even eight o'clock. Thoughts of Casey came to mind and Julie wondered how she had tolerated it as long as she had.

"We had to drop that…" Mr. Whitley stuttered, frustrated as he tried to remember Calandra Kosta's name. "…that woman that…" Spit spewed like venom from Mr. Whitley as he rant and raved about a client Julie was unfamiliar with.

"Casey?" Julie sat up straight as she questioned where Mr. Whitley was heading with his tirade.

Quickly, Mr. Whitley made himself perfectly clear. "Yes…No. I'm speaking of that Greek woman. Whatever!" He waved his hand it the air, as if he was swatting at an irritating fly. "No more projects for under ten thousand dollars. Do you understand me, missy? Last's quarter's profits were pitiful. Our purpose is profit. That is the bottom line. Now, if you want this promotion, you're going to have to earn it. Do you understand?" Mr. Whitley leaned over the desk, his beady eyes narrowing to slits.

Julie stood up trying to ignore Veronica, who sat in a cubicle just outside of Mr. Whitley's office, silently mimicking him. Holding her head high, Julie simply replied, "Crystal clear." Turning on her heel, she returned to her desk. After signing onto her computer, Julie began to update her resume.

Casey returned from the kitchen with her breakfast. As she sat down at the table that seated four, she quietly asked Michael, "Would you like anything?" The she took a bite of her toasted bagel.

"No, the coffee's fine." Michael stated flatly as he joined her at the table by turning a chair around backwards and straddling it.

"Make yourself at home." Casey noted sarcastically as she glared at Michael's actions.

He did not comment nor changed his position. An uncomfortable silence grew between them and Casey was getting frustrated. "Guess who I ran into?"

She questioned trying to hide her agitation.

"Hhmm, Valerie Sorrenson?"

Casey's eyes widened, "How did you know?"

"She called me at the office."

"Oh no Michael, I'm sorry. I told her not to call you." Casey stated in a sing-song voice then added, "I swear I didn't give her the office number." Casey defended herself.

"Don't worry about it. It's not like we're not listed. We do advertise." Michael's words dripped with sarcasm, then his tone changed, "I did a side job for her and her husband, a sunroom, just before the reunion. It turned out really nice. Mostly brick with lots of windows. They get a nice western exposure even in the winter." Michael's eyes lit up when he talked about creating original designs for residential projects.

"So what did she have to say?"

"Not much. At first it was idle chit-chat until she finally came around, slinging questions at me about my marriage. Which didn't surprise me. But then she caught me off guard when she starting asking about you."

"Me? And what did you tell her?" Casey's voice was shaky and her heart was pounding realizing nothing about this conversation was going to be simple. Then she tried to rationalize away the situation before Michael responded. Did it really matter what Michael told Valerie? Valerie always believed what she wanted to, truth or not. Besides, there really wasn't anything to talk about. The situation between her and Michael was strictly professional. Casey needed a job and Michael wants to expand his company. What's wrong with that? A smile ran across her face as Casey slowly bit into a piece of honeydew.

"I told her we were back together." He teased, curious of her reaction.

"You what!" Casey's voice raised an octave as her brown eyes exploded with fury.

"Casey, I'm kidding. I told her we were back together professionally and that there was nothing to tell nor to write about for the newsletter. End of story."

"And that was it?"

"That was it. Valerie sounded disappointed. But even if there was anything going on between us other than business, do you really think I would tell *her* let alone let her publish it in our alumni newsletter? Please, give me some credit." Michael shifted in his chair. He began to fiddle with a worn thread that dangled from the rip in the knee of his faded jeans. After a long silence,

Michael looked up at Casey and simply asked, "Why does it matter to you so much?"

Casey sat back, reliving her meeting with Valerie. Drawing in a breath then exhaling, the words flew from her mouth, "I just don't like being the object of someone's gossip, especially when it's not true. And…she did want to know what your wife thought about her husband working with…" Casey trailed off not wanting to pursue the current topic of conversation any further.

"Well, since I don't have a wife, I don't think my wife's opinion about who I work with really matters. I think, however, that Valerie is just playing with you." He stated coolly.

"Really? How can you be so nonchalant about it?"

Michael twisted the silver chain that hung on his wrist then looked up at Casey's twisted expression. He again replied with a steady tone, "Valerie Sorrenson is not worth getting upset. She's a gossip and believes what she wants to. She was like that in high school. Besides, there are more important things in this world to get riled up about."

Sipping his coffee, Michael had finished his sentence yet to Casey she was waiting for him to expand on his last comment. Then again, it was too early in the morning for mind-bending philosophy. With that observation, Casey opted to simplify the conversation. "I wonder if the weather is going to clear up."

Glancing out the window, Casey flashed back to past Memorial Day weekends that her and Michael had spent together at Hidden Springs Lake, when they were in college. Remaining silent as her eyes locked with his, Casey could feel herself getting lost in a sea of green as a twinge caught her in the stomach. Her fork slipped from her hand and clinked on the plate, bringing her back to reality. She lowered her eyes to her half-eaten breakfast. Picking up her fork, Casey took another bite of melon, not daring to look at him again.

Michael fidgeted as he raised the cup of coffee to his mouth, even though it was empty. Intently, he watched Casey close her mouth around the fork and he too felt a twinge in his abdomen, remembering what it was like to kiss those lips. He wanted to do that right then and there, but refrained from such an aggressive move. He imagined his hands entwined in her red curls. Then, silently he berated himself for his thoughts and pushed the image of his actions out of his mind. "Restroom?" Was the only word he could utter.

"By all means." Casey pointed down the hallway.

"Thanks." He mumbled gruffly. Michael put down his cup, retrieved his bag and disappeared down the hallway. When he returned, he had changed into a fresh tee shirt. His wavy hair, still damp, was combed straight back. "So, what are we going to do today?"

"We?" Casey raised an eyebrow. "I'm going to finish my laundry, clean and start packing my car."

In that moment he knew he had made a bad choice. He should not have come to the Lake. Michael drew back the shear drapery, keeping his back to Casey. He did not want her to see his disappointment. "It looks like it's clearing up, maybe we could do something later. I noticed a sign on the way in, something about riverboat cruises?"

"Yeah, I think they run every hour." Casey stated matter-of-factly, opting not to finish the last bit of her breakfast.

"Well, I'll get out of your way. I'm going for a walk."

"Michael, that isn't necessary. Why don't you just relax?" Casey stated calmly as she picked up her dishes and headed towards the kitchen but his response stopped her.

"I think it is necessary." He mumbled, refusing to turn and face her.

"Michael, why are you here?" Casey blurted then wished she had kept her question to herself.

Finally turning to face her, every muscle was taut in Michael's body as he crossed his arms against his broad chest. A muscle twitched in his cheek as he tried to conjugate a sane answer. "You know why I'm here."

"Do I?" Setting her breakfast dishes back down on the dining room table, Casey too, folded her arms across her chest, raising an eyebrow to his comment.

"Eric and I had to pick up the sketches for his meeting this afternoon." He reasoned through a clenched jaw.

"Eric could have done that on his own. And I really don't buy the excuse that you don't trust courier services."

"Casey this is a rather remote area. A resort area at that." He knew he was pulling at strings and if anyone could see through his ridiculous reasoning, it was Casey.

"You're not telling me something and I want to know what it is."

Michael's grip tightened on his upper arms. Clearing his throat, Michael rubbed his hand over his brow. Digging the toe of his boot into the carpeting, Michael defensively stated, "Casey, I told you I can stay at one of the lodges. I didn't have any intentions of staying here with you."

"You already told me that. But you've been here before. You know how crowded this place gets on holiday weekends." Casey was beginning to regret her decision, even though she needed the job. How were they going to keep it professional? "It's just…you've just been acting strange since you got here. So, I'm just curious, what's going on?"

"I…ah…" In any given situation, Michael was quite articulate, displaying that he was a well educated man but when it came to Casey Andrews, he was usually rendered speechless. Then he turned the tables on Casey, "Strange? Me? You're the one that has been short with me. Constantly reminding me, I'm getting too personal. Cutting off conversations, hanging up on me. Don't you think your actions and lack of professionalism, is making this personal?"

Raising an eyebrow, Casey found herself rolling her eyes but when she realized Michael was right, at least about her attitude, Casey softened her tone. "Michael…maybe I place too much value in my career but I'm all I've got. I don't have the luxury of falling back on someone else's paycheck. And…" Casey trailed off. Suddenly, she felt this need to sit as she positioned herself at the table. Slowing her pace, she continued. "I've never been fired in my life. It threw me for a loop. And you…running into you and offering me a chance to be a Design Manager…for you. To create an entire department from scratch… I'm just…"

Michael was drawn to her worried expression and he started to move closer. "… just what Casey?" he questioned quietly.

"Well, it's just plain weird! I mean, weird in a good way, but weird nonetheless. Don't get me wrong, I really want to do this, despite what happened between us. I just hope and pray you didn't hire me out of pity. I want to believe you hired me because I can do a great job. I need for you to believe in my expertise. But most of all… I'm afraid I'll disappoint you."

"Casey, Eric and I both poured over your portfolio for hours. You're resume is impressive. We don't gamble when it comes to the company. And if you don't trust that, trust this; Eric was the deciding factor. If he didn't want you to join the firm, we would not have hired you." Michael drew in a breath, "And this is the exact reason why I'm here. I *need* to know that everything is all right between us."

Taken aback, Casey rose and took her empty dishes to the kitchen. Returning to the living room, Casey abruptly marched across the room then poised herself in the recliner. Pulling her knees close to her chest, she wrapped her arms around her legs. "And why wouldn't it be?" Casey's words were tart.

Michael tried to remain on an even keel but his replied was fierce. "Listen to what you just said. This is what our conversations have been like all week…less than amicable. I can't have this going on in the office. You have this wall around you, that you won't let anyone get through. Where is the confident woman I use to know and…" Michael abruptly stopped realizing Casey had indeed changed and digging up his feelings from the past was not going to resolve the situation at hand, so he quickly shifted his approach. "To answer your question, I am here Casey because I didn't want to discuss this on the phone." He paused then questioned, "I need to know, after all these years, are you still angry with me?"

Casey's nervously twirled a piece of hair around her finger. "No, Michael, I got over you when you boarded the plane to California. This is an entirely different situation. And it's just awkward. This was our dream a long time ago and who knows where we would be had we done things differently. I just need time to adjust to the fact that you are my boss and I'm not your business partner." Casey was strong with her words, and as she made her confession, a sense of relief washed over her.

"Oh." Michael was so stunned he could only give her a one word response.

"It's silly, I know." Embarrassment reigned over Casey but she knew she had to speak the truth. "Maybe I'm still a little angry but I'm committed to the challenges that lay ahead. Like I said before, I will do whatever you want me to, whenever you want me to. Just understand, I'm just a little overwhelmed and…" Casey drew in a breath, "…while I like to think that I bounce back pretty easily, I just needed time to myself. Can't you understand that?"

"Eric and I really need to land this project. It's our top priority right now. Can you understand that?"

Casey understood perfectly. He was here because of the business and she completely misunderstood his intent. Finally, her tone softened as she moved closer to him. Suddenly, she felt this overpowering urge to be wrapped in his arms but Casey knew she was acting out of emotion and he was responding on an entirely different level. Resisting the temptation, she rested a hand on his arm, that was still locked across his chest. "Everything is going to work out. All I'm asking for is a little time." She looked into his eyes and became conscious of the heat rising between them.

As she started to pull away, Michael engulfed her in an embrace. The warmth of his breath tickled her neck and his body began to melt into hers. His hands sizzled through the material of her shirt. Then an ache swelled in her stomach and traveled upwards to her chest. He gently whispered, "I'm going for a walk." into her ear, his lips lightly touched her cheek, then he pulled away. Michael straightened up and exited without another word.

Shocked, Casey let him go.

"Good Afternoon, Whitley Designs. This is Julie."

"Just the person I was trying to reach." Eric stated in a low tone.

"Eric." A tickle ran through her mid-section then an inkling of panic struck. "You're not calling to cancel our date are you?"

"No. But I'm going to be a little later than I had expected. The meeting that was scheduled for one o'clock, has been pushed off until two. Can you believe it? And on a Friday before a holiday. It's kind of ridiculous."

"It is. But are you ready for it?"

"Absolutely."

"Then go in there and show them who's ready." Julie encouraged.

Eric liked Julie's upbeat attitude and thanked her. "I'm not sure how long it's going to last but can I call you when I'm done?"

"That's fine. Just call me at home. I'm leaving early today."

Eric paced the hallway outside the conference room at Brookshire Hospital. "So, do you have a few minutes?"

"I'll always have a few minutes for you, Eric." Julie giggled then quietly wished she hadn't said something so silly.

As Eric turned in his path, he recognized the big-bellied man approaching him. Nodding and shaking hands with Clayton Wills, a competing contractor, Eric told him the meeting had been postponed an hour.

"What I meant was…" Julie trailed off trying to regain her composer.

"So, how's your day going?" Eric asked as he watched Clayton waddle down the hall and then turn the corner toward the vending machines.

"Not fast enough."

"Excited about tonight?" Eric teased.

"No…Yes. What I mean is that, Whitley is all over me like a snake attacking a field mouse. I've been updating my resume." Julie let out a breath. "Casey is so lucky she was let go."

"Well, if things work out with Casey and we get the business we're anticipating, I'll bring it up with Mike about bringing you on board as well."

"Oh Eric. That would be wonderful."

"Well, I can't promise anything right now. But let's not rule anything out. In the mean time I'll keep my ears open. If I hear anything, I'll let you know."

A clatter rose from just beyond Julie's cubicle which caused her to turn with a start. Glaring down his long nose at her was Mr. Whitley, his pea size eyes bulging. "Ms. Warren that better be a business call because if it is personal, you can pack up and get the hell out right this instant."

Julie could feel her blood rushing to her face and her heart racing with fury but she dared not show fear to The Snake. Abruptly Julie turned her back to him, calmly but loud enough for Mr. Whitley to over hear, spoke into the receiver, "Mr. Logan. I'm going to have to call you back. My boss just step into my office."

"Hang in there."

"I will. Thank you Mr. Logan." Julie quickly minimized her resume that was up on the computer screen hoping the Snake had not taken notice to what she was really working on. With spite and confidence, she stood to face him head on. "That was a potential client and he heard you." Julie fibbed not feeling an ounce of guilt.

"Are you talking back to me, Ms. Warren? Because the last person that did that is out on the street."

"If you're referring to Casey Andrews, she's not. She's head of her own design department at one of the most prestigious Architectural firms in the state."

Mr. Whitley looked down his nose at Julie, "And what company would that be, Ms. Warren?"

"Sterling Architects and Construction." Julie stated triumphantly.

With that knowledge in mind, Mr. Whitley's eyes widened, he shivered then quietly slithered away.

The air was thick and the humidity hung stagnant as Michael sauntered to the main road. Glancing over his shoulder, he saw the shear curtain fall back into place. Heading towards the lake, he kicked at the pebbles, carelessly walking with no planned destination. It was unbearably warm for May and silently he wished he had packed a pair of shorts.

An hour had lapsed before Michael realized he had hiked half way up Mount Springs. His mind wandering aimless as well as his step, as he moved along one of the more established and well-marked trails. Now resting on the ledge of an outlook, he could barely see Casey's cabin on the opposite side of the lake, the thick foliage obstructing his view. Michael picked up a dried twig, fiddling with it as he drew in the damp mountain air.

Michael was juggling emotions he was not familiar with as questions stabbed at his gut and he couldn't understand why. He had been pretty probing with Casey this past week and he knew she was right. They had both agreed their relationship was to be professional. Yet, why did he want to know her every move? Why did he want to know everything about her? What was wrong with him? Why did he come here? Why the hell did he hug her then kiss her on the cheek? After all, affection was not part of her employment contract.

He stared at the natural environment that surrounded him, perhaps subconsciously believing the answers laid within. The trees had grown thick and dotted the landscape in varying shades of green. Remembering their many trips to Hidden Springs, a smile appeared on Michael's face. The memories of their college days together were fond and Michael felt a swelling ache in his chest. But in the same moment he crinkled his brow. Their last visit to the lake was less than a memorable one. How could he have chosen graduate school and his father's money to pay for it, over spending a lifetime with Casey? Yet, why didn't Casey have enough faith in their love that they could have survived the time and the distance? At that point, they had been together for seven years and they both knew there was no one else but each other. However, Michael failed at keeping in touch nor did he look her up when he returned home. Now it didn't seem to matter that he had gone to the same college as his father. They had an estranged relationship and he had given up the one woman he had ever really loved. When the answers wouldn't come Michael decided it was time to head back to the cabin but he found it difficult to budge from his spot. "*A few more minutes.*" He reasoned to himself as he picked up another twig. As he twisted it around, a red-shouldered hawk, race across the sky, no doubt on his way to lunch, followed by two brightly colored Blue Jays. Out of the corner of his eye, Michael watched a few squirrels chase each other around, in a friendly game of tag, then they raced up an oak tree and disappeared. For a brief moment, the sight lent a minimal level of peace, causing Michael to boast with laughter until thoughts of Casey drifted back in. He tossed the mangled twig to the ground, stood and stretched his stiff back. The only conclusion Michael could manage was to keep his distance from Casey and opted he would take that riverboat cruise without her.

As he wandered down the trail, back to the main dirt road, he witnessed a young boy with his back to him. Next to him, was a young girl, probably not much older than fifteen. She hit the young man on the shoulder with the back of her hand and whispered, "Someone's coming."

"Don't let me stop you." Michael entertained and let out a chuckle. Paying more attention to the trail then the two teenagers, Michael continued on, all the while trying to stifle his laugh. But something on the trunk of the tree caught him right in the gut. Stopping in his tracks, Michael took a sharp turn and approached the two teens.

"Oh, we're in trouble now. I told you!" The girl turned and hid her face in the boy's shirt.

Oblivious to their presence, Michael reached out and touched the craved bark. He traced the outline of the initials that had been put there when he was a teenager. He felt his blood pulsing through his veins as memories of that day came rushing back.

"Hey, mister. You all right? You're not gonna like get us in trouble or nothin' are you?" The boy asked as he held his girlfriend close to his side.

Finally acknowledging their existence, Michael replied, "Heck no, it's cool." He stared at the initials again. "You know, twenty years ago I did the same thing with my girlfriend. Looks like history repeats itself."

"Wow, you're old." The girl stated. " I mean, like are you here with your kids or somethin'?"

"Not exactly."

"So, ah, who's C.A. and M.S.?" They inquired.

"I'm M.S.…." Michael introduced himself, then added, "And C.A.…" he touched the initials again feeling a throbbing pain in his chest, " …was the love of my life." Michael finally admitted it, knowing he could probably never capture with Casey what they once had.

Casey had all the windows opened and a light breeze was billowing the curtains when Michael returned to the cabin. It was just passed noon when he politely knocked before entering.

"Casey?" Michael called out.

"Hey, you're back." She said breathlessly, her arms full of folded laundry. "Gosh, where did you go?"

"I hiked up the mountain. Sorry, I lost track of time."

"That's okay." Casey disappeared into her bedroom and returned quickly. Still out of breath she brushed her hand over her crown of curls, "You want to grab something to eat then go take that riverboat cruise?"

Michael was delighted by her suggestion but hid his enthusiasm. He was feeling like that boy back in high school when they had first met. Excited, confident, nervous and scared. "That would be great. Do you mind if I take a shower or do you need help with something?"

"No, we can grab sandwiches at the Country Store. Go ahead. There are fresh towels in the hall closet."

"Thank you." Michael smiled as he brushed by her.

The scent of his cologne mixed with the woodsy smell of Hidden Springs Lake swirled in the air igniting all of Casey's senses. *No! You're the one that said strictly professional!* Her mind scolded her. *You are not falling for him again!* She stood motionless as Michael entered the bathroom and closed the door behind him, separating the two of them. Out of sight, out of mind, at least for a few minutes, Casey rationalized as she heard the water running.

The morning clouds had given way to the afternoon sun and the Riverboat Cruise ended up being the perfect activity. Catching the glint in his eyes, Casey was suspicious of his changed mood. Although, mountain air was known to have a rejuvenating effect on people and that did not rule out Michael Sterling, she concluded, as Michael handed a twenty dollar bill to the river boat attendant. Casey welcomed Michael's friendly gesture as he assisted her on board. Her hand fit perfectly into his and chills tickled her spine as her fingertips lingered in the warmth of his grip. A spark ignited deep inside her and she wondered why she was still attracted to him after all these years? And was it just her? Was he feeling the same spark? As they took a seat near the front of the boat behind the captain, Casey doubted it, chalking it up to left over feelings from a teenage crush, that was long since over.

It was a beautiful cruise that lasted almost two hours. The host pointed out various types of wildlife, foliage and refurbished historical landmarks. Not many people were on board and Michael relished the time they were spending together as he casually draped his arm over the back of the bench. He felt the electricity rising between them without even touching her and he wondered why was he still attracted to her after all these years? And was it just him? Was she feeling the same electricity? As the boat swayed and his fingers brushing again Casey's shoulder, Michael doubted it, chalking it up to left over feelings from a teenage crush that was long since over.

As she blotted the tissue to her lips, there was a knock at the door. Eric had arrived earlier then he said he would and Julie was relieved she had dressed first before styling her hair. "Eric, hi. Did you have any trouble getting here?"

"Not at all. Ah, here." Clenched in his fist was a bouquet of tulips, sprayed with sprigs of baby's breath and evergreen.

"How sweet." As Julie pushed her straight blond hair behind her ear she buried her face in the flowers and inhaled. "Hhmm...smells just like spring." She giggled.

"Are you ready to go?"

"Give me just five more minutes." Looking over her left shoulder, she expected Eric to be behind her. Instead he politely stood in the open doorway. "Eric, you can come in."

Mesmerized by the slight sway in Julie's hips, Eric blurted out, "You look great!" Blood surged to his cheeks but because of his deep tan Julie did not take notice.

She had taken care to pick out just the right outfit and Julie was glad Eric noticed. Wearing navy blue shorts, a white short sleeved silk blouse and a blue and silver floral vest, Julie blushed at Eric's observation. "Thank you, so do you." Julie slipped into the kitchen, retrieving a crystal vase from the cabinet above the stove. "Could you put these in some water for me?" Julie returned to the bathroom, applying a second coat of black mascara. When she returned, Eric had sent the vase of flowers on her coffee table in the living room. "Should we go?"

Unlocking the door to his truck, Eric assisted Julie into the passenger seat. As he walked around the front of vehicle, Julie noticed the loose fit of his jeans and the tight fit of his dark maroon shirt. She leaned across the bench seat and unlocked the door for him. "Thanks." Eric smiled.

Eric decided to take Julie downtown. The sun was still shining bright and an arid breeze filled the night. *It's perfect.* Eric thought to himself. "Dinner downtown? Maybe at one of the outdoor cafes and then a movie? How does that sound?" Eric politely inquired.

"Sounds like a plan to me." Julie responded cheerfully.

"So, did you grow up here?" Eric questioned, trying to fill the uncomfortable first date silence.

"No, Tennessee, Indiana, then here."

"What brought here?"

"Followed a guy." Julie stated matter of factly.

"Oh." There was disappointment in Eric's voice.

"But he's no longer in the picture." Julie responded quickly. "He went back to Indiana after six months. He hated it here plus I wanted to get married, he wanted to start dating men. Life goes on." Julie shrugged.

"Wow!"

"What?"

"You don't seemed bother by…" Eric found it difficult to form the right sentence.

Julie giggled, "I learned that life-goes-on attitude from my brother, Jared. He always says, 'Build a bridge and get over it.' So far, it's worked for me. Besides I couldn't make that guy love me especially when he wanted to be with someone else." Julie raised an eyebrow.

"You have a brother?"

"And a sister, Jill. They're twins. What about you, any brothers or sisters?"

"Three sisters and three brothers."

"Seven kids? Oh my gosh, your poor mother."

"Mom wanted more, it's more like poor dad." Simultaneously, they laughed.

"Did your day get any better after we hung up?" Eric was so nervous he was verbalizing every question that came to mind.

"I had the pleasure of telling Mr. Whitley about Casey. He looked pretty angry. I think I need to get out of there and fast. When Casey was around I could tolerate the Snake, as Casey and I so affectionately refer to him, but now, I'm being attacked all the time. Whitley is not the nicest person in the world. He's too regimented and not a people person at all. I don't know how Casey lasted as long as she did." Julie sucked in a short breath not wanting to rehash the misery of her employment situation so she changed the subject. "So what movie are we going to see?"

"*Last chance.* Is that okay?"

"You want to go see a chic flick?"

Eric shrugged, "Well, I doubt you want to see an action movie so, why not? I'll try to be open minded." Eric smiled.

"Okay but can we go to the late show? I worked through lunch so I'm hungry."

"No problem." Eric muttered as he found a metered spot a few blocks from the movie theater.

They dined at The Director's Chair Restaurant, a small side-street café. The black and white abstract wallpaper contrasted with the heavy red drapery that bordered the large front bay window. Just in front of the window was a small platform with a baby grand piano. Dressed in a black tuxedo was a silver haired gentleman moving his fingers over the ivory keys. Various black and white photos of movie stars from an era long since passed, added to the ambience. As they were enjoying the gourmet cuisine, a client of Michael's interrupted Eric and Julie's dinner.

"Mr. Logan, don't you two look so cute?" Melinda stated mockingly then leaning over whispered, "Where the hell is Michael? Lyle and I need to discuss the resort project. Tell him, if he wants to stay in business, he better call me." With that statement, the woman stood tall, turned and disappeared into the night.

Chapter 9

Earlier in the day, when Casey and Michael had grabbed lunch at the Country Store, Michael had noticed numerous flyers advertising the "Memorial Day Dance Under the Stars" and had enticed Casey to attend. "It will be the end to a perfect day. Besides, we have to celebrate your new job." He encouraged. And Casey could not resist. She had a reason to where the sundress Hannah had encouraged her to purchase.

Casey laid on the sofa, her eyes closed as she drifted into twilight. A Top-40 love song reverberated from the radio when Michael made his appearance from the spare bedroom. Casey's eyes drifted open as Michael stood before her. More then his green eyes and his clean-shaven face captured her attention. Stonewashed jeans hugged his strong thighs and were pleasingly cut across his washboard stomach. He tossed his jean shirt over the arm of the sofa, then tucked his dark purple polo shirt into the top of his jeans. Fastening the button at the waistband and buckling his belt, a sigh escaped Casey's lips. A tingling sensation started in her mid-section then raced down her legs to her toes causing a knee-jerk reaction.

"Oh, did I wake you?"

"Hhmm, no, I was just ah…resting."

"Well, it's your turn. Are you going to get ready?" Michael questioned as he squeezed and wiggled her toe.

Casey sat up with a start, surprised by his touch and her physical reaction. Was he flirting with her? Shaking her head and fluffing her curls, Casey was on her feet, heading to the bathroom for a long awaited shower. Their bodies brushed against each other as Casey squeezed by. Again, a physical reaction took her by surprise as she felt it ten-fold. Engulfed by the scent of Michael's cologne, chills spiraled down her spine, tickled her mid-section then raced down her legs, then her knees buckled. Steadying herself in order to turn and close the bathroom door, she raised an eyebrow to Michael, wondering what was causing her to melt in his prescnce. "I think I need a cold shower." She mumbled.

Michael chuckled at her comment wondering if she was flirting with him. Just the simple touch of wiggling her toes caused heat to rise from just below his belt, grip him in the stomach and race to his fingertips. This was getting ridiculous. They were mature adults and should be able to control themselves yet, at least physically, it seemed as if something was still there.

The cold shower did little to ease the fire that burned inside Casey. Her heart was beating furiously and this was getting silly. They were no longer two high school kids yet there was no doubt about it, something was still there, at least physically.

Forty-five minutes had lapsed when Casey appeared from her bedroom and Michael's mouth fell open.

Conscious of the expression on his face, Casey instantly questioned, "What?" As she fumbled with the silver earring she was trying to fasten to her earlobe.

"You look…amazing."

She struggled to say thank you then jokingly added, "Hannah told me not to wear this dress around you."

"And why is that?" Michael's curiosity was piqued.

"When I tried it on, she said I looked irresistible but I don't know about that."

"Well, sister don't lie to each other, now do they?"

All Casey knew was that when her and Hannah had gone shopping and she saw the white sundress with bright purple flowers in the window, she had to have it. The scalloped v-shaped neckline laid gently against Casey's skin. The bodice of the dress hugged her torso, where it was gathered at the waistline then flared. The hemline danced just above her ankles. As Casey slipped on her white sandals, Michael was very aware of her every move.

Casey pushed back her hair, wondering if she should tie it back, then opted not to. Her red curls gently fell over her bare shoulders, hiding the thin purple straps of the dress that laced down her back.

Michael noticed that the bow at the small of her back had come loose and he immediately stood behind her. "Let me tie this for you." He whispered as his breath cascaded over her bare shoulder.

"Thank you." Casey stuttered as his fingertips brushed against the material and seared right through to her skin, sending heated current through her body.

"You're welcome." Michael stumbled in a small voice as the heat that radiated from Casey ignited his masculinity on fire. Drawing in a breath, he fought the temptation to wrap Casey in his arms. Clearing his throat, he mustered, "Ready?"

The daytime heat had dissipated into a warm summer night. The sun was just above the mountain peaks as Casey and Michael walked to the Welcome Center. The outside wooden deck was to the right of the main entrance and was decorated with streamers and silver glittered stars. Helium balloons, in every color added to the décor. There was a live band playing at the edge of the dance floor and a full buffet had been set up inside the Center's lobby.

Casey ran into the Kirby's and Nancy invited them to join her and Sean at an outside table. "My! You are not the young man I remember." Nancy teased.

The dance was underway as Michael offered to get them something to drink. Returning with a plate of finger sandwiches, fresh cut vegetables and two wine spritzers, Michael scooted his seat closer to Casey.

"Michael, Nancy knows Eric."

"Really?"

"Eric's non-profit organization is refurbishing housing in the downtown area for moderate income families. Certainly, you knew that the Hearth and Home Project was Eric's, didn't you?" Nancy raised a questioning eyebrow to Michael.

Michael shook his head, "No, I didn't." Embarrassed, he lowered his head, wishing he knew Eric on a more personal level. They had spent a considerable amount of time together in the office but ninety percent of the time conversations were about business.

"Really Michael, maybe you should get to know your business partner better." Casey teased.

"We could use an architects input on the next project, if you're interested." Nancy encouraged.

Michael nodded, considering Nancy's offer but before he could respond, a high-pitched voice interrupted them, "Michael Sterling, why as I live and breathe. What are you doing here?"

"Hello, Valerie." Michael stood and was taken aback by her overpowering embrace.

"Well you two look awfully cozy. Are you sure it's just professional, Casey?" Valerie teased.

Casey gritted her back teeth and slowly stated, "Michael came up for the day to discuss business. We're heading back to the city tomorrow."

"An overnight visit, how interesting." Valerie snickered.

"It's not like…" Casey's temper was about to short circuit when she was interrupted by Nancy.

"Hello, I'm Nancy Kirby and this is my husband Sean." Shaking Valerie's hand with a firm grip, Nancy added, "…and you are?"

Taken aback, she stammered, "Valerie Sorrenson. We all went to high school together."

"Well that's nice Valerie but this really is business." Nancy emphasized. "Michael's company and my women's group are working together on a housing project. We were just discussing the details so if you don't mind perhaps we can all visit later. It was nice to meet you."

Valerie turned on her heel, heading in the opposite direction, calling out her next victims name.

Taking his seat again, Michael glanced at Casey, both of them holding their laughter and hiding their gratitude for Nancy's assertiveness. Valerie Sorrenson had finally met her match.

"Sometimes it pays to be an ornery old crow." A burst of laughter echoed into the night air where stars now lit the sky and the moon was full.

"That's my Nan for you. Always able to put people in their place." Sean stood and held out his hand, "Come on lady, you deserve a whirl around the dance floor for that performance."

Taking his hand, Nancy smiled, "Why Mr. Kirby…"

Casey looked on in envy. "Aren't they cute? I hope my marriage is like that when I am their age."

"I'm sure it will be." Michael mumbled. He was taken in by the sparkle in her eyes and how the moonlight danced off her fiery curls. The need to reach out and caress her sun-kissed skin started to consume him. He wanted to feel again what they had shared so many years ago. But Michael knew it was going to a take more than a simple touch and a sweet kiss to convince Casey Andrews that they were meant to be together.

"Michael, woo-hoo, Michael…" Casey was waving her hand in front of his face. "You didn't hear a word I said did you?"

"Huh? I'm sorry, I was thinking about how Eric's meeting went." Michael fibbed.

Casey looked at her silver watch, "Well, you're off the clock and you talked me into coming to this dance, so let's go dance."

Before Michael could object, Casey had him by the hand and was leading him to the dance floor and before she knew it, she was wrapped in his embrace as the music slowed.

As they exited the downtown movie theater, Eric asked, "So what did you think of the ending?"

"It was good, but I don't know of any man on the planet that would give up his career for a woman. It was a little unrealistic."

"Yeah, but he could always get another job."

"I know, but he worked so hard to build his business. I just don't think people are like that. Maybe I'm cynical but I don't know anyone who would make such a sacrifice in the name of love."

"You sound a little jaded, Julie. Not all us guys are bad. Maybe you just haven't met the right one." Eric could no longer resist; he had to kiss her. He leaned forward to touch his lips to hers but instead ended up kissing her nose.

"Eric what are you doing?" Julie squeaked out in surprise by his bold move.

Stumbling over his words, he managed, "Well, I was trying to kiss you, but I ah… Could I try again?"

Julie nodded and then was on her tiptoes so she could reach her arms around Eric's neck. Their lips met in a sweet kiss.

Eric took Julie by the hands, "I must be crazy for saying this but I don't want this night to end. I really like you Julie Warren."

Julie smiled, "Well, then why don't we go get a cup of coffee or something?" Hand in hand they walked to the downtown waterfront.

"Got it!" Valerie squealed. "I can't wait to get this one developed. You two can argue with me later whether or not it's personal or professional because one thing is for certain, pictures never lie."

"Great." Casey moaned. "Just what we need, our lives in print."

"Who cares, Casey. We're not doing anything wrong." Michael continued to move Casey around the dance floor.

"I care. I don't want it to effect business. Doesn't it bother you?" While Casey stiffened, she still remained in his embrace.

"No Casey, it doesn't."

"Why not?"

Michael didn't even have to think, because deep down inside he knew why. "Casey, when I went for that walk, earlier today, I saw our initials carved in the sweetheart tree. And I finally confessed, to two teenagers if you can believe that one. They asked who C.A. was and I couldn't help myself. I told them you *were* the love of my life."

Casey's eyes widened, "No, Michael, don't!"

"Don't what? Let me just finish." Michael cut her off quickly, wanting to say what needed to be said along time ago. "… but it's not true."

"What!" Casey pushed herself out of his embrace. "You're telling me now, that you never loved me? That's really cruel, Michael. Just down right cruel!" Casey turned her back to him, wrapping her arms around her waist. It didn't even take a moment for Casey to digest it all. So, there it was, after all these years, she meant nothing to him.

"Casey!" Michael whirled Casey around.

"What!"

"Casey... I love you. I've... always... loved... you."

As Michael stepped towards Casey she, took a step back, "No, you can't do this to us. We agreed. We agreed to keep our relationship strictly professional." As she continued, her tone slowly raised an octave. "It's the moment, the mountain air, the summer night, the moon, the stars, the... it's not true. It can't be...." Tears choked off Casey's words as she ran off into the night.

"Where's Casey going?" Nancy inquired.

Michael had stunned even himself. Had he been too aggressive? Had he said the right words? Was his timing all wrong? Yet, what did it matter? He had said it. It was now out there, like a breath hanging in the air on a cold winter night. As he pondered his thoughts, it dawned on him, he felt alive for the first time in years. He had said 'I love you' to Casey Andrews and it was the truth. His mind was yelling at him to go after her, but his feet would not move.

"What did you say to her!" Nancy demanded.

"Nothing I can take back. She'll probably never speak to me again. Shoot, she'll probably quit her job before she even starts working for me."

"Ah, I know Casey pretty well. She's like a daughter to Sean and me and it takes a lot to shake her up. Tell me, maybe I can help."

"I told her...how I felt about her."

"And what is that Michael?"

"That I love her."

"Well, that's obvious and there is only one thing to do." Nancy gave him a hard look. "What are you waiting for? Go after her, before it's too late." Then she gave him a good nudge.

The full moon lit the main road as Michael headed towards the cabin. He wasn't sure if that's where Casey had headed but that was the first place he planned to look. He didn't care if it took all night, he was going to find her and help her understand.

Even though there was no evidence of life in the darkened cabin, Michael still tried to open the front door when he had reached the porch. But it was locked. *"She can't be that angry with me."* Michael hoped. The chirping of crickets and frogs echoed through the still night. In the distance ahead, Michael strained to hear a muffled sound that resembled a cry. Turning towards the lake he saw Casey silhouetted in the moonlight, on the dock overlooking Hidden Springs Lake.

Casey looked up as Michael slowed his pace. "Go away, Michael." She commanded in a shaky voice. It wasn't only her voice that was shaking as she turned her back on Michael.

The night mountain air had grown chilly so Michael removed his jean shirt, draping it over Casey's shoulders. The feel of her skin under his fingers caused Michael to shutter. He wanted nothing more than to take her in his arms and chase away the chill that had her shivering.

"Casey, I'm sorry." Breathing heavily, Michael swept his hand through his hair. "Am I going to be apologizing to you forever?"

Letting out a small laughter laced with tears, Casey turned to face him. "Why? I just need to know why, Michael?"

"You were right Casey, it was the moment. But for me it was the right moment. It sounds crazy but it hit me so hard when we were dancing and I was telling you about our initials carved into that tree trunk. I know we were meant to be together."

"Michael we haven't seen each other for at least ten years, if not longer…" Casey realized her throat was dry as she lost her concentration.

"That's not true." Michael stated abruptly still keeping a fair distance between them.

Casey crossed her arms over her mid-section, nibbling on her lower lip. A perplexed expression fell across her face and her tone became harsh, "What's that supposed to mean?"

"Casey, do you remember my sister, Amy?"

"Of course, but what does she have to do with this?"

Michael inched a little closer, "About a year ago, Amy died and…"

Casey gasped as she stepped forward, "What! Why didn't you tell me? Oh my God, I am so sorry… what…"

"Casey…" Michael cut her off, "I'll tell you about it later but what I do want to tell you is, her last wish was that I find you and I did shortly after she died."

"So you knew that I was working for Whitley Designs? When we ran into each other?"

Michael could no longer keep his secret, "Yes. Yes, I did and my meeting with Whitley Designs was no mistake. I wanted to see you again and working with you was the only way I thought I could get close to you again."

"Why now, Michael? I mean, you've been back for a long time. You're business is well established, you were engaged! For Christ sake! Why now?" Casey choked, desperately trying to hold her tears at bay.

Crossing his arms over his chest, Michael looked down and kicked at nothing impractical on the dock. He knew he was risking it all but he continued, "I denied it. Even when Amy reminded me. When it comes to love there is only one person for me and that's you." Michael looked deep into Casey's eyes, begging for understanding. When she did not return a comment he continued with his story. "Amy only had one regret and that was that she had never loved anyone the way I love you. Like Amy, I don't have any regrets except..." Michael paused, choosing his words wisely, "Except... I let you go."

"No, Michael, that's where you are wrong!" Casey gritted her teeth, remembering the day he left for California. The pain that clutched her heart was almost equivalent to what she felt then. Drawing in a breath, Casey tried to maintain her composure. "You didn't let me go, you left. There's a difference." Her body tensed as she breezed past him; her heels clicking on the boardwalk, resonating sound across the glass-like lake. To his surprise as well as her own, she whirled around, "Michael, death changes people. Believe me, I know. But how could you say what you said? How can you be so sure? How do you know that what you are feeling is real and not some dumb high school fantasy we left behind a lifetime ago? But most of all, how do you expect me to trust you again, that you won't leave me?"

The moonlight caught the amber flecks in her eyes revealing the pain he had put there so long ago. Summing up the courage he could only speak from his heart, "Casey, I'm never going to leave you, again. I came back. I'm settled here. I've worked hard to build a reputable company but...that doesn't matter. What matters is that I'm nothing without you." Crinkling his brow, Michael inhaled deeply then slowly exhaled. "Don't you understand, some things never go away. They get buried or put away or hidden or even lost but they never go away. And as far as trusting me, I'll have to earn it." Michael cast a gaze to her quivering lip as he witnessed the anguish on her face. Tears welling in her troubled eyes.

"I...ah..." No words would come. Casey spun on her heel and started to sprint towards the cabin.

"Casey!" With a trembling voice that carried across the lake, Michael yelled, "Trust this...I love you!"

Michael's declaration stopped Casey in her tracks. Standing motionless, it felt like an eternity had passed when she finally summed up the courage to turn back around. Her body shook as tears stained her cheeks. The urge to run into Michael's arms gripped her heart while fear and longing played a tug o' war in her head. Inching forward, Casey was captured by the spark in Michael's green eyes and an old familiarity came back. It was the way he looked at her when they were young. And in love. As the gap between them lessened, so did the hurt of the past. Michael reached out for Casey's hand, sweeping her into his arms. The intensity of his strength and the warmth of his embrace erased the doubts that had gripped her heart for so long.

Raising his hand to her cheek, Michael brushed his thumb over Casey's tears, "I never did like to see you cry." His tone low and sincere.

Their gazes locked as another tear escaped the corner of Casey's eye. Michael dropped his eyes to her lips, tracing his fingertip across them. Their lips came together in a sweet kiss. At first, slow, tender, and forgiving then the heat between them ignited and it was no longer a kiss like they had shared in their youth. But a kiss shared by two adults who had grown up, grown apart and grown together again, in order to reunite in this moment.

It was the gentleness of a caring man that now held her close as his shirt that had protected her from the brisk night, fell off her shoulders and tumbled to the ground. He trailed a gentle hand down her back as she caressed the back of his neck.

The sounds of the summer night embraced them, as the flames slightly subsided. Michael gently touched his lips to hers, whispering, "I love you, Casey Andrews."

"I love you, Michael Sterling." Casey returned and the moment was filled with hope, promise and love.

Michael held Casey close, wrapping his shirt around her, then escorted her to the cabin. Before she could manage the lock, he lowered his mouth to hers. Drinking in the sweet taste of his breath, their mouths danced together, sparking the embers that had been laying dormant for too long. Casey twisted the doorknob, while Michael trailed kisses against her neck. Her nerve endings became raw as her mid-section clenched tight. Once inside, she reached for the light switch.

"No..." Michael whispered. "Dance with me."

Her eyes sparkled in the moonlight that trickled in through the front window. "Michael, there's no music. Do you want me to turn on... I just bought a new CD..." Casey's rambling was stopped by Michael crushing his lips to hers.

"We don't need any music..." He whispered. Again covering her mouth with his.

He slipped his shirt from her shoulders, tossing it over the back of the recliner. Trailing light feathery caresses over her bare shoulders and down her arms, Michael wrapped Casey in his embrace. She responded by pulling him closer as she encircled her arms around his neck, tangling her fingers in his sandy brown curls. They swayed back and forth to a beat only they could hear. As the heat rose from their cores, Michael and Casey knew there was no extinguishing the flames that burned between them.

Sweeping Casey up into his arms, he carried her to her bedroom. There, he gently lowered her onto the cotton quilt. Running a fingertip down her leg, Michael removed her sandals, aimlessly tossing them aside then he slipped out of his boots. Nibbling on her ankle, a giggle escaped Casey's rosy lips as Michael languished her with kisses all the way up her legs. Slowly maneuvering himself onto the bed, Michael came to rest next to Casey. Brushing his lips with hers, he reigned kisses across her cheek, then began to nibble on her earlobe. Breathless, he whispered, "I want to be with you Casey."

Abruptly, Casey sat up with a start. "I have to tell you something..."

A sudden wave of worry consumed Michael. "What is it?"

Curling her legs underneath her, she lowered her head, twisting her fingers around the hem of her dress and quietly said, "Michael, I'm embarrassed to tell you this but, it's been a long time since..." she trailed off, dreading his reaction to her confession.

"A long time since you made love with someone?" Michael finished her sentence for her. "Believe me, I understand." Michael ran the back of his hand over her cheek, "You have nothing to be ashamed about."

Casey straightened as she slid off her bed. "No, Michael when I mean it's been a long time..." She trailed off then blurted out, "Michael, you're the only man I've ever been with."

Crinkling his brow, Michael tapped his thumb to each of his fingers.

Crossing her arms over her chest, Casey harshly stated, "No need to count. I know it's been almost..." Twirling on her heel, Casey heading for the living room, neutral territory, she reasoned. Tossing her head around to face Michael, she huffed, "I know you think it's funny... oh, just forget it!"

Michael jumped off the bed, cutting her off at the doorway. Gently resting his hands on her shoulders, he gazed into her deep brown eyes, "Casey, I don't think it's funny at all. I find it admirable and somewhat flattering." Michael gently touched his lips to hers. "We don't have to do anything. Let me just stay with you tonight. All I want is to be near you."

Casey caught the spark that danced in his eyes and she hugged him for being so understanding. "Thank you." She whispered in a sultry tone, then they kissed, again and again, holding each other until moonlight became sunlight.

Chapter 10

The small architecture firm had been awarded the multi-million dollar expansion project for Brookshire General Hospital. As a result, it allowed Eric to expand his construction crews, adding two new superintendents, one being Clayton Wills, who Eric had been bidding against for several years. In his youth, Clayton had been employed by Eric's father, which allowed him to fine tune his construction skills, over the years. Having stayed with Bucky Logan until his retirement, Clayton ended up shifting from job to job in order to pay his children's college tuition. When Clayton lost the Brookshire Hospital bid he realized he was getting too old to be climbing ladders and that's when he sent his resume to Eric Logan. Content to be working for a second generation Logan, Clayton had to constantly remind himself, he wasn't working for Bucky. Even though Eric was a carbon copy of his father, both in looks and personality. To Clayton Wills that was a good thing. Clayton took up the slack on smaller construction sites while Eric focused his attention on the daily operations at Brookshire Hospital.

Because they had landed such a high profile project, Michael hired two Junior Architects assigned to proposals and projects, mostly residential, that were twenty-thousand square feet and under. Even though new names and faces had been added to the Sterling Architects directory and Michael's responsibilities had shifted greatly, his professional philosophy remained intact. "Give as much attention to the thousand dollar clients as one would to the million dollar clients." Michael lectured during orientation, believing the dollar amount of a project should not determine how a client is treated. In his eyes, all their clients were equals.

With all the changes that had taken place in a matter of a month, Michael and Eric were observant of the work load that had been thrusted upon Casey in such a short time. She had easily settled into her position as Interior Design Manager and had met all her deadlines with no problems. Still they offered to hire her an assistant. Immediately, Casey suggested bringing Julie Warren on board as a designer. Eric had given Casey the nickname of "little lucky charm" since business had more than double with the acceptance of her contract. But Casey argued that it wasn't luck at all, it was hard work and dedication. As a result of their booming business, Casey also suggested promoting Maggie Cowan to assistant designer for her and Julie. Taking her advice, Eric and Michael agreed. Now all they needed to do was fill Maggie's position, as receptionist.

It was early Saturday morning when Julie stopped by to pick up Casey and meet Eric downtown at the Home and Hearth Housing Project. Some of the women from Women of Hope were going to be there, including Nancy Kirby, assisting with the exterior and interior painting. Julie decided to lend a hand and it also allowed her and Eric to spend more time together, especially since the hours at the office lately had been long and exhausting. Eric had called earlier, asking Casey and Julie to stop by the hardware store to pick up extra paintbrushes and paint rollers.

As they entered the hardware store, Julie could no longer contain herself, "So how are things with Michael?"

"You should know, Julie, you work in the same office." Michael and Casey had agreed to keep their personal life just that, personal, in the hopes they would not become the brunt of office gossip.

"That's not what I meant and you know it. So, tell me."

"Tell you what? There is really nothing to tell." Casey remained cool, but the guilt of lying to Julie, her best friend, was starting to get to her. She occupied herself, looking through the bins of various sized brushes.

"Okay, I'll let it slide for now. But I just know you two belong together."

Casey smiled and headed to the check-out register.

When they arrived at the site, Eric and Nancy were already there, organizing the volunteers. Eric greeted Julie with a little peck on the cheek. As Casey busied herself opening cans of paint, that she had selected, she noticed that Eric and Julie were engaged in deep conversation.

"She's in total denial, Eric."

"What are you talking about?"

"Casey…and Michael. She says they're not together but I don't buy it for one minute. All those lunch meetings, alone. All the late nights, alone. Something has got to be going on."

"Julie, they work together. It's strictly professional. Besides, their relationship really isn't any of our business, so quit meddling." Eric chuckled.

"I know, I just want them to be as happy as we are." Julie glanced at Casey and then looked up at Eric, batting her long lashes. He bent and kissed her again on the cheek.

"Oh will you two cut it out and get to work." Casey shouted in a teasing manner. At that moment Nancy approached Casey.

"How are you, sweetheart?"

"Good. Is Sean coming out today?" Casey squinted against the summer sun.

"He'll be here later to pick up me and my granddaughter, Nicole. How are you and Michael getting along?"

"Wonderful but we can barely get any time alone outside the office. Since we were awarded the Brookshire General Hospital project, we've been working around the clock. See the blonde girl with the ponytail over there, with Eric?" Casey pointed in Julie's direction. "That's Julie Warren. She was my assistant at Whitley. Not that it was difficult but to lure her away from The Snake..." Casey continued to tell Mrs. Kirby of the changes made at the office. "...but Michael doesn't even have time to interview for a new receptionist." Casey picked up two open paint cans and handed them to a volunteer that was standing near by.

"Well, honey you have to make the time. Cut out a little early on a Friday and go to the Lake or the beach or something."

"I know. We're trying to get away for Fourth of July weekend, but once again, we're not going to be alone." Casey paused then added, "Nancy, no one knows Michael and I are together. I mean we work with these people. Michael owns the company and I am Julie's supervisor, so I would appreciate it..."

"You're secret is safe with me, no need to worry." Nancy reassured Casey, "But why isn't Michael here, with you?"

"He had to meet with a client about a new project. We're not sure if we're going to submit a bid but Michael feels he's not in a position to turn away business right now."

"You know, it just dawned on me, Nicole is looking for a job, at least for the summer. She's planning on taking a few classes this Fall; maybe she could help you out?" Nancy handed a can of paint and a brush to another volunteer. Then the two women picked up the last of the paint and headed into the house. It was a little cooler inside the three-bedroom row home. Heading upstairs to the master bedroom, Nancy and Casey continued discussing Nicole, while they painted the trim work, eggshell white.

Eric and Julie had gone to the house next door and were working on the exterior when Michael showed up later that afternoon.

"Well speak of the devil." Julie nudged Eric.

"Hey Mike, how's it going? How was your meeting with Melinda?"

"Don't ask. Is Casey here?"

"Yeah, she's next door, upstairs with Nancy." Eric pointed.

"Thanks." Michael quietly walked away.

Eric looked at his watch and turned to Julie. "Wow, it's getting late. I think we better wrap things up for today. I know Nancy wants to meet with the volunteers before we leave." Eric gathered up the brushes and put them into a bucket of water while Julie hammered the lids onto the cans. They put everything in the back of Eric's pick up truck then met up with Nancy, Casey, Michael and the others.

After everyone had cleaned up, the group assembled outside. The sun was now descending and perspiration laid across Casey's brow as the night air grew heavy. Michael stood next to Casey with his hand gently resting on the small of her back as he pulled his hanky from his back pocket. Patting the cloth to Casey's face, she whispered into Michael's ear as Julie looked on.

"Not together, my foot!" She thought but before she could say anything to Eric, Nancy was addressing the crowd.

"I just wanted to let you all know that Women of Hope will be hosting a Charity dinner scheduled for late October. It's a fundraiser so that we can furnish these homes and the new owners will have a place to sleep by Christmas. We still have quite a bit to do here but we need to know who can volunteer for the organization committee. So, if you are interested, please call Eric Logan or myself. That's it. And thank you for coming out today. Good work." The crowd clapped, cheered and quickly dispersed.

Casey and Michael approached Nancy. Sean had arrived and was waiting while Nancy introduced Nicole to the couple.

"I understand you might be interested in a job, Nicole." Michael inquired.

"Yes, my grandma told me about it. I'm trying to save some money for college." The young gal was very poised for her age. Her long black hair was pulled back into two french braids and a splotch of white paint contrast against the dark color of her bangs. She had a lanky stature of five foot seven and braces on her teeth.

"What computer applications are you familiar with?"

Nicole's list was long and then she added, "I'm very organized and I like dealing with the public."

She kept rambling until Michael politely cut her off, "Okay, okay. Do you think you can be at the office Monday at nine? And can you e-mail me a resume before then?" Michael retrieved a business card from his wallet and handed it to the young girl.

"Sure." The teenager could hardly contain her excitement.

"Casey or I will show you around and then we'll talk salary." Michael stopped then continued, "If you work hard, we'll see what we can do to help you out with tuition."

"Thank you!" Nicole repeated three times and abruptly shook Michael's hand. She turned to Nancy and gave her a big hug, "Thanks for bringing me out here, grandma." Her excitement was cute and contagious.

"Way to go, my little one." Sean gave Nicole a hug and took his granddaughter's hand as well as his wife's.

"What was that all about?" Eric asked.

"We got ourselves of a receptionist." Michael smiled at Casey then kissed her on the cheek.

"The little lucky charm comes through again." Eric teased as Julie stood speechless.

"Stop calling me that. I'm just looking out for our best interests and besides, we've been too busy to even think of hiring a receptionist let alone actually do it. With Michael in meetings half the time, you're on site, Julie and Maggie always have overtime and…" Casey sighed, "It just so happens that Nicole was looking for a job."

"Okay, okay, enough about business. You two want to go grab dinner downtown or do you have plans?" Eric winked at Julie.

"Yeah, let's go to the Waterfront. It'll be so nice downtown. I just don't want to go home yet." Julie stated enthusiastically.

Not wanting to fuel Julie's suspicions they agreed, even though it was the first opportunity Casey and Michael had to be alone since the night of the dance at Hidden Springs Lake.

They arrived just in time to be seated at an outside table at Harbor House. They ordered a medley of seafood appetizers and a couple dozen crabs. The sun was now a red thin line on the horizon as a soft breeze came off the water, cooling their exhausted bodies. Relaxing comfortably in the warmth of the summer evening, Julie exclaimed, "So how exciting is that? A Charity dinner? We're going aren't we, honey?" She addressed Eric.

"Of course. This is my project, my baby. Besides Nancy will probably volunteer me to give some speech or something." Eric chuckled.

"Casey, we have to go shopping."

"Definitely. And by then, the new fall fashions will be out." There was a twinkle in Casey's brown eyes. Shopping was one of her favorite past times and she had not had the luxury of a leisurely shopping trip since her visit with Hannah in South Carolina.

"I'm excited." Julie's blue eyes widened. "I've never been to a black tie dinner before."

"You haven't? Wait until the Christmas party. We go all out, making it as formal as possible." Michael grinned.

Julie eyed Eric elbowing him in the rib, "I have to go to the ladies room and freshen up, I'll be right back."

"Me too." Eric jumped up from his seat and disappeared inside with Julie.

Michael eased closer to Casey. "I missed you today." He took her by the hand and brushed his lips across hers.

Casey felt like she had butterflies in her stomach when Michael kissed her. And her heart raced at his touch. Michael gently swept the back of his hand down Casey's cheek and their gazes locked. Responding to each other with a kiss, their lips parted, welcoming each other. Michael drew Casey into his embrace and trailed kisses across her cheek to the side of her neck. As the embers inside them became inflamed, Casey gently pushed against Michael's hard chest. "Michael, they…" she could barely catch her breath, "…they'll see us."

"Who cares. I want the whole world to know I love you."

"Michael that's sweet but…" He continued to nibble on her neck.

"But what?" Michael finally stopped and looked deeply into Casey's eyes. "We can't keep this a secret forever."

"Believe me, I know. Julie is already asking questions."

"You too? Eric has been drilling me on a daily basis. I guess all those late nights look suspicious."

Again they looked at each other. Michael raised his brow, as Casey tried to hold back a smile. "They know." Spoken simultaneously, they laughed and kissed again.

Just as they were about to make their way across the terrace, Eric pulled Julie back inside. Julie was not surprised as she eyed Casey and Michael. "I knew it! They are together." Julie placed her hands on her hips. "They can try to hide it all they want, but I know the truth." She stated victoriously.

"Aw, let's give them a minute. They haven't had anytime alone."

"No way. I am confronting them once and for all." Julie bounced forward too quickly for Eric to stop her.

"Hey, love birds." Julie snuck up behind Michael and Casey. "Nothing to tell, huh Casey?"

"Julie!" Casey stated nervously. She looked at Michael and shrugged then addressed her best friend. "Please don't tell anyone at the office."

"I think it's a little too late for that." Eric chimed in as he stretched his long legs over the bench seat. "I think the whole office knew the day you started, Casey."

Surprised by Eric's comment, Michael replied, "We've been so discreet trying to keep our relationship out of the office. How could anyone know?"

A silent relief washed over Casey as she placed her hand in Michael's.

"You're kidding, right?" Eric concluded as he popped a piece of shrimp into his mouth. "Pretty much everyone figured it out by the end of Casey's first week. Everyone was cheering for you two but I have to admit Casey, I was reluctant bringing you into the company. Mike and I have worked hard to build this business to what it is today. I even told Mike I would be keeping an eye on you two. What I didn't expect was to see sparks fly when you two look at each other. It so obvious how you feel about one another." Eric cleaned another piece of steamed spiced shrimp and took a bite before continuing. "And obviously it's good for business, so do us all a favor; stay together forever. Because Mike has never been happier." Eric chuckled.

Chapter 11

Many nights Eric had reprimanded Casey and Michael for staying too late. Tonight was no exception as Casey exited her office. Heading downstairs to the reception desk, an eerie feeling trickled down her spine causing her to shiver. It had been so quiet all afternoon, it was nearly deafening. But the abandoned offices, after all, was her doing. Casey had managed to coax Michael and Eric into closing the office for a few days. Yet it was nearly six-thirty and she was still burning the midnight oil. As she tugged the chain on the little brass lamp on Nicole's desk, she quickly sealed and addressed the package then left a note for Nicole to mail it Monday morning. Since, they did not foresee any problems arising in the immediate future with business, Michael, Casey, Eric and Julie, along with the rest of the staff, were excited about the long Fourth of July weekend and a much needed break.

With her things-to-do list at the office now complete, Casey's thoughts became more personal. She imagined at this time tomorrow night, her and Michael would be snuggling together in the hammock, sipping on Margaritas. While her sister and friends indulged themselves in a variety of activities, they would all be anticipating the fireworks spectacle Hidden Springs sponsored every year. It was by far the best display of patriotism in the area. And this year held a very poignant meaning. Happiness tickled her funny bone and Casey could hardly wait to get out of dodge.

As she rose, so did a clap of thunder rumbling in the distance as the front door swung open, cutting into her fantasy. Lighting flared in the evening sky, silhouetting the person that now stood in the lobby.

"We're getting ready to close for the weekend…" Casey managed but a smoky voice stopped her dead in her tracks.

"Where's Michael Sterling?" The thick smoke from the attractive brunette's cigarette wafted towards Casey, causing her to cough.

"Excuse me?" Casey questioned as she reached for her bottle of water on the reception desk.

"Michael Sterling. You know, the owner, your boss. Where is he? I need the plans for Hidden Springs Lake…tonight. The dozers are ready to move in first thing Monday morning." As the woman stepped forward, menacing shadows were cast across her sharp features, by the tiny desk lamp. "Oh…you must be Michael's new secretary. I wasn't expecting someone so old."

Startled by the woman's rude remark, Casey felt her throat closing around her words.

"Look sweetie, I don't have all night, go get him. Now!" She demanded as she exhaled. A ring of smoke circled above the woman's head like a halo, but Casey knew in an instant she was no angel.

Michael's sudden appearance interrupted Casey's response. "What are you still doing here? I thought you would have left for the airport by now." Earlier in the week, Hannah had called, informing Casey that Adam had surprised her with an airline ticket to visit for the long holiday weekend.

"I'm trying." Casey stammered. Her eyes widening at the actions from the woman who stood before her.

Without a second thought, the woman stubbed her cigarette in a nearby potted plant. Decked in a red halter dress, along with matching accessories and heels that made her four inches taller than she was, the sultry woman swung her full hips as she sauntered towards Michael. Planting a kiss on his cheek, she left a red outline of lipstick that appeared to be the mark of the devil's mistress. "Darling, how are you? Still all work and no play...you know that makes Mikey a dull boy." Draping her arms around his neck then narrowing her eyes towards Casey, she began to release Michael from his tie, that now seemed to restrict his breathing.

Astounded by the woman's actions, Casey stumbled against the desk chair then fell into it. What did she think she was going to do with him? Seduce him right here in the lobby? Casey tried to shake the idea from her head.

"Did you hear what I said?"

"Huh? Oh, I was getting a package..." A twinge of jealousy kicked Casey in the stomach as she marched past Michael and the brunette without another word. Unable to hold back a reaction, she abruptly turned, casting a cold stare towards the woman that still had her arms wrapped around Michael.

"Casey," Michael called out, "You haven't met Melinda Parker."

As if she were walking a balance beam, Casey cautiously moved towards the couple.

"This is Casey Andrews." Michael paused then added, "Eric and I hired Casey about a month ago as the Interior Design Manager."

Melinda extended her hand towards Casey but she ignored the gesture. "I am terribly sorry about the confusion Cas-sie."

"It's Casey." She clenched her back teeth. "You're head of the Historical Preservation Committee, aren't you?"

"Yes, darling. Among other things." Melinda drew out her words, then addressed Michael, "So I'm still a hot topic of conversation in your world? Either that, or Cassie has done her homework." Melinda was so full of herself she reeked as she tightened her grip on Michael.

"It's Casey! Maybe you should do your homework." She snapped knowing her short temper had no place in her professional life.

Michael snapped a look of curiosity in her direction yet his words remained placid. "You better get going. You don't want to be late picking up your sister, do you?"

Taken aback, Casey fiddled with her necklace, wondering why he was being so dismissive with her? "Of course not." Wanting to pull Michael from the clutches of the devil woman, Casey went to reach for Michael's hand, but as she did so, his came to rest on Melinda's. Stepping back, she held her head high. "I'll see you tomorrow." Casey's poor imitation of Melinda Parker did little to alleviate the pain gripping her heart and the hurt that was consuming her. Dumbfounded that Michael was brushing her off so easily, Casey felt the urge to yell, "What the hell is going on?" but her professional morality prevented it.

How could she have been so foolish? Daring to let her guard down and Michael in, they had not even been together two months and in waltzes Mata Hari. And in an instant, Michael was putty in the hands of another woman. Besides, what business did Michael have with Melinda Parker and plans for Hidden Springs? Michael maintain such a high level of work ethics, Casey found it impossible to believe he was mixed up with the likes of that woman. Something fishy was going on and if Casey had to play Nancy Drew, she was going to get the answers to all the questions that were causing her headache.

Michael pulled himself from Melinda's clutches then peered down the hall before speaking. When he did, his tone cut through to the core of Melinda's soul, or so he thought. "Our meeting's not until the end of next week. You have no business being here."

"I'm not allowed to stop by my own company?"

Michael cringed at her words, praying with all his might that Casey was not within ear shot. "No Melinda, that was part of the deal but you always see fit to break it. And you also seem to forget that it's *my name* on the door, not yours. I'm the one making the deals here, not you!" Michael took a step back realizing his words had not even made her flinch. Once he calmed down, he simply asked, "Why are you here?"

"Because I'm bored and when I saw your office light on...I thought we could go have a drink or something." She whined, winked then kissed his cheek again. This time leaving a mere smudge as she allowed her touch to linger.

"No! Go home to Lyle and have a drink with him." He brutally jerked Melinda's hands from his chest. Swiftly, Michael retrieved his hanky from his pocket, swiping it hard across his branded cheek.

"Oh, Michael, you know that old poop is about as exciting as getting teeth pulled."

"That's not my problem!" Michael shoved his fists into his trousers along with his stained handkerchief.

"Why Michael, I am surprised at you. You've never acted like this before." Melinda stepped back, folding her arms across her voluptuous breasts revealing the curves in her deep cleavage.

Turning away, Michael glanced down the corridor, wishing Casey would reappear and bring this unscheduled meeting to an end. He had had enough of Melinda and Lyle Parker to last him a lifetime. And with the Brookshire General Hospital project taking up most of his waking hours, he needed a break from what had now become the bane of his existence.

"Ooh… I get it now. It's the bottled-redheaded cheerleader down the hall. Huh? Well, isn't it?" Melinda did not wait for an answer. Moving closer to Michael she grabbed at his shirt causing a button to pop off. "You just remember who has been funding this little enterprise of yours. Without the Parkers you'd be bankrupt and in the gutter." She drew in a breath and through clenched teeth continued, "I own you and you will do as your told. You will back up Parker Industries one-hundred percent with the Hidden Springs Project. You have no say in the matter. Do I make myself clear?" Releasing her grip, Melinda's newly manicured finger nails, that matched her red dress, scratched across his chest as she smoothed her clammy palms over the material.

Michael stood motionless at the realization of Melinda's toxic dissertation.

Moving away from Michael, Melinda grabbed her Foreinzali bag from the receptionist desk then and headed towards the door, shouting over her shoulder, "If you get bored, call me." A clap of thunder cut off her laughter then the door swung closed, leaving him shrouded in silence.

Even though Melinda Parker had finally left, the scent of her spicy perfume and cigarette smoke, hung in the air like a thick fog on a chilly morning, and Michael was certain he was going to be sick. Pure evil was the only way to describe Melinda and he was beginning to regret his involvement with the Parkers. Since Casey had come on board, Melinda had made her presences known, even though up until this point, the two had never crossed paths. Her blatant actions and condescending attitude made Michael wonder what she was conjuring up next. Obviously, Melinda did not know the meaning of silent partner. As he straightened his shirt and tie, Michael's blood was boiling. Something had transpired between Melinda and Casey, and he was furious. As he ascended the stairs, Michael was determined to resolve any misunderstanding before him and Casey embarked on their long holiday weekend to Hidden Springs Lake.

"Ladies and gentlemen, this is your captain, please fasten your seat belt for our final descent."

Hannah could hardly contain her excitement as she tightened the belt around her growing mid-section. It had only been six weeks since Casey's visit to South Carolina but she needed an adult weekend. Adam had suggested Hannah visit Casey and she took him up on his generous offer. A smile came to her lips as she thought of her husband. He was a good man. Always attentive to her needs and taking pride in his role as a father, Hannah couldn't have asked for a better husband, then Adam Nayler. Jason and Emily were going to get the royal treatment this weekend with their mother gone. Adam was taking them to the fireworks at the State Fair grounds Thursday night, the beach on Friday and Saturday Adam had made plans to cook out with their neighbors. As the wheels of the aircraft touch down on the runway, silence fell over the cabin as it taxied to the gate. Within minutes Hannah was out of her seat and heading through the airport terminal. With the advanced security measures, Hannah knew Casey could not pick her up at the gate. When she reached the main terminal, Hannah scanned the crowd but Casey was nowhere to be found. Nervously, Hannah continued on to baggage claim.

Casey stood with her tightly clenched fists perched on her hips. Examining the pile of paper work on her drafting table and desk, she wondered what was taking Michael so long. He still had not come upstairs to his office, which only meant one thing, he was still entertaining the trollop downstairs. For all Casey knew, he probably left her there, to lock up, alone and late at night. "Damn her!" Casey cursed as she threw her sketchpad across the room. It ricocheted off the door-jamb, barely missing Michael's head as drawings scattered to the floor.

"Casey!" Michael shouted.

"What!"

"That's not really a good way to deal with this." Leaning against the door frame, he crossed his arms over his shirt that was still rumpled, trying to conceal the now missing button.

Embarrassed, Casey refused to give Michael the satisfaction of her jealousy. "What are you talking about?"

"Don't do this."

"Do what Michael?" She smirked but did not wait for a reply. "Where's Melinda? Oh wait, let me guess. She's probably waiting for me to leave, so you two can be alone. Well, don't worry. I leaving!" Casey's voice raised an octave.

The hair stood up on the back of Michael's neck at the mention of Melinda. "I told her to go home to her husband." He drew in a breath, "What did Melinda say to you?"

"Her husband? That's a laugh. Besides, it's not what she said Michael, it's what *you* did."

"What did I do?"

"Nothing, that's the problem. You let that…that woman, drape herself all over you as if she owns you. And then you had the nerve, the actual nerve to introduce me as your Design Manager." Casey's words cut through Michael like a knife.

He tried desperately to contain his laughter. "That's what this is all about? Casey, honey, that's what you are and Melinda Parker is a client. What was I going to say, that's you're my girlfriend?" Michael reasoned.

"Oh, of course not. It's always what's best for the company. You'll do anything for this place. But never anything when it comes to us."

"Casey, what do you want from me?" Michael's tone had actually softened.

"I just wish you would put as much effort into our relationship as you do with this business." Casey was trying to be sarcastic but when she realized what she had said, she knew she was acting like a spoiled rotten child. Her words were unjust and there was no reason to compare work with their relationship especially after Michael's next comment.

"Business is business and when we're together here, at the office, that's what we have, a professional relationship. You know that. You insisted upon that. I know it's hard right now. We haven't had much time together outside these four walls, but you also know that outside these four walls it's another story." He surmised all the while maintaining a cool demeanor.

Casey stared at Michael knowing full well he was right. And just as she was about to move into the warmth of his embrace and apologize, Michael blew those thoughts right out of her mind. "Casey, your jealously is unwarranted." His words were full of contempt yet his heart was telling him to take Casey in his arms and tell her everything was going to be all right but the ringing of Casey's cell phone held them both captive in their anger.

She wanted to call a truce but the timing and the reason became apparent when Casey picked up the phone on the third ring, "Hello." Her tone was fierce.

"Casey, it's your sister. Did you forget about me or is Michael making you work late, again?" Hannah teased.

"No Hannah. I'm sorry. I'm leaving right now. I'll be there in about twenty minutes."

"That's fine. I'll wait outside baggage claim."

Casey placed the phone back in her purse. After grabbing her keys from her desk, she purposefully stepped over the mess of sketches on the floor and stomped past Michael without another word.

"Casey, wait." Michael grabbed her by the arm and jerked Casey back. His strength, surprising them both.

"Michael. Let me go!" Startled, she reacted with a burning glare as she struggled to be free from his embrace but instead Michael tightened his grip. Before he knew what he was doing, he pressed his lips against Casey's. He had never kissed her like this before.

Confusion made her head spin and her stomach churn. In a sudden movement, she pushed against his chest, forcing Michael to release her. Puzzled by the hurt look on his face, Casey snapped. "Michael, are you out of your mind! A kiss like that is not going to make everything all better. You can't sugar coat this! And for the record, I'm not jealous. I'm angry." As Michael stood motionless, Casey abruptly turned away and ran down the stairs.

The sharp pelting rain stung Casey's skin as she opened the door. Determined to get to the airport, she moved quickly against the harsh elements. As lighting cut through the night sky, Casey could see the steam rise off the hot asphalt. Thunder rolled like a raging locomotive as she stepped off the curb. Inadvertently her feet became immersed in a pool of rushing water and her silk short set clung to her curvaceous body as she blindly made her way across Madison. Her hair, that she had pinned neatly atop her head, now flailed in the ferocious wind. *"Just a little further."* Casey contemplate as the dimly lit parking garage became a blur then went dark. Suddenly, she felt a jolt and extraordinary pressure of something or someone shoving her down. Then a sharp pain stabbed at her ankle. The edge of the curb cut into her ribs as she reached to break her fall. Her hand slipped against the sidewalk as her head collided with the concrete. The last thing Casey saw was a blurred image of her hand, a shoe and the pavement just before everything went black.

The clash of thunder that cracked the sky, had the hair on Michael's neck standing straight on end. Rubbing the back of his neck, he toyed with the idea of going after Casey or waiting for her to cool off. He choose the latter, assuming he would call her in an hours or so, to patch things up. Collecting Casey's sketches, he piled them neatly together and placed them on her drafting table. He lingered at her drafting table for a moment, then decided he'd go to his office, finish signing off on some paperwork and head home. As he began to depart for his office, Michael banged his knee on an open filing cabinet draw. "I deserved that." He mumbled then proceeded to close it but something caught his eye. There, wedged in the front was the picture frame he had sent to Casey, the same day they had "bumped" into each other. To his surprise it did not house the black and white photo of her mother but a picture of them.

He examined the photo for several minutes, pondering where it had been taken. Then it dawned on him. It was the picture Valerie Sorrenson had taken at the Hidden Springs Lake dance. He chuckled thinking, Casey must have moved heaven and earth to get this out of Valerie's possession because, come to thing of it, it never did come to life in there alumni journal. He stared at it just long enough to realize, they had that look it there eyes, like they did back in high school and he finally understood Casey's fears.

Hannah stood underneath the over hang at baggage claim that shielded her from the thunderstorm that now raged. She glanced at her watch, concerned about how much time had passed. Hannah went inside to call Casey again. With shaking hands, Hannah dialed the number, expecting her sister to answer. The voice on the other end was automated. "All circuits are busy. Please try your call again later."

"Damn!" Hannah shouted as she slammed down the receiver on the pay phone.

"You couldn't get through either?" Dressed in an oversized tee shirt, kakhi shorts and sandals with white socks, the young man gave Hannah a sheepish grin as he waited for a response.

"No, my sister is late picking me up."

"Give it a few more minutes." He reassured Hannah, then continued. "The storm has just about shut down the city. I over heard there's a partial blackout."

Hannah glanced at her watch again. Decisively, she called Sterling Architects. When there was no answer Hannah dialed Michael's cell phone, relieved that Casey had given it to her.

Red and white flashing lights caught Melinda's attention as she turned her Corvair into the long driveway that led to the Parker mansion. Her heart began to pound at the sight of two police cars and an ambulance parked in front of her house. As she stepped out of her vehicle, the wind stung against her bare back and whipped around her already soaked curls. Struggling against the wind and the rain that now fell, Melinda dashed up the stone steps to the front door.

The slamming of the door echoed through the large circular entrance and Melinda was surprised that no one greeted her. Her heels clicked against the black and white marble tiles as Melinda shouted, "Jasper? Chelsea?" She started to move up the large circular staircase when there was no answer. Her knees started to wobble as she yelled, "Damn it! Someone answer me!"

"Ma'am come quick." Chelsea met her at the top of the stairs then led her down the long hallway to Lyle's study.

Upon entering, the room was bustling with activity. Several paramedics and a police office stood over Lyle who was laid out on a stretcher. Melinda's purse fell to the floor as she gasped. An oxygen tube was wrapped around his face and two intravenous lines had been inserted into his arm. Melinda rushed to her husband's side as the paramedics raised the stretcher. Tears fell as Melinda gripped Lyle's limp hand. She wanted to say something but the words would not come.

"Ma'am we have to get him to the hospital." One of the paramedics stated, then offered, "You can ride along."

Melinda could only nod as they exited the study and headed downstairs to the waiting ambulance.

Michael stared at the contracts on his desk that needed reviewing. Rubbing his eyes, he concluded it was too late before a holiday weekend to mull over paper work. Besides, a signature tonight or Monday morning would not make a difference. He decided to stuff them in his briefcase and call it a night. By time he got home, Casey and Hannah should be back from the airport and it would still be earlier enough to give Casey a call.

After powering down all the lights, Michael punched the code on the alarm pad and stepped out into the chaotic night. With nothing to protect him from the thunderstorm that went unpredicted earlier in the day, Michael pressed into the darkness towards the garage. The rain swirled around him and the wind whipped at his back, making it difficult to move. As Michael cautiously crossed Madison, he was startled by the motionless figure that laid on the ground. His heart pound with the same fury as the storm when he realized the lifeless body was Casey.

A barbaric tone erupted from his throat and his muscles clenched at the sight of her lying frighteningly still and bleeding. Kneeling by her side, Michael shook Casey, yelling her name numerous times over the roar of the rolling thunder. Again, lightening illuminated the night as Michael gathered her up into his arms, holding her close, trying to protect her from the rain. It was a struggle but Michael managed to get Casey to his car. Before turning over the engine, he retrieved a tattered blanket from the trunk of his car and wrapped it around her shivering body.

Hail battered the hood of his car as Michael whispered, "Everything's going to be all right." Turning right onto Madison, Michael headed downtown towards Brookshire General Hospital. Just then, lightening ripped across the sky. As Michael shifted into second gear the city skyline before him went to black.

The blackout had virtually immobilized downtown as Michael cautiously navigated the city streets that were being patrolled by the local police force. The storm had finally blown through the city, leaving its wake of destruction as thunder and lightening now threatened the distant horizon. Michael parked in the emergency lot, noticing it was nearly full to capacity when he lifted Casey into his arms. As he reached the Emergency Room entrance, paramedics rushed past with in an older man that had suffered a stroke.

Dried blood streaked Casey's face and her ankle had barely stopped bleeding when a rather Romanesque woman came out from behind the desk,

"Oh my, honey. What happen to her?"

Fighting to open her eyes, Casey could not understand the commotion around her and it magnified the pounding in her head. Then a familiar kind-hearted whisper eased her nerves momentarily, "Hey…I brought you to the hospital. You're going to be okay." No sooner had Michael spoken such words of comfort and Casey passed out again.

"She fell. I think."

"Let's get her into this exam room right over here." The nurse moved quickly through the corridor that was lit by generator lights. Drawing back the exam curtain, she instructed Michael, "Place her on the gurney. I'll take her vitals and get a doctor in here as soon as possible." The nurse informed him as she place a blood pressure cuff on Casey's arm and placed the stethoscope in her ears.

He tried to remain emotionally distant, knowing that one tear would not help Casey's condition, yet deep down inside, Michael was riddled with anxiety. They had just found each again. Michael could not fathom losing her, again, this time, forever and having to live a life without her. If that happened, he knew he would die too. Maybe Casey was right. Had he invested more in the company then in their relationship? Maybe he was becoming his father after all, by keeping his emotions down while the fear of hurting Casey ruled his very existence. All he wanted to do was love her for the rest of his life but now it could be too late.

"Viola, what do we have here?"

"Female, Caucasian…" The nurse turned to Michael, "Age?"

"Thirty-two."

"Thirty-two years old. The gentleman here says she fell, Dr. Everett. Her blood pressure is one hundred-fifty over one hundred and her pulse is eighty-eight She's unconscious and…"

"Dr. Everett?" Michael's voice was shaky, "Is she… is she going to die?"

Dr. Everett turned in surprise. "Mike?" He stood a few inches taller then Michael and his physique was comparative. "Friend of yours?"

"Casey Andrews."

"Do you know what happened?"

"I'm guessing she slipped and fell. Her ankle is cut and her head… and she has a bunch of scrapes and… is she going to die, Dr. Everett?" Michael nearly choked as tears burned his eyes.

"Viola, could you get a towel and blanket for Mr. Sterling and show him the coffee machine."

"Yes, doctor."

"But…"

"Don't worry Mike, I'll let you know in a few minutes the status of her condition."

As Michael was escorted out by Nurse Viola, two other nurses slipped behind the curtain to assist Dr. Everett. As they did their work up, Dr. Everett was certain Casey was not going to die as she slowly fluttered her eyes open.

Looking up and into the eyes of the man that stood over her, she was shaken for a brief moment. But his dark eyes and bright smile that contrasted against his dark skin, radiated understanding, easing Casey's senses. "Where am I?"

"Hi, Casey. I'm Dr. Everett. You're at Brookshire Hospital. Mike Sterling brought you here. Can you tell me what happened?"

Her brown eyes grew big because she couldn't remember. "I guess I…misjudged…and lost my balance and fell. I feel really stupid." Casey managed through chattering teeth.

"Is there a chance you may be pregnant."

Alarmed, Casey responded in a high pitched tone. "Absolutely not!"

"All right. You need to stay calm. You're blood pressure is spiked and you need some stitches. I'm going to prop up the gurney a little here." Once he adjusted the bed, he checked her eyes, ears, neck and shoulders. When he examined her arms and wrists, Casey mentioned that she was soar and achy but when he asked her to make a fist, she winced at the pain.

"I assume you tried to break your fall."

"I guess." Casey whispered.

"Do you remember anything specific?"

Casey jerked her hand back when she said, "I told you, I fell. End of story."

When he lifted her blouse revealing a bruise on her right side, his brow crinkled. "Are you having trouble breathing?"

Casey shook her head no.

"Well, that's a good. I want to get a head, chest, and hand x-ray. We can have that done as soon as we are finished here." He moved down to her leg and held her ankle in his lap. He inspected the wound and then began to clean it. "Casey, do you know what you cut your ankle on?"

"It was something sharp. It was raining so hard."

"I'm going to give you a tetanus booster."

"Hannah!" Casey suddenly shouted. She tried to jump from the gurney but Dr. Everett encouraged her to remain still. "No! You don't understand. My sister is waiting for me at the airport. I have to go get her!"

The shrieking from behind the curtain may have been cause for alarm to others but to Michael, he was ecstatic. Pulling back the curtain, Michael was immediately drawn to the fear on Casey's face and he rushed to be by her side. "Casey, Hannah just called me. I told her what happened and Eric and Julie are on their way to pick her up." His words brought her a moment of comfort until she remembered their earlier argument.

Eric dialed the number that he now had committed to memory. Tapping his fingers on the table next to him he waited impatiently as he counted the rings. "Two, three…"

"Hello?" A sweet voice questioned on the other end of the line.

"Eric, this is Julie."

"Oh really?" Julie giggled at the nervousness of Eric's words.

"I mean…" Eric cleared his throat. "Julie, this is Eric." He stated succinctly.

"What's up?" Julie's curiosity was already piqued by his tone.

"It's Casey. She had an accident and Mike took her to the hospital. But that's not why I'm calling. He asked me…ah…us, if we could go pick up Hannah at the airport?"

"Oh my God! A car accident? Is Casey all right? What hospital is she at? Can we go see her?" Fear clung to Julie's questions.

"Julie, Mike is with her. She fell outside the parking garage. She's pretty banged up but she's going to be all right."

Julie let out a sigh of relief. "I should call her. I should go see her; see if she needs anything."

"Mike's taking care of that. We need to go get Hannah. I'll pick you up in a few minutes."

"Oh yeah, Hannah. Right. Okay. See you in a few minutes." Julie hung up the phone and began praying for her friend's recovery. She quickly called the hospital to see if she could get an update on Casey's condition but the nurse would not release any information to a non-relative. Julie decided she would call Michael later.

"What are you still doing here? You can go home." Obviously, Casey was still angry and he could only place the blame on one person, as she watched

Dr. Everett injected her leg with local anesthesia then he informed Casey and Michael he would return in a few minutes.

Suddenly, Casey's breathing became shallow as she white knuckled the edge of the gurney. "I don't feel so well." Then she slowly eased herself down onto the pillow. "Michael." She whispered as she reached for him. Tightening a single handed grip around Michael's fingers, his hand met with her cheek, "Casey, I'm sorry. It's going to be all right. You just look at me. Are you with me?"

Releasing her grip she reached her arm around his neck and pulled him close. As the tears came, she just sobbed, begging Michael, "Hold me."

Dr. Everett returned and sutured her ankle with ten stitches then he tried a new technique on her forehead. After cleaning the wound, he applied a sterile liquid adhesive in place of skin strips. Even though it required three applications, it was less evasive to her skin and would minimalism scarring. "Casey will have to return to have the stitches removed on her leg, but her forehead laceration will heal on its own in five to ten days." Dr Everett explained as he finished the procedure.

Michael stayed close and the warmth of his presence gave Casey strength.

"Okay, Casey I'm finished." He applied a protective bandage to the stitches. "I'm going to send you up to x-ray now. Unless you have a concussion, which I don't suspect you do, I will release you. But you are going to need plenty of rest." The nurse named Viola appeared and assisted Casey into a wheelchair. With Michael by her side, the three of them went to x-ray.

Julie was hanging half way out the window of Eric's pick up truck as she spotted Casey's sister. "Hannah? Hannah!" Julie yelled. Eric stopped abruptly as she jumped out of the vehicle before he could come to a complete stop. Julie and Hannah had only met a few times but Casey talked about both of them incessantly and in this moment they felt like they had been friends for a lifetime. Julie reached Hannah and embraced her.

"How's Casey?" Hannah creased her brow, anticipating the worst but hoping for the best.

"I don't know. The hospital wouldn't tell me anything." Julie rolled her eyes. "But I was waiting to call Michael until Eric and I got here." Julie then reached for Hannah's bag and led her to Eric's truck. He placed Hannah's bag behind his seat then Julie slipped into the back of the extended cab.

Offering a hand to Hannah, Eric boosted her into the passenger seat. Once settled into Eric's truck, Julie introduced the two. Unable to contain her anxiety, Hannah pleaded with Eric to call Michael, immediately.

Hours had passed when Casey and Michael returned to meet with Dr. Everett in the emergency room. Holding Casey's x-rays up to a light board. "Technically, nothing is broken. You're a lucky lady." But the grim expression on his face opposed his words. "However, you have a hairline fracture to one of your ribs. Initially, it's going to hurt if you cough or laugh too hard. It'll take some time to heal. About three months, overall. Same with your hand. Do you work on a computer?"

"Yes." Casey whispered. "It's my job."

Dr. Everett nodded, responding with, "I understand. I'll give you a topographical pain reliever but no computer work for a week. As for the head injury, there is no sign of a concussion but I'd still like to admit Casey for overnight observation." Dr. Everett spoke directly to Michael as if she wasn't even in the room.

Even though her head was spinning and she felt nauseated, Casey still managed a reply. "I have to go home." She tried to hide the pain that retched her battered body as well as the confusion of how she ended up in the emergency room. "Please, I want to go home!"

"Do you have someone to take care of you if I send you home?"

"She can stay at my house." Michael quickly stepped up to the plate, assuming responsibility.

Dr. Everett agreed she could be released, informing them both that if Casey needed any additional medical attention, regardless the reason, to call for an ambulance and page him, right away.

"Thank you, Dr. Everett." Casey whispered.

"Mike, take care of her. Bed rest for at least forty-eight hours." Dr. Everett ordered then the two men shook hands.

As they exited the emergency room, the realization hit Casey hard, "Hannah!" She shouted. "Oh, she must be worried sick. I have to call her." Casey tried to get up out of the wheelchair but before she could, Michael had already dialed Eric's number and handed the phone to her.

Chapter 12

Casey and Michael had argued all the way back to his house. She wanted to go home and he wanted to take care of her. Her stubbornness was as unrelenting as his, forcing Michael to put his foot down. For the next forty-eight hours, if not the entire four day weekend, Casey was his responsibility.

As Michael cradled Casey in his arms, ascending the stairs to his master bedroom, she tried to put up a fight but as battered and bruised as her body was, her stamina was feeble. Easing her onto the bed, Michael propped pillows under and around her aching body. Still in her damp clothes, she shivered against the chill of the air conditioning. "Leave... me... I'll... take... care..." She expelled incoherently through chattering teeth wondering where she was and why couldn't she wake up from her nightmare.

Sweeping aside the damp curls that were matted to her face, Michael offered what comfort he could. "Casey, shh... you're at my house." A hush touched her ear as darkness fell around her. Obviously, she was worn out and sleep was the best remedy. Retrieving a blanket from his walk-in closet, Michael spread it out over her shaking body. Quickly, he changed out of his rain-soaked clothes then retrieved an oversized tee shirt from his dresser. He eased himself onto the edge of the bed, contemplating his next move. Time seemed to stand still as he found himself staring at her, memorizing every feature and regretting his every word as he recalled what, or rather who had caused their earlier argument. Smoothing a gentle hand down her cheek, Michael shuttered. Feeling Casey's skin beneath his fingertips caused his pulse to quicken, his heart to race and his mind to skip back in time, to more innocent days.

The brilliant colors of autumn decorated the ground as Michael held Casey's hand in his. It was the perfect fit. In the two months that they had been dating, ever since Casey had bumped into him, he couldn't help but notice that her tomboyish figure was beginning to mature. At times he found himself confused and curious but she would have to take the lead. He really liked her but his parents taught him well, never to pressure a girl into anything she didn't want to do.

They were walking to Casey's house, as they did everyday after school, but something was different about her. She was jittery and

Michael couldn't help but wonder why. Casey unlocked the front door, leading Michael to the kitchen. "You want something to drink?"

He answered her question with a question, "Where's your mom and Hannah?"

"Mom has play practice with her students and I think Hannah is with her friends decorating the gym for the dance tomorrow night."

"So we're alone?" Michael choked as he tugged at his shirt collar that suddenly felt too tight.

"Yeah." Casey shrugged and smiled as she handed him a glass of soda. "Come on." She mumbled as she led Michael to her bedroom.

"Casey, what are you doing?"

"Nothing. We have to study, don't we? We do have mid-terms on Monday and you're not doing so great in Biology." She reasoned.

Michael was too nervous for words.

"We'll just study in here." Casey popped on the radio and planted herself on the bed with her notes and text book. "Come on Michael." She patted the empty space next to her.

Clearing his throat, Michael managed, "Casey, I don't think this is such a good idea."

Jumping from the edge of the bed, Casey stood before him, eye to eye and simply asked, "Why?"

There was no doubt about it, she had that goofy-girlish look in her eyes begging him to make the first move. He wanted to kiss her but he couldn't.

And as he stood there motionless, Casey slipped his books from his hands, tossing them onto the bed, she reached for his hand then leaned forward. Her lips barely met his. Gently, softly, sweetly, they kissed for the first time.

The feathery touch stirred movement from Casey as she mumbled, "Hidden Springs plans."

Shaking his head, Michael was back in the present. As he moved off the bed, he didn't think twice about Casey's ramblings. They had been talking about Hidden Springs Lake for a month now and here it was, their long awaited weekend together. More than likely it was going to have to wait. He couldn't really concern himself with it right now. Casey needed his undivided attention and the idea of a long, relaxing weekend moved to the bottom of his priority list.

He pause, knowing he had no choice, Casey's damp clothes had to come off. Hesitantly he reached for the buttons on her blouse. Casey's nakedness was revealed as the material fell to either side causing Michael to draw in a deep breath. Slowly, easing Casey up, he propped a few more pillows behind her head. After removing her wet garments, Michael stretched the collar of the old tee shirt over her head. With trembling hands, he slid the material down her barely tanned skin. Unintentionally, the back of his knuckles came in contact with body parts he had not touched in a rather long time. He grew nervous as he cautiously maneuvered the zipper and buttons on her shorts. With the slightest of hand, he pulled the clothing passed Casey's hips, down her legs and over her bandaged ankle. Tugging on the hem of the tee shirt, he covered her as best he could.

Michael stood breathless for a moment, taken in by Casey's mere presence. She had become his world but had kept it to himself. Maybe they were both guilty of building walls around themselves and not letting each other in but that was going to change.

Despite her bruising, she was still beautiful as ever causing a pounding in Michael's heart as a dull ache swelled in his chest. He hated seeing her like this and he was determined to do something about it, but this too would have to wait. Finally, with Casey resting, Michael pulled the blanket up over her body then attended to the soiled clothing that was now piled up on the floor.

Returning to the bedroom with another blanket, Michael slowly laid down next to Casey. Propping himself up on one arm, Michael looped a red curl around his finger, as memories of Memorial Day weekend wandered about in his thoughts. Just as he started to drift into a slumber the door bell rang. "Damn." Michael grumbled, forgetting that Eric and Julie were on their way over with Hannah.

They impatiently stood at the front door waiting for Michael to answer. When he finally did, Hannah pushed past Eric and Julie and into the foyer, with no hesitation. "Where's my sister?" Her words were packed on ice as she paced back and forth.

"Nice to see you too, Hannah." Michael greeted sarcastically.

Hannah turned towards Michael. "I'm sorry, Michael. I want to see Casey. Now!" Hannah crossed her arms over her stomach and began tapping her foot. Hannah's stare was so sharp it could have cut the tension that was emanating between them.

Michael gently placed his hands on Hannah's shoulders, "She's sleeping." Michael could see the concern in her eyes, eyes that looked exactly like

Casey's. Finally he gave in, "Upstairs, the bedroom to the right." Michael barely completed his sentence and Hannah had disappeared.

Eric and Julie dropped off Hannah's luggage then decided to call it a night despite Julie's hidden reluctance. She wanted to see Casey, too.

"I'll call you if anything happens but what Casey really needs right now is sleep."

"It has been an rough night for you both." Julie patted Michael on the shoulder. "We'll come by tomorrow."

"Thanks for picking up Hannah. I'm sure Casey appreciates it."

"Not a problem buddy, but you think you can handle both of them?" Eric teased.

"Do I have a choice?" Michael smirked, raising a brow. "I just need to get some shut eye. I'll talk to you in the morning."

As Julie and Eric said goodnight, Hannah may have been moving slowly, but confrontation was written all over her face as she descended the stairs. "Michael, we need to talk. Now!" With her jaw tightly clenched she tugged on the sleeve of Michael's tee shirt.

"Hannah? It's really late. Can we talk about this in the morning?"

"Michael, my sister went to the hospital tonight and you were the last person to see her before…well it looks like she's been beaten. And now she crying. Just what the hell happened tonight?" Hannah was revved up and sleep, at this point would be impossible until she was satisfied. "I'm trying to make sense of it all. Casey is rambling about Hidden Springs plans and some woman? Who is she talking about Michael? Why is Casey so upset? I want to know and I want to know right now!" Hannah had a certain skill for getting her point across without having to raise her voice. Yet given the circumstances, she didn't feel it was out of character.

"Casey's crying?" Michael started to ascend the stairs but Hannah stepped in front of him before he made it to the first step.

"Not anymore. She's so exhausted, she finally went back to sleep."

Michael cautiously swept an arm around Hannah's shoulder, "Let's go into the living room."

Before Hannah had returned, Michael's tension had started to subside, but as she bombarded him with question after question, he could feel the muscles in his neck contracting again. He, too, felt like he had been hit on the head and his headache was the result of it.

They each sat on opposing sofas as Michael carefully chose the right words with the hope that Hannah would see it from his perspective. "I think that there has been a big misunderstanding and until I talk to Casey, I'd prefer not to discuss this with anyone else. This is between me and Casey."

Hannah swept her hand through her hair in the same manner as her sister did when she was nervous. Looking directly at Michael, she retorted, "Oh come on, Michael. Don't you want to know what happened tonight?" Then she stood up and began to pace. "If you ask me, this was not just the result of some clumsy fall."

He knew a fight was about to unravel but it was not going to be with Hannah or Casey, if Michael could prevent it. Visions of the night flashed in his mind and he knew Casey was upstairs, lying in his bed because of his actions. Maybe if he had gone after her, this would not have happened. Shaking his head, Michael realized he had become too laxed when it came to Melinda Parker. She defined evil whereas Casey was quite the opposite and it was never his intention for their paths to cross. "I don't know what you are implying, Hannah, but I would never lay a hand on your sister, let alone…" He was on the defensive simply because he felt backed into a corner, and it showed.

"You're misunderstanding what I'm saying, Michael. I'm not accusing you of anything like that but aren't you the least bit suspicious of Casey's injuries?"

Michael remained silent for what seemed like an eternity. Edgy and aching for sleep he finally blurted out, "It is my fault! I did this to Casey. There. I confess. Are you happy now?"

"You what!" Hannah was so shocked by his confession that her knees buckled and she nearly ended up on the floor. As she caught the edge of the sofa, Michael jumped up, escorting her to a near by chair. Swatting at Michael, Hannah yelled, "Don't you touch me!"

Michael threw his hands up in the air in defeat. "Look, Hannah…"

"I don't want to hear it. I'm calling a cab. Casey and I are going to her house. And there will be no argument from you." She stated firmly as if she was disciplining one of her children.

Michael moved forwarded, blocking Hannah from getting out of the chair. "No! You're not." From the wild-eyed look on Hannah's face, Michael had been too aggressive but what was it going to take for her to listen?

Slowly easing back, Hannah had never felt so fearful of someone, especially someone she knew. This was the man her sister was in love with? Casey must be out of her mind! But before Hannah could plan her escape, Michael eased up. Kneeling before her, he hesitantly took Hannah's hands in his. "Look…" Michael's tone had taken a hundred and eighty degree turn. "A client came by earlier this evening and I think Casey misunderstood and we had an argument. I should have gone after her…" He trailed off, hanging his head low.

As Michael divulged the unpleasant details of the evening, Hannah realized being scared of Michael Sterling was uncalled-for. She had always been protective of her sister when it came to him, remembering she was the one who helped Casey pick up the pieces when he had left for California. There was an undeniable bond in sisterhood that could not be broken and was often misunderstood by outsiders. But as Michael and Hannah talked into the late hours, they knew their arguing and yelling was because they both loved Casey. However, Hannah could not refrain from giving Michael her two cents worth about business. "I know you love your work Michael, but don't sell your soul to the devil just because he's the lowest bidder because Casey will be the one to pay the price. And believe me, you think I've been tough on you tonight, you just wait, Michael Sterling." Hannah's words were so sharp she surprised even herself.

"Hannah…" Michael spoke barely above a whisper. "I know what I need to do and I will take care of everything, including your sister." He paused then added, "I promise." His words were sincere but his thoughts were quite different as he moved into the kitchen. "*I did sell my soul and for what?*" Michael knew he had dug himself a grave with Lyle and Melinda Parker. But from tonight's events, he was determined to stand by his convictions. He was going to get out of this, no matter what, without losing Casey or his company. And he knew exactly how.

When Michael returned to the living room with two glasses of iced tea, there he found Hannah curled up on the sofa, fast asleep. Quietly, he set their drinks down on the coffee table. Digging through the hall closet for a blanket, Michael came upon a Christmas blanket Amy had given to him when he bought the house several years ago. He surmised it would have to do as he spread it out, over Hannah. As he eyed the decorative pattern, Michael had not realized how much he missed his sister. And in that moment, he fully understood where Hannah was coming from.

Exhausted himself, Michael climbed the stairs to his bedroom. Surprisingly, Casey had slept through World War III, and he was relieved. As quietly as possible, he slipped beneath the covers and before his head hit the pillow, he too was asleep.

Melinda Parker extinguished her cigarette and returned to the emergency room lobby, where she approached the nurse on duty. "When am I going to find out about my husband?" Glancing at her watch, Melinda was agitated by how much time had passed without a word from any of the staff at Brookshire General. "This is unacceptable. It's been hours. I want an answer, damn it!" She pounded her fist on the counter top just as Dr. Everett appeared.

"Mrs. Parker, I understand you're upset but please do not bully my staff or I'll have you removed from the ER. Is that understood?" He raised an eyebrow to her. "Please, come over here and have a seat." Leading her to the chairs off the main lobby, Dr. Everett gestured for Melinda to sit down first, before he did.

Offering her coffee, Melinda declined because all she wanted to know was, "What's wrong with Lyle? Is he going to live?"

"He's stable now, but he suffered a stroke. He will probably not fully recover but with long term physical therapy he should regain most of his faculties."

"Will he be able to talk? Will he be able to go back to work? What about brain damage?" Melinda knew words were pouring out of her mouth but it all seemed so surreal. "Isn't Lyle too young to be having a...stroke?" She could barely form the word on her lips. He may have not been her world but he had certainly created a world for them that she had been accustomed to all her life. Raised by a doting father, and a mother borne of royalty, Melinda had never known the taste of hunger. And she wasn't about to find out what that felt like. If she had to move heaven and earth, to maintain it, Melinda Parker was determined to remain on the Top Ten List of America's Richest Couples, even if it killed her.

"I won't know that for at least seventy-two hours. Why don't you go home, get some rest and come back tomorrow. I will know more after I run some more tests. In the meantime if you need anything, page me." Dr. Everett handed a card to Melinda and disappeared down the hall.

Melinda remained motionless.

Hours later Casey finally woke up. A murmur escaped her lips, instantly waking Michael from his slumber. "Hey..." Michael's tone was soft.

Confusion consumed her. "Where am I? What are you doing? What's going on?" The pitch in her voice grew increasingly demanding. She lifted the blankets and gasped, "Where are my clothes?" Casey's voice cracked then she reached her hand up to her head. "I have the worst headache. What the hell happened?"

At that moment Michael was on his feet. "Casey, you need to stay calm."

"Calm? Calm down! You have some nerve…" The pounding in her head intensified, preventing her from moving another inch.

"Casey, don't you remember? I took you to the hospital?" For a brief moment worry wash over Michael. Casey had not been able to dispel any of the details of her fall and it was troubling.

Pain retched her body as she tried to turn away from Michael. "I remember, all right." But what she was really remembering was Melinda Parker draped all over him.

He sat down on the bed and reached for Casey's hand. "Hannah's here."

"I know. I've ruined everyone's weekend." Tears burned her cheeks as Casey stifled what she yearned to say. The warmth of Michael's hand possessed her as she faced him. The light that danced in his eyes drew her in. Reaching to trace his lips with her fingertip, Michael brushed away her tears. His touch sizzled on her skin and he moved closer. Anticipation grew until the sweet tenderness of his lips touched hers. Casey drew in a breath and winced as his lips lingered over hers. "Be with me. Hold me." Casey pleaded in a rough whisper as she willingly parted her lips welcoming the passion that set her aching body on fire.

Michael's hand caressed her curves causing her to shutter from the pain and pleasure. Speaking softly into Casey's ear he compassionately cradled her, "Casey, I want to. Believe me I do. But I won't take advantage of your emotions." Their gazed locked and Michael simply said, "I can't…"

Casey rolled away from him, pain gripping her. "I should have known…"

Michael could not find the words to console her bruised feelings.

With nothing said, Casey curled up underneath the blankets and cried until she fell asleep.

The late morning sun streamed in through the bedroom window as Casey struggled to sit up in bed. "Michael, I want to go home!" Casey pouted as she flipped the blankets down to her waistline. Agony escaped her lips as she slowly inched herself up.

Hannah came in and placed the tray she was carrying on the bed. "You're not going anywhere, Casey." Hannah scolded, acting as if she was the older sibling.

"I'm fine." Casey did everything to hide the anguish on her face. Pain consumed her body from head to toe but her stubborn nature took over, refusing to complain. "But, I can go home and you all can still go to the Lake."

"Nonsense. We're not going to leave you alone."

"But I'm fine. Really." Casey tried to get up out of bed but as she did her head began to spin and she felt dizzy.

"Casey Marie Andrews! You are so pigheaded! Now get back into bed." Hannah scolded.

"Really, Casey. Eric and Julie are coming over." Michael added. "We'll all be together. What does it matter whether it's here or at Hidden Springs?"

Michael's question went unanswered. "Then I want my car and my clothes." Casey whined then thought to herself, *"I'll go home and take care of myself, you'll see."* Her eyes narrowed as she stared at Michael. Her hurt had turned to anger. The Hidden Springs Lake development and Michael's grotesque display of affection with Melinda was taxing Casey's brain. He was the last person she wanted to be around, let alone take care of her. Even though she kept her words to herself, she was ready to fight but then realized her energy was depleting quickly. *"He's just lucky Hannah is here."*

Sensing the tension between them, Hannah turned to Michael, "Why don't you go downstairs and have breakfast." Then she whispered, "Let me try to talk to her."

Michael wanted to object but given Casey's obvious hostility towards him, maybe Hannah was the best candidate for mediation. If she was able to smooth thing over, then perhaps he would have his moment alone with Casey to clarify what really happened with him, Melinda Parker and the firm.

As he glanced over Hannah's shoulder, Casey abruptly turned her gazed away from his in a grand gesture. He got the picture; Casey was not ready to deal with what had happened last night. Reluctantly, Michael nodded knowing if he was put off much longer, he would not be able to repair the damage that had been done.

Hannah watched Michael close the door, then turned back to Casey. "He's gone, now eat your breakfast. You need to regain your strength." Hannah demanded. As Casey nibbled on her toast, Hannah continued the conversation. "Now what is going on with you two? Is this all because of work or have you gotten too personal? And no skating around the subject anymore Casey. I know you too well for you to keep the truth from me."

"There's nothing to tell. We were together for a few months but I'm pretty sure it's over. It's no big deal."

"No big deal? I think we have been down this road before and I remember it well." Hannah tapped her index finger to her lips, "As I recall it was a pretty hellish summer – for all of us. You're first job out of college, your first apartment and many nights crying yourself to sleep in your old bedroom."

"Really Hannah, that was then. This time, I'm not going to fall to pieces. It was nice while it lasted but Michael and I are through. And this time it's for good!" Casey's voice raised an octave as she noticed the concern on Hannah's face. "I'm fine." Casey lied as she reached out to pat her sister's hand. Ironically, she was comforting Hannah when she needed the comforting. Yes, Casey was struggling to figure out what hurt more, her head or her heart. She tried to rationalize that it didn't matter but it did. But that's where she intended on keeping it, to herself. Casey knew she would always love Michael Sterling. And while it seemed that the bad times out weighed the good, the sweet memories of then and now, were engrained in her brain. And there they would stay. No one needed to know her true feelings. For now, Casey had to get well and get out of Michael's bed, as soon as possible.

Restless and unable to sleep, Julie pulled back the lavender sheets and stepped onto the plush carpeting. The fibers tickled her toes as she started to unpack her travel bag. It had not been mentioned, but Julie assumed that their trip to Hidden Springs Lake was cancelled. It would have to wait until next year. As Julie busied herself, the early morning sun had warmed her apartment to an uncomfortable temperature. The thunderstorm had done little to dispel the summer's drought as anticipated by the local weather forecasters, which forced Julie to close up her apartment and crank up the air conditioning. As she was locking the window sash in the living room, the phone rang.

"Good morning." His voice was too cheery for this hour, Julie thought but found it endearing.

"I just hung up with Mike. Casey must be feeling better because she's insisting we get her car and she wants *her* clothes. The bag she packed for the weekend is in the trunk." Eric chuckled.

"Well Eric, I guess there isn't anything that can keep Casey down for long. I'll be ready in an hour."

Stepping into the shower, Julie adjusted the shower massage so the water beat on her back but did not ease her stress. She had certainly been worried about her best friend yet she sensed there was more to last night then what was being said. Or rather, what wasn't being said. Short of Michael pushing her and Eric out the door last night, Julie wondered if any of this had to do with Melinda Parker. Details of Melinda confronting Eric on Michael's whereabouts were still clearly etched in her mind, even though that was nearly two months ago. Back then, Julie assumed it was a dissatisfied customer and had not mentioned it to Casey. Now she wished she had and it made her wonder if it was a sign of things to come. Julie and Casey had been friends for more than three years and naturally she didn't want her friend to get hurt. Someone had to get to the core of what really happened and Julie was pretty good at sleuthing. It was just part of Julie's nature, revealing the truth.

When Eric arrived, earlier than anticipated, Julie was still wrapped in her bath towel. Grabbing her robe she ran to the front door, "Eric, you've got to stop doing this to me."

"What?" He smiled then leaned down and kissed her cheek.

"You're always early. Even when you tell me you're going to be late." Breathless she grasped her robe closed.

"Maybe you're internal clock needs to be adjusted." Eric saw the look on Julie's face. "Just kidding."

Twenty minutes later, Eric and Julie were on the interstate heading towards Sterling Architects.

"Wait!" Julie shouted as they exited onto Madison Avenue.

"What?"

"Keys." Julie batted her long lashed at Eric. "How are we going to get Casey's car?"

"Relax. Mike told me he has a set of Casey's keys in his office." Eric parked in a metered parking space at the main entrance of their office building. As he assisted Julie out of his truck he handed his keys off to Julie. "I'm going to run to The Corner Café and get us something to drink. Why don't you run upstairs and get Casey's keys. Mike said they were in the credenza, behind his desk. First drawer on the right."

"Okay." Julie turned towards the front door then paused, "Ah Eric, could you get me a lemonade, if not, iced tea?"

"Sure." Eric winked.

Julie let out a sigh of relief as she stepped into the lobby. The early July temperatures were well above normal and she welcomed the coolness of the air conditioning. After turning off the alarm, she went upstairs to Michael's office. Placing her purse on the corner of Michael's desk, she went directly to the credenza. Opening the first drawer, the only thing she found were closed out job files, so she continued on. As she rummaged through just about every drawer, all she found were more files and drawings but no keys. When she reached the last drawer, Julie pulled it opened causing a set of keys to clink against the metal. "Finally! And it was the last drawer on the left!" Julie grumbled to no one. Surprisingly, she also came across a lone file, a rather thick file and temptation got the best of her. Glancing over her shoulder to assure herself that she was alone, Julie riffled through its contents. As she glared at the photo Eric quietly entered Michael's office.

"Did you find what you were looking for?"

Startled, Julie threw the file and photo back into the drawer and slammed it shut then dangled the keys in Eric's face. "Right here." Julie faked a smile as blood surged to her cheeks, turning them bright red.

"What is it? You look like you've seen a ghost or something."

"Nothing." She stammered.

"You don't look so good, maybe you should sit down." After placing the drinks on the desk, Eric guided Julie over to a Michael's desk chair.

"It's the heat." Taking a sip of the cold lemonade, Julie drew in a deep breath and returned to the credenza. Slowly reaching into the drawer, with trembling hands she picked up the black and white photo.

"What is it?" She handed the picture off to Eric. "Oh, that's Melinda Parker." He rolled his eyes as his words dipped with sarcasm.

"Yeah, but that's Michael she's kissing!"

"On the cheek. It's no big deal. She's a client. You know, the hoity-toity…well, you know what she is. She's the one that approached us at dinner that one time…"

"Approached? That's putting it mildly. What is she doing kissing Michael?"

"Oh, it was some ridiculous publicity hype for the Historical Committee or Parker Industries, who knows. Besides, that was a long time ago."

"You mean Melinda Parker is Parker Industries? You've got to be kidding me. Does Michael know who he's messing with? She is, after all, married."

"Michael is not *messing* with Melinda. And it's best if you don't mention this to Casey. Or Michael, for that fact. This is none of our business." Eric stated knowing that if Casey ever met with the likes of Melinda Parker, it would be ugly.

A shiver ran down Julie's spine despite the summer sun that warmed the office. Julie had never been formally introduced, other than their one chance meeting and as she stared at the photo, she knew there was nothing good about this woman. At Eric's suggestion, Julie returned the photograph to its original place. As she walked around the other side of Michael's desk, she accidentally knocked her purse to the floor, spilling all the contents across the carpeting. "Agh, I hate it when I do things like this."

Eric bent down to assist Julie with her belongings. As they gathered up pens, pencils, receipts and her wallet, a small piece of metal caught Eric's eye. Lifting a key chain, he dangled it before Julie's blue eyes. "C.M.A.? Jeez, how many sets of keys has Casey handed out?" Eric grumbled. "You had these the whole time. Didn't you?" He teased in a more light-hearted manner.

"Oh my gosh, I completely forgot!" Julie's hand flew over her mouth.

"Sure you did." Eric gave Julie a playful nudge.

"No really, Eric. I borrowed Casey's car like, six months ago when she was out of town on business and mine was in the shop... oh I feel like such..." Julie's words were ceased as Eric gently laid a finger on her lips.

"It's okay, Julie. I'm just teasing you. You make it so easy, sweetie." Quickly, Julie put her belongings back into her purse. As she started to get up, Eric did too and the two of them bumped heads causing Julie to drop her purse, again.

"Oh! I'm sorry Eric! Are you all right?" Julie held her head as she reached for his.

"I think I need a kiss." He announced and swept Julie into his embrace, pressing his lips to hers.

Julie giggled as her nervousness subsided. Breathless, she whispered, "Well, Eric, I think we should go." Looking up at him with her baby blues.

"Yep." Eric could not extinguish his exuberance.

Hannah busied herself in the kitchen, cleaning up the breakfast dishes even though Michael insisted he would take care of it. But she dismissed him, so he went upstairs, took a shower, dressed then he checked on Casey. Maybe this was his chance. Disappointment washed over him when he saw that she was sleeping again, even though he knew she needed the rest. Closing the door more than half way, disturbing her was the last thing he wanted to do. Maybe she would wake up later, he reasoned as he made his way downstairs, where he found Hannah curled up in a chair, out on the covered deck.

Deeply engrossed in a book, Hannah did not acknowledge his existence. Agitated, Michael did not know what to do with himself. He was so used to being busy with work that the word relax had practically been removed from his vocabulary. Plus, this was not what he had had in mind for the weekend. If he had the power to turn back time, everything would be different from what it was right now. But that was wishful thinking. All he could do was change the future or at least influence it and that's when Michael decided, when Eric and Julie arrive, he would have some unexpected business to take of. No sooner had the thought entered into his mind, when the door bell rang.

Hannah jumped from her seat when she realized it was Eric and Julie and a little sigh of relief washed over her. Not that she minded Michael's company alone, after all, they had come to a cordial understanding in relation to Casey, but that was it. Casey was the only thing they had in common and she was in the mood to talk about anything else, other than her sister.

Julie, Eric and Hannah made themselves comfortable out on the deck while Michael put together some snacks and served up drinks. Eric shuffled a deck of cards with a certain madness causing them all to laugh but Michael was far from a laughing mood, so he quietly excused himself, encouraging his friends to make themselves at home. Quietly, he slipped out of the house and headed downtown.

Payne Claiborne sacrificed yet another holiday to be at Melinda Parker's beckon call. But as they sat in Lyle Parker's office, he was not prepared to hear what Melinda had to say. "You need to bring me up to speed on all of Lyle's business. Current contracts, meetings, contacts, what's pending, what are his plans for the future and what needs immediate attention? Lyle's going to be out of commission for a long time and I'll be damn if I'm going to let a stroke ruin this company. We are, after all Parker Industries."

"Mrs. Parker, I'm more than capable of taking over, temporarily of course."

"I bet you are." Melinda snipped knowing Payne was acting a little too kind for her blood.

"I beg your pardon, Mrs. Parker, but how are you going to handle your job at the Historical Preservation Committee and Parker Industries, while dealing with Mr. Parker's recovery?"

Payne's words cut into her like a sharp knife but she refused to let any emotion rear its head, especially to a man after her age. "I can take a leave of absence. The committee will understand." She shrugged then added, "Besides, it's not my career, it's a hobby. It keeps Lyle and I in the limelight as do-gooders."

Her words did not surprise him. "Well, then should we get started?" Payne jumped from the leather chair.

At the same time so did Melinda, "What the hell is this?" She held the file out to Payne. "Were you investigating Casey Andrews? For my husband? Why? I want to know now and I want to know why?"

"Mrs. Parker, I assure you that any investigating I do for you or Mr. Parker is never questioned. I'm sorry, you're going to have to ask your husband."

"Ask, my husband! You twit! My husband can't sit up. He can't hold a fork. He can't speak!" Just then tears slid down her cheeks and Payne swore he would never live to see the day that Melinda Parker would cry. But he was wrong. And there was only one thing he could do, he pulled her into his embrace and let her cry.

Downtown was congested with tourists and holiday celebrations. With all the chaos that had ensued in the past twelve hours, Fourth of July had completely slipped his mind. As he entered the parking garage next to Empire Tower, he doubted Parker Industries was open for business, yet something kept nudging him on. As he drove to the top level, he practiced the speech he had been writing in his head, on the drive, one more time. Most of the business he had conducted with the Parkers was through Melinda, but after last night, she had forced his hand. He had to go to Lyle. Michael had several proposals in mind and whichever one Lyle Parker decided to choose, did not matter, because they all resulted in Michael regaining ownership of Sterling Architects. Once he had gone down three flights of steps and across a covered walkway to Empire Tower, the security guard didn't even flinch as Michael took a detour to the men's room. Riddled with anxiety, he was not himself. When it came to business, Michael knew how to keep his wits about himself, thanks to his father's regimented teachings but this time it was different. He had more than a company to lose, he could lose Casey. Glancing in the mirror, Michael looked and felt like he had aged ten years in the past two days. Splashing cold water on his face, then reaching for a paper towel, Michael silently wishing he had not dressed so casually. Taking in a deep breath, he eyed his reflection, "It's now or never." As he was giving himself a mediocre pep talk, days of when he played soccer in college popped into his head. And there was Casey, cheering him from the sidelines. Suddenly, his lost confidence was found and he knew he had to play Lyle like he was playing soccer. "Use strategy and defend your goal." With that in mind, Michael made his way to the elevator but the security guard stopped him. "Where you headed?"

"Parker Industries." Michael stated in a confident manner.

"Yeah, they never close, not even for Christmas. It's the only damn reason I'm working a holiday. That and double time and a half." The guard grumbled then questioned, "Doesn't anyone take time off anymore?"

Michael shrugged as he pressed the up button. The ride to the twenty-third floor seemed endless. When the doors finally fell open, Michael was shocked to see Melinda Parker wrapped in the arms of another man.

Hannah, Julie and Eric had only plaiyed two rounds of gin rummy, when from a distance, Hannah could hear her sister calling out her name. In an instant, she was out of her seat but she was not able to move at lightening speed. "I'm coming, Casey."

Julie on the other hand, dashed up the steps, two at a time, greeting Casey with a flabbergasted smile. "You're up. I was so worried about you. How are you feeling?" Julie was at Casey side.

"Like I've been hit by a Mac truck." Casey sighed then added, "Do you think you can help me?" Embarrassed, she pointed to the bathroom.

"No problem." Julie jumped up and slid the covers off of Casey.

Slowly she inched herself around to the edge of the bed. Along came Hannah as well, helping Casey and thanking God it was a short distance.

"Is Casey okay?" Eric burst through the bedroom door.

"I'm fine." Casey shouted from behind the closed bathroom door that didn't remain closed for long.

"Eric, get out of here." Julie playfully shoved Eric out of the room, closing the door in his face.

Casey lingered in the bathroom, wondering if there was any feasible way for her to bathe. The three of them put their heads together and while it was a task, had managed just fine without getting any of her stitches wet.

Dressed and feeling refreshed, Hannah combed then loosely french braided Casey's curls while Julie applied a new bandage to her ankle, carefully following the instructions Dr. Everett had given Michael. "Wow! I feel so much better." With that confirmation, Eric had returned and carried Casey downstairs to the patio. "I bet you never had this in mind." Casey giggled, again embarrassed by all the attention everyone was reigning on her. Surprisingly, she had not even noticed Michael wasn't home until Eric dealt their third game of cards. Relieved for the moment, she kept her thoughts about Michael to herself.

As the afternoon wore on, it became partly cloudy, stirring a warm summer breeze that cut through the screened in porch. Julie had brought along Monopoly and while they were all deeply engrossed in the game, Casey's thoughts were elsewhere. It seemed like Michael had been gone a long time and she wasn't sure if she should worry or wonder where he was. The front door was right in her line of vision and no sooner did she glance in that direction when Michael walked in carrying several bags of groceries.

Upon his return, he was surprised to see Casey sitting out on the deck and smiling. Before he was able to greet her, Julie intervened. "Michael, Hannah and I helped Casey with…well you know, girl stuff, like washing her hair. It's put her in a better mood but I think she still might be pretty angry about last night, so go easy on her, okay?" Julie's suggestion didn't even phase him as she helped Michael put away the groceries.

Accepting his fate as it was, for now, he decided to be the perfect host, knowing two things were certain; eventually, everyone would have to leave, giving him and Casey time alone and first on his agenda Monday morning was to call a private investigator.

The rest of the weekend played itself out and was far less eventful then what had happened mid week. They had a cook out, played cards and various board games, and even rented a few DVD's. Since Casey was still on strict bed rest, they watched the Capitol fireworks on TV. Every now and then, Michael would catch her staring at him and a slight smile would appear but nothing more came of it. Her words to him were few if any at all and remained rather superficial. The tension was obvious and in various private conversations, over the course of the weekend, Julie put forth all her effort to convince Casey that Michael still loved her.

But Casey always came back with, "You didn't see him with Melinda the other night. I know they are together and there is nothing more to discuss."

Knowing otherwise, Julie felt the battle may have been lost but not the war and she began plotting her next move to reunite Michael and Casey.

As for Hannah, she had tossed in the towel, like Eric had, concluding Michael and Casey had to resolve their own problems. And before too long, Hannah had to return home to Adam and her children. After a tearful good-bye with Casey, she reassured her sister they would see each other in two months. Then Julie took Hannah to the airport.

It was now Sunday night and while Casey had managed to get herself out of Michael's bed by sleeping on the sofa for the remainder of the weekend, it was now time to get out of his house.

However, he had a different plan in mind. They were finally alone and Michael was hoping they would be able to clear the air but Casey picked up right where they had left off almost a week ago. "Michael, if you don't take me home right now, I will drive myself."

"Casey, I really wish you would stay here. It's closer to the office and I can come by at lunch to check on you." Michael pleaded knowing if he let her go, nothing would be right between them ever again. "Besides, you know you can't drive. You could tear your stitches."

"Then I highly suggest we get going." She huffed as she struggled with her crutches to get to the front door.

"You are so stubborn!" He gritted his teeth.

"Michael, please...there is nothing you can say or do right now that is going to make everything all right. So please, let's just leave it in the past. I just really want to go home."

For the time being, Michael knew Casey was right but he didn't want to let her go. But he couldn't keep her where she didn't want to be. As he held open the front door, Michael fought all emotion to sweep her into his arms and beg for forgiveness but he knew it would take more than words and gestures of affection to convince Casey what had really happen the night Melinda Parker came to their office.

Chapter 13

The file was packed, jam-packed but it still lacked the proof he needed. Since the night of Casey's accident, the Parkers seemed to have gone into hiding, plotting and scheming their next hostile take over, Michael assumed. He had made several attempts to contact Lyle Parker, to arrange a private meeting but every time he called Parker Industries, Payne Claiborne answered. Michael wondered, if perhaps Lyle's protégé, or was he Melinda's, had taken over. Suspicious, he knew something was brewing, simply because Payne's excuses as to Lyle and Melinda's whereabouts were flimsy at best. As he flipped through the file, most of the pieces were there but they didn't quite fit together. Even though Michael had witnessed the trump card he needed to play against Melinda, the snap shot of that image remained only in his mind. If she had become involved with Payne, she was indeed clever at covering up her indiscretion. Closing the file folder, Michael shoved it off to the side and returned to the Hidden Springs Development file Melinda had given to him back in June. As he surveyed the land specs, Michael contemplated how could he design and develop a resort that didn't effect the one person he loved the most?

Oh, how he missed her, even though she was in the office right next to his. Two weeks after her recovery, Casey had initiated they meet at Imperial's. Little did Michael realize it was to end their personal relationship, vividly recalling the scene.

It was an ugly gray day as Michael climbed the steps to Imperial's yet he was smiling when he saw Casey. Julie had temporarily taken up residence at Casey's apartment during her recuperation period, which forced Michael to stay away. It was a welcome relief when she had finally called, inviting him to lunch. Before he sat down, Michael greeted Casey with a kiss on her cheek. "You look great. You must be feeling much better?"

But Casey's response was cold. "Michael, I didn't ask you here so we could discuss the status of my health. I'm sure Julie had kept you well informed."

Taken aback, Michael nearly fell into his seat. "Casey...I know you're still angry with me but I can explain."

Holding up a hand, she refused his explanation. "It doesn't matter to me anymore what is going on with you and Melinda Parker. I just would appreciate a little respect and ask that you not bring her to the office. I signed a contract and I'm still obligated to work for you but that's it. Anything personal between us is history."

"There is nothing going on between Melinda and myself other than business and that's it."

"And you expect me to believe you? After the way you treated me..." Casey trailed off, stunned that he would lie to her. Sipping her ice water, Casey grabbed her purse and stood up. "You know what, Michael? I can't do this anymore. I may have healed physically but emotionally...well let's just say the damage has been done. I'll survive. I always do but do not pursue me outside of the office. Understood?" With her strength intact, Casey did not wait for his response.

"Mr. Sterling..." Nicole's youthful voice resonated over the intercom as she announced, "You have a call."

She knew what she was doing was wrong but she couldn't help herself. She was a woman of need and with the stress of Lyle's slow recovery, taking over Parker Industries and leaving the Historical Preservation Committee, if only temporarily, Melinda Parker had to indulge herself. And Payne Claiborne had become her indulgence since her husband's stroke almost two months ago. Payne and Melinda had taken up residence in one of the many guest bedrooms of the Parker mansion. Impeccably decorated with white on white satin wallpaper, oak crown molding, and period furniture from the Victorian era, Melinda felt like a queen in the four-poster bed as Payne massaged her feet with coconut scented oil. The touch of perfectly applied pressure, sent waves rushing to her womanly core. He had surprised her with his maturity between the sheets and supplicated a passion in her that she had not experienced since her days as a newlywed. "Young man, you're spoiling me."

"That's my intention, Lindy." Pride radiated from his boyish smile with the use of the nickname he had conjured up for her.

And Melinda didn't seem to mind. She found it endearing and to put it simply, it was something only the two of them shared. "So what are you going to do to me this time? Got any new tricks up your sleeve?"

He raised an eyebrow. "Now how is that possible, Lindy, when I don't even have a shirt on?" Payne replied roughly.

"Indeed you don't." His comment made her smile, something she hadn't done in years and for a brief moment she felt close to Payne's age.

When Payne finished massaging both her feet, he commanded Melinda to lay back on the satin pillows. She stared up at him, contemplating his next move. "Close your eyes." His voice was deep and confident.

"I'm afraid." Again, words that Payne never expected to hear out of Melinda Parker's mouth.

"Now, Lindy…" He soothed, "Have I ever given you reason to be afraid of me?"

"No, Payne. You surely haven't." She proclaimed in a raspy voice.

"Then close your eyes, relax and trust me." Once she had done so, he retrieved the box from under the bed he had placed there earlier that morning.

The crinkling of tissue paper piqued Melinda's curiosity but she did not peek.

Payne had special ordered all the rose petals he could afford. Quietly, he sprinkled them all over the bed. Drawing in a deep breath, her senses told her, she was being bathed in delicate passion, something her husband never would have considered, at least not for her. Next came an even greater surprise, Payne gently clutched a single red rose in his hand. First he tickled her toes with the silken petals followed by his kisses. As he followed the outline of her curves up her legs to. the hem of her silk robe, Melinda imagined, if only for a brief moment, Michael touching her in a way she had never been touched before and the thought made her pulse quicken.

Sliding his strong hand across her mid-section, to the sash on her robe, in one fell swoop, Payne exposed her voluptuous body causing her to arch her back. "Oh, Lindy." His voice was deep… smooth…and Payne's. Still, desire ignited the embers of her soul that she thought were long since burnt out. Michael or Payne? What did it matter? Especially since her womanly desires were being satiated, in various ways. Blazing a trail of rose petals from her navel to her neck, followed by his mouth tasting the sweetness of her wet skin, Melinda was captivated by his technique. Tracing the lines of her neck with the delicate petals, followed by the tenderness of his lips, Melinda's body was on fire and she could not resist his maneuvers. As the rose bud found it's resting place on the pillow next to her, Melinda fluttered her eyes open in total ecstasy. With a smile decorating her lips, Payne knew he had taken her, yet again, to a place of euphoria.

Melinda rolled over, reaching into the nightstand for a cigarette. As she exhaled, she requested, "Honey, can you go down to the wine cellar and find us something decent to drink?"

Surprised, Payne wanted to kick himself for forgetting the champagne. "What if one of the servants sees me."

Sitting up, Melinda cupped his boyish face in her hand. "I'm no fool. I gave them the day off. You're secret is safe with me."

Quietly, Payne dressed while Melinda basked in the glow of their meeting. Once he closed the door behind him, she picked up the phone to call Michael.

While Julie and Maggie were meeting with Calandra Kosta, at her new restaurant location downtown, Casey took advantage of her time alone in her office. Secretively, she made a few inquires about the land development at Hidden Springs Lake. However, this phone call, like all the others, had resulted in another dead end. With nothing on paper to solidify the deal, all fingers pointing to Melinda Parker as the source of the rumor. And she may have slipped up when she revealed to Casey that bulldozers were moving in after Fourth of July weekend but as of yet, nothing had happened. Casey speculated that Melinda had conjured up the whole idea just to keep her and Michael apart. But why? Willing to conduct a little investigation of her own, Casey was ready to call Melinda Parker's bluff.

With Labor Day weekend just around the corner and her family already at the Lake, Casey felt confident that opportunity would present itself. And maybe, her and Michael could get back on track. Oh, how she missed him, even though he was in the office right next to hers. But there was no time for regret. As she finished her weekly report and printed it, Casey gathered up her belongings. Anxious to beat the holiday weekend traffic, she had opted for working a half day and it was time to go. As she headed to Michael's office, Casey was puzzled by the words that stung her ears.

"It's over Melinda! I have had enough. And I mean it this time." Michael's words were harsh.

Casey's heart began to pound as she moved slowly towards Michael's office door. It was open just enough so she could clearly hear Michael's end of the conversation. Holding her breath, Casey listened intently.

"I don't care if I lose the business. If it'll get you off my back and out of my life, then so be it." Michael practically choked on his words. *"What does*

Michael's relationship with Melinda have to do with him losing the business?" Trying to stay as still as possible, Casey feared Michael would sense her presence.

"Hey Casey, I thought you said you were leaving early." Eric startled Casey.

Casey whirled around, her red curls swaying to one side, as she held her index finger to her lips. Then she gestured to Eric, motioning him to move closer. In the softest of whispers, Casey's mouth was only inches from Eric's ear. "What does Melinda Parker have to do with this firm?"

Eric pulled Casey into her office and closed the door. "Why do you ask?"

"I just overheard Michael tell Melinda that it's over and that he doesn't care if it costs him the business. You know when I met that woman something about her just didn't seem right. But then when I saw her hanging all over Michael, I assumed he knew a side of her no one else did."

"What are you talking about?" Eric crinkled his brow, pursing his lips, confused as to where Casey was headed with their conversation.

"Michael and Melinda. Their involvement."

Eric folded his arms over his chest then fingered the bridge of his glasses, pushing them up on his nose. "What involvement? I've known Mike for years and he has never ever been involved with Melinda Parker other than business. Where are you getting your information from?"

"That's what I'd like to know?" Slamming open the office door, Michael's quick movement and angry tone alarmed her. "Into eavesdropping now, Casey?

Swallowing hard she retorted, "Hey, I'm getting tired of this Michael. You're getting to be unbearable." Casey's sharp toned surged through his veins. "I was coming to your office to give you the file on Calandra's restaurant renovations and my weekly report. I can't help it if your voice carries out into the hallway. It's not my fault I just happened to over hear you breaking up with Melinda." Shoving the files into his hands, Casey smirked, "I'm sorry." And it wasn't their break up she was sorry about.

Throwing his hands into the air, Eric raised his voice, something Michael had never witnessed before but certainly caught his attention. "This is exactly what I was afraid of! The tension between you two the past few months is intolerable and it is effecting this company. I've invested my blood, my sweat and my wallet and I'll be damn if it's going to get washed drown the drain because you two are too damn prideful to reconcile your differences." A vein pulsed in Eric's neck as he turned his harsh tone towards Casey, "Now, I don't know what you heard, but Melinda Parker does not effect nor influence this company in any way. We've been awarded a few projects here and there in relation to the Historical Preservation Society but other than that..."

Casey cut him off, "Oh really now? Then why don't you ask Michael about the plans to develop the land at Hidden Springs Lake? Something about a resort?" Narrowing her eyes, Casey cast a piercing glare in Michael's direction before perching her fists on her hips.

"It has nothing to do with you. It's a business deal between the Parkers and myself." Michael's words were terse.

"The hell it isn't. The only plot of land large enough to develop a lake front resort would be right where my mother's cabin is. And the Kirby's."

Eric's eyes widened as he questioned Michael, "What is she talking about?"

Changing his toned, Michael stated, "I need to talk to the both of you." Michael exited Casey's office and led the two of them to his.

After Casey and Eric sat down across from Michael, who was now seated behind his desk, with no hesitation Michael simply stated, "I'm resigning."

The pain in Casey's heart felt like someone had taken her very breath from her. "Michael..." sympathy resounded in her voice, "You can't be serious. This is your life, your dream, for as long as I've known you..." Trailing off Casey could not find the words he needed to hear.

Then Eric cut in, "Mike, this is yours. You can't walk away. Brookshire General Hospital has put us on the map. Come on...what's really going on here?"

Michael shook his head and looked down, then confessed, "It's not mine. Sterling Architects is silently owned by the Parkers."

"What? How did they ever become involved?"

"Around the time I became engaged, I had made some bad investments. Legitimate, but they didn't pan out. And you both know how the economy in the construction and architectural industry fluctuates. After that, I asked my father for a loan but he turned me down flat. Then, out of the blue Melinda Parker showed an interest in the business and brought her husband, Lyle on board. It was supposed to be to everyone's benefit, with Lyle being a properties manager and Melinda working for the Historical Committee. The bottom line is, is the loan wasn't really a loan. They bought fifty-one percent of the company but I would still manage it. Silent partners or so they said."

"Michael, we can buy them out."

"No, that's the problem, Melinda refuses to sell. Now they want to build a resort at Hidden Springs and she has threatened to shut us down if I don't design the plans. But that's not the worst of it. It involves the demolish of all the cabin's on the main road, including Casey's and the Kirby's."

Again pain ripped through Casey. She would die to save the cabin. Not only was it hers and Hannah's but her mothers and her grandparents as well. They had worked and saved for so many years so there would always be a place for the family to call home. Pushing aside her anguish, Casey stood up and leaned against Michael's desk, "We have to stop them, Michael."

Shaking his head, Michael questioned. "How? The Parker's possess two attributes: money and power. Besides, if they have any questionable business deals out there, I'm sure they have covered themselves. Lyle and Melinda are too smart to get caught." Eyeing both Casey and Eric, he considered sharing the file of documents he had collected on the Parker's but as Eric broke in, the idea quickly diminished.

"There's got to be a way. Somehow…if we put our heads together…" Thoughts were turning in Eric's head.

Casey glanced at her watch, "Look, I'm going to the Lake for the weekend. Let's do some digging. There has to be a way to stop them once and for all." She turned to Eric, "You and Julie are still coming up tomorrow, right. You'll help me?"

"Of course. Count me in." Eric stated enthusiastically

"Wait, both of you. You don't know who you are dealing with." Michael tried to discourage them.

"Michael…" Casey's words were soft, "You can't give up. Come to the cabin this weekend." She pleaded.

He resisted with every fiber of his being but those sparkling eyes could not be denied. A glimmer of hope sprang into Michael's heart, maybe too, this was their chance to reconcile and possibly turn something professionally wrong into something personally right.

The afternoon sun was still warm despite the predictions of an early fall and a cold, wet winter. The valley below was dotted with varying shades of green and Casey smiled as deer grazed in the lush grass. Taking in the fresh mountain air, she marveled at the beauty of the landscape. Easing up on the accelerator, she took the Mountain Road exit that led her to Hidden Springs Lake. Excitement and anxiety swirled inside her as she pondered the up coming weekend. The Lake was her sanctuary when life in the city became too tumultuous, yet what laid ahead could turn out to be just the same. With a house full of relatives and friends plus a weekend full of investigating, unanswerable questions kept stabbing her mind. Melinda Parker had managed to get on Casey's last nerve and without really trying. But determination had always been Casey's strong suit and she was not about to give up now as she kept reminding herself that the truth always won out in the end.

Parking in the grassy lot between her family cabin and the Kirby's, Casey found Emily and Jason playing badminton or at least trying. Greeted once again with shouts from her niece and nephew, laughter echoed through the trees as the two youngsters covered their aunt with hugs and kisses.

About to enter her third trimester, Hannah slowly made her way over to her sister. Hugs were exchanged as Adam joined them as well. "What took you so long? We expected you an hour ago."

"Oh, Michael, Eric and I had a quick meeting." She quickly stated, keeping the true details to herself. "They're coming up tomorrow, along with Julie."

"Michael is coming up here? Why?" Hannah smirked as she crossed her arms above her swollen mid-section.

"Hannah, trust me, it's business and let's just leave it at that." Casey brushed off her sister knowing that when it came to Michael, they would always disagree.

"Well, ladies, chef Adam is at your service. I have the grill all fired up and ready for shrimp and chicken and hot dogs for the munchkins." Adam chuckled.

"Daddy, I'm not a munchkin. I'm a big girl. When are you going to stop saying that?" Emily chimed in as she stood in the same posed position as her mother, her brown eyes glazed with tears.

Adam scooped the lanky little girl up into his arms, "Emily honey, even when you are my age, you will always be my... daddy's little girl. No matter how old or tall you are. When I call you that, it's because I love you. But if you want daddy to stop..." Adam started to choke on his words as he perfectly explained to his daughter his words of affection.

Emily glanced around, first at her mom then her aunt. Pondering his words, Emily's doe eyes lit up then she smiled. "Oh!" Flowed from her tiny mouth with the sweetest of innocence then she planted a big kiss on Adam's cheek. "I love you too, daddy."

After placing Emily gently on the ground, Adam dabbed the corner of his eye. Turning to his wife, he pursed his lips then smiled. "Now about dinner..."

After a late dinner, Adam put the kids to bed and joined Hannah and

Casey on the front porch. "I just don't get it Casey, Michael was never honest with you about his involvement with this Parker woman and now you want to risk it all to help him save his business?"

"Hannah you have it all wrong. Michael was never *involved* with Melinda in that way. I was the one who assumed that and pushed him away…again."

"Again? How can you say again? He was the one who choose graduate school over you."

Casey was starting to despise having the same relentless conversations with Hannah. She knew her sister meant well but when it came to Michael Sterling, Hannah did not want to see it from her perspective. Casey had a history that was not as easily erased as Hannah wanted it to be. "Hannah, I did push him away. I'm the one who broke it off. I'm the one who didn't believe that we could maintain a long distance relationship for two years. And isn't it ironic, I'm working with him anyhow. Our dream of running our own company one day still came true.

"That's nice, Casey. But you should be one of his partners. You have brought in quite a bit of business for him. When is he going to add *design* to the company name?"

"I don't know. Why don't you ask him when he gets here?" Casey's words dripped with sarcasm.

"Maybe I will." Hannah returned quickly then added, "I just don't trust him. It's taken him months to tell you the truth. And it seems he is a little too willing to bring you and Eric down with him." Hannah argued.

"It's not like that at all. Michael is opposed to the idea of going up against the Parkers. But Eric and I practically begged him to come up here. We all have a vested interest here and you should too. Do you want to see mom's cabin bulldozed and the Kirby's?" Casey was on her feet, pacing the length of the porch. "You know, Michael gave me a job and the opportunity to advance my career. He has been very supportive. And he was also there for me when I had that stupid accident. I can not turn my back on him now. Besides, I'm the one that wants to get to the bottom of all this and find out what makes Melinda Parker tick and why she has her claws dug into him so deeply."

"Hannah…Casey can take care of herself." Adam reassured as he sipped his iced tea.

"Thank you, Adam." Casey smiled at her brother-in-law.

"I just hope you know what you are doing." Hannah stated in a sing-song voice.

"So do I!" Casey thought to herself. "Why don't we play that board game you all have been raving about?"

Casey was up with the morning sun, a habit she could not seem to break. She decided to take a walk before her relatives woke for the day. When she stepped outside into the fog-laden morning, she was surprised to see Michael sitting on the front porch swing.

"How long have you been here?" Casey's leather tennis shoes squeaked against the dew-drenched floorboards as she approached him.

"About a half hour. I didn't sleep much last night." He paused then continued, "Casey, I've been thinking and I think we should just forget…"

Casey held a hand up, "Don't even say it Michael. You don't want me to investigate the Parkers. Well, it's too late. I'm part of it and there isn't anything you can say that will change my mind." Casey sat down next to him, realizing this is the closest they had been in months and suddenly she felt that old familiarity of wanting and needing him. She had been loving him for a lifetime and whether or not they ended up together, Casey knew Michael would always hold a special place in her heart.

He gazed into her eyes and saw that sparkle that always caught him in the chest. "What have you told Hannah?"

"We have business to take of. Why?"

"Why? Because your sister doesn't like me, that's why."

"It's not that Hannah doesn't like you. It's just that she doesn't want to see me get hurt."

"Well, I can't blame her in that respect. I've certainly have been the soul contributor of that this year, haven't I?" Michael reached out and gently placed his hand on top of Casey's. "I'm sorry." Michael's sincerity was real but his words felt hollow, even though they weren't. Holding back his emotions, Michael refocused his thoughts on everything he loved about Casey. Seeing her in the office always brightened his day. And that he loved how her eyes lit up when she smiled. That he admired her creative talents and independent spirit. And when she got nervous, she always played with her hair or bit her lower lip. But he knew deep down inside, despite the fact that he would always love her, at this point, he would rather hurt and live without her than risk ever hurting her again.

"Michael." Casey interrupted his thoughts, "Do you want to go for a walk?"

He smiled and nodded thinking to himself, *I would follow you to the ends of the earth, if you asked me.*

By the time they had returned from their morning expedition, Eric and Julie had arrived. Julie was pleasantly surprised to see Michael and Casey together and to top it off they were smiling.

"Hey bud, what's going on?" Eric greeted as they slipped in through the front door.

"We just took a walk around the Lake." Michael shrugged. "Then Casey introduced me to Adam and the kids."

Hannah nodded then asked, "Don't you all have work to do?"

Quickly Casey intervened. "Not exactly but we are going to take care of it this morning and get it out of the way."

"Good. It is after all a holiday. Don't you ever just relax?" Hannah teased.

Julie eyed Eric across the room, then looked at Casey and Michael. A small giggle escaped her lips. Shrugging her shoulders, Julie raised an eyebrow, "We work hard; we play hard."

Casey glanced at Michael who was sitting quietly in the recliner. "It may not seem like it, Hannah, but we do. However, I have to go talk to Mr. Miller. If we want to keep this cabin, dear sister, then yes, we have our work cut out for us. If anyone knows anything about this place, it would be Mr. Miller." Casey claimed.

"Well, Eric and I were thinking about going boating, everyone's invited, unless you want us to go with you, Casey."

"I'm going with Casey." Michael had remained quiet until now.

"As much as I'd love to go, I think I'm staying on land. I don't think the kid can handle it." Hannah rubbed her stomach, "I'm going to take Adam and the kids lunch."

The clock struck one o'clock, when Michael peeked his head into the kitchen. He saw Casey attending to the lunch dishes and without being asked, grabbed a dish towel and started drying the plates. Silence enveloped them and Michael felt uncomfortable that they had nothing to say to one another. They had been left alone by the others and temptation was pulsing through Michael's body. He wanted to hold Casey and kiss away all the pain but instead he simply asked, "Are you about ready to go see Mr. Miller?".

"Absolutely. You know you don't have to go. This concerns me more than it does you."

"But it does, Casey. If I can find a reason to break ties with Parker Industries, then I need to know first hand. You don't know them the way I do and they don't play by the rules."

"Suit yourself." Casey shrugged her shoulders as she rung out the dish towel, hanging it over the edge of the sink to dry.

Michael remained silent as he watched Casey exit the kitchen. Glancing over her shoulder, she casually asked, "Aren't you coming?"

Conversation was minimal as they walked to The Country Store. Mr. Miller was finishing up with a customer when Casey and Michael arrived.

"Afternoon, Casey. " Mr. Miller greeted. "It's been awhile, how's that new job of yers goin'?"

"Busy." She hesitated then asked, "Mr. Miller do you have a few minutes, I need to talk to you."

"Why sure." Then he shouted. "Mrs. Miller!"

"What is it dear?" A stout little woman came running from the store office. "Land sakes, give me a heart attack why don't you."

"I'm sorry honey. Casey and her friend here need to chat with me. Can you watch the register?"

"Of course dear." Mrs. Miller rolled her eyes but then a smiled graced her face as her husband stepped out from behind the counter.

Clouds shadowed the afternoon sun as they stepped out onto the porch. "What do you need to talk to me 'bout?" Mr. Miller smacked his lips, then reached into his pocket and pulled out his pipe.

"Mr. Miller, have you heard anything about developers building a resort?"

His aging eyes grew wide. Mr. Miller rubbed the graying whiskers on his chin, "Whelp, now I don't see how that's possible. The lake itself is state park property and it's protected by some government agency or someone like that." He shook his head in disbelief that the same hideous rumor had once again reared its ugly head. "Nope, no one can develop anythin' commercially here. Why do you ask?"

"I've been approached by Parker Industries to design a hotel resort but in order to do that, all the cabin's along the main road would be torn down, including Casey's." Michael informed Mr. Miller.

"Them again."

"What do you mean?"

"If anyone knows this place can't be developed its that Parker woman and her assistant."

"Her husband, Lyle?" Michael asked.

Mr. Miller thought for a moment, rubbing his chin, before he answered Michael's question. "If my memory serves me right, I think his name is Blaine, Cain...no..." Mr. Miller snapped his fingers when the name came to mind. "Payne. They were up 'bout a month ago. Young man. Prob'ly half her age. Anyhow, a few years back, some of the buildin's 'round here were considered historical properties, like my store that was actually built in 1923. They can't be touched, no sir-e-e. Not to mention what them nature lovers would have to say 'bout this."

Casey's eyes lit up as she glanced at Michael. She reached out and patted Mr. Miller's arm. "Oh, thank you so much!"

"You're welcome dear." Mr. Miller exhaled on his pipe, pleased he could help the young couple. Then he added, "Casey, if you need proof of what I jus' told you, you might want to do some digging at the local newspaper or library or something like that."

"We will." Casey and Michael stepped off the porch and started back towards the cabin when Mr. Miller called after them, "Casey, I'm not gonna tell you what to do but if I were you, I'd stay away from them Parkers. They're mean spirited." Mr. Miller raised his hand to the couple and then slowly returned to his pride and joy, The Country Store.

As Michael and Casey sprinted down the dirt road, the rain began to fall.

Since the summer sun had baked Julie's delicate skin, her and Eric decided to cut their boating trip short despite the rain. Needing to cool off, Julie went to the kitchen and made a large pitcher of lemonade. When she returned, Eric could not resist eyeing Julie as she moved across the room. Nestling close to him, Julie sipped on her drink while he gently rubbed aloe lotion on her shoulders and the back of her neck. Even though it stung, Eric's touch tickled Julie's senses causing her to giggle.

The creaking of a bedroom door made Julie sit up with a start, taking her breath away for a brief moment, but it was only Hannah entering the living room.

"Did we wake you?" Eric inquired.

"No, the rain did and so did the baby." Hannah winced as she felt the baby nudge its foot against a rib. "Adam's not back with the kids yet?"

Julie shook her head while Hannah peered out the window. "How was your day?" She struggled to get out her question.

"It was fun. Eric caught a fish, but the nice guy that he is, threw it back."

Julie smiled as she glanced over her shoulder at him.

"Eric, that was supposed to be dinner." Hannah smiled teasingly.

"Really?"

"I was kidding." Hannah stated as she positioned herself in the recliner then began to massage her stomach. "Is that fresh lemonade?"

Julie jumped up in an instant. "I'll go get you a glass. Eric, you want another beer?"

Eric took the last sip and handed the empty bottle to Julie. "Actually, one is plenty. Would you mind getting me a glass of ice water, sweetie?"

"Not at all." Then Julie disappeared into the kitchen.

"Are Casey and Michael back yet?" Hannah questioned as Julie handed her, her drink.

Julie shook her head, saying nothing more.

Quickly, Hannah caught on to the tension brew between them. Rolling her eyes, Hannah continued, "Don't get me wrong, but Michael has really sucked Casey in this time and for what? His love? Please."

"Hannah, Michael really loves Casey and they're happy when they are together." Eric defended Michael.

"He has a strange way of showing it." The ice cubes clinked against the glass as Hannah took a sip then abruptly added, "They're back together? Casey told me that it was over."

"I'm sorry but I can't talk about Mike and Casey like this. Whatever has happened between them should stay between them. It's really not our business." Eric's tone surprised both Julie and Hannah and before either of them could respond, Emily and Jason came running in with a very drenched Adam right behind them.

"We've got her, Michael! I'm not going to lose the cabin after all." Casey shouted over the pattering of the rain echoing through the mountainside.

Michael picked up Casey and swung her around then gently placed her back down on the ground, "I couldn't have done it without you. How am I ever going to repay you?"

Casey pulled out of his embrace, "Michael, you don't owe me anything just next time choose your business associates a little more wisely."

Her words stung but Michael knew she was right, "Thank you." He pulled her back into his embrace and kissed her on the forehead. There was a glint in his green eyes as he wiped droplets of rain from her cheek.

Michael's affections were making her uncomfortable. "Michael too much has happened. If you really want to repay me, then set up a meeting with Melinda as soon as possible." The latter half of her sentence was filled with urgency.

Michael released her from his embrace and took a step back, folding his arms across his broad chest. "Casey, I'll take care of this. You've done enough. There's plenty of time to confront the Parkers. Let's just enjoy the weekend. Okay?"

"How can you be so matter-of-fact about this? The firm is your life. You know they are up to something and we need to get to the bottom of this." There was a sorrow in her brown eyes as she looked at him, knowing it was Melinda who had driven them apart. And Casey wanted to know why. What was it about Melinda Parker that stopped Michael from being the strong, confident, self-assured man she knew and loved? He said he had never been involved with Melinda but on some level was Michael in love with her? Numerous questions stirred inside Casey but when she noticed a woman with a bright red umbrella approaching her and Michael, she knew the answers would have to wait.

"Casey! Michael! You two look so cute playing in the rain." Valerie taunted. "Actually, I'm glad I ran into you."

Giving Valerie a sour look, Michael immediately interrupted, "I'll see you back at the cabin, Casey."

Michael's curt departure threw Casey off yet Valerie continued as if he had not even been there. "Casey, have you heard of Parker Industries? And have you heard they want to build a resort here?"

"Don't worry, Valerie, it's not going to happen. Michael and I just talked to Mr. Miller. We need to find some documents…" Casey proceeded to repeat the same information to Valerie.

"Well if that's the case, then why would such a rumor like that be going around?"

"That's what I'd like to know. My guess it has something to do with Melinda Parker…and Michael but I can't seem to put the pieces together."

Valerie pursed her lips then replied, "Well, I just have to tell you this. I did a little digging myself and you will never guess what I found out?"

"Is it really important Valerie because I have a house full of guests. I really have to get back." Casey wanted nothing more than to avoid gossiping with Valerie Sorrenson.

"Well, I just have to know Casey…" She huffed. "…did you know that

Melinda Parker has a sister?" Valerie drew in a breath, placing a hand on her hip.

Casey's crinkled her brow at the information, "And?"

"Half-sister actually. It seems Melinda's father had an indiscretion outside the marriage."

"Really?" Casey nodded. "Thanks." Not waiting for her reply, Casey left Valerie standing in the rain. As she sprinted towards the cabin, Casey made it to cover just as it began to pour.

Chapter 14

Even though it was business as usual after the Labor Day weekend, Valerie's comment left a gnawing feeling in the pit of Casey's stomach. And she couldn't leave well enough alone. Knocking on Michael's office door, she peeked in. "Michael, is there anything you need before I leave?" She nibbled on her lower lip.

"Where are you going?" There was a sternness in his voice.

"A design seminar."

"What seminar? You didn't tell me about it." He looked up from his paperwork trying not to stare. *Damn, she looks irresistible!* Michael thought to himself as Casey stood in the doorway dressed in a business suit. The silky emerald green material hugged her curves and was a pleasing contrast to her fiery red locks. Michael caught the slight shimmer on her lips, which tipped her just towards seductive, yet in a classy manner. In his mind, no other woman could hold a candle to Casey Andrews. And without a doubt, Michael or any man for that fact, would have to be dead, not to notice her innocent allure.

"Oh, I read about it in the paper a few weeks ago. I thought I told you about it." Casey hated lying to him but she felt she had no choice.

"No, I don't remember you mentioning it." Michael cleared his throat then asked, "Are Julie and Maggie going with you?"

"No, this is something I want to do on my own." She stated, then started to fiddle with her car keys.

Michael eyed Casey inquisitively but then abruptly asked, "Why?"

Casey grew nervous as she nibbled her lower lip, "I can't spend every waking moment with them. Besides, they have enough work to keep them busy. We can't all be away from the office at the same time, anyhow. It's just not good business." Casey reasoned as she ran her fingers through her thick curls then asked in a softer tone. "Did you talk to Melinda yet?"

"She's not in her office. Something about some meeting downtown. Which really doesn't make any sense, because I just found out she's taken a leave of absence from the Preservation Committee." Michael shrugged then added, "Her secretary said something about her and Lyle are off to Europe or something like that, I wasn't really paying attention. But I'll take care of it." Easing back in his chair, he rested his hands behind his head, "I'll see you tomorrow." Michael stated flatly not wanting to have another conversation or confrontation about the Parkers. Deciding it was his fight, he did not want Casey nor the rest of the company involved. Leaning forward, Michael stared down at the stack of papers on his desk, praying Casey would leave it to him to resolve the issue at hand.

"Fine." She smirked and exited his office. He looked on, intently. Letting out a hard sigh, Michael was relieved she was gone for the day. Watching out his window, Michael patiently waited for Casey to drive out of the parking garage. Once he saw her make a right onto Madison and disappear into the bowels of the city, Michael reached into his desk drawer, grabbed his car keys, a few files then he too, was gone from the office for the rest of the afternoon.

Garrick Mansion stood high on a grassy knoll that overlooked the water. With its finely manicured gardens and resorted 19th century architecture, the Mansion was indeed a welcome addition to the upper side of the Waterfront district. And that was were Casey was headed. The weekend rain had dissipated the summer humidity and now a cool breeze cut across her open car windows as she selected a parking space across the street from the Mansion. Making her way over to the crowd, Casey stood at the bottom of the semi-circular steps that lead to the Mansion's main floor, a story above ground. It appeared as though every reporter in town was present and it made her wonder why Melinda Parker would draw such media attention. Uncertain of how this was going to play out, her mid-section aching and despite Michael's warnings, Casey was still determined to the put the missing pieces of the puzzle in their place.

Impatiently waiting for the ceremony to begin, she stood behind the group of journalists, knowing she would have to wait until the end of the ceremony to confront Melinda. Suddenly her thoughts shifted when out of the corner of her eye, someone in the distance was waving to her. At first she could not make out the figure that was now moving towards her.

"Casey…Casey!" She recognized the singsong voice in an instant. "What are you doing here?" Valerie greeted her with a hug, as if she hadn't seen her in months, yet it had only been a few days ago at Hidden Springs. "Isn't it exciting? Anybody who is someone is here today."

"So, what are you doing here, Valerie?"

"Oh, I forgot to tell you, I got a job! Yes, you are looking at The Weekly

Times society reporter. It's only part-time but it's work, none the less."

"Well, I'm happy for you." Casey managed.

"So, is Michael with you? How's he doing? He ran off so quickly I didn't get a chance to talk to him. Do I hear wedding bells?"

"We're not together, Valerie. Sorry to disappoint you."

"Well, don't give up. Oh, look they're starting. I have to get back up front, I have some serious questions for Melinda Parker, especially after what we talked about."

Casey's eyes widen, "Valerie, I was wondering could you ask her..." Casey leaned towards Valerie and whispered in her ear.

"Consider it a done deal. Why don't you come up there with me? If anyone asks, you're my assistant. This is going to be good." Valerie's navy blue cotton dress swayed in the breeze and her brown ponytail, that was tied up with a white ribbon, bobbed up and down as she wove a path to the front of assembled reporters.

Michael parked his car in a metered spot around the corner from Garrick Mansion. With the Parkers headed for Europe for an extended vacation, he knew that time was not on his side. They had narrowed the window of opportunity and Michael had finally accepted the fact that he had to randomly chance a meeting with Melinda in order to get his company back. Straightening his red silk tie and sweeping his hands through his curly waves, Michael sighed, reaching for the door handle. As he stepped up to the curb to feed the meter, his cell phone rang. "Not now." He mumbled but answered it anyway. "Michael Sterling."

"Mike, it's Eric."

"I'm getting ready to go to a meeting, what is it Eric?"

"We need you at the Rezabeck site. He thinks we've gone overboard with the construction materials and he wants me to use different materials to cut costs. I've explained it to him over and over about the building codes, but he won't listen to me. Mr. Rezabeck said he wants to meet with you right away."

"I'll give him a call."

"He's here now, Mike."

"Put him on the phone." Michael insisted.

"He wants to see you in person." Eric paused.

Aggravation gripped Michael's muscles as he debated the situation. *The Parkers or Mr. Rezabeck?* He questioned in his mind.

"Mike he's ready to pull us off the project."

With Eric's last statement, Michael replied, "Mr. Rezabeck is a reasonable man, tell him I'm on my way." Tossing the file into the passenger seat, the black and white photo, that had arrived on Michael's desk just this morning, of Melinda Parker and Payne Claiborne fell to the floorboard. Cursing under his breath, Michael started his car and put it into reverse. At the stop sign, he impatiently waited for on-coming traffic to clear before he could make the left turn. Glancing over at the ceremony, he saw an older woman standing on the platform, then his grip tightened and his eyes narrowed at what he saw next. The woman dressed in green looked too familiar but he couldn't be sure. Making the turn, Michael struggled to get a glimpse of the ceremony but the distance, trees and traffic impaired his view. A horn blasted from behind him, forcing Michael to accelerate with this thought in his mind, *That couldn't be Casey, I told her to leave Melinda Parker alone.*

"Ladies and gentleman, it is with great pride that I introduce to you the President of the Historical Preservation Committee. Without her hard work and dedication, today would not be possible. Let's all give a round of applause for Mrs. Melinda Parker." The elderly woman stepped to the side of the podium.

As the crowd roared and whistled, Melinda stepped up to the microphone, dressed in an elegant bright yellow dress with red accents. Her long strand of red beads swayed across her chest with each move. Lifting a hand to the crowd, Melinda's red bracelets clinked together as she actually smiled when she said, "Thank you." She repeated. "Ladies and gentleman, we fought a good fight and won." The crowd cheered at her words. "It has been two years, a lot of long hours and many employees since we took on this project to have Garrick Mansion deemed a historical property and renovated for public use. As you may know, this was once the home of Colonel William Paul Garrick, who played an integral part in the ending of the Civil War in President Lincoln's cabinet. It will now serve as a museum for the community and the Historical Preservation Committee will work in cooperation with the City Tourism Counsel to sponsor annual cotillions. Proceeds will go to educational programs and the upkeep of the mansion and it's gardens. Now, before the Mayor cuts the ribbon, I'd like to thank the Preservation Society for allowing me to participate in this dedication, since I had to take a leave of absence." Melinda glanced at the older woman who had introduced her. They both nodded and applauded each other while mouthing the words, "Thank you." Melinda was in her glory as she once again spoke to the crowd, "Ladies and Gentleman, I give you Garrick Mansion." Applause was returned as the elderly woman handed the pair of scissors to the Mayor.

Once the ribbon was cut, there was a rush from the group of reporters calling out Melinda's name. It was Valerie who was first to be recognized, "Mrs. Parker, did you take a leave of absence from the Historical Preservation Committee so that you could be a part of the resort development that Parker Industries is planning at Hidden Springs Lake? Do you realize that it will effect a dozen families that have been vacationing there for generations?" Valerie held out her micro-cassette recorder as a hush fell over the crowd.

Mr. Rezabeck was an older man though no one would have guessed with his thick brown hair and gray eyes. He sat quietly at the table while Michael reviewed the list of materials and costs that Eric had presented to him upon his arrival. As the minutes passed, Mr. Rezabeck's assistant entered his office with a fresh pot of coffee. Michael declined while Eric dressed his coffee with sugar and cream.

Finally, Michael cleared his throat. "Mr. Rezabeck, I've looked this over and I assure you that the cost of materials is correct. We're building an assisted living community and the specs require certain materials for handicap specification. We don't want to go against the law now, do we?" Michael's words were strong but smooth in his delivery. While he was addressing the situation at hand, thoughts of Casey and Melinda kept seeping into his head.

Mr. Rezabeck sipped his coffee, a perplexed look souring his face. "No, Mike. We don't want to go against the law." He stated in a low voice as he rubbed his index finger and thumb against his chin. Mr. Rezabeck felt he had no choice but to be truthful. "I do understand Mike, but the cost is eating me alive. I'm sorry but it's true."

"Mr. Rezabeck if finances are the issue, we can come to an agreement." Michael sat up straight as he reached for a coffee mug.

"That would be mighty nice of you." Mr. Rezabeck smiled as he reached for his project file.

Melinda's eyes narrowed as she glared down at Casey. Her response was concise, "What my husband does is not my business." Melinda cleared her throat and smoothed her hands over her dress. Publicly Melinda always maintained her decorum. Quickly gathering her thoughts she continued, "What

173

I meant to say…I've taken a leave of absence for personal reasons. As for development of a resort at Hidden Springs, I assure you, I am uninformed."

"I have documentation that some of the buildings at Hidden Springs Lake, that have been there since the 1900's, have been deemed historical properties. Wasn't this under your presidency that the Historical Preservation Committee deemed them Historical Lodging Properties of America and could not be demolished?"

Casey was taken aback by Valerie's efficiency in performing her job. She was direct yet held a cordial air about herself.

"I don't recall. I would have to check our records and I'll be more than happy to assign a staff member to it right away." Melinda lied. "Now let's continue with the dedication of Garrick Mansion. Mr. Mayor, would you like to address our guests?" Expecting the Mayor to save her from the scrutiny of the reporters, the Mayor simply lifted a hand with a shake of his head. Silently, he had made his point; he did not want to get involved. "Well, ladies and gentlemen, refreshment and drinks…"

Valerie pushed on, "Mrs. Parker, according to my resources, plans have already been developed for a resort complex which really isn't necessary considering the Lodge at the Welcome Center has one hundred thirty rooms plus numerous hotels off the interstate as well as cabins and camping grounds. Would you care to comment?"

Melinda became flustered and suddenly lack poised, "Surely, I don't know what you are talking about?"

Valerie turned towards Casey and winked. "Well then, can you answer this question? Are you aware of the detrimental effects it will have on the environment if that land is developed?" The crowd remained silent as Valerie dominated the question and answer session.

Melinda started to shake. The flashes from the photographer's cameras were starting to give her a headache. Gripping the podium, she could barely reply, "I don't believe you have a reliable source, but as I said before, I will get my staff right on it. And thank you ladies and gentleman for your patience and time." Melinda exited in haste into the mansion and disappeared out of sight.

"That will be all. Refreshments are being served on the back terrace. Thank you for coming." The elderly woman stated and exited as quickly as Melinda had.

Valerie turned to Casey and squeezed her arm, "So, how did I do?"

"I got to hand it to you Valerie, I'm impressed. You were good and I especially liked the environmental part, nice touch."

"Thank you." Valerie was smiling ear to ear then added, "You're not the only one who has something to lose at Hidden Springs." Her tone was somewhat sharp until she asked, "Could I buy you a cup of coffee or something?"

"I'd really love to Valerie, but now it's my turn to confront Melinda Parker, once and for all."

"Do you mind if I tag along?"

"Not at all." Casey smiled in return.

There were awkward silences between Casey and Valerie while they waited for Melinda Parker to show herself. Valerie reasoned now was as good a time as any to return Casey's check to her. Reaching into her little over the shoulder pocket book, Valerie retrieved the uncashed check she had been carrying around all summer. "Here."

"What's this?" Casey unfolded the piece of paper.

"Casey, I was wrong and I'm sorry. I shouldn't have charged you for the picture and negatives of you and Michael at the dance. I don't know why I do stupid things like that. I was just trying to impress the old high school gang."

Surprised by her gesture, Casey was hesitant. "But Valerie, if I take back this check, then there's no guarantee you won't print it in our Alumni paper."

"I'm not going to cash it." Valerie reassured. "And I'm not going to print your picture either. If what you and Michael have is more than professional, then it should be between the two of you."

"Then the coffee's on me." Slipping the check into her pocket, Casey simply added, "I really appreciate it Valerie, especially since Michael and I are no longer together."

"You mentioned that earlier, but when I saw you two at Hidden Springs..."

Casey shrugged, "I know what it looked like but I decided we're better off just being friends."

Valerie felt a sadness in her heart about the news of Michael and Casey's break up. Even though she had snooped into their personal lives, deep down inside she still wanted them to be happy. "Friendship could be a good thing." Valerie mustered then shifted the conversation, talking about her children and the start of a new school year. Casey could barely get a word in edgewise but for the first time Casey was content on listening and was really enjoying Valerie's company. Silently, she declared that she would be more patient and continue to get to know Valerie better when Melinda finally appeared.

"Oh God, are you two vipers still here? Haven't you done enough damage for one day?" Melinda's heals clicked against the pavement as she made her way down the cascading steps.

"Why won't you let Michael buy you out?" Casey shouted then turned towards Valerie when she heard a stifled gasp.

"Look...." Melinda stopped herself mid-way on the steps, still placing herself well above Casey and Valerie. "I have a plane to catch. Besides, I don't owe you an explanation. Now get the hell out of my way!"

"No! Not until you get out of Michael's life."

Melinda continued her descent, her heels once again clicking against the concrete. As she reached the sidewalk that led to the Mansion's elaborate gardens, Casey gasped, nearly choking trying to catch her breath. "What the hell is wrong with you?" Melinda tone was vile.

From out of nowhere, Casey grabbed Melinda by the arm.

"Get your hands off of me you little twit! Or I'll have you arrested for assault. You don't know who you are messing with little girl." Melinda's words were full of grit yet she was trembling as she reached into her red bag, retrieving a cigarette. Once lit, it was as if Melinda had inhaled confidence, as she stood tall, glaring at Casey.

"Too bad, I sent my photographer to go back to the office. This is going to make a great front paper headline." Valerie roused.

Stepping back, Casey stood wide-eyed and silent. And it was suddenly so overwhelming, as if someone was running a movie trailer on fast forward as flashes of the first night she met Melinda Parker, bombarded her.

Oblivious to Casey's state of being, Melinda's tone flared even more as she narrowed her eyes on Valerie. "Alright! I'll tell you. But it stays out of the damn paper. Got it? The last thing I need is you two little busy-bodies ruining my reputation." Melinda clenched her teeth together then blurted out, "It's never going to happen."

"What?" Valerie pursed her lips feeling she had already conquered the almighty Melinda Parker, without even hearing the whole story.

"The resort at Hidden Springs Lake. I know the property can not be developed." Her words were icy as she continued, "It was an excuse to get close to Michael. He's the only man that has ever been nice to me without trying to buy me. I wanted to drive a wedge between little miss cheerleader here...and him." Melinda stubbed her cigarette out on the ground with the point of her red stiletto.

Snapping out of her shocked state, Casey attacked Melinda, "You! It was you! You're the one who put me in the hospital. You pushed me! And stepped on my hand, with that very shoe." And with those words, the memories came flooding back, not in bits and pieces, but the whole picture.

Startled by Casey's words, Valerie patted her shoulder. "What are you talking about?"

"I'm sure you don't know what you're talking about." Melinda lied as a tiny beads of perspiration broke out on her upper lip.

"It was the night of that thunderstorm... when we had the black out downtown..." Casey shook as her words came to fruition. "I remember it as if it was yesterday. It was Fourth of July weekend and I was in a rush to get to the airport. But I never made it because I was assaulted and Michael ended up taking me to the emergency room." Drawing in a deep breath, Casey finished telling her story to Valerie, "And the last thing I saw before I passed out, was a red heel crushing my hand."

Melinda poised herself accordingly as she carefully responded, "Yes, it was dark that night from the black out, therefore it could have been anyone." Melinda cackled then added, "It's not my fault you slipped on the sidewalk."

Valerie crossed her arms across her chest, "And how would you know that?"

"Looks like you just incriminated yourself." Casey raised an eyebrow, waiting impatiently for a reply. When Melinda reached for another cigarette without a word, Casey knew she had found her window of opportunity. But Casey was not satisfied, she had to know why. Why would Melinda intentionally hurt her without even knowing anything about her?

"Because if I can't have Michael, no one can! It was so easy to get rid of the other one." Melinda blurted through gnashed teeth.

"What did you do Melinda, pay off your own flesh and blood?" Valerie interjected.

Shrugging, she simply replied, "Something like that."

Shocked by her answer Casey concluded, "Oh my gosh! You're in love with Michael, aren't you?"

Melinda folded her arms across her voluptuous chest, her cigarette dangling from her bony fingers.

"Well, Melinda, since you don't have anything to say, here's the deal. Michael will buy back his fifty-one percent of the company at a reasonable and fair market price, giving him soul ownership of Sterling Architects and then he will never have to know who put me in the hospital." Casey crossed her arms over her chest and began tapping her fingers on her forearm. Again Melinda had nothing to say but Casey did. "Actually, I'm feeling rather generous, I won't press charges either."

That clinched it and it showed. A tiny vein pulsed at Melinda's temple as she inhaled. "Oh, all right. Besides, this works out for the best for everyone. Lyle and I don't have time to bother with the measly little operation that Sterling Architects is." Melinda's words dripped with sarcasm. Glancing at her diamond and ruby watch, Melinda had to go, if her and her husband were going to make it to the airport on time. As she eyed Casey and Valerie, who were looking rather triumphant, Melinda's temper caught fire and she had to add one last dig. "It'll have to wait until the Charity dinner project Mr. Logan is head of. Lyle and I are going to Europe on an extended vacation until October. We'll take care of it then." Melinda huffed then abruptly turned away.

Casey was disgusted and wanted it all to just go away, including Melinda Parker but she had one last question, "You're invited to the Charity Dinner?"

"Of course, Lyle and I got an invitation. I had to pull some strings but we got in. We are, after all, the most prestigious couple in town. I'll call Michael when we return. He can name his price." Melinda raised an eyebrow. "In fact, I'll donate Michael's paltry little check to Mr. Logan's little house thing. At least I'll get good press coverage out of this." And on her final word Melinda walked away for good.

Casey began to shake as she watched Melinda fade into the distance. Turning to Valerie, anger surged through her body, "God for bid that woman ever does something unselfish." The pain that had been gnawing at her stomach, now consuming her body.

"Casey, you know this is not about the money. It's about control. I remember learning about this in my psychology class in…" Valerie trailed off as she turned towards Casey. "Are you feeling okay? You're as white as a ghost." Draping her arm around Casey, Valerie trying to ease her despair. "It's going to be okay." She said in a motherly tone.

"I don't feel too well." Casey stood tall as she concentrated on her steps across the lawn of the Garrick Mansion. "I really didn't like doing that and you know what, I actually feel sorry for the woman."

"She brought it on herself. It just a good thing we didn't have to play all our cards. Melinda was probably thinking in the end she would get Michael. But that's where she was wrong. Michael doesn't love her. He loves you."

"I don't know about that." Casey raised an eyebrow then her expression turned to curiosity. "Valerie, what are you talking about? Play all our cards?"

"Melinda's half-sister." Judging from the look on Casey's face, Valerie knew that now was not the time to reveal the information she had been sitting on for days. Quickly, she returned with, "Oh, it's not important. I'll tell you about it later. The bottom line, Melinda Parker probably had a bad childhood." Casey glanced at Valerie and couldn't help but smile. Then the two giggled.

"So, do you want to go get that cup of coffee?" Valerie asked.

"That would be nice, but I think I'll have a ginger ale."

With his curiosity pique, Michael could not resist returning to Garrick Mansion. Impatiently waiting at the traffic light, with one car in front of him, and pedestrians in the cross walk, with every fiber of his being he wanted to believe Casey would not betrayed him. Refusing to let Casey Andrews rescue him, he knew he got himself into this mess and it was time to get himself out of it. But when the light changed, a woman out of the corner of his eye caught his attention. There was no doubt about it, the red cascading curls, the green silk suit and Valerie Sorrenson by her side. Michael's blood began to boil as he made a right hand turn and parked. Hastily, he filled the meter with several coins, then made his way across the street, following the same path Casey and Valerie had.

The aroma of Valerie's coffee tickled Casey's nose. She was feeling much better, since she had taken several sips of her ginger ale and nibbled on crackers and chicken vegetable soup. "Valerie, I really appreciate you staying with me today."

Patting Casey's hand, Valerie beamed. "Believe me, the pleasure was all mine." Then Valerie bit into her tuna salad sandwich.

Now that Casey's nerves were steady, she had to ask, "So what did you mean by…"

"Casey." His voice was strong and undeniable. Startled, she couldn't help but turn, coming face to face with Michael.

"What are you doing here?" She stammered, wondering how on earth he tracked her down.

"That's what I'd like to know." His tone was above normal volume, giving cause for the other patrons to stop and stare.

"She's having dinner with me." Valerie quickly jumped in, then pulled out the chair next to her, patting the vinyl cushion. "Care to join us, Michael?"

Not wanting to cause a scene, Michael took the seat Valerie had offered him. "How was the design seminar?"

Casey nearly choked on her soup with his probing question but it was

Valerie who caught on quickly and answered, "Boring."

"And what were you doing there, Valerie? No one to gossip about this week?"

"Michael!" Casey was taken aback by his snide comment.

"Well, Valerie's not a designer so what would she being doing there?"

"Covering a story for The Weekly Times." Valerie fibbed, guessing Michael would hit the roof, if he knew that her and Casey had bargained with Melinda Parker.

Casey's calmness was turning to agitation, "What's your point Michael?"

"Oh, I'm just wondering how you two ended up over here, across the street from Garrick Mansion. I do believe Melinda Parker was there."

Casey felt caught between a rock and a hard spot. She didn't want to lie to Michael, but she had to keep her word with Melinda and leave it up to her to follow through with their deal.

"She was. I ran into Casey at the design seminar and asked her if she wanted to join me at the dedication of Garrick Mansion. Life of a busy reporter. And then we came here to grab a bite to eat. That's it." Valerie insisted.

"That's it?" Michael wanted to believe that was the truth but he had his suspicions. Casey was far too silent but for now he would accept Valerie's quick explanation until he could get Casey alone.

Michael ended up staying and ordering a sandwich, while telling Casey and Valerie of his meeting with Eric and Mr. Rezabeck. Conversation remained on business as Valerie chatting away about her new position as a society page journalist. Before they knew it, it was nearly seven o'clock when the check came. "I'll get this." Casey smiled at Valerie.

"Well, I have to scoot. My husband is with the kids, getting them ready for school tomorrow. He's probably in need of some back up." Valerie giggled as she stood to exit. "Well, Casey. Thank you for joining me today. It was fun. I'm so glad I ran into you. I'll call you. Maybe we can get together again for lunch next time." Valerie's perkiness was contagious.

"Sure that would be nice. And thank you." They had an unspoken understanding now as Casey winked, concealing her disappointment that she was unable to learn more about Melinda's half-sister.

Turning, Valerie held out her hand to Michael, "Good night." And with that she exited.

Casey had finished the last of her ginger ale when Michael attacked. "Since when have you become so buddy, buddy with Valerie Sorrenson?"

Casey looked into his troubled green eyes. There was no doubt, his suspicions where running high. "Since today. I guess." Casey shrugged then added. "She apologized for taking that picture of us at the dance at Hidden Springs. She even gave me the picture and negatives."

"I know. I saw it in your desk a few months ago. What did she do, persuade you to pay her to keep it out of the Alumni paper?"

Michael didn't miss a beat when it came to Valerie but after the day they had with Melinda Parker and with their friendship starting to blossom, Casey wanted to give Valerie the benefit of the doubt. Deep down, she believed Valerie was truly sorry and until she proved otherwise, Casey was going to leave it between her and Valerie. "Not exactly." Casey motioned the waitress for another ginger ale, to go.

Once the check was paid, her and Michael made their way across the street. Michael was finally easing up as he opened Casey's car door for her. He caught a glint in her eyes, realizing this was the perfect opportunity for them to spend some time together, alone, away from all the hustle bustle and drama of the office and the Parkers.

As Casey rolled down her car window to say goodnight, Michael leaned in. "Do you want to go do something?"

"It's kind of late Michael." She saw the look in his eyes, wondering what his intentions were. "What did you have in mind?"

"Maybe a movie or a walk down by the Waterfront. Or we could rent a movie and pop some popcorn."

"That would be nice." Casey smiled as she shifted her car into gear, following Michael back to his house.

Chapter 15

September had quietly passed, with summer slowly fading into fall. The office had fallen into a steady routine of meetings, proposals and design projects. Construction for the Pediatric Oncology Wing at Brookshire General Hospital had broken ground, keeping Eric in the field most of the time. At first it was an adjustment for Julie, still they managed their relationship well and had grown closer over the months. They were tossing around the idea of buying a house together, but the notion of them merging their lives had not come to fruition, yet.

Even though Casey and Michael's relationship had moved to a new level of mutual consideration, they were still distancing themselves emotionally. When a colleague of Michael's was unable to fulfill his part-time obligation, teaching at the local University, it presented a challenge Michael had never considered. It was only one class and he was happy to take up the slack to fill a void that had been there since the summer.

As for Casey, she found solitude in seminars and design shows where she crossed paths with Bill and Veronica, who were still employed at Whitley Designs. "Honestly, Casey. He has changed…for the better." Casey knew Veronica would not lie to her yet she found it hard to believe.

And Bill backed her up. "Veronica is right. He has changed. Dare I say it, he's become…nice." And the three of them broke out into laughter. Before they went their separate ways, they agreed it had been too long since they had spent anytime together and agreed to meet for happy hour the following week.

Since the drama had died down, Casey could breathe a sigh of relief. Yet thoughts of Melinda Parker found their way into the forefront of her thoughts, remembering how much that woman had turned their lives upside down. She loathed the woman and the absence of the Parkers did not seem to make much of a difference, except to Valerie. The society pages of The Weekly Times needed to be filled and there was always someone or something to write about, keeping Valerie on the run. And tonight was no exception.

As the limousine pulled into the circular drive of the Waterfront Convention Center, that old uneasy feeling crept its way back in, gripping

Casey's mid-section.

"Are you all right?" Michael's deep voice was soft as he moved across the bench seat, narrowing the distance between them. Loosely draping his arm around Casey's bare shoulders he stated, "If you're not feeling well, I'm sure Eric will understand."

"Don't be silly, Michael." Casey mustered. "Julie, Valerie and I spent all day getting ready and I don't want to disappoint Eric." Looking down, Casey fiddled with her white sash. "Besides, I don't want this dress to go to waste." She pursed her lips, raising an eyebrow to Michael, letting out a small sigh. There was no doubt in Casey's mind, she wanted to be at the benefit dinner but why had she agreed to go with Michael? Their history spoke for itself and it was senseless to be around him in any other manner than professionally. Again, she asked herself why. And when Casey felt Michael's touch on her face, she knew the answer to her question.

Gently lifting her face towards his, the moonlight through the limousine's open roof caught the flecks of gold in her brown eyes. "Did I tell you…you look absolutely beautiful this evening?"

Casey batted her eyes as her cheeks grew warm from his compliment. Gazing into his eyes she started to thank Michael and found herself wanting to kiss him. As if reading her mind, Michael leaned forward, pressing his lips to hers. Without hesitation, she parted her lips, welcoming him in. Sliding her hand down his tuxedo shirt she felt his taut muscles beneath the stiff material as Michael trailed his fingertips down her bare back igniting the embers inside.

"Sir." The single word sentence uttered by the chauffeur, Mr. Clark, that Michael had hired numerous times before for such events, brought their aching passion to abrupt halt.

Stepping out into the crisp October evening, the moon illuminated the starry sky as Michael reached out his hand to assist Casey. After slipping a folded bill into Mr. Clark's hand, Michael offered his arm to Casey. Together, they slowly ascended the stone stairs, leading to the Convention Center Banquet Hall. A professionally crafted sign, billowing in the breeze, hung across three marble archways, advertising tonight's event: A Charity Dinner by the Woman of Hope, for the Home and Hearth Project.

The softly lit banquet hall bustled with hundreds of guests as Casey was drawn in by the elegant atmosphere that was unfolding before her. "Do you know where we are supposed to be seated?" Looking up at Michael, the ambience reflected in Casey's eyes and for a brief moment he wished they were the only ones in attendance.

"Ah, I thought I'd be a nice guy and let you two sit with the guest of honor." Eric greeted with a chuckle.

"Eric! You look…"

"…stupid?" He cracked as he fumbled with his bow tie.

"So handsome!" Casey's eyes flew opened as she marveled over him, from head to toe. His black tuxedo and red bow tie were a great contrast to his daily construction wear of worn jeans, dirty tee shirts, and work boots.

"So, you actually own a razor?" Michael jumped in ribbing Eric.

"Gee, thanks man." Eric smiled

Shaking hands with many of the volunteers as they moved to the front of the banquet hall, it was a sight to behold. Hundreds of tiny white lights hung across the high ceiling, reminiscent of the Winter Wonderland dance Casey and Michael had attended in high school. The round dinner tables seating eight, where conservatively decorated with deep red linen table clothes and pure white cloth napkins. The centerpieces displayed on each table consisted of a white vase with a single red rose, white daisies and greenery. The full dinner settings comprised of white china accented in gold and enough utensils for an eight course meal.

Casey moved quickly towards Julie as she saw her rise from her seat. "You look wonderful!" Casey shouted above the noise of the crowd as she hugged her best friend. The soft lighting reflected perfectly off of Julie's pale green sequin gown causing highlights to bounce off her blonde spiral curls.

"So do you!" Julie beamed. Casey's simple-cut gown of velvet softly accentuated her shapely figure. A month ago, she had carefully selected a maroon sleeveless gown. The bodice hugged her torso and at the waistline draped into a full skirt. There was a slit straight up the front revealing layers of white chiffon. To complete her ensemble a long chiffon sash bordered the scooped neckline and the ends of the scarf fell over her shoulders and down her back.

Casey and Michael sat down next to Julie, and Eric seated himself on the other side. "Have you heard from Maggie?" Casey questioned.

"She called me this afternoon. Little Joey has the chicken pox so her and her husband can't make it." There was disappointment in Julie's voice. "I really was hoping they would be here."

"Me too." Casey agreed.

Waiters dressed impeccably in white tuxedos and black trousers served appetizers consisting of miniature quiches, shrimp wrapped in pea pods and bite size pastries stuffed with crab. The waitresses sported in white tuxedo jackets and black skirts, were serving a variety of beverages to the guests.

As she sipped her drink, Casey's nervousness was starting to subside. Glancing around the banquet hall, there was no sign of Melinda Parker nor her husband. As she eased back in her chair, Casey found herself staring at Michael, as him and Eric engaged in conversation about Mr. Rezabeck's project.

"You still have it bad for him, don't you?" Julie whispered into Casey's ear. "Don't lie to me Casey Andrews, I see it in your eyes." Her voice now above a whisper.

"Lie about what?" Michael questioned.

Casey turned towards him and was caught by the spark in his green eyes. "I don't know." Casey stammered.

"Tell him." Julie nudged Casey.

"Tell me what?" Again Michael eyed Casey as he flashed his bright smile.

Casey's eyes widened and heat from her mid-section surged to her cheeks turning them a bright shade of pink.

"If you don't say anything then I will."

"Julie!" Casey voice cracked.

"Michael, you two belong together and that's all there is to it. There, I said it for you."

"Really Julie, leave them alone." Eric chimed in. "What goes on between Mike and Casey is their business." He raised an eyebrow, knowing they had had this conversation too many times before.

Before Julie was able to defend her intentions, Nancy and Sean Kirby arrived. Casey let out a sigh of relief as she admired Nancy's long black satin dress that was accentuated with an ornate pattern of silver sequins. Her husband, Sean wore a black tuxedo with a white tie. Behind them stood, Nicole. The slender teenager's dress was made of shimmering silver rayon imprinted with red roses, that hung just above her knees. Her long black hair had been French braided and tucked under at the nape of her neck which was secured with a large rose barrette.

"Eric, honey, are you ready to make your speech?" Nancy had inquired.

"No, I think you should give it Nancy." Eric joked.

"Absolutely not young man. This is all your doing." She teased back then added, "Well, they're going to start serving the dinner soon so I better introduce you."

"So, Nicole, how did your mid-terms go?" Casey inquired.

Sean nestled into a chair next to his granddaughter, half listening to Casey and Nicole's conversation, while watching Nancy out of the corner of his eye, who was now approached the podium with Eric Logan.

"I know I passed but my Physics and Calculus exams were hard. I was the last one to finish, on both exams. All I can do now is keep my fingers crossed." Nicole indicated, mature beyond her age.

"I'm sure you did fine." Casey reassured as she patted Nicole on the arm.

"I'm sure you did, too." Sean agreed.

The music subsided and the microphone reverberated as Nancy began to speak. "Good evening ladies and gentleman, and thank you for coming tonight." There were claps from the audience, then she continued, "The Women of Hope Auxiliary is proud to sponsor this evenings charity dinner. And I would like to introduce to you the founder of the Hearth and Home Project, Mr. Eric Logan." The crowd cheered and applauded as Eric shyly stepped forward.

Pride swelled inside Julie and she could hardly contain her excitement as she stood, clapping the loudest. Others followed her lead, giving Eric a standing ovation.

Overwhelmed by the response Eric grew nervous. "Ah…thank you…" His voice cracked as he spoke into the microphone. "Please…" Eric motioned. "Thank you." Eric stammered as he gestured to the crowd, to take their seats. Clearing his throat, Eric continued with his speech, "Thank you for such a warm welcome." Again clearing his throat the inflection in his voice grew strong. "Three years ago, when I was overseeing a job site, I encountered a homeless family for the first time, up close. A father, a mother and their two boys living behind the construction dumpster. My first instinct was to call the police and have them arrested for trespassing. After all they weren't my problem."

Eric drew in a breath as whispering ensued through the banquet room. "Or were they? After speaking with the father for thirty minutes, he convinced me to give him a job. So, I did. I also offered to put his family up in a hotel, until he got on his feet. He refused. Even though he was homeless, he still held onto his pride. When I asked him where his family was going to sleep, he begged me not to ask him again. He worked harder than anyone I had ever met in my life. He was always the first one on site and the last to leave. After a few weeks he was able to rent a two bedroom apartment and get his boys back into school. And to this day he is my best foreman. So many times I have wanted to ask him, how did he ever get to the point that he did?" As Eric paused an eerie silence fell over the room.

"But you see ladies and gentlemen, it doesn't matter how. In our society he never should have gotten to the point of having to struggle to survive on the streets with his family. That's when I realized I had to do something, so I approached him and asked him, what could be done to make difference. And that's when Hearth and Home Project was born. Hearth and Home Project buys condemned properties at a low market price, renovates and refurbishes them to assist families with dependents in order to get them off the streets and into a warm and safe environment. And that is where you come in. Your generous contribution in attending tonight's dinner will furnish five houses and allow Hearth and Home Project to purchase three more homes. I would like to thank all the volunteers for their hard work this past summer." Eric paused as the crowd applauded. Finally continuing, Eric added a very special thank you to, "…Mrs. Nancy Kirby and the Women of Hope Auxiliary for creating, donating and collecting linens, pillows, blankets and kitchen items to the project. Their contribution has turned seven houses into homes for many families. Again, thank you, everyone for your time and effort. You should be proud. Thank you." As Eric stepped away from the microphone there was not a dry eye in the room and the audiences ovation lasted almost ten minutes.

After the applause subsided Nancy stepped to the podium, "Ladies and gentlemen, dinner will be served momentarily, in the meantime I would like to acknowledge and thank the Lyric Chamber Orchestra for volunteering their time and providing tonight's entertainment." Again the audience clapped and the conductor took a bow. "Enjoy the rest of the evening and bon appetite." Applause filled the banquet hall as Nancy returned to the table and the music swelled.

Julie dabbed the corner of her eyes as Eric moved towards her. Reaching for him, Julie kissed him. "Eric, I'm so proud of you." She boasted. "I love you, honey." A soft whisper tickled Eric's ear.

"Congratulations, Eric." Casey's voice cracked as she looked around the table. She was not only proud of Eric, but proud to be a part of this group as well as the Hearth and Home Project. Silently she smiled, casting a glance towards Nancy. "Thank you." She mouthed. It was a blissful moment for her as emotion struck. Thanks to Nancy Kirby's encouragement, Casey had found a way to fill the void that had been empty for so long.

"Way to go." Michael shook Eric's hand intensely, slapping him on the back in a manly gesture. Then leaning down, he whispered to Casey, "I'm proud of you, too." His breath tickled her neck, sending a familiar sensation down her back. "Would you like to dance?" Michael took Casey's hand, directing her to the dance floor where he swept her into his embrace.

As they moved across the dance floor, Valerie had approached the table and introduced her husband, Mark Sorrenson. "Eric, that was some speech. I will make sure tonight's dinner makes tomorrow's headlines. Would you and Nancy mind posing for a photo?"

"That isn't necessary, Valerie…" Eric shook his head, embarrassed by all the attention.

"Oh yes it is." Nancy insisted. "Come on handsome." Nancy teased as she hooked her arm into his.

As Eric and Nancy walked to the back of the banquet hall, Julie caught a glimpse of Casey and Michael out of the corner of her eye, then did a double take. *"I don't care what they say, they still love each other. They undeniably have stars in their eyes."* This time Julie kept her thoughts to herself.

"What is it, Casey?" Michael asked as he gently placed his hand on the small of her back, pulling her closer to him.

"Nothing." She whispered as she looked up into his eyes.

"I think I know."

"Know what, Michael?"

"What Julie said earlier. We belong together. You know it's true. You still look at me the way you did in high school. And, Casey, there will never be another. I will always love you."

Casey's cheeks flushed as Michael glided across the dance floor causing her to look away. As she did so, Casey noticed her friends looking on.

"Julie, stop staring at them." Eric teased after returning from his photo session with Nancy. "You have to get over it, honey. They're friends, business partners, end of story."

With her aging hands perched on her hips, Nancy wanted to argue with Eric and defend Julie but her words were soft and motherly, "No, Eric, it's not the end of the story." Nancy shook her head as she once again witnessed Michael and Casey dancing cheek to cheek. "They still love each other. I remember those two as teenagers, when they use to come to the Lake…I thought nothing would ever tear those two apart." Nancy stated.

"There is one person…" Valerie interjected, "…and there she is."

A sudden hush fell over the banquet hall as Melinda Parker entered the room with her husband. Whispers ensued as she made her way to the edge of the dance floor, pushing Lyle Parker in his wheelchair. An instant smile decorated her face as photographers swarmed around them, lighting up the room with their flashes. While Melinda drank in the attention, Payne Claiborne silently hovered in the background.

"Mrs. Parker, can you tell us why your husband is in a wheelchair and how does this effect Parker Industries?" One reporter shouted.

"My husband suffered a stroke in July, the night of that retched thunderstorm." She was all drama and anyone who knew Melinda Parker knew she was playing it to the hilt. "While Lyle and I were in Europe, Parker Industries was left in the capable hands of Payne Claiborne, my husband's Senior Executive." Melinda turned to Payne and although she was smiling at him, it was forced.

Payne waved to the crowd, "I assure you Parker Industries is still the same company and I have not made any decisions that Mr. Parker himself would not have made." Payne was a natural for the cameras.

And Melinda knew he was only speaking truth. Payne had managed to keep the Parker empire well afloat and turn a nice profit in the process. Of which Payne Claiborne managed to acquire a reasonable percentage. And it showed from head to toe, in his newly tailor Christian Dior suit to his authentic Italian loafers. He reeked of wealth and power.

Melinda turned away from the inquisitive group of reporters, addressing only Payne. "You can go, now." Her icy words were a sharp contrast to what her and Payne had shared over the past several months and it hurt, but only for a brief moment. When he locked eyes with Nicole Kirby, Melinda Parker quickly became his past.

"Now where was I?" Melinda faced the reporters again, "As I was saying, Lyle's team of doctors are the best in the world. They anticipate a full recovery. And they are certain he will be back in the driver seat in no time." Melinda smiled, placing a hand on her husband's shoulder but her eyes followed Payne as he escorted Nicole to the dance floor.

Julie now stood next to Valerie, "His team of doctors, the best money can buy, please. That woman won't stop at anything."

"Too right."

Julie glanced at Valerie, who was just as hooked as she by the viperous woman who had them all cast in her spell. "Why aren't you over there? Aren't you covering tonight's event?"

"Casey and I got this story a month ago." Valerie casually stated.

"What?" Wide-eyed, Julie was taken aback by Valerie's statement and had to inquire.

"Oh, it's a long story. We'll tell you about it later. I'm going to dance with my husband."

"But…" Julie was unable to finish her sentence as Mark and Valerie also headed to the dance floor.

"Can you believe this? My God that woman always has to be in the limelight." Eric loathed Melinda Parker and while he was always cordial to her, he never hid his feelings.

"Let's go dance, honey." Julie lead Eric to the dance floor while numerous reporters continued to inundate the Parkers with questions.

Michael was still waltzing Casey around the dance floor as if they were the only two that existed. He stared down at her lips, his body aching to kiss her. As he leaned towards Casey, the commotion of the Parkers impromptu press conference captured his attention. Realizing it was Melinda, Michael abruptly abandoned Casey on the dance floor.

"Don't let her come between you two. Go after him and stop him."

"Forget it Julie, after tonight it will all be over." Casey mumbled.

"What are you talking about? Valerie mentioned something… what have you two been up to?"

"Just enough to get her out of our lives once and for all." Casey felt her stomach clench as she watched Michael approach Melinda.

He had quietly waited for their return from Europe and while determination welled in Michael as he moved towards the crowd that had gathered around Melinda and Lyle, he had no intention of making a scene. Yet the questions that had been tormenting him for over a month now, needed to be answered. Why had Melinda lied to him about the Hidden Springs Lake resort? What was her motivation? And when would he be given the opportunity to buy out the Parkers share of his firm? Shoving his fists into his pockets, Michael pushed through the crowd of reporters that were beginning to disperse. At the sight of Lyle in the wheelchair, Michael was taken aback and in an instant lost his nerve as sympathy took over.

Lyle's sky blue eyes were now gray and slightly sunk in. His normal skin tone was ghostly pale and Michael noticed across his chest was a Velcro strap that held him up right. Even though the Parkers had put him through hell over the years, still he could not find it within himself to wish ill will on anyone, no matter how much he despised their tactics.

Sorrow grabbed Michael in his chest as he greeted Melinda "Why didn't you tell me? I could have helped." Michael leaned down, shaking Lyle's weak hand. Lyle tried to smile, but the man could barely manage to part his lips.

"Oh please Michael, don't be silly. You have the firm to run especially since you landed the Brookshire project. You need not be bothered with my problems." Melinda flipped her head as the last photographer snapped a picture. Then her eyes narrowed towards Casey who looked on from a distance.

Casey wasn't surprised by the pleasantries that were being exchanged between Michael and the Parkers especially when she caught a full glimpse of Lyle in his wheelchair. Ebbing between sadness for Mr. Parker and hope for Michael, she trusted he would handle the situation with dignity and respect. Yet she still found herself inching forward, wanting to witness the conversation taking place between Michael and the Parkers until someone stopped her.

"Miss Andrews." The scratchy voice verbalized.

Casey let out a gasp at the sight of the man standing before her. "Mr. Whitley." Casey stammered as she took a step back, offering a fearful look to the elderly man she always referred to as The Snake.

"How are you, my dear?"

"Good." Casey crinkled her nose at his question, then out of the corner of her eye, noticed that Melinda and Michael were standing even closer. The green-eyed monster of jealousy kicked Casey in the stomach as she caught Melinda reign Michael with inappropriate affection, especially in front of her incapacitated husband.

"Michael, we can't be involved with the firm anymore. Lyle's health is top priority." Swallowing her pride, Melinda made mention of the expense of their trip to Europe. "Offer whatever amount you feel is suitable. I trust you'll come up with the right figure." There was a twinkle in Melinda's eye as she touched her hand to Michael's shoulder, then slowly slid it down the sleeve of his tuxedo jacket as she gave him the once over. *"Damn, he is so handsome."* She thought to herself as the same old feelings surfaced. Giving Michael's hand a gentle squeeze, Melinda was caught between emotion and commitment, knowing her place was by Lyle's side. It was now her responsibility to take over Parker Industries and keep them accustom to the lifestyle she was use to.

Surprised by her gesture, Michael simply stated, "I'll have a check sent to your office next week. And…thank you."

"Don't thank me, thank your meddling little girlfriend." Melinda callously called out over her shoulder then gracefully turned and pushed her husband over to a table near the main entrance of the banquet hall.

Watching Michael and Melinda over Mr. Whitley's shoulder, Casey missed his question when he asked in a small voice, "Did you hear what I said, Miss Andrews?"

Casey did a double take as Mr. Whitley finally captured her attention. "What? I'm sorry but I was looking for a friend of mine."

"I said, I was wrong…for firing you and I was wondering if you wanted to come back to Whitley Designs?" He politely inquired.

Casey observed the elderly gentleman with caution, his cordial manner placing her on guard. Even though Bill and Veronica had told Casey the Snake had changed, she found it hard to believe he wasn't ready to attack his prey. "You're serious?" Mr. Whitley now had her undivided attention.

"I am. After you left and then you lured away Miss Warren…well, I had to reassess the situation and …" Mr. Whitley struggled to get out his words. "Esther, my brother's widow, stepped in. You see, Arthur wrote into his will that if you left the company, she was to take over. She told me to change my ways or leave." Mr. Whitley lowered his head, then added, "My brother thought of you as a daughter. Did you know that?"

Casey stepped back in disbelief, struggling to form a coherent sentence but when the words didn't come, the only gesture she could manage was a slight shake of her head.

The older man stepped closer to Casey, continuing, "Esther and I have decided to expand the company and we're opening new offices as far south as Georgia. The choice is yours."

From a distance, Michael saw Casey speaking with an older gentleman and at the given moment he didn't care what he was interrupting. Melinda's last statement had bowled him over. Valerie and Casey had certainly fabricated their story well to cover their tracks but now Michael had confirmation that Casey had over stepped her bounds. With his blood boiling and his anger difficult to control, Michael rudely interrupted Casey and Mr. Whitley.

"So where did you learn how to dance?" Nicole questioned as Payne held her a respectable distance from him.

"My mother. She is a professional ballroom dancer and has been in competitions since I was three. She's quite good."

"I can see that." Nicole smiled as Payne led her into another turn.

"Perhaps, you would like to accompany me to one of her competitions?"

"Maybe."

Payne smiled. It wasn't a 'no'. As the music subsided, Payne escorted Nicole to the open bar. Handing her a drink, Nicole hesitated. "Payne, I'm not of legal drinking age." She tried to hand him back the drink and order a soda, but Payne was ahead of the game.

"It's lemon-lime soda. I don't drink." He raised an eyebrow and his fluted champagne glass to Nicole's. "Shall we go out on the terrace?"

Glancing over Mr. Whitley's shoulder again, Casey saw Michael approaching with purpose. She expected him to be smiling but the expression on his face stated otherwise.

"Excuse me. Casey, I need to speak with you. Now!" She had never heard such contempt in his voice.

"Of course." Looking directly at Michael, she had expected his eyes to be dancing with happiness but when burning anger flared, Casey knew she had to excuse herself.

"I appreciate your offer, Mr. Whitley, but thank you, anyway." Embarrassed by Michael's behavior, Casey quickly turned on her heel and followed Michael, not waiting for a response from Mr. Whitley.

Walking past the dance floor, Casey held her head high, even though she knew something was not right. As she reached for the door to exit to the outside terrace, Michael had her by her upper arm and whirled her around.

"You were at the dedication for the Garrick House, weren't you?" Michael's voice was well above normal speaking level, prompting guests around them to stop and stare.

"You know I was with Valerie." Blood surged to Casey's cheeks causing her to feel lightheaded. "Can we please go outside? People are staring." Not waiting for an answer Casey slipped through the side door.

"I want an answer and I want it now! What happened at Garrick Mansion?"

Casey retorted with the same level of harshness. "Valerie asked me to meet her there." She knew it was wrong, but Casey refused to alter what her and Valerie had already told him about that day.

"Don't you dare put this on Valerie."

"I thought that is what you wanted. Your company back..." Hanging her head down, Casey fiddled with the end of the sash on her dress.

"I did, I mean I do. But I specifically told you this was between me and the Parkers." Michael emphasized. "Melinda told me everything."

"Everything?" Casey's eyes widened.

"She said that if it wasn't for you, she never would have considered selling the firm."

"Did she tell you why she wants to give up her half of the company?"

"Because Lyle fell ill and they're in need of the income for his medical expenses."

"Medical expenses…please, Michael, the Parkers have more money than…" Casey trailed off then questioned, "Is that all she said?"

"It was enough. Her husband has been in physical therapy for months. Good God Casey, of all the people I know, I thought you would be the one to have some compassion for what she's going through, but I guess I was wrong."

A chill fell over Casey and it was not from the autumn breeze that rustled the trees. It was obvious to her that Michael was fond of Melinda for what reason she could not fathom but despite all of Melinda's lies, she would not hurt him with the truth. Instead Casey remained silent.

"Don't you have anything to say?"

"No." She whispered.

"Well then listen to me and listen good, don't you *ever* get involved in my business, personally or professionally ever again. And as far as I am concerned, we're through!"

"Michael don't do this…" Casey choked on her words as she fought the tears that burned her eyes.

"And don't bother coming in on Monday."

Tears were now streaming down Casey's cheeks at the harshness of Michael's words. She desperately tried to speak but she had been rendered speechless. The hurt surging through her body was so painful that impulsively, Casey turned away from Michael and ran down the stairs that led to the sidewalk below.

Shocked by his own words and Casey's actions, Michael was immobile. Never once did Casey look back and in an instant had disappeared into the night. Clenching his fists by his side, Michael immediately regretted his anger as his head started to pound. Standing motionless, Michael tried to determine who he was angrier with, Casey or himself. Had he found other means of financing the firm, he probably wouldn't be in this mess now but at this given moment he was finding it hard to forgive Casey for interfering. Especially since, he had made it perfectly clear he would take care of it. Michael remained outside in the chilly night air trying to decipher what had happened between them since their reunion back in May. He played every event over in his mind, both good and bad and nothing changed. He was still angry and Casey was…*gone!* He had done it again. He had pushed the one woman he always loved right out of his life, again! He cursed under his breath. *"Why? I was supposed to be righting a wrong. What the hell is the matter with me?"*

Glancing at his watch, Michael realized that he had been outside for almost thirty minutes pondering every thought, every word, every action. Drawing in a deep breath, Michael concluded he would call, no, he would go see Casey tomorrow and set things right this time. As he reached for the door, the realization hit him like a Mac truck. Casey had beaten him to the punch with the Parkers and he now understood his anger. Foolish pride, once again had gotten in the way of what he really wanted. Casey. He turned and whipped the door open with unnecessary force and was greeted by Valerie.

"Who was that? I thought he was never going to leave." Payne inquired as him and Nicole stepped out of the shadows.

"Believe it or not, those two are my bosses." Nicole cautiously proceeded to tell Payne what little she knew about Michael, Casey and Melinda Parker. "So you see, Payne, it's more personal than professional. I just hope Casey and Michael can resolve their differences. They belong together." A chill ran down Nicole's back causing her to shiver.

Payne had listened intently, not surprised by Melinda's actions and now that the picture was so crystal clear, he knew he had to do the right thing. "Well, perhaps I can help?"

"How?" Nicole questioned as Payne removed his jacket, retrieving an envelope out of the breast pocket then draping his jacket over Nicole's shoulders. He tore the envelope in half again and again until it was practically confetti.

"What was that?"

"An investigative report on one of your bosses. Both Melinda and Lyle asked me to investigate…" Payne trailed off as Nicole's eyes widened in horror. "It doesn't matter. It's not important anymore. What I know, I'll take to my grave." He stated with confidence as the tiny pieces of paper fluttered into the trash and the information on Casey's father became history.

"Where's Casey? I've been looking everywhere for her."

"She left."

"Why Michael? The night's still young."

"It doesn't concern you Valerie, so please just leave me alone?"

"I can't Michael. Casey is my friend and if something is wrong, I want to know."

"This isn't high school Valerie and I am tired of Casey and I being the object of your gossip." Michael started to head towards the exit when Valerie shouted above the music.

"Amanda Carlyle."

Caught off guard, he turned and quickly escorted Valerie outside. "What did you say?"

"Amanda Carlyle." She stated sheepishly.

"What about her? What do you have to do with Amanda?"

"Not me. But she has everything to do with Melinda Parker." Valerie was deliberately being vague.

"All right Valerie, quit with the games. Out with it."

"Did you know that Amanda and Melinda are related? Did you know that they are half-sisters? And did you know that Melinda and Lyle paid Amanda to call off your marriage to her?"

Bewildered by Valerie's words, Michael could barely utter, "What did you say?"

Valerie moved closer to Michael. "Oh, you heard me loud and clear Michael. But for the record, I'll repeat myself. Amanda Carlyle is Melinda Parker's half sister. Born out of wed-lock and from the wrong side of the tracks. Didn't you know that Melinda's maiden name was Carlyle?"

"I'm not a gossip columnist like you."

Gritting her teeth, Valerie snapped, "I'm not a gossip columnist! I'm a society reporter and I'm damn good at it. When I heard that the Parker's were trying to develop the land at Hidden Springs, I did some digging on my own. It was pretty easy finding several articles linking Edwin Carlyle and Melinda Parker…"

Furrowing his brow, Michael cut Valerie off, "Why would you lie like that? It's not true."

Valerie's voice became high pitched. "I'm not lying Michael." She stated as she shook her head. "And it wasn't that difficult to put two and two together. You remember the day I ran into you and Casey at the Lake? When you were coming back from Mr. Miller's?"

Michael nodded.

"Casey and I talked about the Parkers and their plans to develop Hidden Springs Lake. Well, being the reporter that I am, I did my research. That's when I confronted Melinda at the Garrick Mansion ceremony, not Casey. I just wanted her there as a witness." Valerie paused as she softened her tone, "You know, my husband and I have worked really hard to build our cabin at the Lake, so that our children would have safe summers with good memories. So, when I heard the rumors that Parker Industries was going to tear it down, I did what I had to do, even if it meant humiliating Melinda Parker."

"But why didn't Amanda tell me her and Melinda were related? Why would Melinda not let Amanda marry me?" Michael's stomach tightened as he crossed his arms over his chest.

"Isn't it obvious, Melinda Parker's in love with you. But if you ask me, that's not how someone should treat someone they love. And..." her voice trailed off then she added, "...Casey. I see the way she looks at you... she still loves you Michael."

"I have to go." Again Michael cut Valerie off as he ran down the steps.

"Where are you going?" Valerie shouted.

"To find Casey."

A gust of wind sent a shiver down Casey's spine as she slowed her pace at the corner of Madison and Calverton. The autumn evening had unexpectedly turned chilly as the wind stung her exposed skin. Folding her arms around her, she was all too familiar with her surroundings. Passing by The Corner Café, Casey noticed that it was filled to capacity with its usually Saturday night crowd. Out of breath and her feet aching, Casey rationalized, "*I have to stop.*" When the sign for Sterling Architects and Construction came into view, a mixture of emotions stirred inside of her. All the events of the past six months swirled in her head, making her feel ill. Decisively, she sat down on the step that led to the front door of the firm. Staring out into the distance, sweet memories of Michael danced before her as well as disturbing nightmares of Melinda Parker. The cold of the night was engulfing her and Casey was on the edge of tears when the calling of her name startled her back to reality.

"Casey!" The deep male voice was sharp. Holding her breath, she recognized the familiar voice and wanted to run but her body would not move. Again a voice called out, but this time it was soft and melodic. Casey let out a breath and stepped forward, relieved to see Julie.

Running towards Casey, Julie wrapped her arm around her best friend. "Thank God you are all right. We've been looking for you for hours."

Casey wanted to apologize but as she started to speak the only thing that came were the tears.

Eric jumped out of the limousine. Removing his tuxedo jacket, he draped it over her shoulders then escorted Casey towards the waiting sedan. The warmth inside the vehicle blanketed Casey but she still shivered not from the chill of the evening but from the tears that would not subside.

"Everything's going to be okay." Julie hugged her friend again. "Nicole told us everything and we talked to Michael and…"

"I don't want to see him." Casey choked.

"Casey…" Julie pronounced in her sing-song voice.

Eric handed Casey his handkerchief. As she wiped her stained cheeks, looking straight into Julie's eyes, there was a determined harshness to her words, "I don't ever want to hear that name ever again. I don't want to see or talk to Michael Sterling ever again! I just want to go home."

"Casey, Michael knows he was wrong."

"Yeah, he told me to tell you to come to work on Monday." Eric encouraged.

"Absolutely not!" Casey's hurt twisted into anger. "You two weren't there!" Casey shook her head. "He made it perfectly clear that we were through. He doesn't want me there and I don't want to be…" Drawing in a deep breath, she raised her shoulders then exhaled. Spite entwined her words, "In fact, I think I'll take Mr. Whitley up on his offer."

"What!" Julie shrieked.

"I ran into Mr. Whitley this evening and he asked me to come back to Whitley Designs and I'm…"

"You can't be serious! The Snake! Are you out of your mind? You can't, Casey, you just can't." Julie was practically on the brink of tears when Eric gently wrapped his arm around her.

Casey narrowed her brown eyes, "You just watch me."

"But…" Julie started.

Casey held up her hand, cutting Julie off. "Look, I know you mean well but I think it is best for everyone that there needs to be a lot of time and distance between us, him, you know who…so please, don't make any attempts at trying to get us back together."

Julie folded her arms across her chest in defeated.

Snuggling into the comfort of Eric's jacket, Casey was firm, "I need some time to myself. Can you please just respect that?" She didn't wait for a response as she stared out the window at the blurring neon. But it wasn't from the speed at which the limo was progressing, it was from the tears Casey fought to hide.

Just before the driver pulled up to Casey's apartment complex she suddenly realized she had left her belongings at the Convention Center, with her abrupt exit. She turned to Julie, "I left my purse at the Banquet Hall. We have to go…"

Before Casey finished her sentence, Julie held out a small maroon satin bag. Not another word was spoken between them until the driver opened the car door. Returning Eric's jacket to him, Casey simply stated, "I'll talk to you next week." Waiting for a response from Julie, she hesitated getting out of the car. When Julie refused to reply, Casey stepped out of the vehicle, shut the door, turned and walked to her apartment building.

The flashing red light in the darkness of the one bedroom apartment was the first thing Casey noticed as she opened the door then tossed her keys onto the end table in the living room. Relieved to be home, she turned on various lights then crossed the room to her answering machine. Depressing the button the automated voice echoed, "You have seven new messages…" The first message was from Julie. "Casey, Eric and I are looking everywhere for you. If you're home call one of our cells phones. We know what happened. Bye."

The second was a hang up. "Mike is really worried and so are we. We tried your cell phone but you must have it turned off. Where are you? Please call." Eric had left the third message. The next message came from Valerie, "Casey, I am so, so sorry. I told Michael that this was my doing. Call him when you get this and me too. Hang in there. Don't give up. I'll talk to you later. Bye."

As the machine played out the recorded calls, Casey moved over to the sofa and surrendered to the exhaustion that now swept over her. Removing her high heels, she began to rub her aching feet as Michael's voice filled the room.

"I'm sorry…"

"You should be…" Casey stated sarcastically as she threw her shoe across the room but it missed the answering machine.

"…Casey. Please call me. I was wrong…about everything. We really need to talk… "

"No we don't." Casey replied as she turned off the machine refusing to listen to anything more Michael Sterling had to say. Meandering into her bedroom, Casey slipped out of her red velvet gown and crawled into Michael's tattered soccer shirt. As she grabbed the crotchet blanket, her mom had made for her when she was sixteen, from her bed, the phone rang. But Casey put forth no effort to answer it. She just let it ring as she turned on the television and surfed the channels. A few minutes had passed and the ringing finally stopped. Opting to leave on the Home and Garden channel, Casey curled up on the sofa and cried.

Chapter 16

As he listened to her voice mail, a flicker of hope still burned inside him, believing this time Casey would answer her phone. But when she didn't, Michael cursed today's technology as he placed the receiver back in its cradle. Yet he knew he couldn't really blame it on the phone company's technical advancements because her silence said it all. Days had turned into weeks, weeks into a month and Casey had ignored his every move. He concluded it was time to throw in the towel. And while it pained him to have to sever all ties with Casey Andrews, her lack of response hurt even more.

For now, Michael had to address the issue of the minor dent that was left in his company's assets after the repurchase of the Parker's fifty-one percent. After printing several spreadsheets, he went to meet with Beth Smith, his in house accountant, since Sterling Architects had been established. Together they spent hours examining line item after line item. Because of Beth's meticulous records of every penny ever spent and earned, including Michael's short lived game of Russian roulette with the Stock Market, he realized she was on top of her game.

"Michael, I promise you that we are operating in the black."

Rubbing his eyes, he agreed. "I know. Your attention to detail shows."

"You know, the revenue that Casey generated shouldn't be overlooked either, since she…" Beth did a double take as she noticed the dismal expression on Michael's face. "I'm so sorry. That was very insensitive…"

He stopped her in mid-sentence. "She's still part of this company. Don't worry about it."

"And you don't need to worry about the financial statements. With the exception of the few clients we had to set up on a payment plan, we're set." Beth affirmed confidently.

Still, Michael made it his soul purpose or rather his excuse to rebuild the company's cash flow to a level he was use to. He had been here before, giving it his all, so the extra hours and the numerous meetings, including wining and dining clients, did not fetter his spirit. Falling into bed each night, exhausted, to him was therapy. The busier he was, the less time he had to think about Casey.

As the morning hours slipped into afternoon, Michael accepted the fact that Beth had everything under control and it was time to return to his office.

After setting up a few meetings with potential clients, Michael instinctively dialed Casey's extension. But when Maggie answered the phone, he realized he had already broken his resolution. And in an instant a dull pain throbbed in his chest, reminding him she was working at home.

Still in the dark as to how Eric had convinced Casey to finish out her contract, Michael continually begged him for an answer but he always got the same response. "I convinced her to stay on. It's not important how, so let's just leave it at that." Eric was torn both personally and professionally between the two of them. Unless it was business related, he refused to divulge the details of any conversations he was having with Casey.

Michael tried to shake off the emptiness that brewed inside of him. Caught up with the nitty-gritty details of his daily responsibilities, he considered calling it a day. But that thought was dashed when Eric strolled into his office.

"Man Mike, you look like you're sick or something." He observed as he positioned himself in a chair across from Michael's desk. Crossing one leg over his knee, Eric tugging at a thread that hung from the hole in the knee of his worn jeans. Eric did a double take as he eyed the photograph of him, Julie, Michael and Casey, arm in arm, grinning from ear to ear. Nicole had taken it upon herself to photo journal the progress of Hearth and Home Project. But what Eric didn't know, was that Nicole was putting together several scrapbooks and journals, her latest hobby, for both him and Nancy, as a Christmas present. Smiling, Michael's response to his comment did not quite register.

"Nah. I skipped breakfast. I just need to grab some lunch." Michael reasoned knowing full well it had nothing to do with food.

Eric chuckled at their four smiling facings that were spattered with paint. He knew it was a childish thought, but they had become the four musketeers if only for a brief moment. The Charity Dinner was that last time they had been together. If only Melinda Parker had kept her mouth shut. If the opportunity ever presented itself, he had a thing or two to say to that villainous woman. And he wasn't the only one either. Both Julie and Valerie had verbalized, on several occasions, their thoughts about the infamous Melinda Parker. Yet they knew better. They could not get involved.

"You want to go to The Corner Café?" Michael questioned noticing that Eric was staring at the framed photo that was perfectly positioned on the credenza behind him.

"I can't. I have a meeting downtown. You want to go with me? It'll get you out of the office for awhile."

"No. I have a ton of paperwork to go over. I was just going to run out and grab something to go." Michael rubbed his brow. "She won't return my calls."

"Mike, I really don't want to get in the middle of this." Actually he did but he wasn't going to tell Michael or Casey how he felt. Eric had grown fond of Casey over the past six months and he knew it had all been a series of misunderstandings that could be cleared up, if only he could get them in the same room together. With that in mind, it was like a light bulb had lit up a windowless room and the wheels began to turn in his mind.

Michael ignored Eric's comment as he continued. "The only contact we've had is e-mail. And she's keeping it very professional." Michael paused, wishing Eric could give him an unbiased opinion but when his business partner remained unobtrusive, Michael pressed on with the conversation. "Jeez, her e-mails start out with 'Mr. Sterling, As per your request...' and she signs them, Casey Andrews, Sterling Architects, Interior Design Manager. It's nerve racking. Without saying a word, I'm hearing her loud and clear."

Eric raised a brow to Michael. "Are you finished?"

Michael nodded.

"Can I ask you a question?" Eric didn't wait for a response as he broke his vow. "Do you love her? Because if you do, find a way to tell her. Quit burying your head in your work. Either you need to show her or tell her how you feel or you need to let her go. The choice is yours. But I wouldn't wait much longer if I were you because the end of the year is coming fast and so is her employment. Julie and Maggie are up to speed on all her projects and they're ready to take over. Rumor has it, she's taking a job with Whitley in South Carolina. So time is not on your side my friend." Eric stood and shrugged. "It's up to you to make your feelings known."

"Casey would never go back to her old job. She hated working for Mr. Whitley. Don't her and Julie refer to him as the Snake?"

Eric ignored Michael's question as he stood to exit the office.

"What would you do?" Michael abruptly asked.

Pondering for a moment, Eric simply replied, "Something completely unexpected."

Michael had been racking his brain for a week. He thought all his previous gestures had been something completely unexpected and now he was at a total loss. Too much time had passed and Casey had returned every gift, unopened, every letter, unread and every phone call, unanswered. It was now the day before Thanksgiving and Michael was looking forward to his ski trip, alone. Away from the constant reminder that Casey was no longer a part of his life.

"What time does your flight leave?" Michael dropped his pen on the paperwork and shoved it off to the side, as Donna, brought them their lunch.

"I think five thirty." Eric eyed his watch then dug into his sandwich. Propping his elbows on the table and eyeing Julie, he bragged, "Yeah buddy. This time tomorrow we'll be drinking in the tropical breeze, basking in the rays of the Bahamian sun and sucking on Bahama Mama's." Eric's mood shifted as he imagined Julie in her bikini and a smile ran across his face. If Casey had not accepted Michael's offer to work at Sterling Architects, Eric may have never met the woman he wanted to marry... someday.

"Sounds nice." Michael stated quite matter-of-factly.

"Michael, Casey and I went shopping this weekend." Julie smiled as she tasted her salad.

For a brief moment, Michael wondered why Julie would make such a comment. Then it dawned on him, "So you two are friends, again? Not just co-workers?"

"Oh yeah. We worked that out awhile ago."

Eric eyed Julie wondering why she would be sharing any information about Casey to Michael when they had agreed to not get involved or at the very least, not to mention their involvement with each of them. It was no surprise to Eric that Julie had cooked up a fool proof plan to get them back together. Now he was just hoping she wouldn't expose them.

"Well, I'm glad you're friends again." Michael questioned as he bit into his sandwich.

"Yeah, I ended up buying the cutest little skiing outfit." Julie stated so matter-of-factly.

Michael creased his brow. "What are you talking about?"

"We're thinking about going skiing for New Year's." Eric lied trying to cover Julie's slip up. "Maybe we could all go. Make it an office trip."

Michael simply nodded as he continued with his lunch. Quietly, he gave Julie and Eric the once over, wondering if they were plotting something and not letting him in on it. But that thought seemed unreasonable since Eric had repeated himself over and over that him and Julie were remaining neutral.

Eric had quickly finished his sandwich while Julie pushed away her half eaten salad. "We better get going." Eric turned to Julie as he reached into his back pocket for his wallet.

"I'll take care of this." Michael held up his hand, motioning for Eric to put away his money, then added, "You can get it next time. You two, go. Have fun."

As Julie stood she slung her purse over her shoulder, asking, "When do you leave for Blue Mountain Lodge?"

"Anytime I want to." Michael was a tad bit sarcastic but he quickly changed his tone. "After I take this paper work back to the office with me. I want to get a few runs in before it gets too dark."

"Good." Julie's over enthusiastic smile left Michael curious.

He knew her a little too well. With his curiosity piqued, he wondered what she was up to.

"Have fun skiing." Julie shouted over her shoulder just before the door closed to The Corner Café.

Drawing in a breath, she tried to tame her excitement. "I know this is so deceptive but it's going to work out. Mark my words."

"Honey, I know you mean well, but don't get upset if this little scheme of yours backfires. You almost gave it away."

"I know. I can't help myself." She admitted, placing her hand in Eric's as they crossed the street to the parking garage. But then she had to reassure Eric if not herself, "It just has to work."

Sighing as he climbed the stairs to his office, Michael paused. Looking around the office that was now expanded and occupied by Julie and Maggie, there was little evidence that Casey had been its original occupant. He fought to keep the words from spilling from his mouth and sounding like a hopeless idiot, especially since he had let everyone leave at lunchtime. But before he could stop himself, his confession rolled off his tongue. "Everything reminds me of you." He missed her bursting into his office, interrupting important phone calls with a new idea. The long hours working together, stealing sweet kisses, and the playful laughter that followed. He missed her sparkling smile and her kind-hearted nature. And as if Casey was standing before him, he spoke aloud. "Casey Andrews you may think it's over, but I still love you. And I miss you like crazy." And for the first time since their explosive argument back in October, Michael allowed emotion to well at the corner of his eye. And that's when he realized, her mere presence put him on cloud nine but since her absence, Michael felt like he was living in hell.

Casey had been so engrossed in the CAD drawing she had been working on, she didn't even realize it was twenty minutes past mid-night until she glanced at the clock on the wall. Time seemed to have slipped by. And indeed it had. Having disconnected herself from Michael, she found it hard to believe she hadn't spoken nor seen him in over a month. As she reflected on the past six months, Casey wondered what she could have done differently. It certainly had been a whirlwind of events and a roller coaster ride of emotions. As she shut down her computer, she shook her head.

Meandering into the kitchen, Casey filled the kettle, turned on the burner and waited for the water to boil. Quietly reflecting, if she had to do it all again, she wouldn't change a thing. Her tumultuous romance with Michael, even if it was only for a few months, was worth it, because for a brief moment he had loved her again.

Spooning sugar into her tea, a sadness fell over Casey. The holidays were approaching rapidly and she dreaded spending them alone. And right now Thanksgiving was looking pretty bleak. Casey went through a checklist in her head, of whom she could have spent the holiday with but then it dawned on her, everyone had travel plans. While shopping last weekend, Julie had made it a big deal about her and Eric going skiing while Hannah, Adam and the kids were driving to Georgia to be with Adam's parents. Julie had also mentioned that Michael was flying to Key West to go sailing with a rather wealthy client. At one of their many lunches they had share over the past month, Valerie had begged her to come to Hidden Springs Lake to see Mr. Miller's Veteran's club re-enact the first Thanksgiving Dinner. Since she was not ready to face the memories that still shrouded her mind. Casey turned down Valerie's invitation as well. Her final invite came from Nancy Kirby. The Women of Hope Auxiliary were serving Thanksgiving dinner at one of the local homeless shelters then her and Sean were headed to Hidden Springs as well, where evidently a rather serious Payne Claiborne and Nicole, along with her parents, were joining them on Friday. Contemplating it was too late to accept anyone's invitation, Casey chalked it up to her dark mood.

After finishing her tea, Casey went to her bedroom. Feeling restless, she knew sleep was going to elude her, so she picked up the novel off her nightstand, trying to remember where she had left off. Unable to concentrate, she rationalized, *"There are others worse off then me...maybe I can go to a movie or start packing. Packing...how am I going to tell Michael I'm moving to South Carolina?"* She tossed the question around for another minute then pushed it from her mind. It was not going to be easy to say good-bye to her friends but all the tell-tale signs were apparent. It was time to move on. Eventually she would have to give Michael her two week notice. She dreaded the idea but she owed him a respectful and reasonable notice, if nothing else. Returning to her reading, the hours passed. Finally her eyelids grew heavy and her book tumble to the floor.

Morning came too soon. Snuggling underneath the warmth of her comforter, Casey wanted to remain in the protective cocoon. Barely past seven, she tried to fall back to sleep but the ringing of the phone startled her.

"Happy Thanksgiving! Did I wake you?" Julie's voice was too perky for this time of day.

"No, I was just laying in bed." Casey yawned then added, "Why are you calling me at the crack of dawn?"

"Well, Eric and I talked about it again last night and we want you to come skiing with us. No one should be alone on Thanksgiving or any other holiday for that matter." Julie crossed her fingers as she eyed Eric. "We have a two bedroom suite at Blue Mountain Lodge, so there is plenty of room."

Casey rolled her eyes. "Julie, we've been over this enough. I've spent holidays alone before and I've survived. Besides I'm not in the mood for driving."

Julie sat up in bed as Eric handed her a freshly brewed cup of coffee. Taking a sip, she quickly commented, "Well you're going to have to get in the mood."

Casey sat up with a start. Her comforter fell from her shoulders causing a chill to race through her body. "What are you up to Julie Warren? This better not be some elaborate plot to get Michael and I back together."

Almost choking on her coffee, Julie cleared her throat, "Now what makes you think that? You made it perfectly clear that we're to stay out of your affairs…I mean business. Besides, I told you he's in the Keys." Julie set her mug on the nightstand then looked up at Eric with wide eyes. "Casey if you leave by nine, you can be at the Lodge by lunchtime. Now get your butt in gear."

"Are you sure he's in Florida?" Casey questioned suspiciously but then again why would Julie lie?

"As far as I know, that's where he is. Enough about Michael. So, we'll meet you in the lobby around noon."

"You're not going to take no for an answer, are you?" Casey was finally letting her guard down. She didn't have any other plans and skiing would be fun. Plus, maybe the mountain air would clear her head. "All right. I'll see you later." Casey smiled as she hung up the phone and headed to the shower.

"Jeez, she is a tough sell." Julie commented to Eric as she placed the phone down on the receiver.

"Well, she bought it and that's all that matters. Are you ready to go get breakfast and then hit the beach?"

"Absolutely. But let me call Blue Mountain Lodge. I want to make sure Michael checked in last night."

Eric shook his head. He had to hand it to her, Julie's hope was unrelenting.

An hour and a half later, after Casey had tossed some sweaters, jeans and the essential clothing to go skiing into her small suitcase, she was well on her way to Blue Mountain Lodge.

It was a quiet drive as Casey progressed northwest towards the mountains. Snow started covering the landscape and the roadway became difficult to navigate. Easing her foot off the accelerator, Casey dropped her speed to thirty-five miles per hour, slowing down her trip significantly. When she spotted the road sign that read, Blue Mountain Lodge, 3 miles, Casey was relieved. Still, the last three miles to the Lodge's parking lot took almost a half hour.

Slipping from the driver seat, the chill of the mountain air caught Casey by surprise as well as the snow. But then she reminded herself, she was three hours north of the city. And snow in November was not unusual for the area. Wrapping her pale pink scarf around her neck, she zipped her winter coat up to her chin. Digging her mitted hands into her pockets, Casey made her way through the icy parking lot, towards the oversized double wooden doors. Peering inside, Casey was unable to see if Eric and Julie were waiting for her in the lobby because the bay window was steamed over.

Content to be in the warmth of the lodge, Casey scanned the lobby. The main lodge was a mixture of modern and rustic décor. While the structure of the building was that of a log cabin, the counter top at the reservation desk and the window sills were finished in white marble with traces of brown and gray. Various brass light fixtures softly illuminated the room. The aroma of hot chocolate tickled Casey's nose causing her to turn towards the group of men and women that huddled around the roaring fire. They sat comfortably on two brown leather sofas, facing each other. In between was a dark cherry wood coffee table, displaying a couple of coffee table books and a whicker basket full of fruits and vegetables. Hand carved signs hung over two opposing archways, indicating the Restaurant and Lounge were to the right while rooming accommodations along with other hotel services were to the left of the reservationist desk.

"May I help you?" A young red headed gentleman asked.

Casey looked around and realizing there was no sign of Eric or Julie and that the reservations clerk was addressing her. Approaching the reddish-orange haired man, she noticed he was in need of a shave. Dressed in a black turtleneck, a red and black flannel shirt and blue jeans, she giggled slightly thinking he looked like the man on the paper towel label.

"May I help you, please?" He dragged out the last word, not amused by Casey's laughter.

"Oh, I'm sorry. I was looking for my friends. I believed they checked in yesterday. Eric Logan and Julie Warren."

The young man quickly changed his attitude and busied himself at the computer, "Yes, you're room is ready for you."

Julie had cleverly placed the reservation in all their names, knowing the hotel could not reveal whether or not they had checked in. She had also managed to leave a message for Casey, upon her arrival.

"I have a message here for you."

Casey read the note that simply stated, "Meet at the chair lift."

Once Casey was checked in the clerk handed her the room key without another word.

"Thank you." She mustered then headed to her room. When Casey opened the door she was puzzled it had been unoccupied and wondered why the clerk did not give her a key to Eric and Julie's suite. Maybe they got a room just for her, Casey reasoned after dropping off her belongings and quickly heading outside. Stepping into the cold of the afternoon, Casey made her way through the snow that was now falling heavier. There was little evidence of footprints in the snow, on the trail that led to the ski lift. Upon her approach, she noticed that the chairs were empty.

"Base one, were coming down the mountain. Did you radio the doc to meet us at First Aid? Over."

"Affirmative, Base two. What is your ETA? Over." A tall broad shouldered man with black hair stood outside the lift ticket booth waiting for a response.

"Eight to twelve minutes. Visibility is decreasing rapidly. Over."

"Copy that. Over and out." He turned and opened the half door to the tiny shelter.

"Sorry, the lift is temporarily closed."

His words caused Casey's mid-section to tighten yet she could not pinpoint why. "Ah, I'm not here to ski, I'm looking for…I don't suppose you would remember a guy…tall, curly hair and a short blonde girl…" Casey asked through chattering teeth. Why didn't Julie and Eric just meet her in the lobby like they said they were going to, unless…

"What's his name?" The man cut into Casey's curious thoughts.

"Logan. Eric Logan and Julie Warren." Casey glanced down at her snow-covered boots, wiggling her toes inside them that were starting to go numb.

"Base two from base one. Over." Again the man was on the radio.

"Go ahead base one. Over."

"Have you established an identity on the victims? Over."

"Affirmative. A Log…" static cut off the rest of the transmission. Anxiety surged through Casey's chilled body.

"Base two, you're breaking up. Repeat. Over." Again static cut off their broadcasting abilities.

"Base two. Repeat. Over." The man waited a few minutes but received no response.

The man shrugged. "Sorry." When he saw the frown on Casey's face, he added, "They're due to arrive in…" he glanced at his watch, "…five minutes, if you want to wait."

Casey nodded. The clouds hung heavy over the mountain top, casting dark shadows on the mountainside. The midday sun was replaced by large snowflakes, blanketing the land. Looking up at the ski lift attendant's dark eyes, Casey wondered, "Can you tell me what happened?"

He looked around to see if anyone else was near, "I'm not supposed to, but two skiers, a male and female collided. The woman is okay but the doc will probably examine her just to be sure. As for the man, he blew out his knee. Rescue thinks he might have broken his leg."

With every fiber of her being, Casey tried to convince herself it wasn't Julie and Eric but with the lack of radio communications and identities unknown, an uneasy feeling fell over her, tying her stomach in knots.

"Base one from base two. Over."

"Go ahead base two. Over."

"We're about two hundred yards out. Over."

"Copy base two. I have a visual. Over." He turned to Casey, "Here they come."

Through the blur of the falling snow, she barely made out eight figures in bright red jackets, skiing down the mountain with two metal stretchers in tow. She wanted to run towards them but her feet would not move.

As a woman approached from behind, dressed in the same red jacket and carrying a radio, the man from the ski lift ticket booth sprinted towards the rescue team, joining in their efforts. Rushing by, Casey failed to get a glimpse of the victims being taken to the First Aid Station and instinctively she followed a few feet behind.

"Aagghhh!" The man let out a boisterous roar of agony as he was lifted onto the exam table while the woman was taken to an exam room behind a closed curtain.

"I'm all right." The woman demanded to an attending nurse but Casey barely heard what she said as commotion enveloped the room.

"Get her out of here!" An older man with silver hair glared at Casey as he placed a stethoscope to his ears then pumped the blood pressure cuff that was on the man's arm.

Then the man from the ski lift booth quickly approached Casey, wrapped an arm around her shoulder and escorted her outside.

"But...I have to know, if it's Eric and Julie!" Casey shrieked trying to look over her should to get a quick look of who was being treated.

The man whirled Casey around to face him. Leaning forward he got caught up in her beautiful brown eyes. Clearing his throat, he said, "Look, if your friends are in there, you have to stay calm. Understand?" He tightened his grip a little more and then added, "I *will* find out what's going on; in the mean time why don't you go wait in the lounge?"

Tears streamed Casey's red cheeks. "But...I need to know, now!" Her words were jagged as she fought her tears.

"My name is Hank. Why don't I go inside with you? I'll come back over here in a few minutes and get their names, okay?" Nodding, Casey sniffed as Hank released his grip and loosely draped his arm across her shoulder. "What's your name?"

"Ca-sey." She struggled through the cold and fear.

The warmth of the lobby embraced Casey and so did Hank. As she wiped the tears from her face, Casey turned into the security of Hank's arms, not noticing the two men standing at the reservations desk.

One of them looked on in disbelief as Hank and Casey disappeared into the lounge. Hank escorted Casey to a small booth in the corner of the lounge. "What do you want to drink?"

"Nothing for me, thanks." With the exception of a few employees that were beginning to set up for the Thanksgiving buffet, they were the only patrons in the lounge.

"Have something. It's on me."

"Ah, hot chocolate…or whatever?" Casey was still distraught not knowing the identity of the ski victims and the fact that Julie and Eric were nowhere to be found. *"Maybe it's just a coincidence."* She reasoned quietly then her thoughts began to snowball. How much more drama could she face in less than a year? And what a year it had been. A new job, a rekindled romance and old friendships renewed, Casey knew change was evident but all at once was almost too much to handle. And sadly enough, two out of the three had not lasted. Was she about to lose her friends as well? With her employment contract coming to an end and Michael completely out of her life, Casey could only hope that a new beginning would bring the histrionics in her life to an end.

"It's going to be okay." Hank's deep tone resonated as he set down their beverages, taking a seat next to Casey.

"I know." But Casey didn't believe him as a shiver emanated down her spine. All the evidence proved it was Eric and Julie who had the skiing accident.

"Your friends are in good hands. But it's not like your boyfriend or brother or sister or someone like that, who got hurt."

Casey gasped at Hank's ridiculous remark. "How can you be so insensitive? What makes you say something like that? They are my best friends. They mean the world to me." Her edginess was apparent as she tightly twisted a lock of hair around her finger that had fallen out of her french braid.

"I'm sorry. What I meant was…it's just that you're pretty upset. And I know your are trying not to cry." At Hank's observation, a tiny tear slipped out of the corner of her eye. He gently touched his fingertip to her cheek, trying to wipe away her anguish. And his gesture was comforting, if only for the moment. "Let me run over to First Aid and find out what's going on." Hank exited not even noticing the man approaching Casey.

"What are you doing here?" His caustic tone resonated throughout the restaurant as she looked up, locking eyes with Michael Sterling. Jumping from her seat, Casey spilled Hank's coffee across the table but gave it no regard as she leaped into his arms, coming to rest her cheek against his chest.

Michael's response, however, was heartless. He jerked her arms from around his neck. Clamping his hands down on her shoulders he sternly asked, "Casey...Casey! What are you crying about now?" Realizing his own harshness, his toned shifted with his next question. "Did something happen?"

"Eric...Julie...they had a skiing accident and they're over in..." Again, she burst into tears.

"Casey...Casey! Eric and Julie are in the Bahamas. Now, what you're doing here and who was that guy?"

Stunned, she fell back into her seat, reeling from his words...and his proximity.

Reaching into the back pocket of his jeans, Michael pulled out his handkerchief, shoving it into Casey's trembling hand.

She managed to utter, "Nothing." as she traced the embroidered initials on the cloth. A smile came to Casey's face, remembering the first time Michael had handed her his hanky.

Again his tone was sharp. "What is going on with you?" He drew in a breath and then moved closer, whispering, "My patience is wearing thin, will you tell me what happened? Was that guy bothering you?" Just as Michael asked the question, Hank reappeared.

Crossing his arms over his chest, Hank grumbled, "Well, it's not your friends. Their last name is Loggias or something like that." He stated firmly as he creased his brow at Michael. The tension between the two of them was so thick, Hank felt like he couldn't breath. "I'm leaving. Casey, I'll catch you later."

Looking up, Casey smiled. "Thank you, Hank."

Just then another voice cut through Casey's anxiety. "Hey Mike..." Eyeing the tall lanky man standing behind Michael, she recognized Scott Rezabeck, Paul Rezabeck's son. Mortified, Casey wanted to crawl under the table knowing Scott had witnessed such an emotional scene. Sweeping her hand over her hair, Casey wished he would stop staring her down. She was embarrassed enough without a client becoming involved in this mess of yet another misunderstanding.

Finally, Michael stepped up to the plate, in his most professional manner, introduced Scott to Casey.

Smiling, he reached his hand out to Casey, giving hers a small squeeze. "Of course. We've met once or twice before but it's been awhile. How are you?"

Looking down, she twisted the end of her braid, whispering, "I think I'm catching a cold. But I'm fine. Thank you for asking." Casey fibbed.

Clearing his throat, Scott patted Michael on the shoulder, "I'm going to look in on my wife. Maybe I'll catch you on the slopes tomorrow." In an instant they were alone.

"Sure thing." Michael shrugged nonchalantly but his response to Scott was quite the opposite of the way he was feeling. His muscles were tense and he ached all over, concluding the achiness was from skiing the previous day but the tension was the mere presences of Casey Andrews. They had not been in the same room since the night of the Charity Dinner.

"We're alone." He reassured then turned on Casey. "Now are you going to tell me what the hell is going on!" Michael was irate and it showed. And it bothered him even more so, since the last thing he wanted was to be cross.

"I thought that..." Unable to finish her sentence, Casey's words were a mix of laughter and tears. "I'm going to kill them when I get my hands on them!"

Michael was so baffled he didn't know what to say as he practically fell into the seat. Settling in across from Casey, he rested closed fists on the table, aware that he was inches away from reaching out and touching Casey's hand. But he held that action at bay.

Finally she laughed. "Well, I'm not really going to kill them." Looking into Michael's irresistible eyes, Casey knew he was still confused. "Eric and Julie called me this morning, inviting me to go skiing..."

As Casey recapped her day, Michael realized it was Eric and Julie who had cooked up something completely unexpected and now it was up to him to follow through.

The set up may have been funny but Casey was starting to see that the joke was on her and it was no longer a laughing matter. "So...this whole time they've been sunning in the Bahamas? So, I've been had by all of you." Shaking her head in disbelief, she laid more napkins over the spilled coffee then concluded. "Well, I'm going home." Abruptly jumping from her seat, Michael caught Casey by her arm. Whirling her around, he demanded, "Sit down. We have to talk."

Wide-eyed, Casey stared him down for what seemed like an eternity. "Get your hands off of me!" Her demand was heard as a scream and in an instant Hank had returned to the lounge.

"Casey, are you all right?"

Looking up into Hank's puppy dog eyes, she begged, "Get me out of here."

Then Hank added, "Looks like you're the one bothering her."

Casey's voice cracked as Hank escorted her to the lobby and the last words Michael heard pass from her lips was, "I am so over this. I can't wait to get out of here."

"Casey, you can't!" Hank persisted as he followed her outside. A gust of wind caught the flailing ends of her scarf as she struggled to zip her coat. Air born, her scarf took off with the increasing winds, then it wafted to the ground, landing at Hank's feet. Immediately, he retrieved it off the wet ground, and in one endless motion, whirled Casey around, wrapping her scarf around her neck.

"Thank you." She chattered as she turned and headed to her car.

"Where do you think your going?"

"I told you. Home!" She abruptly turned. "Look, I really appreciate all your help but I've had enough of this holiday. I just want to go home." Casey's words sounded as if she was on the brink of tears again.

"You can't!" Hank yelled over the howling winter wind.

"Why not?" Casey shouted in return.

"For one thing, you didn't check out. Don't you have your luggage or something?"

"Yes." She pronounced succinctly mostly because she was angry with herself for her absentmindedness.

"You still can't go. The Mountain Patrol just closed the interstate. No one is coming or going until this blizzard is over."

Defeated, Casey's shoulders fell in dismay. "Now what am I going to do?"

"Stay and have Thanksgiving dinner with me." Hank smiled as he draped an arm across Casey shoulders, leading her back to the warmth of the Lodge.

Giving it some thought, Casey's eyes lit up when she said, "I'd love to."

After Hank escorted Casey to her room, she decided to take a long hot bath. The sweet scent of jasmine permeated the steamy air as the bubble bath warmed her through and through. Flipping another page over in the novel she had been sporadically reading, Casey realized, if she didn't get out of the tub soon, she'd turn into a prune. Finishing the chapter, she folded down the corner of the page, then tossed it across the bathroom floor. Wrapping her bathrobe about her, Casey meandered over to the bed and for the first time in a long time, sleep came easily. As she drifted into a deep slumber visions of Michael appeared.

"...Michael, be careful. You're too close. Michael, please. Michael! No!" Casey sat up, her heart pounding. Desperately trying to remember the details of her dream she picked up the phone and dialed the reservations desk. Her voice was scratchy as she spoke, "Michael Sterling's room."

"Just one moment, I'll connect you."

"Oh Michael, thank God you're there. Is everything okay?"

"Yeah, why? Wait, where are you? You ran off so quickly...where did you go?"

"I'm in my room." Casey stated flatly then just above a whisper told Michael, "We do need to talk. Can you come to my room?"

"I don't think that is such a good idea."

"Michael, please."

"Look Casey, I don't know what you want from me. You haven't talked to me in months and then you suddenly show up here, concocting some story about Eric and Julie. Then you're hugging me as if I had been resurrected from the dead. And then you go running off with some guy. I give up. Now, I'm the one that has nothing to say." Michael knew he was being cruel but he too had had enough. Maybe all along his intentions had been wrong. Maybe Casey had been right. Maybe they should have just left it in the past.

"But Michael, I explained what happened." There was a deafening silence on the other end of the line. "Michael?"

"I'm here." His voice was tender and soft, "Why don't we have dinner tonight. We can talk then. I'll come by your room in about an hour?"

"But...aren't you here with Scott Rezabeck?" Then Casey remembered her plans with Hank. Everything was a mess and the room was starting to spin. How did it get to this? There was too much confusion and too much miscommunication and Casey wanted it to end.

Michael interrupted her thoughts, "I just ran into him this afternoon. He's here with his wife and kids."

"I see." Even though Casey had not verbalized it, Michael was not off her list of suspects. His past actions were all about trying to get her attention and now he had it. All she needed now was his confession that he was the one who had conjured up this elaborate plan to reunite them.

"What room are you in?"

"Two seventeen."

Just then there was a knock on the door that adjoined to the next room.

Perplexed, Casey told Michael to hold on. Placing the phone down on the bed, she turned the lock and cracked the door open.

"See you in a little while." Michael smiled then hung up the phone.

Casey crossed her arms over her chest, pursing her lips. "Boy, this was planned just a little bit too carefully."

"Meaning?"

"I'll tell you about it at dinner. I'm going to get ready."

As Casey shut the door to the adjoining room, Michael realized he had been too hard on her. And as the lock clicked he knew he didn't want locked doors or anything else separating them ever again. He wanted her in his life both personally and professionally. Determined to win her heart, Michael grabbed his room key and headed downstairs.

Back at their hotel room, Eric made himself comfortable in the recliner while Julie undressed in the bathroom. With the door slightly cracked open, she called out, "So, do you think our little plan worked?"

"Our plan? I don't know if I want to be included in your little scheme."

"What?" Julie yelled over the sound of the running water. Then she peeked out into the living room. "Come in here and talk to me while I take a shower."

Cocking an eyebrow, Eric was surprised at how relaxed Julie had become with him. Their relationship had certainly moved forward and probably next year at this time, they would be on their honeymoon. Still Eric didn't think it was a good idea and he told her so.

"Oh for gosh sakes, get your butt in here." Julie encouraged then slipped behind the shower curtain before Eric positioned himself on the counter. "Well, I think this is just what they needed." Julie yelled as she lathered her hair.

Rubbing his stubble, Eric decided he needed a shave and busied himself at the sink. "I don't know. We don't even know if they ran into each other."

"It's fool proof plan and you know it. The message I left this morning said to meet at the slopes. And you know, all Michael wanted to do was ski. So, unless something tragic happened, their paths have at least crossed."

As Eric ran the blade down his face, he had to applaud Julie for her efforts. She was a true believer when it came to love. And without a doubt, Eric loved her for it. As he rinsed his face and Julie rinsed her hair, Eric could only hope it would work out for Michael and Casey.

Swiping back the shower curtain, Julie asked, "Could you hand me a towel, sweetie?"

Eric nearly choked at her nonchalant behavior but he held back his reaction as he wrapped the bath towel around Julie.

"Thanks." She chimed as Eric held out his hand then he swept her into his arms.

"You are too much." His lips were close to hers. "Julie Warren...I'm head over heals in love with you."

Julie giggled as she kissed his lips, his cheek and his lips again. "I love you too."

Eric's hands traveled the curves of her body as he reigned her with kisses.

"Honey, we...have...dinner...res...er...va...tions." Julie played along with Eric's affection as she melted into his maneuvers.

Tugging on her towel, he exposed her nakedness. "Well, I think we're going to be a little late." He smiled and Julie did too.

Dressed in a simple black cocktail dress, Casey replaced her gold cross necklace with a strand of pearls. While applying her lipstick, she noted that Julie had not missed one detail, including dinner at the Lodge was semi-formal. Despite Julie's antics, she was looking forward to dinner. *"Elegant, quiet...hopefully they..."* but a knock at the door interrupted her thoughts.

"Oh Hank, I forgot..." Casey frowned.

"You look great. Are you ready to go to dinner?" Hank questioned, ignoring her statement as he let himself into her room.

"Ah, I don't know how to tell you this, but I am having dinner with Michael." Confused, he furrowed his brow. "Who?"

Casey raised a brow, "The guy that was bothering me earlier. Well... let's just say we have a history and..." Casey hesitated. Hank had been so kind to her and she didn't want to hurt him. But she knew the truth was the only answer she could give him. "... we have a lot of things to work out. I'm really sorry. Is there..." There was another knock at the door.

As Michael entered, puzzled to see "that guy" in Casey's room, a twinge of jealousy jab at his gut.

"Michael this Hank, he works here at the lodge."

Each man extended a hand forward and reluctantly shook.

"I was just leaving. I just wanted to make sure Casey was all right. I guess I'll catch you some other time." Hank quietly departed.

As Casey shut the door to her hotel room, she felt bad about Hank, putting her in a far less sociable mood than she had been earlier. But she couldn't back out on Michael anymore.

"You look wonderful. Are you ready to go downstairs?" Michael questioned as he reached his hand out to her.

"Ready as I'll ever be." Hesitantly, she locked her fingers with his. It was always the perfect fit. But how in the same moment, could everything feel so right and be so wrong? The touch of his hand against hers made her heart race and breathing difficult as the spark between them ignited one last time. Could they ever get back what they had months ago? Without all the chaos and drama, could they break through their barriers and make amends? After tonight, she knew it was all going to change but for better or worse was anyone's guess.

In the lounge the hostess escorted Casey and Michael to a table for two by the fireplace. It was obvious the lodging staff had gone to great lengths in preparing the Lounge for Thanksgiving dinner. Each table was skirted twice, first with a deep red linen, then draped with a red, orange and yellow plaid table cloth. Ceramic pumpkins, filled with autumn foliage, cradling red pillar candles, had been strategically placed at the center of each table. Completing the setting, was transparent blue china trimmed with a gold leaf inlay, creating a glamorous yet cozy feel. As Michael held out her chair, Casey was smitten by his gentlemanly gesture. They allowed the ambiance to encircle them, blanketing them in a comfort they had not felt in a long time. The menu consisted of traditional Thanksgiving fare, so Casey suggested he choose for both of them.

The flames of the fire danced in her eyes, catching Michael in the chest. He wanted to reach out and take her hand in his but he refrained as she finally broke the silence. "I was pretty angry this afternoon but I'm glad I'm here now."

"I'm glad you're here, too. We really needed this time alone."

In an instant, tension came back to Casey's neck and shoulders. "Michael, don't spoil this evening with serious conversation. I'm really not in the mood right now to rehash the past." Casey folded her hands into her lap as their waitress brought them each a glass of wine. Quickly, she took a sip hoping it would relax her.

"I'm sorry." Michael paused, then inquired, "But there is one thing that has me truly stumped."

"What's that?" Casey responded with ease.

"How did Eric and Julie get you up here especially since they flew to the Bahamas yesterday afternoon?"

Pursing her lips, Casey crossed her arms over her mid-section. Raising a brow to Michael, she commented, "Are you trying to tell me you had nothing to do with this?"

Michael nearly choked on his wine with Casey's question. "Absolutely. I'm in the dark as much as you are."

Nodding, Casey wondered for a moment if he was indeed telling the truth, but in hindsight, and knowing Julie, she had always been in the corner, cheering them on. "I'll give you the benefit of the doubt, for now." Casey giggled and it was like music to Michael's ears.

"It's good to hear you laugh." Michael leaned back in his chair as the waitress served their salads along with a basket of rolls.

Casey smiled answering his question. "I'll tell you what, Julie should have been a lawyer. She had me convinced you were going to Key West with some rich client to go yachting, no less. I even went shopping with her last weekend and she bought a skiing outfit."

"I know. I heard about it. I had my suspicions yesterday when we had lunch at the Corner Café."

"Really?" Casey took a bite of her salad. "And what else has been said, not in my presences?"

"Nothing. Actually, Eric and Julie have been putting forth almost too much effort to stay out of the situation between us." Michael commented, choosing his words carefully.

Casey knew in a heartbeat where their conversation was headed. They would recap all the events and all the misunderstandings, why they broke up and why they should get back together. True to her earlier words, she wasn't in the mood and before she could stop herself, the words blurted out of her mouth, "Stop right there."

Taken aback by her tone, Michael dropped his fork into his salad. Another couple sitting near by, glared at them causing embarrassment to surge to each of their cheeks. Casey reached for her wine, sipped it, then whispered, "Sorry." Nibbling on her lower lips, she pondered her next sentence. "Can we talk about something else, at least until we're done with dinner?"

Conversation through dinner was light and they talked about everything and everybody except what was in both their hearts, each other.

Michael had abided Casey's request until their pumpkin pie was served.

"Casey, I don't know about you but we need to figure out where we're headed. Don't you think so?" Michael knuckled the box in his pants pocket that was starting to feel like it was burning a hole right through to his skin. *"Just do it."* The words echoed through his brain but why couldn't he bring himself to do what he should have done years ago? He knew he couldn't live without her and despite the angry exchanges earlier this afternoon, Michael was bursting at the seams that Casey was actually at Blue Mountain Lodge. Hope had sprung forth that they were finally alone, away from the drama and trauma of the office and Melinda Parker. No one here would come between them…well almost no one.

"I know where I'm headed." Casey kept the thought to herself, simply stating, "Not right now." There was no doubt in her heart, she would miss him and she desperately wanted to tell him so. But if she revealed that she had accepted a job with Whitley Designs, it would spark another argument and Casey was emotionally exhausted. For now, she would enjoy his company, keeping it strictly professional. It would have to wait until the Christmas party. After all, Casey did tell Michael from the beginning she would only work for him for six months and she was right on target. She just never thought it would be South Carolina.

"So, what was that guy doing in your room earlier?" And no sooner did Michael pose the question when he wished he could retract it, especially after he caught a glimpse of the expression on Casey's face.

"Michael, please. He bowed out gracefully without making a scene. I was going to have dinner with Hank until I had that stupid nightmare about you and…" Her cheeks grew red but Michael did not take notice. The glow of the fire illuminated her bare skin and all he wanted to do was hold her in his arms. Sipping on his second glass of wine, he quietly asked, "So what was this dream about?"

"Oh it's silly." Casey suddenly became timid feeling as if she was sixteen again and they were on their first date.

"Come on, tell me." Michael cajoled.

"We were on this sail boat drifting towards the sunset but it was also raining then it turned to snow. And you were trying to pull a fish out of the water. But not with a fishing line, with your bare hands. And you were leaning over the edge and I told you to be careful but then you fell in. Then I heard was this wicked laughter. It was horrid sounding and I'm trying to get to you but I couldn't because Melinda was standing on the deck yelling, 'There are other fish in the sea.' Over and over. Then I woke up."

Michael creased his brow, "Hhmm, that about sums up this year."

Casey gave Michael a sour look but then was caught off guard by the glint in his emerald eyes. His mood had softened and at that given moment she wanted him to hold her, if only for one last time. "Well, Michael, I'm ready to call it a night. I'm tired."

"I'll walk you to your room."

"That isn't necessary. I'll see you in the morning."

"I'm going that way, anyhow. My room, after all is right next to yours." He reasoned.

Michael unlocked Casey's door and led her inside. Half way in, she abruptly turned and said, "Well, good night Michael." Her mouth only inches away from his and their bodies uncomfortably close. Before another word was spoken their lips came together. Casey rested her hands on his shoulders as he wrapped his arms around her waist pulling her close to him. Michael parted his lips and Casey followed his lead. Swept up in the heat of the moment she never wanted it to end. But it had to, before it began. Slowly pulling away, Casey whispered, "Michael, let's just say goodnight."

"Casey…"

"Michael, I really don't have anything to say." But she did and continued with, "Eric and especially Julie must have really put some thought into concocting this little plan of getting us together but it's not going to work. I'm going home tomorrow so let's not spoil the evening with what ifs."

"Casey, will you wait a minute! Just hear me out." Michael's eyes begged as they locked with hers. "We have been going around in circles since the Fourth of July and you were the one that called me earlier saying we had to talk. Now you're being completely evasive and your actions contradict your words. Can't we at least try to work this out?"

"There's nothing to work out Michael."

"But I still love you. And I always will."

For a brief moment his words hurt more than they helped. But then she realized, "I never stopped loving you either, Michael. But the one thing we did, we betrayed each others trust." Emotions swirled inside Casey as she drew in a breath to prevent her voice from cracking. "Granted, I admit I should not have gone after Melinda Parker. You were right and I was wrong to get involved. After all, Sterling Architects is your company." She commented more sarcastically then she had intended. "I guess I was jealous.

She's so beautiful and powerful and..."

"So, not my type." Michael cleared his throat. "You don't even know, I had Melinda Parker investigated myself. That's why I went to Garrick Mansion because the proof had come in just that morning. But then I got a call from Eric and I had to go to the Rezabeck site."

"Why did you have Melinda investigated?"

"Before everything snowballed about Hidden Springs, I saw her with Payne Claiborne. What we found out at the Lake wasn't enough. Melinda has always played hardball with me and I was a fool to play along. I guess after I was left at the altar, I was in fear of losing my company as well. What I didn't realize was I had so much more to lose." Michael confessed then added, "That aside, the one thing I know about her is that she loves her husband's checkbook. So, I had her investigated. It seems she shared a little indiscretion with Payne while Lyle was recuperating from his stroke."

"You mean, Nicole's boyfriend?"

"Yes. But I think he's crossed over to the right side. It seems he's left Parker Industries and is working for some competing company and doing quite well for himself."

Casey eased herself onto the bed as she began to slip out of her heels. "Boy, I've missed a lot since I haven't been in the office." A sadness fell over Casey, aware, she really missed being there.

"Then why don't you come back to work?" Michael was on bended knee, assisting Casey with her dress shoes. He ran a smooth hand over her ankle and began to massage her feet.

Arching an eyebrow, Casey managed, "Is this your way of getting me to say yes?"

Michael shrugged, "Whatever works."

"I'll be there... on... Monday..." An ache swelled inside her core and shot straight to her heart. Leaning back, Casey arched her back, "Oh, Michael." She moaned and felt herself slipping into the abyss of pure pleasure. Then somewhere in the back of her mind, and alarm went off. *"You have to stop!"* But the words never formed on her lips. She really wanted to believe her and Michael could reconcile their differences. But she was painfully wrong.

A yearning swelled just below his belt and shot straight to his heart. Leaning forward, Michael passed his hands over her legs, above her knees, searching. "Oh, Casey." He mustered and felt himself slipping into a bottomless cavern of pure indulgence. Then somewhere in the deep recesses of his mind, a neon sign flashed. *"Stop!"* Luring Casey into the clutches of ecstasy was not going to reconcile their differences and he knew he had to return the ring. How had he been so painfully wrong?

Chapter 17

Even though truths had finally been revealed and misunderstandings had been clarified, Michael and Casey had not reconciled, at least not personally, but professionally they were back on track. Following their Thanksgiving weekend together, Casey felt obligated to return to the office, even though it was agreed upon in the heat of the moment. In the weeks that followed, incoming business had plateau, allowing the staff to finalize completed jobs, focus on current projects and prepare for the company's annual Christmas party.

Casey had volunteered to coordinate decorating while Eric and Julie had been assigned to hiring caterers and the musical entertainment, Michael, of course sparing no expense. Clients had been invited to drop by but for the most part, it was an opportunity for the staff to celebrate a rather successful year at Sterling Architects and Construction. Judging from the staff now joining the band in a contemporary rendition of "Jingle Bells," it showed.

Casey quietly moved towards the bar. "Can I have an egg nog with a couple of cubes?" She sheepishly asked the handsome caterer as she admired her decorating job. It had taken almost an entire weekend to get it just right and that was enlisting the help of Julie, Maggie, Nicole and Valerie. Thousands of tiny white lights perfectly intertwined with evergreen garland ran the perimeter of each office and hallway on three floor. Poinsettias, candy canes and sprigs of holly were all strategically placed throughout the entire building. And pulling it all together was the seven foot fir tree, impeccably decorated, standing majestically in the first floor bay window.

Ice clinked against the glass as the gentleman filled her request. The bartender handed Casey a napkin and her drink.

Turning on her heel, she slammed right into Michael, the creamy liquid instantly staining his blue dress shirt. "We've got to stop bumping into each other like this." He chuckled.

"Oh, Michael, I'm so sorry." As Casey blotted her napkin over the wet material she couldn't help but feel Michael's taut chest. Looking up into his eyes, she knew it was a good thing she had spilled her third drink because she could barely feel her knees, going weak.

The electricity had not died between them and Michael could feel it every time he was in a room with Casey. His muscle would tense and he found it hard to breathe, just like now. He was certain it was the egg nog that encouraged him to sweep Casey into his arms.

"What are you doing?" Her tone was low and teasing.

Pointing a finger towards the ceiling, Michael whispered, "Mistletoe." Then he pressed his lips to hers. Brushing his tongue over her quivering lips, Michael encouraged her to part them. Tightening his embrace, Casey instinctively wrapped her arms around his neck, entwining her fingers through his curls that laid just below his shirt collar. Feeling like Michael was touching her soul, the sweetness of their kiss flared into passion as their breath became one.

"No!" Her head was screaming but her heart was telling her "Yes!" But before she could vocalize the positive the negative became a declaration as she pushed him away.

Bewildered Michael didn't even acknowledge Julie's comment as she and Eric stepped up to the bar. "That was some kiss." Julie giggled.

Casey grabbed at more napkins, noticing that some of the egg nog she had spilled on Michael now stained her red dress. "Mistletoe. You know how that goes." Casey managed in a cold tone as she abruptly exited down the hall.

Michael opted not to say a word and ended up right on Casey's heels as he caught her by the arm. "Let's go. Now! My office." Short of dragging her up the stairs, Casey reluctantly followed. "What's the matter you? I just don't understand you anymore. You say you want us to be just friends but then you respond to my kiss as if I am the last man you ever want to kiss. What in the hell is going on?" Michael stared into her eyes and all he could see was her confusion reflecting back at him.

You are the last man I want to kiss! Every morning and every night! The words screamed loud and clear in Casey's head but when she opened her mouth different words fell out. "I...just don't think it's going to work Michael." Casey stuttered, regretting her words as soon as they became audible.

Michael did not believe one word. The flirting, the electricity, the kiss, nothing had changed to give him the indication she only wanted to be friends. But what was it going to take, to prove he loved her and that she loved him? It was too tense between them and Michael had to shift the mood.

"It's a good thing I keep a change of clothes around here." He teased then reached into the credenza and pulled out a white dress shirt. Unraveling the tissue and removing the receipt from the dry-cleaned garment, he turned to face Casey. "What are you thinking?"

"Nothing." Casey flatly lied.

"Don't say that because you always play with your hair when something is bothering you."

Casey tightly crossed her arms across her mid-section when she realized Michael was right about her nervous habit. Contemplating her words carefully, she was ready to explain but Michael jumped in first.

"Instead of it being Christmas Eve, let's pretend it's New Year's Eve and were making resolutions."

"Michael, I'm leaving. I wanted to give you a two week notice but I really think it would best for both of us if today was my last day." She blurted out in a fluster. But Casey could not determine if it was because she had finally told Michael she was quitting or that he now stood before her revealing his stunning physique. Easily, she imagined herself tracing those muscular lines with the tip of her fingernails. And tasting his skin with her lips. And following the trail of curls that ran from his chest to his navel then disappeared below the belt.

As they locked gazes Casey recognize the confused look in his green eyes. Trying to compose herself, she dragged her hand through her red long tresses. Standing up straight, Casey continued, "Michael, I received an offer I could not refuse. I'm heading up a division of Whitley Designs in South Carolina."

"What! You can't be serious!" Michael moved from behind his desk like a locomotive out of control. "You swore you would never work for The Snake again, as you so affectionately refer to him. Please tell me this is a joke."

"I'm totally serious." Perching her fists on her hips, his nearness was too close for comfort and she had to take a step back. But when she did, a breath caught in her throat. Michael had yet to button up his clean shirt. Twisting her lower lip in between her teeth, Casey slowly continued. "You remember the night of the Charity dinner? I ran into Mr. Whitley. Well, he offered me the job then." Casey found it difficult to concentrate causing her to divert her eyes away from him. "He's expanding Whitley Designs and he's opening up offices up and down the East Coast. So, I chose South Carolina because of Hannah…"

Michael was fuming. "You knew about this back in October!"

"Not exactly. Actually, I turned Mr. Whitley down until we had that big blow up and…" Casey inhaled deeply, "You did this to me. You're the one that pushed me out of your life, again!" Her tone completely accusatory.

"Jeez, Casey. I thought you were over that." Michael leaned against his desk, running his hand through his hair, finally noticing he had to button his shirt. "I want you to stay."

"Michael, I can't. I've already signed a three year employment contract. It's a done deal."

"What about us?" Michael boldly questioned.

"Michael, it's been one heck of a year but it is time to move on. I need to be near my family. Hannah and Adam are expecting the baby in January and by then I will be settled into my new job. Besides, I'm tired of seeing so little of Emily and Jason. I don't want to be some distant aunt who sees them twice a year. I want to celebrate their birthdays with them and I need to know I have a place to go on holidays. And…" Casey knew her feelings were justifiable yet her reasoning sounded ridiculous.

"Casey…you didn't answer my question."

As if she didn't hear a word he had spoken, Casey went on. "Julie and Maggie are ready to take over. I don't think there will be any problems but if there are, I'll make sure they know where to reach me."

Michael shook his head knowing Casey had made up her mind. Yet he had to ask one more time. He moved to face her, taking her hands in his and in a low whisper, simply asked, "What about *us*?"

Casey saw the anticipation of her answer in his eyes, a smile of hope on his face and an emotional fire rising to engulf them that needed to be left alone. She was speechless from his gaze and weak under his touch as she stumbled into his arms.

Finally the barriers had come tumbling down or so he thought.

"There can't be an *us*." Even though the intensity was mounting between them, physical attraction did not make up for all the mishaps and it was time they faced that reality.

Stunned, he stepped back, crossing his arms over his chest. He was on the defensive and he knew it. "When did you get to be so cold?" Michael almost choked on his question.

"Michael, don't you think our history speaks for itself? I don't want a relationship filled with so much drama. You say you love me but your first love is your company."

"Wasn't your bonus enough?" This was not what he wanted to be saying but the wrong words just kept coming. "You are the Interior Design Manager. You supervise Julie and Maggie. What else is there?" But he knew what she wanted and he wanted to give her the world but not like this, in a state of anger and once again, misunderstanding. Besides Casey had him and herself convince that South Carolina was where she was meant to be.

"I have to go." Casey turned on her heel, making a dash for Michael's office door, that was inconveniently closed. Struggling with the knob, Casey cursed under her breath as her eyes filled with tears.

Michael boxed her in, leaning his body into hers, his lips pressing against the softness of her neck and the warmth of his breath caressed her ear as he whispered, "Please stay."

Casey turned in his arms, tears streaming down her cheeks, "Please, let me go, Michael." Her voice trembled.

And there is was, the pain of the past, present and future, blurred her vision and he knew he had to let her go. "I'm not going to fight you anymore. You want everything wrapped up nice and neat in a little package with a bow on it. And it just doesn't work that way, Casey. All I can say is…good luck." Michael's words were as mean and unforgiving as hers.

"That's not true!" Then she lowered her voice. "I can't keep doing this. It's too much. The one thing I remember my mom telling me about love is that it is never supposed to hurt. And this hurts, Michael." Casey felt as if her heart was tearing in two. She was tired, tired of crying and wrestling with both their emotions to make their relationship work. It was obviously not meant to be and she had accepted that. Why couldn't he? She waited for him to respond, but when he didn't, her words grew harsh. "Fine, Michael, if this is the way you want it to end, then I only have one thing left to say, mail my last check to Hannah's."

Every muscle in his body tensed as the door slammed shut. And in a moment, he realized she was really gone. Michael paced his office, then meandered to the window, staring at the city lights, debating whether or not to go after her. But before he could make his move, Julie and Eric strolled into his office.

"Where's Casey running off to?" Eric's questions dripping with holiday cheer.

"Casey just resigned."

"What?" Eric turned to Julie. "What is he talking about?"

"You know Casey's moving to South Carolina."

"Yeah." Eric admitted. "But I was hoping it wouldn't come to this."

"She's leaving within the next week. Right before New Year's." Julie could see the anguish on Michael's face as he planted himself in his chair.

He could feel a headache coming on and he silently wished he could snap his fingers, transporting him to the comfort of his home.

"Michael, she is going to Hidden Springs first." Julie continued with encouragement. "She's not gone yet. Go after her."

"No. I'm always going after her and I just can't anymore." Michael looked up. "If she wanted to stay she never would have accepted Mr. Whitley's offer."

"Whitley! She's out of her mind. Jeez, Mike give her a reason to stay." Eric interjected.

"Enough!" Michael jumped out of his chair. "I don't want to hear it. It's over. Go enjoy the party."

"Michael, how can you give up like this? This could be your last chance." Julie stated firmly.

"As I recall, you said you wanted to make something personally wrong, professionally right. When are you going to get it through that thick skull of yours Casey wants the dream you're living without her. If you want her to stay, make Casey a partner, for God sake, both personally and professionally."

"Leave it alone." Michael retorted as he crossed his arms over his chest. "Please, eat, drink, be merry…after all tomorrow is Christmas Day. Go on you two, get out of here!" Michael surprised even himself for yelling at them, but offered no apology.

Flabbergasted by Michael's tone, Julie simply whispered, "Merry Christmas." Then turned, placing her hand into Eric's and said. "Let's go. Our work is done." Julie's final words were brutal.

"Merry Christmas." Michael growled as he turned his back on Eric and Julie. He didn't feel very merry, he felt like Scrooge himself. And as he stared out the window again, the weather matched his mood as the snow turned to freezing rain.

Christmas had been a lonely holiday for both Michael and Casey. Ready for the holidays to be done and over with, Casey had rescinded Eric and Julie's invitation to join them for Christmas dinner at Eric's parents house. Feverishly she packed her entire apartment Christmas night which ran into the next morning. Once it was done, Casey knew she could then head out to Hidden Springs Lake and relax at the family cabin for a few days before the movers came to pack out her apartment.

As she dragged her suitcase from the top shelf of her closet, she wanted to take as much clothing with her as possible, both for Hidden Springs and South Carolina. Sweaters, jeans, a few skirts and dress slacks, quickly filled her suitcase and now she was ready to tackle her dresser. Reaching into her lingerie drawer, she scooped out the contents, transferring it over to the bed. The drawer hung open, causing a garment to slide forward, one she did not recognize until she held it up to her chest. It was Michael's age old soccer jersey, that she could not bring herself to throw away, and yet she thought she had. Tossing it into a half packed box, she turned her attention to her suitcase. Breezing into the bathroom, Casey gathered her toiletries, slipping them into various compartments of her overnight bag. Lastly, was the bottom draw of her dresser. Filled with summer wear, she decisively tossed shorts and tank tops into the last open box. Folding the flaps and labeling its contents, Casey felt haunted. Kneeling down, she peeled back the card board. Digging deep, she found the jersey she couldn't seem to let go of. Smelling the April fresh material, Casey slipped it over her head, pulling it down over her tee shirt then wrapped her arms around her mid-section as the sweetest memories of Michael blazed in her mind.

Because of his estranged relationship with his father and his remarried mother living in Europe, Michael felt there really was no home to go to for Christmas except his own. This was the first year he turned down an invitation to Eric's parents house. Previously, Michael would join Eric in the afternoon, after Eric's rather large family had gone to church, had a big breakfast and opened all the gifts. Since he was taking Julie, Michael wasn't in the mood for a Norman Rockwell Christmas.

When he woke up, he didn't bother to shower, tossing on a pair of jeans and tee shirt. He couldn't reason his behavior, only that he was charged with energy and ended up spending most of Christmas morning cleaning out his attic and closets, that had been neglected for years. Now as he sat in his recliner with the television blaring, he was sifting through one last box. He found his high school year books stacked on top of unrecognizable memorabilia, but as he dug deeper he remembered what the contents were.

During his quest for order, Eric had called, but he let the answering machine pick it up. Surprisingly, Valerie Sorrenson had called as well, extending an invitation to join her, Mark and the kids. But he couldn't even bring himself to decline her invitation. He just let the tape play as he delved into the memories of him and Casey that had been packed away for too long.

Emotions twisted through his body as he reread faded notes, examined portrait photos from various school dances, class schedules, a variety of cards, including Valentine's and Christmas and then there it was. He shoved the faded black box into the pocket of his jeans then quickly repacked the box, placing it back on the shelf where it had originated from. Both physically and emotionally exhausted, Michael and Casey were relieved when midnight struck on December 25th.

She should have relaxing at the cabin the past two days but Casey was filled with nervous energy. Feeling this great need to bring order to her life after the year had been so chaotic, it was the perfect ending before she embarked on her newest venture.

Valerie stood in the doorway of the kitchen watching her pull the last sheet over the recliner, then wedged it in a corner. Glancing around the living room, a smile ran across Casey's face as bittersweet memories danced before her. Casey's mother, pickling home grown cucumbers, Hannah as a tot, asleep on the sofa after a full day of swimming in Hidden Springs Lake, and most recently, her and Michael kissing as they danced over the threshold, all the while proclaiming his love. Now the New Year was just three days away and Casey was ready to start her new life, knowing the events of the past year would soon wither and fade away, just as their relationship had.

"Casey can't you stay one more day. Please?" Valerie had to beg especially after the frenzied phone call she had received earlier this morning.

"I can't. Hannah and Adam are expecting me tonight. I've taken care of all my business and it's time to go." Casey approached her friend and gave her a hug.

Stepping back, Valerie tugged on the hem of Casey's shirt. "Where did you get this ratty old thing? It's ready for the rag bin." She teased.

The blood rushed to Casey's cheeks and she found herself looking at the floor as she confessed it was Michael's.

Not the least bit surprised, Valerie was willing to do anything to postpone Casey's departure as much as possible. "Did you say good bye to Michael?"

Casey shook her head. "This is hard enough. I think if I saw Michael, I would fall to pieces. It's a done deal and it's time to go." She hugged Valerie one more time." I promise we'll keep in touch and I'm sure I'll be back for business trips and vacations with Hannah."

"But it won't be the same. Why don't we go over to my cabin and have lunch? For old time sake?"

Casey creased her brow, suspicious of her friend's words and wondering why she was trying to delay the inevitable. Glancing out the window, Casey noticed a few snowflakes wafting their way to the ground. Pulling her cable knit sweater over her head, she explained. "I wish I could but it's starting to snow and I really want to get on the road."

"All the more reason you should stay. At least until it clears up." Valerie reasoned.

Quickly, Casey whisked Valerie from the cabin. After locking the door they said their good-bye. Slipping into the driver seat, Casey started her car and placed it into reverse. As she waved, Valerie felt defeated. Reaching for her cell phone, Valerie carefully punched the keypad. "She just left."

A light snow decorated the bare landscape as Casey maneuvered down Hidden Springs Lane, dabbing at the tears forming at the corner of her brown eyes, again.

"Couldn't you stall her any longer? I'm twenty minutes away." Michael huffed as static crackled on the line.

"I tried. Honestly I did. I don't know what else to tell you."

"Well, I'll drive for another ten minutes and then turn around. If I have to drive all the way to South Carolina to catch up with her, I will." Determination swelled in his voice as he hung up the phone. Just as Michael was about to exit the two lane highway, the car in front of him suddenly fishtailed, striking a car in the southbound lane, causing a domino effect. Within seconds, seven vehicles became lumps of twisted metal blocking both lanes. Witnesses frantically scrambled to get to each car as several cell phone calls where made to Emergency Services. Barely scathing being struck himself, Michael had pulled off to the side of the road, sprinting towards one of the victims. A young man was draped half way out the broken driver side window. Surprisingly, he was conscious. Michael wasn't sure what he could or should do, so he talked to the man for a few minutes, then sprinted back to his car. Retrieving the well worn blanket from his trunk, Michael hastily ran back towards the man and in the midst of all the madness slammed right into a woman, bringing her to her knees.

"Jeez! Why don't you watch where the hell your going!" She yelled, struggling to peel herself off the wet asphalt.

Sirens roared and Michael was unable to hear what the woman was saying as he wrapped an arm across the back of her waist, then reached under her arm and pulled her to her feet. Spinning on her heel the woman came face to face with her assailant.

Grasping and choking at the sight of her, Michael thought for one brief moment he was going to lose it. Blood stained her cheeks and sweater. "Jeez-us! Are you all right?" Michael rushed to her side, wrapping the blanket around her shoulders. "We have to get you to the hospital right away! I'll take you. My car is right over here."

"Michael! I'm fine." Casey swatted at his arm that was draped across her shoulder. A frown darkened her face, "I should have known it was you that plowed me over, again!"

"I was just trying to get to this guy…over there…Are you sure you're all right?"

Casey explained that she had helped someone perform CPR but then some doctor came along and took over. Looking down at her sweater, Casey could understand Michael's concern.

A highway patrol officer approached them, "Are you folks okay?"

"We're fine." Casey informed him as she swept a dirty hand through her matted curls.

"We're closing down the highway for the night, so I'm going to have to ask you to clear the area of your vehicles so we can get Medivac in here." The patrolman informed them then turned towards other witnesses, repeating the same words.

Michael scanned the accident scene, noticing, southbound traffic caught behind the accident was being rerouted northbound and visa versa with the northbound traffic.

"Well, I'm certainly caught on the wrong side of this mess." Casey fussed as she brushed dirty snow off her jeans. "I guess I'm going back to the cabin until tomorrow morning."

As Michael pressed a hand against the small of her back, escorting her over to his car, he realized he was caught on the right side of the accident. He was north of it and the only place he could go was to a hotel near Hidden Springs…or the cabin with Casey. Bravery surged its way through his veins, "Do you mind if I tag along?"

At this point, Casey didn't care. All she wanted was a hot shower and a fresh change of clothes. Then is struck her like a lightening bolt. "What are you doing all the way out here?"

"Folks, please, you have to clear the area, immediately." Again, the same patrolman demanded.

Michael looked at Casey and said, "I'll tell you when we get to your cabin."

Narrowing her eyes, Casey crossed her arms over her chest, "Fine. I'll see you there." She then disappeared to the other side of the highway.

When Casey returned to her car, she rummaged through her purse, searching for her cell phone. Aggravated she couldn't find it to call Hannah, Casey dropped her car into drive, when an officer signaled her to make a U-turn. Michael fell in a few car lengths behind. The snow, the accident and the cell phone; Casey was not one to be superstitious but all the tell-tale signs where apparent that she was not meant to leave for South Carolina today. It's just as well and it was much later than she had anticipated. At this point she would arrive on Hannah and Adams doorstep somewhere around midnight.

The Medivac Helicopter circled over head before descending. Eyeing his review mirror, Michael could barely see the Medivac rescue team jump from the helicopter. It was an awful sight and he would never know what became of the young man hanging out his car window and it shook him to the core. Praying silently Michael hoped he would be all right.

The snow was tapering off and not more than an inch had fallen but it had caused quite a bit of damage out on the highway. Casey parked in front of the cabin, retrieving her tote bag from the back seat. "It's a darn good thing I still have running water." Casey shouted as Michael fell into step next to her. Once inside, she dropped her bag on the floor then went through the kitchen to the laundry room. What she didn't know, is that Michael had followed her. Peeling the stained sweater off her body, Casey laid it flat on top of the dryer, while she healthfully dousing the garment with stain remover.

"Where in the world did you get that?" Michael examined her shirt from behind. The red number twenty-three had faded and was peeling, the gold trim now looked pale yellow and the white was nearly gray.

Startled, Casey's heart fell into the pit of her stomach. As she turned to face Michael, her cheeks grew hot with embarrassment. He was the last person she wanted to know that she was still holding onto his old jersey. Pulling herself together, Casey simply stated, "You should know, you gave it to me." And Michael did know that he was the one who had given it to her for Christmas, their Senior year of college, after Casey had begged him for it for four years.

When he didn't respond, Casey informed him she was going to take a shower. "Make yourself at home. I'll be out in a few minutes. You can pull the sheet off the sofa." She shouted over her shoulder then shut the bedroom door behind her.

Once he heard the water running, Michael retrieved what he needed from his car. While Casey had locked herself in the bathroom, he busied himself rearranging the living room furniture then emptied the bags filled with paraphernalia. Once the task at hand was completed, he patted his jeans pocket, reassuring himself that the answer that had been hiding in a box of memorabilia, all this time, was still there.

Casey reached for the box marked towels from her closet, pulling back the card board flaps, grabbing what she needed for her much needed shower. The heat of the water, relaxed her aching muscles and the scent of coconut filled the air as she lathered her hair. Stepping into her bedroom, a chill ran over her damp skin. Quickly she slipped on a fresh pair of jeans, thankful her mother had taught her to always carrying an extra change of clothing in her toiletries bag. "You never know when there might be an accident." Her mother's exact words resounded in her mind. Laying the jersey across her unmade bed, Casey examined it, hoping it was still suitable to wear. There were no blood stains and she sighed with relief. Pulling the shirt over her head, she was actually surprised to find she was happy that Michael was here. This was their finally opportunity to amicably say good-bye.

After Casey hung the damp towels over the shower stall, she glanced in the mirror and fluffed her curls. *"This is about as good as it's going to get."* She thought to herself, until she passed by her make-up bag on the bed and opted to put a little on. Believing her five minute make-up job did her justice she wondered why she was making such a fuss. It was just Michael. *"It was just Michael."* The statement repeated itself over and over in the forethought's of her mind. *"It was just Michael. It was always just Michael."* His voice, his confidence, his eyes, his charm, his heart, his love…*His love for her!* It was always Michael and Casey knew what she needed to do.

Twisting the doorknob, Casey pulled the bedroom door open, startled to find Michael waiting near the threshold.

"Close your eyes." He demanded of her.

"Michael! What on earth are you doing?" Casey's heart pounded.

"I have a surprise for you so keep them closed." Michael led her to the recliner he had strategically positioned just right.

"Michael, I don't like …" Just then the scent of roses tickled her nose as he laid the bouquet in her lap.

"Okay, you can open your eyes."

The sight took her breath away. "What are you up to Michael Sterling?" Casey narrowed her eyes then a smile danced across her face. Dozens of candles illuminated the living room and there, laying before her was a bouquet of her favorites, roses, daisies and violets, wrapped with a white silk ribbon and Michael down on one knee.

"Read the card." Tucked within the stems was not a greeting card but a business card. Instantly she recognized the design. It was the business card she had created for her and Michael so many years ago. *Sterling Architects, Design and Construction...a family business.*

"Michael..."

"Don't say anything, just read this." He commanded as he handed her an envelope.

Casey's hands trembled and tears edged her eyes as she read through the legal terms of the document. Thirty percent of Michael's company was now in her name.

Handing her a pen, Michael offered, "All you have to do is sign it."

"Michael..." Casey stammered, "I can't sign this..."

"Sure you can or you can wait until after the New Year."

Arching an eyebrow, Casey questioned. "Why after New Year's?"

He was so confident that the words just rolled right off his tongue, "So you can sign it with your new name." He held out the fade velvet box, he had kept so carefully hidden. Lifting the lid, he asked, "Will you marry me?"

A tear slipped from the corner of her eye. It was the ring, her ring, the one Michael had given her in college. The one full of promise and hope that they would always be together. The heart shaped diamond still shimmered as the candle light reflected off the amethysts that surrounded it.

Casey looked into Michael's pleading eyes and there was that look. The spark of love that had sustained itself since their high school days. "Say yes. Be my partner both personally and professionally..."

Casey stopped him as she pressed a finger to his lips then she smoothed her hand over his cheek. Her heart beat with fury as Michael raised his hand to her cheek.

"Casey." He softly whispered, "Thank God I ran into you."

Closing her eyes at the warmth of his touch, all her senses where magnified. Emotion took over when she opened her eyes, gazing into Michael's. "I thought this was going to be our chance to have a proper good bye..." she stammered.

"Casey, I know I've hurt you but I promise..."

"Michael, you don't need to promise because I have always known. It's you. It's always been you. I was just so blinded by my anger and jealousy that I couldn't see the truth. And the truth is, I was so wrapped up in the fear of getting hurt and losing you that I brought this on myself. But most of all, I forgot about the joy of what it is like to love you. Can you ever forgive me?"

Michael shook his head. "Can you ever forgive me?"

Then they quietly whispered to each other, "There is nothing to forgive." And in that moment, understanding knocked down the barriers that had kept them from one another.

"I know you are the one I'm supposed to be with. The one I was meant to love."

Michael took her hand in his. As he slipped the ring on her finger, Casey looked down at her hand in his. It always was a perfect fit. She gazed into his green eyes, the eyes that always captured her heart. "Is that a 'yes'?"

"Yes, yes, yes!" Casey tossed the bouquet onto the coffee table, and fell into Michael's arms causing him to fall back and Casey landed onto top of him. Easing herself up, her red tresses cascading off to the side, she gave him a seductive smile, whispering, "Well, Mr. Sterling..."

"Yes, Mrs. Sterling..." Michael's voice was low and husky as he wrapped her in his embrace, pulling her into the warmth of his body.

"Aren't you going to kiss me?"

Michael turned and in one quick gesture he was on top of her, cradling her in his arms. He lowered his mouth to hers, barely caressing her lips. Then he pressed harder, desire burning between them causing the passion to fully ignite. Separating his lips, Casey welcomed him as she pressed her hand into his. The perfect fit. And there it would stay.

Michael eased himself up. "I love you, Casey."

"I love you, Michael."

"And to answer your question, I will always kiss you and love you forever." And he did.

With the help and understanding of Esther Whitley, Arthur's widow, Casey managed to rescind her employment contract with no repercussions. Surprisingly, Carl Whitley came around, wishing Casey well. With her mind at ease, it enabled Casey to concentrate on their wedding plans. Michael had proposal only three days ago and now it was New Year's Eve. Dressed elegantly in an antique white silk dress with a lace overlay of the same hue, Casey adjusted the wide pearl headband that decorated her long fiery curls. Her satin white heels clicked on the marble floor as Julie and Valerie followed her down the hallway.

"Casey, you're going to need this." Julie handed her the bouquet that Michael had given her back at the cabin. "Now, do you have something blue?"

"Oh come on, Julie." Casey rolled her eyes and giggled.

"No, you need something old, something new, something borrowed and something blue."

Casey indulged Julie. "My dress is new. My pearl earrings, were my mom's…"

"Something old…" they both said simultaneously and once again laughed.

"You're garter is blue and…" Valerie interjected, grinning from ear to ear.

"Something borrowed. I don't…"

Just then Julie handed Casey a small box. Casey opened it, revealing a pearl bracelet. "Oh Julie, you shouldn't have."

Retrieving the bracelet from the box, Julie clasped it closed around Casey's wrist, "It was my grandmother's. She loaned it to her best friend and my mom loaned it to her best friend and now it's my turn to loan it to my best friend." Julie smiled and then said, "You look radiant. Now let's get you two married once and for all."

Casey paused before she opened the door to the judges' chambers. "Thank you, both of you for being here."

"No Casey, thank you for letting me be a part of your wedding. I'm glad we're really friends this time." Valerie gave Casey a hug and slipped inside through one of the double doors.

"What is it Casey? You better not be having second thoughts." Julie questioned.

"Oh no. I was just wishing Hannah was here."

Julie placed her hand on Casey's shoulder, "I know, but just think you'll have the big wedding next year and by then Hannah will have had the baby. Plus this prevents Hannah and I fighting over who gets to be your maid of honor. We both do!" Julie exclaimed. "Besides, you and Michael only gave us three days to pull this off." Julie giggled as her blue eyes sparkled then she added, "Think of it this way, what a better way to start the New Year?" Julie's excitement had softened as she opened the wooden doors, where Eric and Michael stood. Moving forwarded, Julie was followed by Casey. As Casey joined Michael, placing her hands in his, a perfect fit, their eyes sparked with love as their wedding ceremony began.

Epilogue

Six months later.

A bead of perspiration tickled his temple. Dabbing his hanky to his head, Michael Sterling completely disregarded the fact that a warm breeze was trickling in his open office window. The temperatures, the past few days, had soared into the nineties for the early part of June.

"Man, if this weather is any indication of what summer's going to be like, I'm going to Alaska." Eric Logan cajoled as he sauntered into Michael's office, immediately closing the window before taking a seat.

It was the third time Michael had read the paragraph and the words just weren't registering in his brain. He tossed the contract onto his desk, rubbed his eyes, stretched, then finally acknowledged Eric's presences as he clasped his hands behind his head. "What can I do for you Eric?"

He shrugged, "Ah, just came in from the heat. Wanted to say hello. Let you know how things are going with Brookshire. Nothing major."

"Well, that's good to hear. I could use some good news right about now."

"Casey's still not feeling well?"

"It's been almost two months that she's had these flu-like symptoms. At lunchtime, I insisted that I take her to the doctor, but she wanted Julie to go with her, so I just let them go. I'm just so afraid she caught some weird disease when we all went to Jamaica." Michael glanced at his watch, "They should be back by now." No sooner had Michael spoken those words when Casey and Julie made their appearance.

"Eric, sweetie, what are you doing here? You said I wouldn't see you until tonight." Julie commented as she squeezed his hand. She still could not bring herself to display affection to him in the office; it just wasn't professional.

Casey on the other hand, circled around Michael's desk and planted a kiss square on his cheek.

"What did the doctor say?" A perplexed looked danced across his face at Casey's elated mood.

"First, open this." Casey handed him a gift wrapped in pale blue paper with a pink ribbon.

"Casey, I'm not in the mood for games. What did the doctor say?"

"Oh, Michael, you're taking the fun out of it. Just open the card…and the present!" Julie encouraged.

Michael raised an eyebrow and as he looked up at Casey, he noticed a glow that had not been there before. Slipping his finger under the lip of the envelope, Michael ended up tearing the paper to get the card out. On the cover it read, "To my husband, To the man I love..." Michael opened the card and read the three words on the inside and it was signed, "Love Always and Forever, Casey."

"What is this? Some kind of joke?"

"Just open the present, Michael." Casey instructed.

Before he finished tearing off the wrapping paper, Maggie Cowan popped her head into Michael's office. "Casey, how are you feeling?"

"Oh, I'm just fine." She replied quickly as Michael lifted the lid.

There in his hands, Michael beheld the most precious piece of sterling he had ever seen. He shook it. He touched it. He examined it. "Does this mean..." Michael stood and gently kissed Casey on the lips and it still felt as if it was their first kiss. And now they were going to have their first child.

The office erupted with shouts of joy. "A baby! I can't believe it!" Eric boasted as he shook Michael's hand, "You old dog you." Then Eric looked inside the card, that read Happy Father's Day.

"Well congratulations, you two." Maggie added.

"I hope it's a girl." Julie interjected. "I'll get to spoil her."

"And you wouldn't spoil him if it's a boy?" Casey asked as Michael wrapped his arms around his wife.

"Well, yeah, I would." Julie giggled.

As the hugs, kisses, handshakes and laughter died down, Nicole called Michael over the intercom. "Mr. Sterling, you have a call."

"Who is it Nicole?"

"She wouldn't say. Should I take a message?"

"I'll take the call, Nicole. Thank you." The perplexed look had returned to Michael's face as he pressed the lit extension line.

"Here we go again." Casey mumbled then she slipped from Michael's embrace.

Julie moved to Casey's side. "I know what you're thinking... that it's Melinda Parker but we haven't heard from her in almost a year."

"Casey, Julie's right. Besides, I think her and Lyle are in France or England or something like that. More specialists." Eric barely took a breath. "And you know what? You have nothing to worry about. You've got the ring on your finger to prove it."

"And you and Michael are going to have a baby. So, smile."

Silence fell over the room as Michael picked up the receiver. "This is Michael Sterling. May I help you?" His voice was as calm and confident as it was the first day Casey had met him. As he eased back into his leather chair he turned towards Casey and winked, struggling to maintain a professional composure. There was silence on the other end of the line. Again, Michael repeated himself.

"Michael?" The voice questioned on the other end of the line.

"Yes, this is Michael Sterling."

"Michael? It's Amanda. Amanda Carlyle."